Arturo's Island

ELSA MORANTE

Arturo's Island

A Novel

TRANSLATED FROM THE ITALIAN
BY ISABEL QUIGLY

STEERFORTH ITALIA

AN IMPRINT OF STEERFORTH PRESS · SOUTH ROYALTON, VERMONT

Originally published in Italian in 1957 as *L'Isola di Arturo* by Giulio Einaudi Editore

Copyright © 2002 Elsa Morante Estate. All rights reserved.

Steerforth Press edition copyright © 2002

English translation originally published in 1959 by William Collins Sons & Co. Ltd.

Translation copyright © 1959 Alfred A. Knopf (U.S.) and HarperCollins (U.K.)

For information about permission to reproduce
selections from this book, write to:
Steerforth Press L.C., P.O. Box 70,
South Royalton, Vermont 05068

Library of Congress Cataloging-in-Publication Data

Morante, Elsa, ca. 1912–1985.
[Isola di Arturo. English]
Arturo's Island : a novel / Elsa Morante ; translated from the Italian by Isabel Quigly.
p.   cm.
ISBN 1-58642-041-0 (alk. paper)
I. Quigly, Isabel. II. Title.

PQ4829.O615 I813 2002
853'.912—dc21
2001057752

Even though the places named in this book really exist on geographical maps, it was not in any way intended that these pages should give a documentary description, for in them everything — beginning with geography — follows the design of the imagination. This story is wholly imagined and does not portray real places, real facts, or real people.

FIRST STEERFORTH EDITION

To Remo N.

That which you thought a little spot of earth
was everything.
A unique treasure never to be taken
by your eyes, jealous even when sleeping.
Your first love will remain inviolate.

Virgin, she has wrapped herself in night
like a Gypsy girl in a black shawl.
Star hanging in the northern sky
forever: no scheming can touch her.

More beautiful than Alexander and Euryalus, young friends,
Beautiful always, protect my sleeping boy.
The sign of fear shall never cross the threshold
of that small, celestial island.

Nor will you ever know the law
that I, with multitudes of others, learn:

there is no paradise except in limbo.

(translation by H. W.)

If I see myself in him, I am content . . .
from *Il Canzoniere,* by Umberto Saba

CONTENTS

King and Star of the Sky

A Winter Afternoon

Family Life

King and Star of the Sky

. . . Paradise,
very high up and vague . . .

from the poems of
SANDRO PENNA

King and star of the sky

FIRST OF ALL, I was proud of my name. I'd found out early on (from *him*, I have a feeling) that Arturo is the name of a star — the fastest and brightest in the figure of the herdsman, in the northern sky. And ages ago there was some king called Arturo as well, who had a group of loyal followers; and, as they were all heroes like himself, he treated them as brothers and equals. The pity of it was, as I later discovered, this famous old king of Britain wasn't proper history at all, but just a legend; and as I thought legends were kids' stuff, I dropped him for more historical kings.

There was another reason, though, why this name Arturo had a sort of heraldic ring to it, and that was that it was chosen for me by my mother, who can't, I suppose, have known all it symbolized, being a simple, illiterate person (though to me, she was more than a queen). I knew very little about her, hardly anything, really, because she died the same moment I was born: I was her first child, and she wasn't yet eighteen. The only picture I've ever had of her was an ordinary, faded, almost ghostly postcard; but I worshiped it all my childhood. It was taken by a traveling photographer in the first months of her pregnancy, which you can already see through the folds of her loose dress. Her two small hands are clasped in front, in a timid, modest way, as if to hide it; she's very serious, and there's not just submission in her eyes — you can see that in all the country girls around here — but a questioning look,

surprised and faintly frightened, as if, among the usual fancies of
motherhood, she already suspected her destiny of death, and of
eternal ignorance.

The island

The islands of our archipelago, down in the sea of Naples, are all
beautiful. They're of volcanic origin, mostly, and wild flowers that
you never see on the mainland cluster in thousands around the
old craters. In spring the hills are covered with broom, and if
you're out sailing in June, you can smell its elusive, caressing
scent as soon as you get near the shore.

On my particular island, up on the hills outside the town,
there are small lonely roads shut in between old walls, and beyond them orchards and vineyards that look like imperial gardens.
There are beaches of fine white sand, and smaller beaches covered with pebbles and shells, hidden between great cliffs that
overhang the water. Seagulls nest in the rocks there, and wild tortoises, and in the early morning you can hear the birds' cries,
sometimes gloomy, sometimes gay. On calm days the sea there is
gentle and cool and touches the shore like dew. If I could only get
back there to splash about in those waters, I'd gladly become any
sort of creature: not a gull or a dolphin or anything beautiful, but
the ugliest thing in the sea, which is the scorpion fish!

Around the port there are sunless alleys between rough old
houses that, though they're painted in wonderful shell-like pinks
and grays, look grim and sad. The windows are narrow as loop-
holes, with carnations sometimes growing in milk cans on the
windowsills, or tortoises languishing in cages the right size for
crickets. The shops are dark and sinister as robbers' dens. In the
café there's a charcoal stove where the owner makes Turkish
coffee in an enameled blue pot. She's an elderly widow and always wears mourning — black dress, black shawl, black earrings
— and beside the till, festooned with dusty leaves, her husband's
photograph hangs on the wall.

The man in the wineshop, which stands opposite the statue of Christ the Fisherman, once kept an owl chained to a shelf high up on the wall, a delicate black and gray bird with a dashing tuft of feathers, blue eyelids, and big reddish brown eyes flecked with black; one wing was always bleeding where he pecked at it. If you held out a finger to tickle his breast, he bent his head down, looking surprised. At evening he'd start struggling, try to fly, flop down, and sometimes end up fluttering upside down on the end of his chain.

The church on the port is the oldest on the island and has some small wax saints in it shut up under glass covers. They have skirts of real yellowish lace, mantles of faded brocade, real hair, tiny rosaries of real pearls hanging at their wrists, and red nails painted on their dead pale fingers, very minutely.

The sort of smart boat that sails for sport or pleasure, and crowds the other island ports, never turns up at Procida. Apart from the local fishermen's boats, you find nothing there but lighters and merchant ships. Most of the day the square is almost empty. On the left, beside the statue of Christ the Fisherman, a single cab waits for the steamer to come in; but it stops for only a few minutes, and only three or four passengers, generally islanders, disembark. Even in summer there's never the holiday hubbub you get on the other island beaches, which are crammed with people from Naples and other places — in fact, from anywhere on earth you like to think of. Outsiders disembarking at Procida are amazed to find none of the gay, promiscuous life that Naples is famous for: no animation, no chatting in the streets, no songs, no guitars and mandolins, nothing but closed doors and windows and people living inside their own four walls, minding their own business. Procidans are dour and silent; they don't like being friendly. A stranger excites no curiosity, only suspicion. They hate being questioned, they hate anyone spying into their secret life.

Procidans are small and dark, with long black Oriental-looking eyes, and are so much alike that you'd think they were all related. The women live cloistered like nuns, the way they always have. Many still wear their hair long and braided, shawls on their heads, long dresses, and in winter clogs over thick black cotton stockings. In summer they go barefoot; and as they pad swiftly and silently by, avoiding everyone, they have a sort of polecat look about them. They never go down to the beaches: it's a sin for women to swim in the sea, or even to watch other people bathing.

The houses of old feudal cities are often scattered about the valleys and slopes below a castle that towers above them; in books, they're compared to flocks around a shepherd. Well, that's just what they look like on Procida, at the foot of the castle — crowded around the port, sparser on the hills, isolated in the country. The castle stands on the highest hill, which looks like a mountain compared with the others; a building that has been added to so often through the centuries that it's now like a gigantic citadel. When ships pass the island, especially at night, there seems to be nothing there but the great dark hulk, making it look like a fortress set in the middle of the sea.

For nearly two hundred years the castle's been used as a prison, one of the oldest in the whole country, I believe. People who live far away often think of Procida as just the name of a prison.

From the west side of our house, which looks out to sea, you can see the castle several hundred yards off as the crow flies, across a number of small bays where fishermen's boats tie up at night with their lamps lighted. It's too far to make out the window bars, or the movements of the guards around the walls; and so, when the weather's misty and the prison is half-hidden in cloud, it looks like some deserted grange in an ancient city: a fantastic ruin where nothing lives but snakes, and owls, and swallows.

About Romeo, the man from Amalfi

Our house stands alone on top of a steep hill, on untilled ground strewn with lava stones. It faces the village, and on this side the hillside is reinforced with an old rock wall, where the blue lizard lives, which you won't find anywhere else on earth. On the right, a flight of steps made of stones and mud leads down to the roadway.

Behind the house there's a wide courtyard, and below it the ground turns rocky and unusable and falls down steeply to a little triangular beach of black sand. There's no path down to it; but it's easy to jump down barefoot from rock to rock. Down there just one boat used to be tied: it was mine and was called *The Torpedo-boat of the Antilles.*

Our house isn't far from an almost urban little square — which even boasts a marble monument — and the clustering houses of the village. But as I remember it, it was quite isolated, ringed around by an enormous empty solitude. There it stands, malevolent and marvelous, like a golden spider that has spun its iridescent web over the whole island.

It's two stories high, apart from the cellar and the attic (houses with twenty rooms, which would seem small in Naples, are called palaces in Procida), and, like most of the island houses, it's at least three hundred years old. A rough, square house, built without any pretensions to elegance and painted a faded pink, it would look like any old clumsy farmhouse if it weren't for the imposing front door and the curved baroque ironwork protecting all the outside windows. The only decoration on the front consists of two small iron balconies in the front of two blind windows. These balconies were once painted white, like all the ironwork, but now they're all stained and corroded with rust.

On one side of the front door is a smaller door, and that's the usual way into the house; the main door is never opened, and the enormous locks that once bolted it from the inside have rusted into uselessness. Once through the front door, you come into a long windowless hall with a slate floor, at the end of which a gate opens into an internal garden, as happens in all the large houses on the island. This gate is guarded by two painted, but rather faded, terra-cotta statues of hooded figures, but whether they're monks or Saracens, no one can tell. And beyond it, shut in between the courtyard's four walls, lies the garden, triumphantly unkempt.

There, under the fine Sicilian carob tree, my bitch Immaco-latella is buried.

From the roof you can see the dolphin shape of the island lying below, with its small gulfs, its Penitentiary, and, not very far out at sea, the purple-blue shape of Ischia; silvery shadows of islands farther off; and at night the firmament, where the herdsman wanders with his star Arturo.

For more than two centuries after the house was built it was a monastery, which is something quite common on the island, and not the least bit romantic. Procida has always been an island of fishermen and peasants, and its few large houses were all inevitably convents, or churches, or fortresses, or prisons.

Later the monks went away, and the house ceased to belong to the church. For a while, during and after the wars of the past century, it was used to house soldiers; then it was left empty for a fairly long time, and, finally, about fifty years ago, it was bought by a rich shipping agent from Amalfi who was passing through Procida. He made it his home and lived there in idleness for thirty years.

He altered the inside of the house a little, especially the upstairs floor, where he pulled down the old convent partitions dividing it up into lots of cells, and papered the walls that were left. In my time, though it was dreadfully dilapidated and growing progressively more so, the house was still arranged and furnished as he had left it. The furniture, picked up from small dealers in the junk shops of Naples, showed a crude though attractive taste and gave the rooms a kind of picturesque, countrified air, an atmosphere that evoked a past full of great-aunts and grandmothers and age-old women's secrets.

Yet the fact was that from the time it was built until the year our family went to live there, not a single woman had ever been inside it.

When my father's father, Antonio Gerace, returned with a modest fortune from America, where he'd emigrated from Procida, the man from Amalfi was still living in the house. He was old, and had gone blind, which people said was a punishment sent by Santa Lucia for his hatred of women. Ever since he had been a young man he'd hated them, hated them so much that he refused to see his own sisters and kept out the nuns who came begging for alms. This was why he'd never married; and he never went to church or to the shops, where he'd be likely to meet women.

It wasn't that he disliked company; on the contrary, he was rather openhanded and often gave dinners and even fancy dress parties, at which he was so wildly generous that he became a legend on the island. But no women were ever invited when he entertained; and the Procidan girls, who envied their boys and brothers those mysterious evenings, maliciously called the man from Amalfi's house the House of the Guaglioni (*guaglione* means "boy," or "young man," in Neapolitan dialect).

When my grandfather Antonio disembarked at Procida after a good many years abroad, he obviously never thought that fate was reserving the House of the Guaglioni for his family. He hardly remembered the man from Amalfi, and had never been the least bit friendly with him; and the old monastery barracks set there among thorns and fig trees certainly wasn't the home he'd dreamed of during his exile. He bought himself a small country house with some land, in the south of the island, and went to live there with just his tenants, as he was a bachelor and had no near relations.

Actually, he did have *one* near relation in the world, one he had never seen. This was a son born during the early years of his exile to a German schoolmistress he'd had an affair with and soon deserted. She had kept on writing to him for several years after he'd left her (after a short time working in Germany, he'd emigrated to America), begging him for help, as she was out of work, and trying to move him with marvelous descriptions of the child. But the emigrant was so wretchedly poor himself at the time that he even stopped answering her letters, and in the end the girl grew discouraged and stopped writing too. And when he got back to Procida, old and without an heir, Antonio had a search made for her and discovered that she was dead and had left the son, who was then seventeen, in Germany.

So Antonio Gerace sent for his son, to give him his rightful name and inheritance at last in Procida. And the man who was to become my father landed there dressed in rags like a gypsy (as I afterward heard).

He must have had a hard life. And his child's heart must have resented, not only his unknown father, but all the other harmless Procidans as well. Maybe the islanders did something, behaved in some way, that right at the start and forever offended his prickly pride. However that may be, his cool, offensive manner made everyone detest him. And though his father tried to win him, the boy remained cruelly remote.

The only person he saw much of on the island was the man from Amalfi. It was some time since the old man had entertained or given parties, and he lived shut up in his blindness, proud and disagreeable, refusing to receive callers, and shaking his stick at anyone who came up to him in the street. Everyone hated his immensely tall sad figure.

His house was open to one person only: Antonio Gerace's son, who became so friendly with him that he spent his whole time there, as if the old man was his real father instead of Antonio Gerace. The old man's affection was concentrated and tyrannical: he couldn't, it seemed, live a single day without him. If the boy was late for his daily visit, he went out to meet him and stood waiting at the top of the road; and as, for all his blind anxiety, he couldn't see when the boy finally appeared at the end of it, he kept shouting his name in a hoarse, already gravelike voice. If someone passing by told him that Gerace's son wasn't there, he flung coins and banknotes down on the ground, scornfully and carelessly, so as to pay anyone who happened to be there to go and fetch him. And if they came back later and said they hadn't found him at home, he made them search the whole island, and even unleashed his dogs to join in the hunt. There was nothing in his life but the companionship of his one friend, or waiting for him to come. Two years later he died and left the boy his house on the island.

Not long afterward, Antonio Gerace died too; and his son, who had married an orphan girl from Messa a few months earlier, moved into the man from Amalfi's house with his young wife, who was already pregnant. He was then about nineteen, and his wife wasn't yet eighteen. It was the first time in the three centuries of its life that a woman had lived in the old house.

In my grandfather's house, and on his land, the tenants stayed, and still live there, on the *mezzadria* system.*

The House of the Guaglioni

My mother's early death at the age of eighteen, when her first child was born, obviously confirmed, if it didn't originate, the rumors that the dead owner's hatred made the House of the Guaglioni fatal to women who lived there or even went inside it.

My father had a small scornful smile for this old wives' tale, so that right from the start I learned to regard it with the scorn it deserved, as the superstitious gossip it was. But it was so firmly believed on the island that no woman would ever agree to work for us. When I was small, we had a boy servant from Naples, called Silvestro, who was fourteen or fifteen when he came, a short time before I was born. He went back to Naples to do his military service, and one of our tenants took over from him, coming for just a couple of hours a day to cook. No one took any notice of the muddle and dirt the house was in, which to us seemed as natural as the uncultivated growth in the garden within the walls of the house.

It's quite indescribable, this garden (Immacolatella's cemetery). Among other things, rotting around the full-grown carob tree, lay moss-covered skeletons of furniture, broken pots, demijohns, oars, wheels, and so forth. And right in the middle of the stones and rubbish grew plants with great swollen spiky leaves, sometimes as strange and gorgeous as exotic plants. After the rain, hundreds of rather distinguished flowers came up from old seeds and bulbs that lay buried there from heaven knows when. And everything was burned like a bonfire in the dryness of summer.

---

* System of farming widely practiced in Italy, in which the tenant lives on the land and works it, dividing the expenses and the profits with the landowner.

Although we were fairly well off, we lived like savages. When I was two months old my father left the island and was away for nearly six months; and he left me in the care of our first boy servant, who was very serious for his age and brought me up on goat's milk. It was he who taught me to talk, and to read and write, and afterward I taught myself, out of books I found about the house. My father never bothered to send me to school; I was always on holiday, and my vagabond days, especially when he was away, had no rules or fixed hours at all. When I was hungry or sleepy I knew it was time to go home. No one ever thought of giving me money, and I never asked for it; anyway, I didn't need it. I don't remember ever possessing a penny during my whole childhood.

The land my grandfather Gerace had left us provided enough for the cook to feed us with — at any rate, his cooking was a primitive, barbarous business. His name was Costante, and he was as disagreeable and rough-hewn as his predecessor Silvestro — whom you could call my nurse, in a way — had been kind.

On winter evenings, or when it rained, I spent the time reading. After the sea and wandering about the island, reading was what I liked best. Generally I read in my rooms, lying on the bed or on a sofa, with Immacolatella at my feet.

Our rooms gave on to a narrow passage. At one time the monks' cells, about twenty of them, had opened out on to it; but the previous owner had knocked down most of the walls between the cells, to make the rooms bigger. Some of the old doors had been left as they were, though, in a row along the passage, maybe because he liked the carved lintels: so my father's room had three doors in a row, and five windows, all in a row as well. One cell had been kept at its original size between my room and my father's, and when I was a baby it was Silvestro's room. A kind of camp bed he used is still there, and so is the old soapbox, now empty, where he used to keep his clothes.

My father and I, though, didn't keep our clothes anywhere in particular. There were plenty of chests of drawers and wardrobes in our rooms, and when we opened them they threatened to crash down on our heads. Smells of their past owners floated out, but we never used them ourselves, except to throw in occasional bits and pieces that were cluttering up the rooms — old shoes or broken harpoons, a shirt in rags — or something we'd collected, like a fossilized shell from the time when the island was a volcano under the sea, empty cartridges, the bottoms of bottles colored by the sand, bits of rusty machinery, or underwater plants and starfish that afterward dried up or rotted in the drawers. Maybe this is why I've never been able to discover the smell of our rooms anywhere else — certainly in no room where people live, and not even in animals' dens; but sometimes I've found something like it at the bottom of a boat, or in a cave.

These enormous wardrobes and chests of drawers took up most of the space along the walls and hardly left room for the beds, which were iron bedsteads, decorated with mother-of-pearl and painted landscapes, the sort you find in every bedroom in Procida or Naples. The blankets we used in winter — I used to sleep wrapped up in mine as if I was in a sack — were full of moth holes, and the mattresses were as flat as flaky pastry, because they never got shaken or carded. I remember that occasionally my father, with me to help, used to sweep the cigarette butts from around his bed into a pile in a corner of the room, to be thrown out of the window afterward; we'd use an apron or an old leather jacket of Silvestro's as a broom. It was impossible to say what the floors were made of or what color they were, because they were completely hidden under a hard crust of dirt; and the glass in the windows was all blackened and opaque. Hanging in corners and between the window bars, glistening spiderwebs sparkled in the light.

I think that spiders, and lizards, and birds, and all nonhuman beings in general, must have thought of our house as a tower uninhabited since the time of Barbarossa, or even as a lighthouse. Along the outside walls, through cracks and secret passages, lizards darted out as if they came from holes in the ground. Thousands of swallows and wasps made their nests there, and foreign birds crossing the island as they migrated would stop and rest on the windowsills. And even seagulls, after plunging in the sea, would come and dry their feathers on the roof as if it was the mast of a ship, or the pinnacle of a rock. At least one pair of screech owls lived inside our house, quite definitely, though it was impossible to discover exactly where; but it's a fact that as soon as evening fell you could see them flying out from the walls with their whole family. Other owls, large and small, used to come from a distance to hunt on our land, as if it was a forest. One night an enormous screech owl perched on my windowsill. I thought for a moment, from his size and kingly look, that he was an eagle, but his feathers were much lighter, and besides, I recognized his small straight ears.

We just forgot some of our unused rooms, and their windows stayed open all summer, and when we came in suddenly after a lapse of several months we might find a bat there, or hear mysterious squeaks from a nest hidden behind a bench or between the beams of the ceiling. And strange creatures that had never been seen on the island would turn up too. One morning I was sitting behind the house throwing stones at the almond tree when I saw a very pretty little creature, something between a cat and a squirrel, pop out on the slope below. He had a big tail and a triangular face with white whiskers, and he peered closely at me. I threw him a peeled almond, hoping to catch him, but my movement scared him and he ran away. Another time, at night, I saw a very white quadruped about as big as a middle-sized tunafish, with curved horns like two new moons on his head, coming up from the beach toward the house. As soon as he drew near me on the edge of the slope he turned back and disappeared among the rocks. I had a feeling he was a kind of sea horse, a rare sort of amphibious ruminant that some people say never existed and others say has disappeared. A lot of sailors, though, say they've seen more than one of these sea horses for certain, and that they live near the Blue Grotto at Capri; they live in the sea like fish, but love vegetables, and come out of the water at night to go around stealing from people's gardens.

As for visits from humans, either Procidans or foreigners — for years the House of the Guaglioni had never had any at all.

On the first floor, there was the monks' old refectory, which the man from Amalfi had turned into a drawing room. It was an enormous room with a low ceiling, almost twice as low as that of the other rooms, and with high windows looking out toward the sea. The walls, unlike those of the other rooms in the house, weren't papered, but decorated all around with a fresco pretending to be a loggia, with columns and a vine and bunches of grapes painted on it. Against the far wall was a table more than six yards long, and scattered about everywhere were sofas and half-broken armchairs, chairs of all kinds, faded cushions. One corner was taken up by a big stove that we never lit. And an enormous stained-glass lamp, all covered in dust, hung from the ceiling, but as there were only a few blackened candleholders left on it, it wasn't worth more than a candlestick from the point of view of light.

Here the young men had gathered in the days when the house belonged to the man from Amalfi. There were still traces of their parties, their noise and singing, about it; it was rather like a room used by occupying troops in wartime, or one of the great rooms in a prison, or anywhere where young men get together without women. The dirty, ragged material of the sofas was burned by cigarettes, and on the walls and tables there were scribbles and drawings — names, signatures, jokes, even melancholy remarks about love, and bits of songs; a pierced heart, a ship, a football player balancing a ball on the tip of his toe, and funny drawings too — a skull smoking a pipe, a mermaid under an umbrella, that sort of thing. Lots of other drawings and scribbles had been scratched out — by whom I don't know: on the plaster and on the wooden tables you could still see the marks of erasures.

There were traces of other past guests in the other rooms, too. For instance, in a little room we didn't use, above an alabaster holy water stoup that remained from the convent days, you could still read on the wallpaper, though it was faded, a signature written in ink with plenty of flourishes: *Taniello*. But apart from these unknown signatures and valueless drawings there was nothing left in the house to recall the parties and their guests. I heard that after the man from Amalfi's death a lot of Procidans who had been to the parties when they were young turned up at

the House of the Guaglioni to reclaim things and take away me-
mentos. They all said, and all supported each other in saying it,
that the man from Amalfi had promised to give them to them
when he died. So the house was sacked, you might say; and
maybe it was then that the costumes and masks they still talk so
much about on the island were taken away, and the guitars, and
the mandolins, and the glasses with toasts written in gold on the
crystal. Perhaps some of them are still kept in Procida in the huts
of the peasants or fishermen; and the women in the family, now
old, look at the relics with a smile, and feel again their old childhood jealousy of the mysterious parties from which they were excluded; and perhaps they're almost afraid to touch these dead
objects, that may carry in them the evil influence of the House of
the Guaglioni!

Another thing that ended mysteriously was the man from
Amalfi's dogs. Everyone knows he had several and loved them.
But at his death they disappeared from the house without leaving
a trace, and some people say that after their master had been
taken to the cemetery they refused all food and just let themselves die. Others say that they began wandering around the island
like wild beasts, snarling at anyone who came near them, until
everyone got furious, and that the police captured them one by
one and killed them and flung them down from a cliff.

And so everything that happened in the House of the Guaglioni
before I was born filtered down to me in an uncertain sort of way,
like adventures that had happened centuries ago. Take even my
mother's brief stay there — I've not been able to find a single
trace of it in the house, except for the famous picture Silvestro
kept for me. It was from Silvestro, too, that I heard how, one day
when I was about two months old and my father had just left on
his travels, some relations who looked like peasants turned up
from Massa and took away everything that had belonged to my
mother, as if they had the right: the household things she had
brought as a dowry, her dresses, even her little clogs, and her
mother-of-pearl rosary. Obviously they took advantage of the fact
that there was no grown-up in the house to stand up to them, and

at one time Silvestro was afraid they'd want to take me too; and so he made some excuse, ran into his cell, where he'd left me asleep on the bed, and hid me hurriedly inside the soapbox with his clothes. Air could get in through the broken lid, and he put my bottle, full of goat's milk, beside me, so that if I woke up I'd be quiet and not give a sign of life. But I didn't wake up and stayed quietly there the whole time my relations were in the house; and anyway, they weren't very eager for news of me. Only just as they were ready to leave with their bundle of stuff did one of them — more from politeness than anything — ask if I was growing up well and where I was, and Silvestro answered that I was out to nurse. They were quite satisfied with that and went back to Massa forever, and they've never given a single sign of life since.

And so my solitary childhood passed, in the house where no women were allowed.

In my father's room there was a big photograph of the man from Amalfi: a thin old man bundled up in a long jacket with rather narrow old-fashioned trousers that showed his white socks. His white hair hung behind his ears like a horse's mane, and the high, smooth, gleaming forehead seemed unnaturally white. His wide-open, extinguished eyes had the expression some animals' eyes have — bright and bewitched. He had taken up a studied, arrogant pose before the photographer, standing with one foot forward and smiling gallantly, as if in greeting. In his right hand he held a black, iron-tipped stick, as if he were in the act of twirling it, and with his left hand two big dogs on a leash. Under the portrait the old man, half illiterate and blind, had traced a dedication to my father in his shaky writing:

To Wilhelm
ROMEO

This portrait of the man from Amalfi reminded me of the figure of the Herdsman and his star Arturo, as they were drawn on a great map of the Northern Hemisphere in an astronomical atlas we had at home.

Beauty

What I know about my father's origins I found out when I was
quite big. Ever since I was small I'd heard the island people
calling him *bastard*, but it sounded to me like a title of authority
and mysterious prestige, something like *margrave,* or that sort of
thing. For years no one told me anything about my father's past, or
my grandfather's. Procidans aren't talkative, and besides, I followed my father's example: I wasn't friendly with anyone on the
island and didn't go around with anyone. Costante, our cook, was
more an animal than a human being: in all the years he worked
for us I don't remember ever exchanging two words of conversation with him; besides, I saw him very rarely. As soon as his work
in the kitchen was done, he went back to his land, and as I came
home whenever I felt like it, I'd find his disgusting dishes waiting
for me, cold, in the empty kitchen.

My father spent most of the time away. He'd come to Procida
for a few days, then leave again, and sometimes he'd stay away for
a whole season. If at the end of the year you added up his rare
fleeting visits to the island, you'd find that out of twelve months
he'd spent maybe two at Procida with me. And so I spent nearly all
my time in absolute solitude, a solitude that, as it had started in my
early childhood, when Silvestro left me, seemed to me my natural
condition. Each visit my father paid the island seemed an extraordinary favor on his part, a special concession I was proud of.

I think I had only just learned to walk when he bought me a
boat. And when I was about six years old he took me out to his
land one day, where the tenant's sheepdog was nursing its month-
old pups, so that I could choose one. I chose the one that looked
wickedest and had the friendliest eyes. It turned out to be a bitch,
and as it was as white as the moon, it was called Immacolatella.

Clothes and shoes and things, my father didn't often remember. In summer I wore nothing but a pair of trousers: I used
to swim with them on, and leave them on me to dry afterward.
Just occasionally I wore a cotton shirt too, but it was too short, and
hung around me in tatters. My father had a pair of canvas bathing

trunks as well, but apart from this he wore nothing in the summer either but some faded old trousers and a shirt without a single button, open on his chest. Sometimes he tied a flowered handkerchief around his neck — one of those that peasants buy in the market for Sunday Mass — and on him this cotton rag seemed to me a sign of his eminence, a garland of flowers decorating a splendid conqueror!

Neither of us owned an overcoat. In winter I wore two sweaters, one on top of the other, and he wore a sweater underneath and a check woolen jacket on top, a shapeless old thing with excessively padded shoulders that made him look taller. And as for linen, we hardly knew it existed.

He had a wristwatch that showed the seconds and could be worn even in water; it had a steel case, and the strap was of heavy steel mesh as well. He had an underwater mask too, a gun, and a pair of sea binoculars with which you could make out ships at sea, and even the sailors on deck.

My childhood is like a happy country, of which he is the absolute king! He was always just passing through, always leaving; but during his short visits to Procida I followed him about like a puppy. We must have looked a funny pair to anyone who met us — he walking resolutely along, like a ship in full sail, with his blond foreign look, his puffy lips and hard eyes that looked no one in the face; and I tagging along behind, my dark eyes darting proudly to right and left as if to say, "Hey, you Procidans! My father's going by!" I wasn't much more than a yard high then, and my dark hair, which was as curly as a gypsy's, had never been cut by a barber. When it was too long, I hacked at it energetically with the scissors, so that people wouldn't think me a girl. I remembered to comb it only very rarely, and in the summer it was almost encrusted with salt from the sea.

Immacolatella nearly always ran ahead of us and dashed backward and forward, sniffing at all the walls, poking into every doorway, greeting everyone. Her friendliness toward our fellow islanders often made me cross, and I'd call her back to the ranks of the Gerace with imperious whistles. This gave me a chance to practice whistling. Ever since I had lost my first teeth, I'd been expert at it: with my first and second fingers in my mouth I could make the most martial noises.

Also, I could sing not too badly and had learned several songs from my nurse. Sometimes as I walked behind my father, or went out in the boat with him, I'd sing "The Ladies of Havana," "Tabarin," or "The Mysterious Mountain," over and over again, or else Neapolitan songs — for instance, the one that goes: "You're a canary, you are my love!" hoping my father would secretly admire my voice. But he never gave a sign he'd even heard it. He was always silent, quick, gloomy, and hardly gave me a glance; but I thought it a tremendous privilege that mine was the only company he put up with on the island.

In the boat he rowed and I steered, sitting astern, or else astride the prow. Sometimes, drunk with divine happiness, I got beyond myself and, enormously presumptuous, started giving orders: "Forward, right oar! Forward, left oar! Backwater! Backwater!" But if he looked up at me, his silent splendor would make me feel my littleness, and I felt like a shrimp in the presence of a great dolphin.

The main reason for his supremacy was his difference from everyone else; this was the most wonderful, the most mysterious thing about him. He was different from all the men on Procida, which was like saying from everyone I knew in the world, and even — which made it so galling — from me. What set him above all the islanders was his height, first of all, but you noticed it only when you saw him beside other people: alone and isolated he was so well proportioned that he looked almost small. Then, besides his height, his coloring set him apart. In summer his body seemed to drink in the sun like oil, and glowed, darkly, caressingly; in winter it grew as pale as a pearl again. And I, who was dark in every season, felt that it showed an almost unearthly descent: as if he was brother to the sun and moon.

His soft straight hair was blond — of a dense fairness that gleamed and glowed in particular lights; and at the nape of his neck where it was shorter, almost shaven, it was actually golden. And his eyes were a violet blue like the sea at moments, darkened by clouds.

* * *

This beautiful hair of his hung down, always dusty and untidy, over his frowning forehead, as if to hide his thoughts. And his face, which through the years had kept the form his adolescent sufferings had set on it, looked arrogant, shut in. Sometimes his jealous secret thoughts seemed to flash across his face — quick, strange, smug-looking smiles or small insulting grimaces, or a look of unexpected ill temper, without any apparent reason. And I, who couldn't attribute any human caprice to him, found his sulks as majestic as the darkening of the day — a definite portent of mysterious happenings, as important as the history of the world.

His reasons for all this were his own business: I sought no explanation for his silence, his pleasure, his scorn, his torment; they were all for me like sacraments, great and grave, beyond all human measure and human littleness.

If I'd ever seen him drunk or delirious, I certainly wouldn't have imagined him subject to the usual weaknesses of mortals. As far as I can remember, he never seemed ill, but if I'd happened to see him ill, his illness wouldn't have seemed to me one of the usual accidents of nature. To me it would have seemed almost like a mysterious ritual, of which Wilhelm Gerace was the hero and those called in to help him would have seemed privileged, consecrated. And I certainly shouldn't have failed to suppose that some upheaval of the cosmos, from here to the stars, would have accompanied such an event.

On the island there is a piece of level ground lying between high rocks, where you find an echo. Sometimes, when he turned up there, my father amused himself shouting in German. Though I didn't know what he meant, I understood from his arrogant air that what he was saying must be terrible, and bold: scornfully, almost blasphemously, as if violating a law or breaking a spell, he flung out the words, and when the echo returned them, he laughed and shouted others still more brutal. Out of respect for his authority, I never dared lend him a hand, and though I was trembling with aggressive longing to join in, I listened in silence. I didn't seem to be attending the usual game of echoes that boys play often enough, but an epic duel. We were at Roncesvalles and suddenly on the terrace Roland would appear with his horn! We were at Thermopylae, and behind the rocks were hidden the Persian horsemen in their spiked caps.

When, as we wandered about the countryside, we reached a hill, he'd grow impatient and go dashing off, as stubbornly as if he was doing something really important, as bravely as if he was up on the mast of a sailing ship. He never bothered in the least to find out whether I was behind him or not, but though my legs were shorter than his, I followed him as fast as I could, my blood pumping with joy. For me it was no longer one of the usual walks I took any number of times a day, roaming around with Immacolatella. It was a famous journey; and down there a cheering crowd was awaiting us, and all the *thirty million gods!*

His vulnerability was as mysterious as his casualness. I remember that once he touched a jellyfish while we were swimming. Now everyone knows what will result when that happens: the skin turns red, but there are no bad or lasting effects. He must have known that perfectly well, but when he saw the marks on his chest — those red stripes — he was overcome with horror, and even his lips turned pale; he ran to the bank and flung himself flat on the ground, his arms flung out like a man who had fallen overwhelmed by nausea, by agony! I sat beside him: more than once I myself had been the victim of sea urchins, jellyfish, and other sea creatures, and I'd never bothered in the least about their attacks. But today, because he was the victim, I had a solemn feeling of tragedy. A great silence reigned over the beach, over all the sea; and the cry of a passing seagull seemed to me like the lament of a woman, a Fury.

The absolute certainties

He scorned to conquer my heart. He never taught me German, his native tongue, but always spoke Italian to me, an Italian that was different from the language Silvestro had taught me. All the words that he used seemed newly invented, still in their wild state;

and even my own Neapolitan words, which he often used, grew bolder and newer when he said them, like poetry. This strange language made him seem prophetically beautiful and wise.

How old was he? About nineteen years older than me! His age seemed to me as solemn and impressive as the Prophets or King Solomon. Everything he did or said had a dramatic fatality; in fact, he represented certainty to me, and everything he said or did was the response of a universal law from which I deduced the basic commandments of my life. This was what made his company most fascinating of all.

By birth he was a Protestant, but he professed no faith and displayed a nonchalant boldness toward eternity and its problems. I'm a Catholic, though, through the initiative of my nurse Silvestro, because when I was a month old he had me baptized in the parish church down at the port. This was, I think, the first and last time I have ever visited a church as a Christian. Sometimes I liked to linger in a church for a moment, as I would in a beautiful room, in a garden, or in a ship; but I would have been ashamed to genuflect or to go in for any other ceremonies of the kind, or to pray, even in my thoughts, as if I really believed it was the house of God, and that God was in touch with us, if he existed at all!

My father had some education because of his mother, the schoolmistress, and he owned some books, most of which she had left him, among them some in Italian. Besides this small family library, a good many other books had been left in the House of the Guaglioni by a young literature student who'd been a guest of the man from Amalfi for many summers. There were some children's books, detective stories, and adventure stories of various kinds as well, so I had quite a decent library to draw on, though the volumes were old and shabby.

They were mostly classical works or school textbooks: atlases and dictionaries, histories, poetry, novels, tragedies, collections of verse, and translations of famous books. Apart from those that I couldn't understand (written in German, Latin, or Greek), I read and studied them all, and some — my favorites — I read so many times that even today I remember them almost by heart.

I had the opportunity to learn a lot and chose to learn what attracted me most, what best answered my own feelings about life. These, and the basic certainties my father had already inspired in me, formed in my consciousness, or in my imagination, a kind of Code of Absolute Truth, whose most important laws might be listed like this:

1. The father's authority is sacred.
2. A man's true greatness consistes of courage in action, scorn of danger, and valor in combat.
3. The greatest baseness is betrayal, and to betray your own father, your own chief, or a friend, etc., is the very lowest depth of infamy.
4. No one living on the island of Procida is worthy of Wilhelm Gerace and of his son Arturo Ggerace. for a Gerace to become friendly with a Procidan would be degrading.
5. No love in life equals a mother's.
6. The most obvious proofs and all human experience show that God does not exist.

The second law

For a long time these childish certainties of mine were not just something I honored and loved — they made up my only possible idea of reality. It would then have seemed to me, not just dishonorable, but simply impossible, to live without my great certainties.

But as I had no one to talk to confidentially, I never said a word about them to anyone on earth. My Code remained my own jealously guarded secret. This kept it exclusive, proud; but it presented difficulties, too. Another difficulty was my Code's reserve; none of my laws, I mean, mentioned the thing I most hated: death. This reticence showed my sophisticated scorn of the thing I hated, which could only creep slyly in among the words of my laws, like a pariah, like a spy. In my own natural happiness, I chased all my thoughts away from death, as if it were something impossible — a dreadful amalgam of vices, hybrid, complex, full of evil and shame. But at the same time, the more I hated death the more I exaltedly enjoyed giving proofs of my own temerity: no game was enough fun if it lacked the fascination of risk. And so I grew up paradoxically, loving risks while I hated death. But maybe it wasn't a paradox, after all.

All reality seemed to me clear and certain: muddied only by the complex stain of death. And so, when I reached it, my thoughts scurried back in horror. But I was horrified, too, when I thought I could read in this a fatal sign of my own immaturity, like fear of the dark in ignorant women (immaturity was what shamed me most). So I waited for the darkness of death to dissolve in the brightness of reality, like smoke in the transparent air: this would be a sign of my own marvelous maturity.

Until that happened I couldn't consider myself anything but an inferior being — a child; and this mirage ahead seemed to beckon me, cunningly, to *cut a fine figure* (as my father put it) in every kind of childish daring . . . Yet daring like that, of course, wasn't enough (and well I knew it) to promote me to the envied position of maturity, nor to free me from my own deep and basic self-distrust. In fact, it was all a game, at heart, and death seemed always remote, an unlikely fancy. How would I behave, though, when it came to the test? In war, say, when I really saw — rising, growing, darkening before me — that monstrous horror?

And so I was skeptical as I played, skeptical even of my own courage; challenging myself, provoking myself, behaving like my own rival. Maybe this was all just because I was vain and nothing else, as W. G. once accused me of being; or maybe this precocious feeling of mine toward death, this glowering bitterness that tempted me to take risks, was nothing but the longing to love myself to the point of perdition — the same longing that ruined Narcissus.

Or was it all an excuse, maybe? There's no answer. And besides, it's my business. Well, anyway, in my Code the second law (where that unspoken fear lurked most naturally, as if in its den) seemed to me the most important of all.

The fourth law

The fourth law, which my father's attitude had suggested to me, was obviously the original reason for my solitude on the island — together, perhaps, with my own natural inclination. I can still see my small self wandering about the port, moving through the traffic and the bustle of people with an air at once shy, and hostile, and superior, like that of a foreigner who has happened among unfriendly natives. The nastiest thing I noticed about these people was their everlasting dependence on the practical necessities of life; a characteristic that made my father's difference stand out even more gloriously! Not only the poor, but the rich as well, seemed perpetually taken up with their daily interests and earnings; every one of them, from the urchins diving for coins or scraps of bread, or little colored stones, to the fishing boat owners who haggled over the price of fish as if it were the most important thing in their lives. Obviously not one of them was interested in books, in stirring deeds! Sometimes a master lined the schoolboys up in an empty space to do some military drill. But he was a great lymphatic oaf, the boys lacked ability and enthusiasm, and the whole spectacle — uniforms, movements, behavior — seemed to me so unwarlike that I'd look away at once with disgust. I should have blushed with shame if my father had turned up just then and found me watching a thing like that, people like that.

The rock of the Penitentiary

The only people on the island who seemed not to arouse my father's scorn and dislike were the invisible anonymous inmates of the Penitentiary. In fact, his romantic and disreputable outlook made me feel that a kind of brotherhood, or bond of loyalty, bound him not just to them but to all outcasts, all prisoners. And, of course, I felt drawn to them too, not just in imitation of my father, but from my own natural inclination, which made the prison appear a monstrous injustice to me, something absurd, like death.

The citadel of the Penitentiary seemed to me gloomy and sacred, and therefore forbidden; and I never remember going there alone during my whole childhood. Sometimes, as if fascinated, I started going up the slope that led to it, but as soon as I saw the gates, I always fled. Once or twice during walks with my father I remember we passed through the gates into its lonely precincts. And these rare trips stand out in my memories of childhood like visits to somewhere a long way from the island. I would follow my father down the wide deserted road, peering at the windows called *wolves' mouths,* and behind a barred window at the hospital would catch a glimpse of the mournful white of a convict's uniform, and look quickly away. The curiosity, or just the interest, of those who were free and fortunate seemed to me an insult to the prisoners; the sun shining on the road there seemed an affront; and the chickens clucking on the terraces of the huts, the doves cooing along the gutters, annoyed me with their chatter and their complaints. The only thing that didn't seem offensive was my father's freedom; on the contrary, it seemed reassuring, like a certainty of happiness — the only one up there on that gloomy hill. With his quick, attractive walk — rather rolling, like a sailor's gait — in his blue shirt puffed out by the wind, he seemed to me to bring victorious adventure, magical power, in his wake. Deep down in me I almost believed that only his mysterious disdain, or just thoughtlessness, prevented him making a heroic exercise of will, flinging down the prison gates, and freeing all the prisoners. I really couldn't imagine any limits to his power. If I'd believed in miracles, I'd certainly have believed him capable of performing them; but I didn't believe in miracles, as I've already said, or in the occult powers that some people trust their destiny to, the way shepherdesses trust in witches or fairies!

Odds and ends

Needless to say, my favorite books were those that gave either real or imaginary examples of my ideal of human greatness, of which my father seemed to me the living incarnation.

If I'd been an artist and had had epic poems, history books, and so on to illustrate, I think I'd have put my father in as hero a thousand times over; and I'd have had to melt down gold dust in my paintbox, to color his hair. Just as girls imagine fairies, saints, and queens all blond, I used to imagine that great captains and warriors were all of them fair, and looked exactly like my father. If the hero of a book was described as dark and of middle size, I preferred to think the author had made a mistake. But if the description was attested, and there was absolutely no doubt about it, I just liked the hero less, and he could never become my ideal.

When my father left, I was certain he was going off to heroic adventures. If he'd told me he was going to conquer the two Poles, or Persia, like Alexander of Macedon; that out at sea a whole fleet of ships under his command was awaiting him; that he was the terror of corsairs and bandits, or else that he was a great corsair or bandit himself, I'd have believed it all. He never said a word about his life away from the island, and around this mysterious and fascinating existence, in which of course he thought me unworthy to take part, my imagination surged. I respected his will so much that even in my thoughts I had no intention of spying on him or following him in secret. I never dared to ask him any questions. I wanted him to think well of me, perhaps even to admire me, and I hoped that in the end he might one day choose me as the companion of his travels.

In the meantime, when we were together, I took every opportunity to show him my courage and fearlessness. Barefoot, almost flying from point to point, I'd cross the burning rocks and dive into the sea from the highest of them. In the water I did the most astounding acrobatics and showed I was expert at every sort of swimming: I'd swim under water until I lost my breath and would drag things up with me when I surfaced: sea urchins, starfish, shells. But it was no use eyeing him from a distance, trying to get an admiring, or at least attentive, look from him. He'd sit on the shore without taking the smallest notice of me; and as soon as I ran up and flung myself on the sand beside him — quite casually, of course, and pretending I didn't care in the least what impression I made — he'd get up, with a kind of capricious indolence, looking

absent, frowning, as if listening to some mysterious invitation murmured in his ear. He'd raise his lazy arms and float away on his
side, and slowly, slowly swim away, in the arms of his bride, the sea.

About Algerian Knife

One day, I thought the chance to prove myself that I'd so long
been waiting for had turned up at last. We were bathing together,
and while we were swimming the famous amphibious watch he
was so proud of and wore even in the water inexplicably vanished.
We were pretty upset about it. He looked disgustedly at the sea,
then back at his bare wrist, and when I offered to dive down and
look for the watch on the bottom, he just shrugged his shoulders.
All the same, he gave me his underwater mask, and, trembling
with ambition and with the honor, off I went, while he waited
there for me on the bank.

I explored the bottom of the area where we'd been bathing.
The water wasn't very deep and was full of shoals and rocks. On
and on I searched, the tall rocks hiding me from sight, and when
I came up for air every now and then I heard him whistling to call
me back. At first I didn't answer, as I was ashamed not to turn up
victorious; but in the end I gave a long whistle from the top of the
rock to reassure him that I hadn't disappeared into the sea like the
watch. He looked at me without speaking or moving, and as I
watched him, golden with summer, a ring of white around his
wrist, I decided: "I'll get the watch back, or else die!"

I put on the mask again and went on exploring. Finding the
watch had become more than a matter of recovering a treasure, or
even just a point of honor. The search had taken on a strange air
of fatality; the time it took seemed immeasurable, its conclusion
the climax of my destiny! I wandered around the seabed —
varied, fantastic, inhuman — burning with the hope of dazzling
him, of seeming extraordinary. Impossible, fabulous stakes to play
for! And there was no one to help me — no angels, no saints to
pray to. The sea was splendid, indifferent; like Him.

It was no use. I took the mask off exhaustedly and grabbed a rock with my hands, so as to rest. The rock hid me from the shore, and hid my dismay from my father. I was alone, without knowing the way out, caught in a maze: I clutched the rock and swayed slowly in the water. And then, as I moved, I suddenly caught a glitter of metal in the sun! I hung on with two hands, jumped up on the rock, and discovered the lost watch sparkling in a dry crevice. It was undamaged, and when I held it to my ear I could hear it ticking.

I closed my hand over it and reached the beach in a few minutes, the mask dangling around my neck. My father's eyes lit up when he saw me arrive triumphant. "You've found it!" he exclaimed, almost incredulously, and as if to show he owned it, or to affirm his right to it, he snatched the watch out of my hand as if it were a prize I might contest with him. He put it up to his ear and looked at it delightedly. "It was there, on that rock over there," I cried, still breathless. I was beyond myself: I wanted to jump and dance, but controlled myself proudly, so as not to make it seem I gave too much importance to what I'd done. My father looked at the rock frowning thoughtfully. "Ah," he said after a bit. "Now I remember: I took it off while we were looking for shells, because I wanted to pull some limpets off the rock. Then you called me to show me a sea urchin you'd got hold of, and made me forget it. If you hadn't been swanking about your blasted sea urchin, I wouldn't have forgotten!"

"Lost!" he continued, sarcastically shrugging his shoulders. "I knew perfectly well it wasn't lost. It's got an absolutely foolproof clasp, it can't go wrong." And, looking very pleased, he put the watch on his wrist.

Well, there was fate mocking me: what I'd done lost almost all its splendor. Disappointment rose feverishly in me, my face trembled, my eyes stung. "If I cry, I'll be dishonored," I thought, and, bringing violence in to counter my weakness, I dragged the useless old mask off my neck and angrily gave it back to my father.

My father gave me an arrogant glance as he took it, as if to say, "Hey, now, what's this about?" And as I couldn't face him after I'd

been so rude, I made a dash for it. But he pinned my bare foot
down with his — fast and playfully — to stop me going, and I saw
his face bent over me, smiling with that faunal look which for a
moment made him look like a goat. He stuck his wrist with the
watch on it under my nose and said harshly: "D'you know what
the make of this watch is? Read it — it's printed on the face."

There on the face, in minute letters, was written the word
AMICUS.

"It's a Latin word," my father explained. "D'you know what it
means?"

"Friend," I answered, rather pleased with my quickness.

"*Friend*," he repeated. "And this watch, with this name, means
something very important. A matter of life and death. Guess."

I smiled, thinking for a minute that my father wanted to make
the watch a symbol of our friendship: in life and death. "There,
you can't guess it!" he exclaimed, making a slightly scornful face.
"Would you like to know? Well, this watch is a present I had from
a friend, maybe the best friend I've got. D'you know the expression 'two bodies and one soul'? Years ago, one New Year's Eve, I
was in a town where I knew no one. I was alone, I'd spent all my
money, and although it was terribly cold I had to spend the night
under a bridge. That night my friend was in another town and it
was a long time since he'd had news of me; so he couldn't know
where I was, nor what sort of a state I was in. But as it was New
Year's Eve, he spent all the evening wondering: 'Where can he be,
tonight? Who can he be celebrating with tonight?' and went to
bed early. Toward midnight he was suddenly seized with shivers
and a freezing cold he couldn't explain; he had no temperature;
he was in bed with good thick blankets in a warm room, but he
shivered the whole night through, no better able to get warm than
if he'd gone to bed on a frozen waste, without shelter.

"Another time I was fooling around with him and fell over by
mistake and hurt my knee on some glass, and he whipped out an
Algerian knife I'd given him and cut his own knee at exactly the
same place.

"When he gave me the watch, he said, 'Look, I've shut my

heart up in this watch. Take it — I'm giving you my heart. Wherever you are, whether near or far, the day this watch stops beating, my heart will have ceased to beat too!'"

It was unusual for my father to talk to me for so long, and so confidentially. He didn't tell me his great friend's name, though: and a name came into my mind — Romeo! Romeo-Boote was actually the only friend of my father's I'd ever heard of, but he was dead, so my father must have meant someone else that day — someone else, who in my mind was called Algerian Knife, lived in the glorious territory my father kept returning to, chief among the satellites that followed the fugitive light of Wilhelm Gerace southward! The one who was privileged! For a moment I caught a glimpse of him: abandoned in some splendid tragic setting, perhaps alone in the Ural Mountains, awaiting my father: with a bewitched, Semitic face, a bleeding knee, and, where his heart should have been, a hollow.

Departures

That day my father left. Immacolatella and I watched him as usual while he bundled buttonless shirts, sweater, heavy jacket, and so forth, into his suitcase. He always left with his whole wardrobe in the suitcase, so you never could tell how long he was going to be away. He might come back in two or three days, or he might stay away for months, until the winter or longer.

He always got ready to leave at the very last minute, moving hastily, mechanically, his face distracted, as if in his mind he'd already left the island. As I saw him shut the suitcase, my heart heaved with a sudden impulse.

"Couldn't you take me with you?" I said.

I hadn't planned this question and I saw at once that he didn't even consider it. He glowered a bit, and his lips moved very slightly, as if he was thinking of something else.

"With me?" he answered, looking me up and down. "Whatever for? You're a little boy. Wait until you're grown up to come away with me."

He tied a rope quickly around the suitcase, which was a very ordinary one, and rather battered, and knotted the rope firmly, with a vigorously efficient sailor's knot. Then, with me and Immacolatella tagging along, he hurried downstairs and left the House of the Guaglioni fast, holding the suitcase by one end of the rope, his cheeks flushed, his eyes dark with impatience. He had already grown legendary and remote — a gaucho crossing the Argentine pampas, lassoing a bull; a captain in the Greek army, dragging behind his chariot on the battlefield of Troy the body of a defeated Trojan; a horseman on the steppes, racing beside a yearling, and ready to mount him at the gallop. And to think he still had on his skin the salt of the Procidan sea, in which he'd been bathing with me that very morning!

Below in the street the carriage that was to take us down to the port was waiting, and I sat beside him on the red damask seat, while, as usual, Immacolatella followed happily down the road, trying to race the horse. She beat him right from the start, easily leaving him far behind, and popped up again at the end of the street, her ears pricked, barking to greet us and provoke him. But the horse took not the slightest notice and carried on at his normal elderly trot, obviously thinking her crazy.

My father was silent and kept looking at his watch, furiously impatient, then at the driver's back, and at the horse, as if to make the driver whip harder, the horse go faster. And my imagination was soaring flamelike toward another departure I'd been promised that same day. I'd be sitting in the carriage beside my father as I was sitting now, but not just to go to the port with him and say good-bye from the quay, while he went off on the steamer. No! — to leave on the steamer with him, to go away with him! Maybe to Venice or Palermo; maybe as far as Scotland, or to the delta of the Nile, or to Colorado! To meet Algerian Knife and those other followers of ours who'd be waiting for us across the sea!

Wait until you're grown up to come away with me. I had a moment of revolt against the intransigence of life, which condemned me to a dead Siberian waste of days and nights before it removed the bitterness of being a boy. Just then I'd even have submitted to a long, long sleep out of sheer impatience; a sleep that would have got me through this miserable age of mine without my noticing it and turned me suddenly into a man, my father's equal. *My father's equal!* Alas, I thought, as I watched him, even when I'm a man, I'll never be his equal. I'll never have fair hair, or violet-blue eyes; and I'll never, never be so handsome!

The steamer that came from Ischia and would be taking my father to Naples had not yet come in. There were a few minutes to wait. My father and I sat down on his suitcase together, and Immacolatella, out of breath from her race, lay down at our feet. She seemed sure that this pause on the dock meant the end of our journey, that we had now arrived at our destination and settled down and could all three of us rest as long as we liked without ever having to separate.

And yet when the steamer had cast anchor, and my father and I got up, she got up too, wagging her tail, and not looking the least bit surprised. Then when my father had left us both and was on the steamer moving away from the dock, she barked loudly and accusingly, but without any serious fuss. She didn't really mind my father's leaving; as far as she was concerned, I was the master. If I'd left, she would have flung herself into the sea and tried to catch up with the steamer, and then, when she'd got back to the shore, she'd have stayed desperately on the dock there, sobbing and calling me until death.

Immacolatella

The very minute he left Procida, my father turned into a legend again. The time we'd spent together was almost present, almost tangible, and seemed still to be swaying before me, dazzling and hazy, to fascinate me with its ghostly beauty; then, like a phantom ship, it vanished with dizzying speed, twirling around and around. A kind of glittering mist, echoes of broken voices, full of manly daring and derision, were all that remained of him. He already seemed like an event beyond time, beyond the history of Procida:

maybe not *lost*, but *nonexistent!* Every relic of him about the house — the mark of his head on a pillow, a gap-toothed comb, an empty package of cigarettes — seemed to me miraculous. Like the prince finding Cinderella's gold slipper, I kept saying to myself, "Well then, it's true!"

When my father had gone, Immacolatella would wander around the House of the Guaglioni with me, worried by my listlessness, urging me to play and forget the past. The nonsense she went in for! She'd jump in the air and fling herself down like a dancer, or play the court fool to my king. And if she saw I wasn't taking any notice, she'd come up impatiently and look at me with those brown eyes of hers. "What are you thinking about?" she'd ask me. "Can't I know what's the matter?" — like women who, when a man's serious, think he's ill, or get jealous because his serious thoughts seem a betrayal of their own superficiality.

And as if she'd been a woman, I'd get rid of her. "Let me alone a bit," I'd say. "I want to think. There are some things you don't understand. Go along and play on your own. I'll see you later." But she was obstinate, and I couldn't get it into her head, and, in the end, with her crazy games, she made me want to play with her and go crazy myself. That would have been her chance to be haughty, but she was a happy soul, without vanity, and she greeted me with a fine frenzy of triumph, thinking my earlier seriousness had all been faked to cut a figure, as in the tarantella.

What a lot of fuss about a dog, you'll say. But when I was a boy I'd no other friend, and you can't deny she was extraordinary. We'd invented a kind of deaf-and-dumb language between us: tail, eyes, movements, the pitch of her voice — all of them told me every thought of hers, and I understood. Although she was female, she loved daring and adventure. She'd go swimming with me, and act as my pilot in the boat, barking when some obstacle loomed up. As I wandered about the island, she'd always follow me; and every day, as we came back through the alleys we'd used and the fields we'd crossed a hundred times, she'd get as excited as if we were two explorers in uncharted country. When we crossed the small strip of water, and disembarked on the little desert island of Vivara, which is just a few yards from Procida, the wild rabbits fled before us, thinking we were a hunter and his hunting dog, and she'd follow them a bit for the fun of running, and then come back behind me, content to behave like a sheepdog.

She was courted a lot, but until she was eight years old she was never pregnant.

Grandson of an ogress?

Throughout my whole childhood, you might say, the only female being I knew was Immacolatella. In my famous Code of Absolute Certainties, there was no law about women and love, because, as far as I could see, there was no certainty (apart from a mother's love) about women. My father's greatest friend, Romeo-Boote, had hated them, but what about my mother? Had even she, being a woman, been repulsed by him? This question caused a kind of uneasiness between me and the ghost of the man from Amalfi, and it always remained unanswered, as I'd never heard a single word from my father either about him or about women; and his smile when the terror every woman felt for the House of the Guaglioni was mentioned wasn't an explanation, but an enigma.

As for my mother, in my whole life I don't suppose I heard him mention her more than a couple of times, and that was only in passing and quite by chance. I remember how his voice seemed to pause almost tenderly on the name, then at once shied off it, quickly, sourly, bashfully, while he looked like a handsome tomcat, exotic, night-wandering, and unpunishable, stopping a moment to consider, with a touch of his velvet paw, the cold pelt of a dead female.

I longed for him, of course, to tell me something about my darling mother; but I respected his silence, understanding perfectly well that it would be too painful for him to remember his wife's death.

There was another dead woman he never spoke about — my

German grandmother. But he must have nursed some terrible grudge against her, or so I deduced, at least, from the single time she came up, in silence, very briefly, between us.

One day we were together in his bedroom; he was smoking distractedly a short way away from me, and I was rummaging through some books in the wardrobe, when I came across a photograph I'd never seen before: a group of girls, all about the same age, one of them marked with a cross in ink. Of course I looked with most interest at her; and, in the moment I saw her, she seemed a perfectly ordinary girl in a blouse and skirt, wearing a ribbon in her hair, and with a large florid bosom inside a high-necked white blouse. She was altogether too big, too heavy and square in both figure and face, for beauty; but her romantic pose betrayed an almost pathetic wish to seem delicate and pretty.

Under the photograph some words were written in German; but apart from that, there was something about her eyes and mouth, some vague resemblance, in spite of her very ordinary appearance, which made me guess at once who she was. Normal curiosity made me run to my father to confirm it; I showed him the photograph at once and asked him if I was right in thinking the fair girl was my grandmother from Germany.

He shook himself out of his thoughts, glanced angrily at the picture I was holding up in triumph, and snatched it brusquely away. "What d'you think you're up to, rummaging about there?" he said. "Yes, it's your grandmother: my mother," he snarled, with an almost vulgar sneer, a look of obvious dislike, and added, his teeth clenched: "Or rather, luckily, it *was*."

And he said no more about it, but went across to the chest of drawers and flung the photograph into the bottom drawer, then kicked it brutally shut, and as he did so, he looked so baleful, so disgusted, that he seemed to be passing sentence on her. "Stay there, you foul, beastly old woman!" he seemed to be saying. "Don't let me ever see you again, from now on!"

That was all. But it was enough to give me a confused suspicion that when she was alive, my grandmother had been an ogress, or something dreadful like that. Later I happened to glance in the drawer again, but the photograph had vanished. My father had obviously put it in some darker hiding place.

Well, as you see, my father's experience did nothing to enlighten my ignorance about women.

Women

Besides, except for my mother's maternity, nothing about their obscure sex really seemed to matter much, and I certainly didn't bother to poke into any of their mysteries. The great deeds I loved to read about were always done by men, never by women. Adventure, war, and glory were all of them manly privileges. Women stood for love, and books talked about splendid, queenly women, but I had a suspicion that women like that, and even that marvelous feeling of love, were just something invented by books, nothing really true. The perfect hero really did exist, I saw the proof of it in my father. But as for wonderful women, queens of love, like those in books — I never saw a single one. Maybe love, passion — this burning business they kept talking about — was something quite impossible, fantastic.

Although I knew nothing about real women, the glimpses I got of them were quite enough to make me conclude that they had absolutely nothing in common with the women in books. Real women, I thought, weren't splendid or magnificent. They were little creatures who could never grow as big as men, and they spent their whole life shut up indoors; that's why they were so pale. All bundled up in the aprons, skirts, and petticoats that had to hide those mysterious bodies of theirs, they seemed to me misshapen, almost deformed. Always busy, bustling, and ashamed of themselves, maybe because they were so ugly, they padded around like downcast animals, without any of the elegance, the casualness, the freedom of men. They'd get together in groups and chatter, waving excitedly, glancing around for fear someone might overhear their secrets. What dull secrets they must have been! Childish things, of course! No Absolute Certainties could possibly interest them.

Their eyes were all the same color — black; their hair was always dark, rough, wild looking. As far as I was concerned, they could keep as far from the House of the Guaglioni as they liked. I'd certainly never fall in love with one of them, or want to marry one.

Sometimes, though not very often, some foreign woman would come to the island and go down to the beach and get undressed to bathe, without the slightest modesty, just like a man. Like everyone else on Procida, I wasn't the least bit curious about these foreign bathers. My father seemed to consider them ridiculous and hateful and avoided the places where they bathed, just as I did; we'd have liked to chase them away, because we felt possessive about our beaches. And as for the women, no one even looked at them. As far as Procidans were concerned, as far as I was concerned, they weren't women at all, but crazy beasts come down from the moon. It never entered my head that their shameless bodies might be beautiful.

Well, that seems to cover almost all my views on women!

I thought of the fate of women. When a girl was born in Procida, the family was upset. As children they were no uglier than boys, not very different, but they had no hope of growing up into handsome heroes; their only hope was to marry a hero, to serve him, to carry on his name, to be his exclusive property, respected by everyone, and to have by him a fine son, just like his father.

My mother hadn't even had this satisfaction. She'd only just had time to see her dark, and dark-eyed, son, as unlike her husband, Wilhelm, as possible; and if by any chance this son was destined (though dark) to become a hero, she wouldn't know it because she was dead.

The Oriental tent

In the photograph, which is the only picture of her I know, my mother seems no more beautiful than other women, but from the time I was quite small, whenever I looked at the picture — as I did again and again — I never wondered if she was ugly or beautiful, or even thought of comparing her with anyone else. She was *my mother!* And I can't say what enchantment it meant to me then, that lost motherhood of hers!

She died because of me: it was as if I had killed her. I was the power, the violence of her destiny, but she consoled me, and healed my cruelty. This was the first sweet bond between us — my remorse, melted in her forgiveness.

Remembering her portrait, I realize she was almost a child, and in fact she was less than eighteen. She looks serious and self-possessed, like a grown-up, but her searching face is a child's, and her shapeless body, clumsily bundled up in her maternity dress, still has a look of childhood. But I saw a mother in the portrait then, and couldn't possibly see her as childish. If I gave her any age at all, it was the age of maturity, boundless as the seashore, as summer on the sea; but perhaps it was eternity too, virginal, sweet, unchanging as a star. She was someone my regrets had invented, with every quality I could wish for, and expressions and voices that kept changing. But above all, in the hopeless longing I had for her, I thought of her as faithfulness, as trust, as conversation, as everything in fact, that fathers weren't, in my experience. A mother was someone who'd have waited for me to come home, who'd have thought of me day and night, someone who'd have approved of all I said, praised all I did, and boasted about the re-markable beauty of dark-eyed, dark-haired people — of medium-sized, maybe even small people. Anyone who dared speak ill of me had better think thrice when she was around! She'd think I was, without question, the most important person on earth! The name *Arturo* would be her golden standard! And she'd think that, as soon as it was mentioned, everyone would know it meant me. Other Arturos who might exist about the world would all have been copycats, second-bests.

Even hens and cats have a special tender tone when they call their young, so you can imagine what a delicious voice she'd have had when she called Arturo. Of course she'd have added all sorts of womanly endearments, and I'd have pushed them elegantly away, like Julius Caesar pushing away the crown. Of course you've got to push away compliments, so as not to get spoiled, but as you can't spoil yourself, a mother's absolutely necessary.

Quite apart from endearments, I lived entirely without kisses and caresses, and out of pride, I had to approve of this. But sometimes, especially in the evening, when I was alone in a room and started to miss my mother, *mother* came to mean precisely *caresses*. I longed for her large, her holy body, for her small silken hands, for her breath. In winter my bed was freezing cold, but to warm me there was only Immacolatella to sleep with, cuddled close.

As I didn't believe in God or in religion, I didn't even believe in a future life and in the spirits of the dead. If I listened to reason, I knew that all that remained of my mother was shut underground in the cemetery. But reason retreated before her, and without realizing it, I actually believed in heaven, because of her. What else was that kind of Oriental tent floating on air between the sky and the earth, where she dwelled alone, idly contemplating the sky with upturned eyes like one transfigured? There, every time I thought of her, my mother came quite naturally to mind. Later, the day came when I no longer looked for her; she had vanished. Someone had folded up the rich Oriental tent and taken it away.

But while I was small, I'd turn to her lovingly at the times when other people pray. My mother was always wandering about the island, and she was so present, suspended there in the air, that I seemed to be talking to her, the way you talk to a girl leaning out from a balcony. She was one of the island's enchantments. I never went to her grave, because I've always hated cemeteries and all the paraphernalia of death; yet one of the spells that Procida wove for me was that little grave. Because my mother was buried in it, I almost felt her fantastic person was a prisoner there, there in the island's blue air, like a canary in its golden cage. Perhaps for this reason, as soon as I had gone a short way out to sea in my boat, I was suddenly seized with a bitter loneliness that made me turn back. It was she who was calling me back, like the sirens.

Waiting and meeting

But there was another reason, actually, another even more powerful reason to make me turn the prow back toward Procida when
I got out into the open sea: the idea that my father might return
while I was away. I felt it unbearable not to be on the island when
he was there, and for this reason, although I was free and loved
adventure, I never left the Procidan sea for other countries. I was
often tempted to flee in my boat, to go and search for him, but
then I realized how absurd it was to hope I'd find him among so
many islands and continents. If I left Procida I might lose him forever, whereas only in Procida was there the certainty that sooner
or later he'd return. One couldn't guess when: sometimes he
reappeared suddenly a few hours after he'd left; sometimes I
didn't see him again for months. And every day, when the steamer
arrived, and every evening when I went home to the House of the
Guaglioni, I hoped to see him. This eternal hope of mine was another of Procida's enchantments.

One morning Immacolatella and I went out in *The Torpedo-
boat of the Antilles* and decided to go as far as Ischia. I rowed for
nearly an hour, but when I turned and saw Procida receding, I felt
such bitter longing that I couldn't bear it. I turned the prow and
we went back.

My father never wrote letters, never gave me any news of himself, never sent any greetings. And to me it seemed fabulous that
all the same he existed for sure, that every moment I lived in Procida he was living in some unknown country, in some unknown
room, among strange companions I thought glorious and happy
simply because they were with him (I never doubted that my father's companionship was the most aristocratic privilege that
anyone living could long for). As soon as I thought: "At this very
moment he . . ." I felt something rent inside me, as if a black
screen had been torn away in my mind; a romantic vision flashed
across it. My father was hardly ever alone in these apparitions;
around him stood the nebulous figures of his followers, and near
him, always beside him like a shadow, the elect of the whole

aristocracy — *Algerian Knife.* My father, waving his pistol defiantly, leaping on the prow of an immense armed vessel, and Algerian Knife, wounded, perhaps mortally, dragging along behind, holding out the last cartridge to him; my father advancing through the dense jungle with Algerian Knife, who, armed with a cutlass, was helping him to hack open a way between the lianas; my father in his tent on the battlefield, resting on a camp bed, and Algerian Knife squatting on the ground at his feet, playing Spanish music on a guitar . . .

Wait until you're grown up to come away with me.

Sometimes, those solitary days, my senses would deceive me, and make me believe he'd return. I'd be gazing out to sea on a stormy day, and, in the thunder of the breakers, would seem to hear his voice calling me. I'd whirl around to face the beach; it would be empty. One afternoon I reached the quay after the steamer had arrived and from a distance saw a blond man sitting at the café in the square. I hurried up, certain I'd find he'd just disembarked and was drinking a glass of Ischian wine, and found myself facing a dark foreigner wearing a straw hat. In the evening, when I was having supper in the kitchen, I'd see Immacolatella prick up her ears and bound across to the window: I'd jump up, hoping to find him outside, turned up unexpectedly, and instead I'd be just in time to see, leaping down from the bars and racing off, a cat that had peered in to spy on us at supper.

Each day Immacolatella and I would go to meet the steamer from Naples nearly every time it arrived. The passengers who got off were almost always people we knew, mostly Procidans who'd left in the morning and came back in the evening: the shipper, the tailor's wife, the midwife, the owner of the Savoy Hotel. And some days, when the ordinary passengers had disembarked, you'd see the prisoners destined for the Penitentiary. Dressed in their own clothes, but handcuffed and guarded, they were quickly loaded into the Black Maria that took them to the castle. As they walked past, I avoided looking at them, not out of scorn, of course, but out of respect.

Meantime, the sailors pulled away in their boat and the steamer left again for Ischia; and once more the blond man I was waiting for had failed to come.

But sooner or later he did come. It might be just on the day when, for some reason or other, I wasn't there waiting. And then when I got home I really did find what I'd always seen in my dreams: him sitting on his bed, smoking a cigarette, with his suitcase still shut at his feet.

When he saw me he'd say:

"Hallo. You here?"

But at that moment, Immacolatella, who'd lagged behind in the street, would dash into the room like a whirlwind, and my father'd start struggling with her as usual, and she as usual would overdo her welcome. "Hey you pup — that's enough!" I'd interrupt, yelling. These idiotic antics seemed to show pretty poor judgment. Who did she think she was? My father must have met a whole heap of better dogs than she was in all this time away! And besides, I had a feeling these tremendous welcomes she gave my father were just an excuse to make a racket. She didn't really care that much about my father's homecoming. I was the master, as far as she was concerned.

At last she'd quiet down, and my father would say to me as he smoked: "Well, what's the news?"

But he didn't take much notice of what I told him. He'd even interrupt me on some other subject, and ask: "Is the boat all right?" or else start listening to the hours striking in the church tower and compare his own watch and protest: "What's that — a quarter to six? What nonsense — it's nearly six o'clock. That clock's getting madder and madder." Then, followed by the pair of us, taciturn, aggressive, he'd start walking up and down the House of the Guaglioni, flinging open doors and windows to take up his ownership again. And the House of the Guaglioni already seemed a great ship in full sail in midocean on a stupendous voyage.

In the end, my captain went back to his room and flung himself down on the bed, looking gloomy and absent. Was he already thinking of leaving again? He looked at the sky outside the window. "New moon," he observed, with an air that seemed to be saying: "The same old moon. The same old Procidan moon!"

More about the man from Amalfi

Meantime, as I watched him, I noticed a few wrinkles under his eyes, among his eyebrows, around his lips. I thought enviously: "They're signs of age. When I've got wrinkles too it'll show I'm grown up and then he and I can always be together."

While I waited for this mythological age, I'd been nursing another hope for some time, something I never dared confess to my father because it seemed too ambitious. In the end I made up my mind one evening. "Couldn't you," I said warmly, "couldn't you bring some of your friends here to Procida sometime?" I said "some of your friends," but I was thinking of one in particular — A. K.

My father didn't answer at first, but scowled so fiercely at me that my very heart turned cold, and I felt so hurt that I wanted to go to my room and console myself with Immacolatella's friendship. But I saw my father's eyes change color and grow cheerful, as if he'd had a change of thought while he watched me. He smiled, and I recognized that faunal smile that reminded me of a goat, and that once before had been the first sign that he was going to speak to me confidentially.

I smiled too, though I was still rather angry. And he frowned and came out with this extraordinary declaration: "Friends, indeed! Don't you know I've only one friend here in Procida, and there must never be another? I don't want anyone else. And that means forever."

When he said this I felt almost transfigured. Who was this single friend of his here in Procida? Could he possibly mean me? Staring at me severely he went on: "Look over there! D'you know who that is in the picture?"

And he pointed to the photograph of the man from Amalfi that was always in his room.

"It's Romeo," I murmured.

"That's right, my lad," he exclaimed, in a tone of biting superiority.

"The first time I came here to Procida," he continued, making a reminiscent face, "I realized at once — and besides, I knew it before I got off the boat — that this was desert island as far as I was concerned. I'd agreed to call myself Gerace because one name's as good as another. It even says so in a poem, one of those that boys write in autograph albums:

> What's in a name: that which we call a rose
> By any other name would smell as sweet.

"To me Gerace meant I'd have land and money coming, so I didn't give a damn about this Procidan surname. But in this empty crater I had only one friend — him; and if Procida became my country, it wasn't for the sake of the Geraces, but because of him.

"I remember when I got off here, and everyone looked at me askance, like some exotic animal, only his dogs treated me as I deserved. There were eight of them, all wicked beasts, and they usually set on anyone who went near them. Instead, when I climbed up here to look at them close (I'd caught glimpses of them from below, and I was interested because they were of various breeds, and fine ones among them), all eight of them came around to welcome me as if they knew me, as if I was already the owner of the house. It was then I met him too, and from then on not a day passed without my coming here. To tell you the truth, I went on coming because I liked playing with the dogs, more than for his sake, because although he made an effort to be very amusing, it wasn't much fun to sit around listening to an old man's chatter, and a blind man at that. But even though I preferred his dogs' company to his, he was quite happy as long as I didn't stay away.

"Sometimes he'd say to me: 'I've always been lucky, and now before dying I've had the best luck of all. The only reason I was sorry not to have married was this: because I didn't have a son I could love as myself. And now I've found him — my angel, my little son; it's you!'

"He said, too, that the night before he met me, he'd had one dream after another, and that they'd all been prophetic. He'd dreamed, for instance, that he'd gone back to the time when he was a shipper, and he'd received, without knowing where it came from, a box of fragrant wood with splendidly colored stones in it, and Oriental spices, scented like flowers. Then he'd dreamed he was still healthy and active and had gone hunting on the island of Vivara, and that his dogs had unearthed a family of hares, but without wounding them, among them a leveret as beautiful as an angel, with gold flecks in its black fur. Then he'd dreamed that in his room there grew a bitter orange tree — enchanted and silvered with moonlight . . . and all sorts of other visions like that.

"I'd retort skeptically when I heard him tell these stories, because I knew perfectly well they were all nonsense. He liked me to believe that since he'd been blind, he'd always had fantastic dreams, much more highly colored than reality, and that going to sleep was like going to a wonderful party for him, a romantic adventure — a second life, in fact. But I could see through his stories and could tell immediately when he was making it all up, to show off. I knew perfectly well they were all inventions of his, that he wanted to cut a fine figure in my eyes and not seem too wretched in his old age. The fact was, actually, that it was too late for him even to console himself in sleep. He suffered from insomnia, as old men often do when they get near their end, and he was ill from stupid manias, frenzies, obsessions, that bothered him day and night. Everyone in Procida knew all this, but he didn't want to confess it to me, first of all out of vanity, and second because he guessed that if he made a habit of weeping on my shoulder I'd pretty soon leave him. I'm made like that, I'm no Sister of Charity. My mother used to yell at me the whole time: 'You're one of those people they talk about in the Gospel — if a friend asks for a piece of bread, you give him a stone.'

"Well, the fact was that for all his boasting, his only beautiful dream was my company. It wasn't hard to see that. And as far as I was concerned, even if I wanted a change, I hadn't much choice of occupation here in Procida. I had no other friend, no other place to go to, and what's more, not a penny in my pocket. Your grandfather never gave me a penny before he left me his money, and I never asked him for money. I preferred asking Amalfi for it, but he didn't like giving it and gave me only a bit at a time — just enough for cigarettes, because he was afraid that if I had plenty of money I might escape from the island.

"So I wandered around and around and around, and every day ended up here.

"Sometimes he said to me, 'Just think, in the past I've seen so many places, so many people, I could people a nation with those I've seen. And the dearest friend of my whole life — that's you — I've met only when I'm blind. If I'd seen just one person — you — I could say I'd known all the beauty of life. But it's just you I can't see. And now, as I think of death, of leaving this life and this beautiful little island of Procida, where I've known all the freedom and joy in the world, I console myself with one hope: some people believe the dead are spirits and see everything — suppose that's true? And if it is, I'll be able to see you here after death, and that consoles me for dying. What do you think of it?' I would answer: 'Hope away, hope away, Amalfi!' (That's what I usually called him.) 'If the dead really see, then you can be happy to die. Because it's certainly worth it if you're going to see me. It's a pity you've got the facts wrong. Like to know the difference between a blind man like you and a dead man?' 'What is it?' he said. 'Tell me.' 'A blind man like you still has eyes, but can't see: a dead man can't see and hasn't even got eyes. You can be perfectly sure of that, Amalfi. You've never seen me, and you never will see me, not if you wait hundreds of years.'

"He kept asking me to describe what I was like — my face and coloring, my eyes; whether I had flecks in the irises or a ring around the pupil, and so on. And so as not to satisfy his curiosity too much, I'd answer him first one way, and then another, depending on how I felt. One time I'd tell him I had bloodshot eyes like a tiger, another time that I had one blue eye and one black eye. Or else I said I had a scar on my cheek and pulled in the muscles of my face in such a way that when he touched my cheek to see if it was true, he'd find a deep gash, and almost be left wondering.

"Then he'd say to me: 'Well, in a way it's best for me not to know what you're doing, after I've died. I could expect nothing but bitter disappointment, because I'd have to see you making other friends and being with them as you used always to be with me. Just think of seeing you with other friends, even in this same island where our friendship is written on the stones, in the air!' 'Well, you can be perfectly sure of that,' I'd answer. 'The dead may be all right for company over there, but I'm *alive*, and I'll find my friends among the living. I'll certainly have something better to do with my days than grow chrysanthemums on a dead man's grave!' He didn't want me to see how much my answer hurt him, but he turned pale and in a moment looked worn out. He suffered more than other people because until these last years of his life he'd never felt any pain. Before that his whole life had been a game, a party; he'd never known that you can suffer because of someone else. Well, that's what happened: I taught him!

"What made him suffer most was fear that one fine day I'd get up and leave Procida out of impatience. If I was just a bit longer in coming than he expected, he began thinking at once that I'd left without saying a word, and even that I was already far away from Procida's shores. But actually I never left the island during the two years he was still alive. And then one night when I was asleep as usual in your grandfather's house, he died here, suddenly and alone, without even saying good-bye. It was very odd next day for me.

"At first I tried to persuade myself, to force myself to believe, that he'd only fainted: and I began beating the doctor, telling him he was nothing but a country quack and a nincompoop and that was why he said there was nothing to be done! But that it was his duty to find a cure immediately! Some medicine, some injection! It was his duty! I ordered him to! I was so much beyond myself, that I actually wanted him to bring him to life that very minute.

And when the doctor had left, and I was alone with the body, I had a terrible nervous collapse — I was still just a boy, remember — and I began sobbing. My tears made me angry, made me insult the dead man; I called him coward, idiot, beast, for dying without even saying good-bye. This seemed to me the very worst thing he could have done, the one thing I just couldn't accept. I don't know why I felt that good-bye was something so unique, so fatal. I was furious when I remembered all the times I'd kept him waiting, whole days I'd kept him without a visit, not because I had had anything special to do, but just because of some beastliness in my own character, or to show off — nothing more. Actually, it was a very good thing: it's best not to spoil people too much, and to tell them to go to the devil every so often — otherwise it would be the end! Life would lumber on, like a boat loaded with ballast, and take us to the bottom to drown . . . But just then I cared nothing for reason, and all the hours, all the days I'd spent wandering about, far from Amalfi's house, just to make him sigh, just to be difficult, now seemed like treasures I'd lost, with nothing in return for them."

(At this point in the story, my father looked up at the portrait of the man from Amalfi with a tender, friendly expression, but immediately burst into an irreverent, theatrical laugh, as if to mock the dead man.)

"I felt then that nothing and no one seemed worth spending my time with, compared with Romeo; I was absolutely certain I'd never meet anyone so marvelous, so fascinating, so entirely beautiful! Yes, there seemed to me not the smallest doubt that he alone could boast of real beauty. If the queen of Sheba, or the god Mars, or the goddess Venus, has turned up in person just then, I'd have thought them vulgar, postcardish creatures compared with him. Who else had his rather febrile, cunning, delicate smile? Or, with such an exaggerated height, those tiny hands that gesticulated at every word, especially when he was telling tall tales? Or eyes with such terrible beauty, terrible because they'd been hurt, because their expression was lost, soulless, mindless, inhuman! And then his manner! Defenseless, unsure of himself, ashamed (he was bit-

terly ashamed of his blindness), but haughty, incurably haughty!
The most beautiful dancers — even angels — weren't as graceful
as he was; they were nothing compared with him — on a different
level altogether!

"Even his gray curls that hung in a mane behind his ears, and
his provincial way of dressing, with those rather ridiculous narrow
trousers, now seemed to me supremely elegant! And his grace, his
elegance, now increased my despair. Stupid, blind idiot! If hell
existed, with all my heart I wished him already there!

"To think that his company, which until yesterday was something certain, dependable, and mine to do what I liked with, had
now become something impossible. The thought of this made me
so desperate, so furious, that I flung myself down on the floor,
weeping and biting the bars of his iron bedstead. 'Amalfi, Amalfi!'
I cried, remembering all the rude things I'd done when he was
alive. I was sorry, but at the same time I almost wanted to laugh
when I remembered, say, the times when I'd creep silently away
and hide in a corner, pretending to melt into thin air, like fog,
when he was in the middle of telling me about his dreams, with
eloquent gestures; and after a bit he'd notice, disconcertedly, that
I wasn't there, and start calling and looking for me around the
rooms, crawling about on all fours and prodding at the walls with
his stick. I'd make signs to the dogs and they'd get excited and
make a pointless racket around him, as if they enjoyed making a
fool of him as much as I did. Well, they must have felt remorse afterward, like me, and maybe that explains their suicide, if it's true
they really did kill themselves, and it seems they did.

"And now it was he who let me call without answering. If he'd
only awakened again, even for an hour, he'd have heard me say
wonderful things, all of them true, without the shadow of a lie,
and he'd have had reason to be proud! But for all eternity he'd see
and hear no more, and I knew it. But all the same, I had to give
him a proof at all costs, a pledge that I was saving our friendship
from death! So I laid the palm of my hand on his stiff little hand,
which was ringed like a sultan's, and swore to him that, however
many friends I might have in the future, I'd always keep them

away from Procida. On this island, which had been peopled for
me only by our friendship, his memory would remain my only
friend. That's what I swore. So here in Procida, where the names
of Wilhelm and Romeo are linked and written even on the stones,
even in the air, no other friend shall come with me; if he did, I'd
be branded a traitor, a perjurer, and would condemn our friendship to death!"

Dreamed by the man from Amalfi

After this solemn declaration, my father eyed Amalfi's portrait
quizzically, as if to say: "Well, are you pleased, you old corpse,
with this homage to your caprice, to your foolishness?"

And then he sighed.

Well, that's how my father's faithful friend on the island was always Romeo, just as Algerian Knife was outside it. The two of
them divided his affection and his secrets, and I knew neither,
and could reach neither. Childhood, I thought with a sigh, was
entirely to blame for my bitter lot. Romeo's death, Algerian
Knife's grown-upness, left me behind, out of my father's enchanted kingdom.

I was silent a bit. "So for two years you didn't leave Procida," I
observed. "Not even once!" (Oh, what a happy time, I thought.
Why wasn't I yet born?)

"Not once," my father agreed. "It was just chance, you see.
Well, not just chance, really. It was Amalfi's doing absolutely. He
was a magician, you know, and he knew how to keep me in Procida. And besides, I thought: he's old, he'll soon be gone, I can
spare him a bit of my time. And what's more, it was in my own interest: apart from everything else, he left me this beautiful house!"
And my father laughed brutally in Amalfi's face, as if he wanted to
provoke him, but then, feeling sorry maybe, looked at him again
with a disarming, childish smile.

"When he made me heir to the house," he went on, looking
back again, "he made a fine speech, like someone in a novel.

'This house,' he told me, 'is the dearest thing I possess on earth, and I'm leaving it to you. I'm also leaving you some money I have in the bank at Naples, so that if you add it to your father's property, you'll almost become a gentleman. The thought that you'll be spared working is a great satisfaction to me, because work isn't for men, it's for donkeys. Hard work may be a pleasure occasionally, because it's not the same as ordinary work. Hard work, an idler's effort, may be useful and pleasant, but ordinary work is useless, it kills imagination. In any case, if by any chance the money isn't enough, and you have to get used to working, I advise you to choose a job that favors imagination as much as possible. Be a shipping agent, for instance. But it's best to live without a job at all. Be content with dry bread, so long as it isn't earned.

"'This house I'm leaving you has been a fairy-tale kingdom, an earthly paradise, for me, and the day I have to leave it I'll be consoled by the thought that it will become yours. There's another thing I'm resigned to as well, and that's the thought that you won't live here alone, but with a wife. Strange though it may seem, you're one of those who, if they haven't a wife to wait for them somewhere, can't keep going. Well, all right; I'm not opposing your destiny, your imagination. Bring your wife here, to this house. I shan't be here when you do — luckily, as I'd sooner breathe my last with a hangman than with a woman. Blind as I am, if I had a woman before my eyes, even death would be a failure; it wouldn't be dying any more, it would be dissolution. You can forgive your neighbor anything (at least on the point of death, you can) except ugliness. No, that you can't! And whatever ugliness I can think of seems to me attractive compared with the ugliness of women. My god, how ugly they are! And where else can you find such bitter ugliness? Such very special ugliness? Even if you don't look at them, even if you don't see them, just knowing they're there puts you in a bad temper!

"'It's better not to think of it. That's enough of that. You'll marry, dear Wilhelm, and you'll bring her here and have a family. It's your fate. I've told you I'll not oppose it; it's your own business and none of mine. Something else I'm hoping will be enough for me: that as far as friendship is concerned you'll reserve this house at least, and this little island of Procida, entirely for me.

"'That's enough, then. This is your house and you'll always come back to it, I'm sure, because one always comes home, and because it's an enchanted garden to you as well, this little island of mine. You'll always come back, yes, but you'll never stop here very long. I mustn't delude myself about that, my dear young master of the house. People like you, who have mixed blood in their veins, never find rest or contentment; when they're in one place they want to be somewhere else, and as soon as they get somewhere else, they want to run away from there too. You'll wander from place to place, as if escaping from prison, or running in search of someone, but in fact you'll only be following the divided destinies mingled in your blood, your hybrid blood — like a griffin or a mermaid. You'll find friends everywhere, but very often you'll be alone. A man of mixed blood is seldom happy with others. Something overshadows him, but in fact it's he who overshadows himself, like the robber and his treasure overshadowing each other.

"'That reminds me. I must tell you about something I dreamed last night. I dreamed I was a gay young spark — I must have become a grand vizier, or something like that, because I was dressed in a gorgeous Turkish costume of silk the color of (this is just to give you an idea), the color of sunflowers. Sunflowers, did I say? What nonsense, I was much more beautiful! I can't think of anything to compare it with at all! I wore a turban with a long feather, and dancing shoes on my feet, and I was going along, humming away, in some beautiful place somewhere in Asia, where there was no one else, through fields full of roses; happy and gay, sweet-mouthed, but around me I could hear sighing. It seemed to me quite natural, though (dreams are so odd that way), and I saw the reason quite clearly in my mind. Even now, after waking, I can remember it, and really there's a logical explanation, a real philosophical concept (I wonder why I always dream such extraordinary things?). Now listen, and see if it isn't a very fine idea.

"'Well, it seems that living souls have one of two fates allotted them: they can be born a bee, or they can be born a rose. What do the bees of a swarm do, with their queen? They go and rob all the roses of a little honey and take it to the hive, into those cells of theirs. And the rose? The rose has its own honey in itself: rose honey, the most adored and precious. The sweetest, most in-amorating thing is what the rose contains within itself: it need not search elsewhere. But sometimes they sigh in solitude, the roses, those divine beings. The roses are unaware; they don't understand their own mysteries.

"'The chief of all the roses is God.

"'Of the two, the rose and the bee, the luckier is the bee, I think. And the queen bee is the luckiest of them all. Look at me. I'm born a queen bee. And what about you, Wilhelm? I think, dear boy, you're born with the sweetest destiny, and the bitterest.

"'You are the bee and you are the rose.'"

One of Arturo's dreams

When I think back over this conversation with my father, and see that distant scene again, everything takes on a new meaning. It reminds me of the hatter in the story, who always laughed and cried the wrong way around; because he could see reality only through a magic mirror.

In those days I could see nothing in my father's conversation (whether it was comic, tragic, or playful in tone) that didn't support my indisputable certainty: that he, that is, was human perfection and blessedness incarnate! Maybe, to be quite honest, he rather liked these childish views of mine and got into the way of showing off a bit when he talked to me. But even supposing (though it isn't very likely) he'd decided to run himself down, and confess the blackest sins to me, and call himself a miserable dog, it would have been just the same to me. What he said was completely divorced, as far as I was concerned, from reason, from earthly values. I heard him as one hears sacred liturgy, in which what is actually spoken is only a symbol, and the final truth behind it is beatitude. This final, real meaning is a mystery that only the blessed understand; it's pointless to look for an explanation of it by human methods. I, like the mystics, wanted no explanation from him; all I wanted was to dedicate my faith to him. What I expected from him was a reward for my faith, and this longed-for Paradise seemed so far off still that — this isn't speaking figuratively — I couldn't reach it, even in my dreams.

Often, especially when he was away, I dreamed of my father; but they were never the sort of dreams that seem to be trying to compensate us for reality (or else just to cheat us) with spurious triumphs. They were always somber dreams that flung back at me the bitterness of my own condition and, without leaving me any illusions, retracted the promises I might have believed by day. And in those dreams I knew sharp, precise suffering, something I was still too young and ignorant to feel in reality.

One of these dreams has stayed in my mind.

My father and I were walking along an empty street. He was immensely tall and covered completely in shining armor; I hardly reached his hip, and I was a recruit, wearing a grayish green uniform too big for me, and my legs were bound up in puttees. He strode along, and for all my enthusiasm I found it hard to keep up. Then, without even looking at me, he ordered me brusquely: "Go and buy me some cigarettes." I was proud of being ordered by him and ran back to a tobacconist's; then, keeping well hidden, I kissed the package of cigarettes before giving it to him.

He hadn't seen me kiss the package, but as soon as he touched it and looked at it, he felt something in it deserved his scorn. And his voice whipped out at me: "You affected little Moor!"

Final events

Well, that was how Arturo's childhood went by. When I was nearly fourteen, Immacolatella, who was eight, found a lover, a curly black dog with passionate eyes who lived quite far away, in a house near Vivara, which he left every evening, just like a regular boyfriend, to come courting. He learned our ways and used to come at suppertime, knowing we'd be in. If he saw that the kitchen window was still dark, he waited patiently, and if it was alight, he let us know he was coming by barking from a distance, and then he would scrape on the door so that we'd open it. As soon as he came in, he greeted us in a high-pitched voice, a sort of squeal that sounded like a flourish of royal trumpeters, and then galloped three or four times around the kitchen, like a champion at the beginning of a tournament. He was clever and polite; he watched us having supper, wagging his tail, but never begging, so that we'd know that only sentiment prompted his visit. If I threw him a bone, he wouldn't touch it — he'd wait for Immacolatella to take it. He must have been partly greyhound; he held his head high, had a bold way with him, and Immacolatella was happy. I'd send her out under the stars to play with him, and keep away, but after a while she'd leave him and come back to me to lick my hand, as if to say: "My life is you."

The time came when Immacolatella was pregnant for the first time in her life. But maybe she was now too old, or had been born with some malformation that made it hard for her. Anyway, she died giving birth to her pups. There were five of them, three white and two black. I hoped to save them at least, and sent Costante all around the island in search of a bitch who could nurse them. After only a few hours he came back with a thin red creature that looked like a fox; but maybe it was too late, because, anyway, the pups wouldn't suck. I then thought of nursing them with goat's milk, the way Silvestro had nursed me, but there wasn't even time to try; they were weak and born before their time and were buried with their mother in the garden under the carob tree.

I decided I'd never have another dog. It was better to stay alone and remember her than to have another in her place. I hated meeting the black dog, who went about without caring, as if he'd never known Immacolatella. Every time he came near me, trying to joke and play as he used to, I'd shoo him off.

When my father came to Procida some time afterward and

asked, "What's been happening?" as usual, I turned away without answering. I couldn't say the words: "Immacolatella's dead."

Costante told him, and my father was sorry to hear it, because he loved animals and was very fond of Immacolatella.

This time he stayed at Procida only an afternoon and a night; he'd come just to get some documents from the town hall. He stayed away about a month and then reappeared, then left again the following day, after he'd got some money from his tenant. But when he said good-bye, he told me for the first time where he was going and when he would be back. He said he'd been engaged to a Neapolitan girl for some months, and that he was going to Naples to marry her. The wedding was fixed for that same week, and immediately afterward he'd come back to Procida with his wife.

And so, he said, I must come and meet the three o'clock steamer the following Thursday, on the dock.

A Winter Afternoon

A winter afternoon

*I*T WAS WINTER, and that Thursday a cold squall of rain was clouding Procida and the bay. On days like that, which come rather rarely, the island seems like a ship that has folded its thousand painted sails and floats soundlessly on the current, toward the Hyperborean. The smoke of the steamers making their usual daily trip, and their long whistles through the air, seem the signals of mysterious journeys, quite outside your own life: the voyages of smugglers, or whaling ships, or Eskimo fishermen: treasures and migrations! They may give you a sense of adventure and gaiety or scare you suddenly, as if they were mournful farewells.

It wasn't long since my fourteenth birthday: only a few days before, I'd learned that from today, with the arrival of the three o'-clock steamer, my life was to change. And as I waited for three o'clock, strung between dread and impatience, I wandered about the port.

When he told me he was marrying this unknown Neapolitan girl of his, my father had said (in a dutiful tone that sounded artificial), "This way you'll have a new mother." And for the first time since I was born I turned against him. No woman could call herself my mother, and there was none I wanted to call my mother except one, and she was dead. Now, in that foggy air, I looked for her again, my one and only mother, my Oriental queen, my mermaid, but she didn't answer. Maybe she'd hidden because this intruder was coming; maybe she'd fled away.

I made no effort to imagine what my father's new wife would look like, or what sort of character she'd have. I pushed off all curiosity. It didn't really matter what she was like — it was all the same to me. All she meant to me was Duty. My father had chosen her, and it wasn't up to me to judge her. Books had always told me a stepmother was beastly, hostile, and hateful. But, as my father's wife, she was someone sacred to me.

When the steamer appeared, I went idly toward the quay. I tried to distract myself by watching the boat being tied up, but the first passengers I saw were the two of them, standing at the top of the ladder, waiting for the gangway to be fixed.

My father was carrying his usual suitcase, and she had one too, about the same size. While my father, who hadn't yet seen me, was looking for the tickets to give the collector, I went up to her and, without a word of explanation, took the luggage out of her hand. I knew my duty. For a minute I felt her resisting; she'd almost taken me for a luggage thief. Then, suddenly realizing something from my movement, she looked at me excitedly, and, pulling gently at my father's jacket, asked him: "Wilhelm, is this Arturo?"

"Oh, there you are," my father said.

She blushed for having thought me a thief, and greeted me in a friendly but self-contained sort of way.

Luckily, it didn't enter her head to kiss me, as relations generally do when they meet. I'd have pushed her off, because really you can't adapt yourself to the idea of somebody being a relation just like that from one minute to the next.

When I'd taken her suitcase, I realized she was carrying a shabby bag as well, bulging so much that it wouldn't shut. I tried to take it from her too, but she refused to give it up and hung on to it more tightly, pulling the lock together with both hands, as if defending a treasure.

The three of us walked along the quay to the square. Although we were carrying the luggage, my father and I walked faster than she did, because she was tottering along on high heels she didn't seem used to, and tripping at every second step. Well, I thought, I'd sooner go barefoot than get used to the sort of shoes that ladies wore.

Apart from those new shoes and high heels, though, there was really nothing very ladylike about the bride, and nothing special about her either. Whatever had I imagined? That I'd see some marvelous being turn up with my father, someone who'd show me that the famous female species I'd read about really did exist? This Neapolitan girl in her worn, badly made clothes didn't seem to differ much from the usual working woman and fishwives of Procida. And a glance had been enough to show me she was ugly, no less ugly than all other women. Like them, she was bundled up, had a full white face and black eyes, and hair (which the shawl tied around her head showed only at the roots) as black as a raven's wing. You wouldn't really have thought that she was a bride. Her figure was quite womanly, but her face (as I guessed at once, unpracticed as I was in guessing women's ages) was still a child's, and a child very little older than myself. Of course it's true that a girl of fifteen or sixteen, which is about what she must have been, is already grown up, while a boy of fourteen is still considered a child. But all the same, my father's idea made me even more indignant; his idea that, apart from everything else, I could possibly accept as a mother someone only a couple of years older than myself, if that.

For a girl she was fairly tall, and I was ashamed and fed up to see that she was quite a bit taller than I was. (This didn't last long, though. It took me only a few months to catch up with her, and in the end, when I left the island, she hardly reached my chin.)

My father waved to the cab, which moved over to us while the bride gazed wide-eyed at the square and the people, as it was the first time she'd been on the island. I sat up on the box beside the cab driver, but facing the pair of them, who sat side by side on the velvet seat. The driver had raised the hood to shelter them from the rain, and as soon as she was sitting under cover, the girl hastened to clean her shoes with a piece of her dress. Those shiny black leather shoes, with their golden buckles, were, I must confess, the smartest I'd ever

seen, but she treated them as if they were absolutely sacred! My father, who was watching her just then, had the ghost of a smile, but
whether of amusement or superiority it was impossible to see. But
she was leaning down over her shoes and didn't notice; otherwise I
think she'd have blushed.

It wasn't hard to see that she had a tremendous respect for my
father. Even when she used familiar gestures that were quite spontaneous, like tugging gently at his jacket as she had a little while
back, she did it with a hesitant and slightly timorous air. And my
father, though he seemed quite pleased to be bringing her home,
was never the least bit familiar with her. I never saw them
whisper, or kiss and cuddle the way people say lovers or couples
on their honeymoon do. And I was glad. He had his usual air of
arrogant withdrawal, and she sat calmly a little way off, holding
her precious bag in her lap, and tugging at the lock with all ten
fingers. Her hands were small and rough, and red with chilblains,
and I noticed that she wore a ring on the left one — my father's
wedding ring. My father wasn't wearing a ring, though.

None of us spoke. She was intent on watching the town. From
her expression you'd think she thought she was entering some historical city, like Baghdad or Istanbul — not just the island of Procida, which isn't all that far from Naples, after all. Every now and
then I glanced at her furtively and saw her large surprised eyes
shining, with the eyelashes sticking out like the points of a star. In
the half-light of the carriage, her face, with its huge wide-open
eyes, seemed jeweled, and the thick, irregularly shaped eyebrows
that met across her forehead reminded me of pictures of savage
women and children I'd seen in books.

At the crossing of the main road, when we passed a niche
where a small picture of the Virgin Mary stood behind a grating,
she raised her right hand and with a grave and recollected air
made the sign of the cross and then kissed her fingertips. When I
saw this, I looked quickly at my father, certain I'd meet at least a
smile of derision or of pity, but he was lolling idly back in his seat,
and took no notice.

When we reached the little square, we saw the great arch of a rainbow rising from the sea, curving up through the air into al-most a complete semicircle. In the bright light and the gleaming rain, the old buildings of the fortress towered close, almost above us. When she saw them, the girl made a movement of fantastic admiration and nudged my father with her elbow.

"Is that . . . is that our house?" she asked in a conspiratorial tone.

I roared with laughter. My father raised one shoulder, and said: "Well, no!" then, turning to me and emphasizing his words, he explained: "*I told her we live in a magnificant castle,*" and smiled at me with an extraordinary expression of childish black-guardly complicity that left me wondering. I didn't like to think that my father might have exaggerated to his wife, or even talked nonsense to her; and on the other hand, I'd never supposed until then that the House of the Guaglioni was a castle!

My stepmother had blushed.

My father raised his eyebrows with a half-indulgent, half-sarcastic air. "D'you know what that beautiful house up there is?" he said. "It's the prison."

"The prison?"

"That's right. The Penitentiary of Procida!"

"So that's the Penitentiary!" she exclaimed, astonished, gazing at the walls with new eyes. "Oh, you told me about it! You said there's not such a huge important prison even in Rome, and they bring criminals there from everywhere! Goodness! I can't bear to look at it! It seems like an insult to think of us passing it here in the cab and up there those poor boys . . ." But when she'd said this, she shook herself, and looked severe, as if to force her feel-ings to take on a high moral tone. "Ah, well, that's justice!" she said. "They've done wrong and now they're paying for it!"

At that I whistled softly because it was just the sort of notion I despised; everyone knows I've always been on the side of outlaws. But she didn't seem to sense my obvious disapproval; maybe, ab-sorbed as she was, she didn't even hear me. It probably wasn't worth whistling softly to convey such a mature idea to a deaf, pre-historic being like her.

When we'd turned the corner toward the bay, the prison in the distance displayed the whole length of its walls, from the ancient fortress to the new buildings, and the pupils of her eyes turned a moment to look there, full of pity and dismay, but with an obvious respect, all the same, for the powers that be. Then, looking away from that enormous punishment block, she sat back in the depths of the cab.

The three of us arrive

On the last part of the ride, I began to get slightly interested. Come to think of it, this was the first time for many years that the House of the Guaglioni had received a woman, and my incredulity was mixed with a curious sense of expectation. What was going to happen, quite soon, when we crossed the threshold with her? I almost began expecting some mysterious warning sign — the walls shuddering dreadfully, say . . . But absolutely nothing happened. As usual, I found the key of the little door under the stone where I'd put it before leaving, and I opened the door gently. And slightly stiff after our cab ride in the open air, we entered the quiet *castle* of the Gerace. The house was empty (Costante had gone back to the farm at midday, as usual), and my father went ahead of us through the cold silent rooms, flinging doors and windows open as he always did when he arrived. Sometimes a door shut, slammed by the north wind that had risen and was lightening the sky.

The bride went through the rooms as if she was visiting a church. I think in her whole life she'd never seen such an imposing house as ours. The kitchen struck her more than all the rest, though. It appeared that a room like that, provided with so many stoves and used only for cooking, seemed to her something marvelous and extraordinary. All the same, she hastened to tell us that a lady her sister knew also had a kitchen in her house where they only cooked and ate, but it certainly wasn't as big as ours. At this my father laughed in his wife's face, and turning to me, explained that the house she'd lived in with her whole family as a girl in Naples had for cooking nothing but a stove on a tripod; in winter they lit it on the bedroom floor and in summer in the street outside the front door. They even made their pasta in the bedroom and hung it to dry on the bedstead bars.

The bride listened to my father's explanation, gazing at us with her big eyes without saying a word. "And she knows nothing," he went on, in the same tone of derision and pity, "but three things — how to make pasta, how to pick the lice out of her mother's hair, and how to say the Hail Mary and the Our Father."

She looked embarrassed at this and nudged my father slightly with her elbow, as if begging him not to go on, because she was ashamed. My father looked at her without taking the smallest notice, and stifled a laugh. "From today on," he continued, with a ceremonious air, "she's a great lady. Signora Gerace, mistress of the whole of Procida." Then suddenly, as if betraying me, he turned on me with an unexpected question. "Hey, Blacky, that reminds me," he said, "when you talk to this wife of mine, what are you going to call her? We must agree about it."

I was silent, cold, proud, and on my guard. She looked timidly at me, and finally smiled and turned very red, and, looking down, answered my father instead of me: "He never knew his mother, poor little boy. I'd like to be a mother to him. Tell him to call me 'Ma' — I'd like that."

This was just about the boldest, most insulting thing the pair of them could have thought up to provoke me! My face must have expressed such savage disgust that even my father noticed, and he said indifferently, almost teasingly: "Nothing doing. He doesn't want to call you 'Ma.' Well, call her what you like. Call her by her name — Nunziata, Nunziatella."

(But this I never did — not that day or any other day. If I wanted to talk to her or get her attention, I'd say, "Listen," or "Hey," or "I say," or even whistle. But *Nunziata, Nunziatella* — I didn't like saying it.)

At my father's words, the girl looked up; gradually the color left her face, until she seemed to me whiter than before, and so frightened that I thought I saw her trembling. All the same, she'd proved her boldness when she suggested I should call her "Ma." Insolently, disdainfully, I looked her up and down. Bundled up in her black shawl, with those big eyes, that waxen moonface of hers, she looked like an owl that never sees the sun. And as for that mangy leather bag, all falling to bits, bulging with important secrets, ever since she had arrived on the dock she'd never let go of it a moment, but had been clutching it between her fingers as if she was scared of being attacked by highwaymen.

She said nothing while I considered her, and hardly dared to breathe. Then suddenly she realized that I was watching her and answered my stormy look with a spontaneous smile that brought a fleeting color to her cheeks. And then, as if to consecrate our family from that moment on, she said, with a sort of solemnity, indicating us one after the other with her small, rough red hand: "Well then, this is Wilhelm, this is Arturo, and this is Nunziata."

My father was leaning against the marble basin, half sitting on it, with one foot dangling and the other on the ground, slackly, absently. Through his half-shut eyelids you could just see the blue of his eyes, the color of water ruffled in winter, in hidden caves no boat can penetrate. His thin hands, with their large neglected nails, were idly clasped, and his hair, in a moment of sunlight, was all flecked with gold.

His wife seemed to be wondering if now, here in the kitchen, we could consider ourselves at home, and the honeymoon over. At first she looked questioningly at my father, but as he was taking no notice of her just then, she decided for herself and resolutely slipped her feet out of her high-heeled shoes. Obviously she was longing to be free of them. Very respectfully she placed them on a chair, and from that moment I never saw them again. She kept them always hidden away, like sacred treasures, with the other bits of her trousseau she never used.

I was glad to see her grow smaller without those high heels. Now the difference in height between us, which had humiliated me so much, seemed almost negligible. Over her silk stockings she wore a pair of dark woolen socks, short and darned; her feet were small but clumsy and inelegant, and her legs, with their rather fat ankles, had an almost childish roughness about them still.

After the shoes, she took off the shawl that covered her whole head and was pinned under her chin; and her hair appeared, pinned tightly up on top with quantities of combs and pins. This made my father notice her again and he began laughing.

"What on earth have you been up to?" he said. "You've put up your hair! That's your mother's idea! No, I don't like it. It's obvious you're not grown up, in any case. Come here, I want to make you look nice — the way I like you."

She looked at him, submissive but hesitant, and her hesitation inflamed my father. With unexpected vigor, he told her to come forward again. Then I realized how terribly frightened she was of him: you'd think she had to face an armed bandit, as she stood there struggling between obedience and disobedience and unable to decide which of the two scared her more. My father took one step and seized her, and she trembled wildly, as if he meant to hurt her.

In the light of the setting sun

Laughing, my father tore out the pins and combs and rumpled her hair with both hands, and pins and combs went flying about the place. A mane of black hair, a great savage pelt of natural curls and waves, fell untidily to her shoulders. Her face darkened, grew almost arrogant, and the gleam of tears lit up her eyes. She didn't try to avoid my father, though; only, when he stopped rumpling her hair she shook her head with the sort of movement you sometimes see horses make, or even cats.

I looked at all those curls with some curiosity, remembering something my father had said a few minutes earlier. He guessed what I was thinking.

"What are you thinking about, Arturo! No, no; they deloused her nicely for the wedding."

He was hanging on to her skirt, but she wasn't even trying to escape. One hand was still clutching her precious bag, hiding it a bit beside her, to protect it from my father's horseplay; and between the two of us, facing the glass door, she stood quietly. The irises of her eyes, which in the half-light looked jet black, gleamed with flecks of color, like cock's feathers; but the ring around them was purely black, like a little rim of velvet, and around it the white of her eyes had a faint mauvish blue tinge to it, the way small animals have. Her cheeks were round and full, as they are in faces whose exact shape of youth isn't yet fixed; and her lips, which were a bit rough from the cold, looked like the red berries (always a bit gnawed by squirrels and wild rabbits) that grow on Vivara. Now that she appeared to me for the first time fully lit, her face looked even younger than I had thought it at first on the quay. If it hadn't been for her tall, well-developed figure, you'd have thought her still a child. Her skin was clear and so pure and smooth that you'd imagine even the cloth she wiped her face with must have been careful not to spoil it. She must have spent all her time indoors, being a girl; and even her forehead, and the skin around her eyes, always wrinkled and marked in anyone who loves the sun, were absolutely untouched. Her temples were almost transparently white, and in the cavity of her eye sockets, under the eyes, her smooth unblemished skin was like delicate petals that, once they are open, cannot last out even a single day, and fade as soon as the flower is picked.

Under the great mop of hair her neck looked rather slim, but from throat to chin was a full, tender curve, even whiter than her face, with a black curl laid alongside it. Two longer tresses hung on one shoulder, and at the nape of her neck, almost under her ears, little curls sprouted, like a goat's. Thick curls clustered on her forehead down to her eyebrows, and fine curls fluffed out at her temples and moved with every breath.

Her hair seemed to have grown by chance, fancifully. I, who had never seen it before, enjoyed looking at it, but she, who must have worn it that way since she was a child, can't have seen anything extraordinary about it: it was just natural. She twirled one curl around her finger, to smooth the mess my father had made of it; and after a bit, ashamed of her untidiness, pushed it back from her face with a practiced movement of her hand. Her ears, tiny, well shaped, and slightly rosier than her white face and neck, then showed: their lobes were pierced, as women's generally are, and she wore two little gold rings in them, the kind girls get as a present from their godmother on the day of their baptism.

While she was tidying her hair instinctively, she still had the same mysteriously frightened air about her, the same scared, lost look near my father. He flapped hard at the piece of skirt he was holding, and let her go. "I got myself a curly girl," he said, in a whimsical, contrary tone. "And I want a curly wife."

"But I wasn't cross with you for untidying my hair," she answered in a mild and tremulous voice. "You tell me what you want, and I'll do it."

"And what are you hiding there?" said my father. "Come on, now, show us your jewels."

He snatched the precious bag from her hand with an aggressive laugh and spilled its contents out on the table. They were jewels all right — a pile of bracelets, pins, and necklaces, nearly all little presents my father had given her during their engagement. I wasn't an expert in such matters and thought at first that they were all real gold, real topazes, rubies, pearls, and diamonds. Instead they were fakes, rubbish bought at fairs and from market stalls. My father had won her with bits of glass, like a savage. Out of all that heap all that was real was a few pieces of coral and a little silver ring with a Madonna cut in it, given to her by her godmother as a confirmation present, which no longer fit her.

(She never wore any of those jewels, but kept them with religious reverence lying in the wardrobe. She never wore anything but her godmother's little earrings, the silver medal of the Sacred Heart threaded on a cord, and her wedding ring. But she didn't think of these as jewels: they were part of her body, like the curls.)

My father amused himself for a while playing with the jewels; then he had enough of it and left his wife in peace. The weather had cleared, and he told us to wait for him and went out toward the edge of the open garden to have a look at the sea. Then his wife, who was alone in a corner, approached the table where the jewels lay, like a defenseless animal emerging from its forest lair the moment the threat of danger has passed.

The glass door was open; and the great sunset across the sea, made brighter than ever by the wind, lit up the whole kitchen with its last lingering rays; even the waves from below sent their shimmering reflection on to the plaster wall, and gradually dimmed. Still scared, she stood beside the table where the jewels were, with the jealous expression of doves and swallows beside their nests full of eggs. Finally she made up her mind, grabbed all her jewels into a heap, and put them in the bag again with a sigh of relief. Then she shot down on the ground, and grubbing about on her knees like an animal, with her hair tumbling down all over her face, she began collecting the pins and combs in her skirt. My masculine duty was to help her. I wasn't a boor and I knew it. But I remembered that not long before on the quay she hadn't trusted me to carry her bag, and scornfully stayed where I was.

When she had finished, she got to her feet again and flung the combs and pins onto the chair beside the high-heeled shoes. Then she tossed her hair back vigorously and gave me a small friendly smile. I looked at her stonily; and she stopped smiling, but didn't seem hurt. Her lashes were still wet with those mysterious childish tears she'd wept before, but tears in her eyes seemed to have none of the searing bitterness of other people's; they seemed just a kind of mistiness playfully lit by her eyes. And the look she gave me, submissive but very frank, very respectful and lit up with joy and a kind of prayer, reminded me of someone — Immacolatella! That's who it was! She had the same way of looking, as if she was always seeing the God of miracles.

I sat down on the steps outside the door to wait for my father. That side of the house was sheltered from the north wind, and the sun lingered there before setting, warming it slightly. After a while, she came and sat on the step beside me and began disentangling her hair as best she could with one of those toothless old combs she'd picked up. We could hear the sea below beating on my little beach and every now and then the north wind whistling over the island. I said nothing.

She said: "Not now, but when she was a girl, my mother had hair just as thick as mine. But my sister's is rather thin." Then, when she'd finished combing hers, she exclaimed: "My goodness! Isn't the sky red this evening!" And she added, sighing, in a grave and fascinated tone, but without bitterness, as if she knew, and was ready to obey, the laws of matrimony: "Just think! This is the first time I've been away from home!"

My father came back from outside, and, as it was getting dark, we took the suitcases that we'd left in the hall upstairs. My father took his own, and I his wife's, as we had done on the dock. And she came along behind us, carrying the combs, the shoes, and the bag of jewels all bundled up in her shawl.

On the upstairs floor

The bride's suitcase was fairly light, but although there couldn't have been much in it, it made me curious. It was the first time I'd lived in the same house as a woman and could watch her life close up, and I had no idea about women's ways and the clothes they bundled themselves up in. I had no idea if they always looked so misshapen and mysterious, even indoors, even asleep. The bride hadn't yet removed the coat she'd worn on the journey, a faded, ill-fitting overcoat that was too short for her and showed a large piece of her full-skirted dress of bright but rather worn velvet below. There was no doubt about it, she looked pretty shabby, but after the surprise of the jewels, she might be hiding the costumes of an Oriental sultana in her suitcase.

For the moment she took out only a pair of old flat, down-at-the-heel shoes that had deteriorated into slippers and put them on at once, looking pleased, although as they were far too big for her she had to drag them around as she walked, and occasionally they slipped off her feet altogether.

My father put his own suitcase in the bedroom and told me to carry his wife's into another room next door, where there was a wardrobe and a small iron bedstead; and a little later he came and took the mattress and the blankets there himself. But when his wife — who at first had seemed delighted to have a room specially for her things — realized she had to sleep in it at night as well, she was frightened; and in spite of her fear of my father, she kept saying obstinately that it was impossible, that she was scared of spending the night alone in a room, and that she wanted to sleep with other people. My father was annoyed, for he was determined not to share his room with anyone; but seeing that she was white with fear, he turned to me and said impatiently, without even deigning to answer her: "All right then, I'll take her into my room with me. Come on, Blacky, help me to lift this bed up." And he and I carried the small white bed into his room together.

She followed us happily. There wasn't room for the new bed beside my father's, as his big bed took up nearly the whole of the end wall, so we put it crosswise, with one end against the longest wall, so that it stood at the foot of my father's bed. As soon as she had seen things arranged, the bride started banging and turning the mattresses and dusty pillows with great enthusiasm, trying to show she was helping us; and as she began on the big bed she re- marked to my father quite naturally: "So from tonight I'll sleep in the double bed with you instead of Arturo. Is that right? And he'll sleep in the single bed?" Obviously it never entered her head that I slept in a room of my own at night; she thought I slept in the same bed as my father.

At this new sign of her ignorance I simply laughed; but my fa- ther, who was already rather annoyed at carrying the small bed, hitched up one shoulder scornfully. "No, madam," he said, his lips curling with mockery. "When I'm sleepy, *you'll* sleep in the little bed. *I'll* sleep in my bed, the big bed, where I've always slept. And *Arturo'll* sleep in his bed, in his room, where he's always slept!" Then, pretending to be angry, he shouted: "Remember you're not living among beggars or in a tribe anymore: you're in the *Castle of Gerace*. And if you say anything else you shouldn't,

I'll send you to sleep up there in that other castle, among the guards and the convicts!"

It was obvious that she didn't understand what she'd done to deserve such fury, but she blushed with shame at having said something wrong and looked at me questioningly, as if wondering what was wrong in a wife sleeping in the same room with a little boy like me.

In the end I got angry too and told her with lively scorn: "I sleep alone, in my own room! I don't need other people near me. If you think everybody's scared like you, you're wrong. I could sleep alone in the middle of the Rocky Mountains, even, or on the steppes of Central Asia!"

When I said this, she looked at me with fervent admiration but kept gazing wide-eyed about the room, as if scared at the idea of sleeping there alone with my father. All the same, between the two fears — that of sleeping all alone or of sleeping alone with my father — she chose the second rather than the first. Perhaps to cheer herself up, she started beating the big mattress even more enthusiastically than ever, and the dust flew out over my father, who'd flung himself carelessly on the small bed.

He jumped up and spat to the side; then, really angry this time, he caught her hand in midair, his face thunderous. "Hey! Will you stop this mattress business!" he exclaimed. "What's the matter with you? When were you ever so mad about cleaning as to go around tormenting mattresses?"

"At home," she murmured, bewildered, "we used to . . ."

"Oh, you did, did you? At home you beat the mattresses, did you? And just when did you beat the mattresses, may I ask?"

"Always. Every year, at Easter. And sometimes even oftener — sometimes oftener, during the year."

He suddenly loosened his grip on her wrists and freed them so brutally that it looked as if he wanted to break them off. "Well," he said, and a humorous note had crept into his anger, "you're not at home any longer. Here we're in the Castle of Procida, this is my marriage bed, and no one's told you to do your spring cleaning today."

Then he spat again and fetched his own suitcase from the corner, took it to the middle of the room and began loosening the rope around it. I'd never seen him turn on anyone so harshly, so malignantly; whenever he'd had to scold me about something, he did it in a quick offhand way — coldly, brusquely, almost absent-mindedly. Now this scene with his wife showed me a new mood of his, as mysterious to me as his justice, and as indisputable. And as I watched him, I felt my nerves contract, as if, this time, I shared his wife's fear. In the end, when he freed her wrists and moved away from her, I felt obscurely freed myself.

He opened his suitcase and half knelt on the floor, and, as he always did, began rumpling up what was in it. His wife meantime stood still beside the bed, gazing around the room. All three of us kept quiet for a while; then she broke the silence by asking curiously why the room had so many doors in a row.

My father, to avoid wasting time on long explanations, said at once, without looking up from his suitcase: "Because every room in this house is guarded by armed sentries, the way it always is in castles — one outside each door. And to prove they never sleep, all through the night they give a blast on their trumpets once an hour, all together."

She didn't dare to contradict him, but looked at me as if to see whether she should believe his fantastic explanation or not. I couldn't stop laughing, and then she blushed a little, and laughed heartily. Just then my father finished unpacking and rose quickly from the floor. Without bothering about the rest of us, he put a heap of stuff in the drawer and kicked the suitcase into a corner; then, cocking his ear for the sound of the bell tolling in the distance, he checked the time on his watch *Amicus*. His wife and I were still laughing at the tale of the doors and sentries, but he had already forgotten it.

He went back to the small bed where he'd been lying down before and sat down crosswise on the edge of the pillow, leaning back against the iron bars. Absent, and rather sleepy, his hair flung over his eyes, he stretched out a foot and with the sole of his shoe rubbed out the marks of his spittle on the floor. Just then the bride looked at the picture of the man from Amalfi and asked: "Who is he?"

"It's a holy picture that protects the castle," he answered yawning. "As in all castles," he went on slyly, lying down on the bed, "there's a dead ancestor who still goes wandering about here. That's his portrait. Be careful the dead man doesn't come and pierce your heart while you're asleep!"

She looked at me as she'd done before, but this time my face showed neither confirmation nor denial. Smiling, she raised one shoulder and murmured: "If my conscience is clear, why should I be afraid of punishment?"

"Because," my father told her, "he hated all women."

"What? He hated all women?"

"That's right. And if he'd been in charge of the universe he'd have abolished the lot."

"But if there were no women, the world would end!"

My father leaned his head on his folded arms and laughed, peering hostilely, craftily, at his wife. "And what d'you think he cared about making the world go on?" he said. "In any case, he's dead. What pleasure does the world's going on give him?"

"He was a Christian soul, and he thought things like that?" she said, crossing her hands on her breast as if to arm herself in the struggle between her shyness and her feelings. Her face trembled so much that, as I watched her, I could imagine her heart beating like a small bird stolen from the nest and shut inside a hand. She tilted her head toward her shoulder a bit and swayed from one foot to the other.

"Why did he hate them?" she asked finally, in a low voice.

"Because," answered my father flinging his head down on the pillow, "he said that women were all ugly."

"All ugly!" she repeated. "What! All of them ugly! But . . . how . . . all of them! Even those in the movies, now, are they ugly too?"

"What d'you know about the movies?" my father drawled idly, stretching himself. "You've only been once when I took you, and it was a picture about Red Indians."

I thought disgustedly that she had beaten me on this point;

because there was no theater on Procida, and I'd never seen a movie in my life.

"My sister's been," she answered uncertainly. "She was taken by a relation of ours at Nola . . . a nice man! She went to see that other film . . . I don't remember the name, but the people in it hadn't got red skins at all. And then you can see the actors on posters . . . you can, all over Naples . . ."

"Carry on. Yes, just keep on chattering about those whores!" my father exclaimed mockingly. "That way, we'll have fun in a minute seeing your tongue drop out. Don't you know the devil makes tongues drop out when they talk about smut and whores? Didn't your mother tell you?"

His wife blushed; my father yawned.

"Shut up, anyway," he went on. "What d'you know about it? You just shut up. I don't want to discuss beauty with you."

Mortified, she tried to produce a worthier example to redeem her from the indecorous example she'd brought up before.

"And what about the queen?" she said. "Is the queen ugly too?"

My father laughed, stuffing his mouth against the pillow with so much enjoyment that he looked as if he wanted to bite it. And I laughed too. She looked from one to the other of us bewilderedly, perhaps searching about, in her submissive mind, for a final defensive argument. In the end her eyes clouded over again as she looked at us, and, her voice trembling and excited, she brought out the supreme argument. "And what about the Madonna?" she said. "Is she ugly? The Mother of God!"

My father shut his eyes. "That's enough," he said. "I'm sleepy. I want to rest for an hour or two. Go away and leave me alone. I'll see you later."

We left the room silently and shut the door. In the passage his wife, in a low voice so as not to disturb my father, asked me to keep her company while she unpacked her suitcase, because she wasn't yet used to the house and was scared of being alone now it was dark.

The suitcase

We went back to the other room, where we'd taken the bed away. There was a rectangle of cleaner floor where it had been, and on it I sat down. The room had plenty of lights in it, but the only one with an unbroken bulb was a kind of metal lantern sticking out high up on the wall. The bulb was so dusty that it gave out hardly any light, so she got up and knelt on the chest of drawers and unscrewed it. Then to clean it, she spat on it several times, and rubbed it with her petticoat.

Opening the suitcase proved a disappointment. The only things that emerged were shapeless old rags, a pair of ordinary clogs, and a light dress of flowery material that was already worn and sweat-stained. Then there was a big head-scarf, but nothing as pretty as those with roses on them that my father wore as scarves. And that was all. The suitcase was practically empty already. All that remained was a layer of newspapers and torn-up paper at the bottom, which was obviously protecting some framed pictures. They were all images of the Madonna, which she brought out with the greatest reverence and put out on the chest of drawers, first kissing them one by one.

It wasn't just one Madonna she believed in, but a whole lot of them: the Madonna of Pompeii, the Virgin of the Rosary, the Madonna of Carmen, and I don't know how many more; and she knew them from their costumes, and diadems, and positions, as if they were all different queens. One I remember was clothed in stiff gold bands like the sacred mummies of Egypt, and, like her baby, who was bandaged up in gold as well, wore an enormous spiky crown on her head. Another was covered with jewels and was black, like an African idol, and held a child, also loaded with shining stones, who looked like an ebony doll. Another had no crown, though, only an airy halo, and, apart from this one sign of her position, seemed like a beautiful blooming shepherdess; she was playing merrily with a lamb and her naked baby, and from under her simple dress peeped a plump little white foot.

Another sat like a great lady on a beautiful carved chair and rocked a cradle so splendid that even a duke's house wouldn't boast one like it. Another one still was dressed like a warrior, wore a kind of armor of precious metals, and brandished a sword.

(From what I could deduce, I think I understood that these Virgins all had different natures from one another. One was rather inhuman, and as impassible as the goddesses of the ancient East; she had to be honored, but it was best not to turn to her for favors. Another was a magician and could do every sort of marvel. Another suffered, and it was to her tragic, holy keeping that passions and sorrows were confided. They all liked feasts and ceremonies, genuflections and kisses, they all loved presents, too, and they all had immense power, but from the sound of it, it appeared that the most remarkable, the most miraculous, and the most courteous was the Madonna of Piedigrotta.

Then, apart from all these Virgins and their babies, and all these saints, male and female, and Jesus himself, there was God. From the tone of voice my stepmother used when she spoke of him, it was clear that to her God wasn't a king, nor the head of the whole Holy Army, nor even the boss of Paradise; he was much more. He was a Name, unique, solitary, inaccessible. You didn't ask him for favors. You didn't even adore him. And basically the task of all that immense crowd of Virgins and saints who collect the prayers, offerings, and kisses is this — to safeguard the inaccessible solitude of a Name. This name is the one unity opposed to the multiplicity of heaven and earth. He doesn't care about the celebrations, or the miracles, or the desires, or the suffering, or even about death: all he cares about is good and evil.

This was my stepmother's religion, or, at least, this is what I have been able to reconstruct from her behavior and from her conversation that day and afterward, during our life together. My reconstruction was necessarily imperfect, though as my stepmother was always inhibited by a kind of modesty in talking of holy matters with other people. And if, on some great occasion, she burst out eloquently on the subject of her faith, she always left some points shrouded in mystery and silence. And so, for instance, it's still hard for me to say today what particular views she held on the Devil, or if she actually believed in his existence at all.)

Some of the virgins brought from Naples (three or four at least) she leaned in a row against the mirror of the chest of drawers. But there were others left in the suitcase for which there was no room there, and these she set, each with a kiss, on the bedside table and the windowsill.

After the jewels, these pictures of the Virgin Mary were definitely the most luxurious thing she possessed. Printed in colors, in gold, in silver, framed and glazed, they were decorated with various ornaments as well. The Madonna of Piedigrotta was festooned with large shells, strips of silk, cock's feathers, and colored glass, which made it look like a banner of barbaric triumph.

In fact, I thought, that suitcase had been pretty surprising, after all. But, dazzled though I was, I made no comment at all.

Eternal life

When she had put down her Virgins, the bride looked around the room again and asked me if I thought my father would allow her to hang one up in the bedroom at the head of the small bed she was to sleep in. I shrugged my shoulders rather skeptically.

"I don't suppose so. We don't believe in any Madonna," I declared severely. "And not even in God," I added.

"But your father's a Christian now," she retorted gravely. (At the time I took no notice of what she said, but later it came back to me, and sounded very surprising. But I'll return to that later.)

Our short talk seemed to take her thoughts back to the ancestor my father had mentioned awhile before; and she asked me, sounding very puzzled, if the ghost who hated women really stalked the castle. At her question I shrugged again and made a face. Her credulity really bored me.

"But can't you see?" I burst out. "It's true that the man from

Amalfi lived here once upon a time, but he's *dead*. Don't you know what *dead* means? Well, anyway, you'd better know that my father doesn't believe in ghosts, nor do I. Ghosts don't exist anywhere. They're romantic legends!"

She came up to me, and very circumspectly, in a solemn whisper, she told me that ghosts did exist. She hadn't ever seen one, but a lady her godmother knew, who was a night nurse at the Hospital for Incurables, had seen hundreds. "But," she said in the end, "even if I see him, what would it matter? They're not frightening." And she explained to me that they're simply unfortunates, suffering sinners who, like poor defenseless beggars, beg for prayers to give them eternal peace. They don't look like people any more, but just like rags of flapping white material. All you have to do is have a requiem said for them, and they go away at once.

I was tempted to tell her the dead, almost certainly, have no spirits, that in death everything is extinguished, and that the only thing that lives on is glory. But then I thought it over and decided that there were some things it would be no good at all telling her about. And, anyway, she'd never attain any glory; so she might just as well be taken in by these notions of hers. So all I said was, sarcastically: "Well, then, if a prayer's enough to chase them away, why are you scared of being alone at night?"

"Oh, I'm not scared of them!" she protested firmly and almost indignantly. "I'd be ashamed to be afraid of them! I'm not afraid of them or of anything else. I'm not like my sister, who's even scared of a cat's eyes at night. I'm not afraid of lightning, or gangsters, or anything. Ask my mother if it's not true that I'm never frightened. Never — not of anything!" (But, I thought without saying it, you're scared of my father.)

"The only thing I'm frightened of," she went on as if forcing herself to explain something rather difficult, that she herself didn't quite know how to explain, "is this: I'm scared of being alone. But not for any special reason. It's just the fact of being alone without anybody near me. It's just the fear of being alone, nothing else at all, that I'm scared of. And then, why are there so many people in the world if we weren't meant to get together?

And not only people! Animals as well — during the day they wander around alone, but at night they all get together."

"That's not true," I retorted firmly. "Some animals can be alone, and are splendid and proud, like heroes! Owls go and settle alone nearly always, and sea horses wander around alone at night; and elephants go off alone, far away, when they have to die. But man has much more heart than all the animals. He's like a king, like a star. That's enough, though. I," I concluded proudly, "have always been alone, all my life."

"That's the lot of those who have no mother," she said with such ingenuous pity that her harsh insipid little voice sounded musical. "Yes," she went on, as if pronouncing some rare philosophical concept, "a mother is one's first friend in this life, and no one can ever forget her.

"My destiny too," she declared majestically, after a while, "was to be an orphan. Because I was left without a father. And without a brother, either. My mother, my sister, and I, just three women — that's all that was left of our family. Before my sister there was a brother, younger than me. He was eight years old when he died. It was five years at Christmas since he died. He died with my father in that famous disaster."

"What disaster?" I asked, suddenly interested. From her impressive tone I expected that the disaster she was talking about must have been due to an air raid, at least, or some other world-shattering event.

"Oh, it was that famous disaster with the load of concrete: people heard about it even in Rome. Four people fell in it, and what a lovely funeral they had! There was even a band, and an official turnout, and the whole thing paid for by the town council — the horses, the crown, everything.

"My father'd gone to work, which was funny. Usually he was on strike, because he got tired . . . he really liked being a gentleman best, that's what he was like . . . But that week he'd felt like it and had gone to work loading concrete. And my brother took him his lunch.

"We had made pasta without sauce, because that's what my

brother liked more than anything. My brother had all sorts of funny ideas — for instance, sauce. He didn't like it a bit. My mother told him: 'First go and take it to your father, and then come back and we'll all eat together.' And he went off grumbling about it with my father's plate tied up in a napkin. And that was the last we ever saw of him. There's fate for you!"

Though it was tragic and moving, I was — to be quite honest — rather disappointed in the story. All the same, so as not to offend my guest, I didn't show my disappointment; no, on the contrary, to show I had the proper feelings, I heaved a great sigh. And, deep in her mournful majesty, she gave me a grateful and trusting look, and, sighing herself, she observed, in the meditative tone of a philosopher: "Yes, as far as death is concerned a grown man and a little boy are all the same. They're all just creatures to her."

As she said this her meager girlhood seemed overlaid with enormous antiquity, full of mysterious and almost regal wisdom. But even as this happened, a childish air of consolation peeped through her mournful expression.

"In the end, though," she said with conviction, "the day will come when families will all meet again in eternal rejoicing!" Here she stopped, as if afraid of spoiling that otherworldly rejoicing with her female chatter; so she just hinted, full of mysterious reverence, as if she was reciting the exotic books of some sacred Sibyl or of the prophet Daniel: "The point is, anyone who's scared of death is really wrong, because it's just a matter of disguise and nothing more. In this world she makes herself look as ugly as a wolf, but up there in heaven she'll show herself as she really is — as beautiful as a Madonna; in fact she changes her name there from *Death* to *Life Eternal*. If you say the world *death* up in heaven, nobody'll understand."

She stopped, hanging her head with a secret, enamored air, as if she could already imagine, though only very faintly, the splendors of the future, which she shouldn't (out of reverence) speak too much about . . . Then finally she spoke again, without shyness. "And so, on the last day, that beautiful *Life Eternal* will turn up smiling at the gate beside the Blessed Virgin crowned, mother of us all like her; and she'll have prepared for them a great feast without end. And there I'll meet my father and my brother, and all my other little brothers and sisters who died as soon as they were born or when they were babies."

Her charming, credulous smile, her fresh and rather untamed joy, made it obvious that as far as she was concerned, the impassable indifference of eternity was turned into a wonderful party full of lights and singing and joyful dances and babies and little boys. She told me (with that important air she often had when she talked about her family) that apart from her — Nunziata — the eldest, her mother had had nine other children, boys and girls. Almost every year of the twelve years she had been married she was pregnant; in fact, people who knew her used to say, "Viulante, your Nunziata won't need any babies of her own because you go making a new one every year . . ." But, alas, God's will was that most of these children should return to heaven before they had learned how to walk on earth.

Luckily none of them had gone without Holy Baptism, and she even began telling me all the names they were baptized with, one by one. There were a Gennaro, two Peppinos, a Salvatore, an Aurora, a Ciccillo, a Christinella . . . At last her face became vaguely puzzled.

"When I remember those brothers and sisters of mine," she said, "I'm afraid I shan't even be able to recognize them, later on. I remember them as if they were all exactly the same, all alike! . . . But obviously up there in heaven we'll know each other without even saying our names — relationships will be written on our foreheads. And you'll meet your mother there again, and we'll all be together in one big family."

A vision of my mother floated through my mind, solitary, disdaining all approaches and, in her splendid Oriental tent, leaving the island of Procida, without saying good-bye.

I answered harshly: "There's no such thing as a family for the dead. You never meet anyone again in death."

She looked at me as a sage looks at a fool, yet with deep respect, all the same, and didn't answer. Only, after a second, twirling a curl around on one finger, she observed in a small dreamy voice: "That brother of mine that I was telling you about had quite special views about things. We called him 'The Arguer' because he was always arguing; and when he talked everybody kept quiet. He was called Vito."

After this we were silent for a bit. And then, gazing at me again with timid pity, she said: "And so, all this time you've been quite alone."

"I should think I have."

"But…what about your father?…Didn't he keep you company?"

"Of course!" I answered. "When he's at Procida, he's always with me. From morning till night. But he has to travel, and until now I haven't been old enough to travel. Soon I'll be old enough, though, and I'll go and travel with him."

"What will you be traveling for?"

"What d'you mean, 'what for?' Well, really! First of all, to visit the geographical wonders of the world! That's logical!"

"What wonders?" she asked.

The double judgment

The subject that her question opened up was too fascinating and had been burning deep down in my imagination too long for me not to burst out on the spot with uncontrollable eloquence. I began telling her enthusiastically about the main marvels scattered about the globe awaiting the arrival of Wilhelm and Arturo Gerace. But, though she'd accepted every word of mine so timidly up to that moment, she was aggressively positive on the new subject.

It seemed that, as far as she was concerned, nothing beyond Naples and its surroundings was worth the trouble of exploring, so that when she heard me rave about these exotic places, she glowered with jealousy for the honor of Naples. Every now and then she'd interrupt to tell me in a grandiloquent yet bitter tone that there was this and there was that in Naples as well . . . as if all the splendor that existed in the rest of the world was rather second-

class, provincial stuff, really, and a citizen of that central, first-
class city could spare himself the bother of traveling. Just being
born was quite enough for him, because the supreme example of
everything could be found under his own roof.

I began boasting of the Castle of the Knights of Syria, where, in
olden times, up to ten thousand knights used to live. And she retorted that in Naples there was a castle (fifty times bigger than my father's here) called "The Egg" because it was completely closed, with
hardly a single opening, like an egg; inside were the kings of the Two
Sicilies, the *Barboni* . . . I told her about the colossal Sphinx of
Egypt, which thousands of caravans came to see from every conti-
nent. And in reply she told me about a church in Naples where
there was a gigantic marble Virgin that sometimes, if you showed
her a crucifix (even a little one, like those worn around the neck as
pendants), shed real tears. She assured me that a great many people
had witnessed this marvel, not just Neapolitans, but Americans,
Frenchmen, and even a duke. And that thousands of pilgrims visited
the statue, and the crosses, hearts, and chains of precious metal had
turned the church into a gold mine . . .

I spoke of the Indian fakirs, and immediately she started
boasting about the marvels you could find in Naples. In a convent
sacristy, there was a tiny delicate nun who'd been dead more than
seven hundred years, but who was still as blooming and fresh as a
rose, and in her glass urn she looked like a doll in a shop window
. . . And in the Piazza San Ferdinando at Naples lived an old man
with a black tongue and black lips who could eat fire. He gave
shows in the café, swallowing handfuls of fire while his grandsons
handed around the plate, yes, that was how that odd old man supported the family.

I let her talk, my attitude being one of magnanimity not
untinged with pity, as to me Naples was just the point of departure
for my travels, the size of a pinhead! While she, condemned to
her inglorious destiny as a woman, would never know anything of
the world beyond Naples and Procida. And so I listened almost re-
morsefully to all that secondhand Neapolitan nonsense which
she believed implicitly and illustrated with gestures of her small

hands . . . then suddenly a mad longing to laugh began tickling at my throat, and I burst out into such a roar of laughter that I actually flung myself flat on the floor on my stomach.

I felt that I'd never known such amazing gaiety, a gaiety that seemed to belong, not just to me but to her and to the whole universe. But she was rather hurt, as it was reasonable she should be. Her boasting suddenly stopped, and I heard her angry voice protesting, mortified: "Ask my mother if I'm telling lies. You can ask the whole of Naples if I've invented all this or if I've been telling the truth."

I looked up a minute, ready to reassure her quite sincerely, because I really wasn't doubting her good faith and felt strangely reluctant to hurt her or be unkind. But as soon as I saw her standing before me, watching me idly and sulkily, my merriment returned like a tune on the brain and took hold of me, so that instead of speaking I laughed more hilariously than ever.

This happened again two or three times over in the space of a minute. Every time I stopped laughing, I glanced at her and then flung myself down and laughed more merrily than before, so that, without my intending it, she grew progressively more and more offended. She looked very grave and pouted alarmingly; and I began thinking: *What will she do?* for the fun and drama of it, the way I used to tease Immacolatella.

At last end I heard her grumbling at me, then suddenly she took a step into the middle of the room and stopped there, and then, with weighty sybilline bitterness, exclaimed: "I swear it. Before all the holy souls in Purgatory! I haven't invented any of it. Let them all bear witness to this oath."

The scene had become so solemn that I turned serious too, at once. But she wasn't even looking at me.

"May my father hear me, too, and my brothers," she concluded. "And may I fall down on the floor this very minute if I invented what I said about Naples! May I fall down dead!"

When the oath was over, she swallowed, and I noticed that her mouth and chin were trembling with the emotion she felt at being criticized. Without looking at me, maybe because she was afraid of seeing me still laughing, she said very softly: "Now you can believe I haven't told any lies."

I had a pang of conscience and regretted my rudeness, and rose resolutely to my feet, and stood before her, angry with myself. Then I exclaimed (and my tone was more than just serious — it was weighty and fateful): "On my honor. May I be struck by lightning if I'm lying! I swear that right from the beginning I believed in the sincerity of every word of yours and that I don't think you're a liar."

In all my life I never remembered such an important ceremony as this one. And for this reason I felt deeply satisfied. She was already completely reassured and smiled at me in a way that seemed to thank me and at the same time to ask: *Well, what was so funny about it, then?* So I said quickly, since I couldn't honestly think of anything better: "I was laughing just like that. Because I felt like it."

This was all the explanation she got, and she asked for no more. She gave a short grateful sigh, all her previous bitterness seemed to have melted, the load to be lifted from her heart; and, shaking her head to deplore her own suspicions, she said happily: "I thought . . . I thought you were accusing me of telling lies."

I shrugged my shoulders. "Oh, get along with you! I know perfectly well you don't tell stories," I exclaimed; adding impudently "I know you pretty well!"

This *I know you* came to me quite naturally. And as I said it, I realized with surprise that, although it seemed odd, it was actually true. Everyone else (and most of all my father) I found mysterious: yet this girl, whom I'd met that day for the first time, I already felt I knew really well. I wonder, was this amazing discovery the real reason why I'd laughed? Anyway, not knowing what else to say, I went and sat on the floor again where I'd been before and said crossly: "Listen, I've sworn on my honor! What else d'you want me to do? Dammit all!"

Her lips made a small, nervous movement, as if she wanted to say: "But I've forgiven you! I've really forgiven you! Honestly!" But instead of speaking, she smiled at me as if asking for forgiveness herself. Then she came up to me eagerly, like a small hen opening her wings as she walks, and, still smiling, stopped a couple of steps away from me. Then I smiled back at her, though with a rather condescending air, with just one side of my mouth.

Something disturbed me — a kind of whimsical confusion that was a mixture of laughing, and looking at her, and not looking at her. I could feel her eyes on me, trustful and protective, and this gave me a strange, funny happiness. After a while she went on, hesitantly, smoothing her hair: "And so, as soon as you're grown up, you'll leave . . ."

"Yes!" I said. And only then, when I was so emphatically making plans, did the thought of her enter my head. What would her part be in the future voyages of the Gerace father and son? "She'll wait for us here alone in Procida!" I decided firmly. But she didn't seem to be wondering what her own destiny would be.

She stood there watching me with those trusting eyes that were at once ancient and childish and that reminded me at the same time of the island's starry nights and of Immacolatella. And after another concentrated silence, she observed again, as if she couldn't resign herself to the idea: "So you've spent all this life of yours without a mother!"

Minerva's ring

"When I was a month old," I answered, lifting my head proudly, "I was already all right on my own. Silvestro went to Naples once for a football game — the finals — and I was alone for a whole day. He tied an unbreakable bottle with a nipple on it around my neck, and laid me on the floor on some rags, so that I couldn't fall."

"And who was Silvestro?" she asked.

"He came from Naples and stayed here until he was drafted. He was a friend of mine. It was he who gave me milk."

"What d'you mean? Gave you milk!"

"He brought me up on goat's milk."

"Well!" she said with deep indignation. "Goat's milk, indeed!

That's not got a human, Christian taste at all. How did you manage to grow up so handsome? In Naples they say goat's milk and sheep's milk is only good for goatherds and shepherds. My brother, if there was even goat cheese on the pasta he wouldn't eat it. And to think that soldier — what sort of a Neapolitan can he have been? — gave you goat milk! Just think of it! If only we'd known. Some years my mother had so much milk her breasts hurt. If only we'd known you were here with a goat in Procida, we'd have taken you home and you'd have grown up with us. Oh, we'd have looked after you well at home. We were so many women, you see. And a baby needs women. But as for that Silvestro of yours — of course he was a boy, but even so! Even a boy could have known better than that! Goat's milk, indeed!"

As she said *that soldier, that Silvestro,* she sounded inexorably antagonistic, as if (quite apart from the scorn he aroused for having given me goat's milk) this unknown nurse of mine had, right from the start, and just because I'd mentioned him, aroused her liveliest dislike. I resented her tone; I couldn't allow my first, my only friend to be attacked without defending him.

"Silvestro," I declared, warmly and resolutely, "is one of the best Neapolitans! And he wasn't just a *soldier,* either. When he was in the army he rose to being a corporal, and if he'd gone on longer he'd have been made a sergeant. He was one of the best in the whole army, and he was a football player too — he was center forward on a real Neapolitan team. He's my faithful old friend. It's eight years since he left, and we've never seen each other again, but he never forgets me. He's sent me lots of postcards all this time: last year he sent me one from Caserta, and his girlfriend signed it too, and so did a sergeant-pilot, and this pilot's sister. And on the 5th of December, which is my birthday, he sent me a colored one with roses on it and a horseshoe. He never forgets to send me greetings for my birthday, every single year. And I keep all his postcards."

She was listening to me intently, but a little peeved, as if, in spite of her obvious admiration for every word I uttered, she couldn't quite hide her unexpected hatred for Silvestro.

"I even had a present from him" I went on. "Years ago, for my tenth birthday. He sent it to me by a man from Naples who was coming here on a trip: it's a German cigarette lighter, a real authentic smuggled one without a state permit. The flint's worn out now, which is a pity, because I can't replace it here at Procida. And I gave the same man a present to take to him — a cameo I found on the beach (it must have been lost by some foreigners), a beautiful stone with the head of the goddess Minerva cut on it. Then he sent me a postcard saying he'd had a ring made of it and that he'd always wear it on his finger; so that's another reason why he could never forget me. And the man who came told me: 'You can be sure Silvestro never forgets you. Often when he's talking about something or other, he mentions *Arturo, Arturo,* as if everyone ought to know who this old Arturo is! And sometimes he says: *I wonder how he's grown up. I really must make a trip to Procida one day to see him.*' And so he would," I went on regretfully, "if it wasn't that his work makes it hard for him to leave Naples. He has a very responsible job in Naples, he's caretaker for a building firm; it's a very fine job, as I see it! He lives in a little moveable hut that's moved about wherever the firm has a job, here one day and gone the next. Once, for more than a year, he was at Pozzuoli, where there are the fields of fire, and another time he was right on the harbor of Naples for about six months, where the warships come, and torpedo boats, and liners. I wonder where he is now! On the last postcard he just sent me his good wishes, without telling me anything."

These last few remarks of mine seemed to reconcile her to Silvestro, at least for a moment, and, her face alight with childish pleasure, she suggested: "D'you know what? One day we'll take the steamer to Naples with your father and go and see him. And you can see the port of Naples, and the liners; and the Pallonetto, too, where my home is. In the Pallonetto," she went on grandly, "even tiny boys play football. They play football matches in all the streets! A sailor we know, called Antonio, has traveled all over the world, and he says there's no place where so many little boys run around as there."

Her eyes rested on me, filled with regret. "Oh, how nice it would have been," she said, "if we'd been related, the way we are now, when you were a little boy. Then of course we'd have known what happened to you, left without a mother as soon as you were born. Then we'd have come, I and my mother and my god-mother, with a lovely flower basket lined with feathers and silk, and taken you home with us."

I would never have been alone, she explained, because her home in Naples consisted of just one room, with the door directly onto the street, so that even if you happened to be alone in the house, there were people walking up and down outside to keep you company.

As I listened to these unrealized plans of hers, I wanted to laugh, because I remembered Silvestro telling me about the time my mother's relations came to the House of the Guaglioni and how he'd hidden me in a soapbox for fear they'd take me away. Well, that's what happened, but, I thought, they hadn't turned up with a flower basket lined with silk and feathers. If these other relations of mine had turned up with such a smart flower basket for me, maybe my nurse would have let me go away with them.

In the moonlight

As I sat on the floor thinking this (without letting her see any of my thoughts, though), she came and sat on her suitcase opposite me. Her straight firm head and shoulders were a little higher than mine; she leaned her head toward one shoulder, crossed her two hands on her knees, and went on talking as if she were telling a fairy tale whose impossibility really fascinated her. Her voice had already grown familiar; it was like that of a girl who hadn't quite finished growing, and it now had a note of incredulity in it — something farfetched, sisterly, and almost bitter.

"If you'd lived there with us," she said, "you'd have had a completely different life. I'd have looked after you, and held you in my arms. D'you know, even when I was tiny I knew how to hold babies.

I had to! Our home was a baby factory. And I carried them all. I could even skip while carrying a baby!"

"Tell me," I asked her at this point, "how old are you?"

"I'll be seventeen in October. What about you?"

"I'll be fifteen in December," I said, and worked it out for myself. Well then, she's sixteen and three months. When I was born she was two. And she thinks she could have carried me at that age. All the same, I didn't point out the unlikelihood of it and let her go on without saying a word.

"You could have been really one of the family, like another brother. We've got a big bed, and there can be as many as six or even eight people in it. You could have slept there with us as well. And if your father had come to see you there after his travels and it was late in the evening, he could have slept in our house as well, if he wanted to, because our bed has two mattresses. We could have put one mattress on the floor for us all to sleep together and then left the bed entirely for him."

I burst out laughing and so did she. But her laughter ended in a small childish sigh, not very well checked, as if she'd grown fond of her story as she went along and was reluctant to end it. I smiled then, with a kind of protective sadness, and her eyes — grave and affectionate and knowing — seemed to apologize and say: I know I'm stupid and I love imagining; but deep down I never forget the real facts.

"Oh, and in the evenings," she said, "my mother, and my godmother and I would have sung you such lovely songs to put you to sleep. You'd have eaten with us every day. Oh, the fun, the goings-on there'd have been if we'd always been together!"

We were silent awhile. And then the island's evening quietness (the blustering north wind had died down almost entirely) seemed to grow around us, so that we really seemed to hear the minutes flowing through the fabulous wastes of time, which rose and fell, rose and fell, in a great calm equal rhythm. She was sitting there on her suitcase, looking very tranquil and peaceful, and somehow innocently impressive too; and as I half-lay on the floor beside her I listened to the beautiful sounds gliding through the night around us — listened without thinking. Then suddenly I heard her observing: "The lamp's getting dimmer."

"That means it'll soon be going out," I said. "Every evening it goes out for a minute when the electricians change over at the main generator."

She was silent again; and for a while remained wrapped in her inspired musing. Only, a second before the light went out, she looked at me and broke the silence again with an observation that was really quite childish and even meaningless; but that, just for this reason, perhaps, sounded like a mysterious answer. "And just think," she said, "all this time, when your father kept saying: *Arturo, Arturo . . .* just think that Arturo was you!"

As the lamp went out, a glimmer of moonlight came into the room through the dusty windows. I flung myself idly on the floor. Beyond where I was lying I could make out her shadow, as she sat there like a statue, and I turned to look at the opaque windows behind me and imagined the slender new moon going down the clear night sky beyond the panes as if dancing on a thread. The darkness in the room lasted only a few seconds, but in those few seconds I suddenly went back and relived one of my memories — a memory belonging to an existence I must have lived a very long time ago — centuries, millennia earlier — that only now rose into my mind again. Not everything was clear in it; yet it seemed so true, so definite, that for a moment it tore me completely away from the present.

I found myself somewhere pretty far away. What the place was, I don't know. It was a clear night, but there was no moon in the sky. I was a hero, walking along the seashore. I'd been insulted, or suffered some loss; maybe I'd lost my dearest friend, maybe I'd killed him (I couldn't remember very well). I called someone and wept as I lay on the sand, and a rather large woman appeared and sat on a stone a step away from me. She was a little girl, yet she had a majestic maturity in her; her mysterious childhood seemed unlike a human age — it was more like a sign of eternity. And she was the one I'd called, that's quite certain, but I now could no longer remember who she was, whether she was a goddess of ocean or earth, or a queen related to me, or a prophetess . . .

I was so drowsy that I didn't notice when the lamp came on again.

"Artù!" she said, "I wonder what the time is now?"

It was the first time she called me by my name.

I shook myself, and sat up, and at once returned to the present — to the lighted room and the bride sitting on her suitcase.

"It must be about half-past six," I said, "because that's when they change shifts."

She leaped off her suitcase. "Half-past six!" she exclaimed. "Well, then, we must hurry and light the fire for supper this evening!"

I told her we never lit the stove in the evening. Every morning Costante cooked the evening meal as well, and today he'd obviously done as usual, and left the supper on the sideboard. But, sounding very important and enthusiastic, she insisted that she wanted to light the stove to warm up the food and even to cook the pasta. So we went downstairs to the kitchen.

The Excellent Condottieri

Costante had left us a roast rabbit for the evening, and potatoes cooked in oil. But when we searched in the other sideboard cupboards, we found a package of store pasta, a jar of preserves, and a piece of cheese, and she declared that with these ingredients we could have pasta cooked for supper as well. So she rummaged about in the kitchen and found some dry sticks, a bucket of charcoal, and some matches and decided delightedly to light the stove at once and put on the saucepan of water, waiting for my father before she put in the pasta. Then she begged me, as she'd begged me upstairs, not to leave her alone in this unknown house. So I stretched out there on the bench, after taking out of the drawer a book I always read while I was eating in the kitchen. But, on that unusual evening, I didn't really want to read much, and I stayed doing nothing, resting my elbows on the book in front of me without even opening it.

She started singing as she prepared to light the stove, and I was startled to hear her, for her voice sounded harsher and wilder when she sang. She went to and fro between the box of wood and the stove, with proud, aggressive movements, frowns, and a quarrelsome air; it looked as if lighting the stove was a kind of war to her, or a celebration.

As she could find no fan in the kitchen, she began blowing on the charcoal herself with enormous energy, and I remembered an illustration in the history of the Crusades, with the north wind, looking like a curly-haired archangel, blowing a fleet of ships along. Because of her hard puffing, the coal finally caught, and so as to liven the fire she picked up the front of her own skirt and began waving it furiously, like a fan, before the stove. A cloud of sparks flew out, but she went on fanning with her skirt with the violent ardor of a gypsy dancer, singing at the top of her voice and forgetting all her shyness, just as if she were alone, or at home in Naples.

She sang, not sentimentally, but boldly, harshly, like a child, her sharp notes reminding me of an animal's harsh cry — a stork's, maybe, or that of some nomad desert bird. When the coal caught, she went to the water jug and poured some water into a saucepan without pausing in her song. I remember one line of one of her songs (which were in proper Italian, not Neapolitan dialect — and were completely new to me):

Perhaps every apache has his knife at the ready now

I asked her, curiously, what *apache* meant (I'd never heard of apaches and gigolettes, whom I later met in hundreds of songs), and she told me that really she didn't know herself. She explained to me that all the songs she knew she'd learned by listening to the radio at a neighbor's house. It was a woman who'd made lots of money in business, and so could afford to spend a bit. And what a nice woman she was! Every time she listened to the radio, she had it on full blast, so all the people in the alley could stand quietly outside their own front doors and listen to the songs.

As she was telling me all this, she finished her preparations and came and sat on the floor beside my bench. She looked at the book that lay before me, still closed, and with difficulty, as the semi-illiterate do, spelled out the title: THE LIVES OF THE EX-CEL-LENT CON-DOT-TI-ER-I.

"*The Lives of the Excellent Condottieri,*" she repeated, and looked at me admiringly, as if the mere fact of reading such a book raised me to the ranks of the excellent condottieri myself. Then she asked me if I liked reading.

"Well, of course," I answered. "Of course I like it."

Then, rather ashamed, yet with the sort of fatalistic resignation of one who recognizes something hopeless and irremediable, she confessed to me that she, on the contrary, didn't like reading; in fact, she disliked it so much that when she had been a little girl and gone to school, just seeing the book in front of her made her cry every morning. At school she'd only got as far as the second grade anyway, and then had left.

At home in Naples they had some books; there was a big novel her godmother had given her, and her sister's schoolbooks (her sister had reached the third grade). But from the time she was a very little girl she'd thought reading books was just a bore and got you nowhere. In books, she thought, there was just a confusion of words, and what was the good of all those words lying there, dead and confused, on the paper? She couldn't see what there was in a book, besides words. That's just about all she could see — words.

"You're talking like Hamlet," I told her.

I'd read *Hamlet* in an Italian translation (besides *Othello,* *Julius Caesar,* and *King Lear*), and I thoroughly disapproved of the way he carried on.

"Who's Hamlet?" she asked.

I made a scornful face. "A fool," I said, and she burst out laughing rather nervously. I didn't see, straightaway, why she was laughing so much; but I soon realized that as I'd called Hamlet a fool, it followed I thought her one as well. At the thought of this, I burst out laughing too. Then I became serious again, and explained: "Hamlet was a fool, I tell you. But you've got nothing to do with him. D'you understand? He was the prince of Denmark."

I saw that she seemed very impressed at this.

"Don't make that servile face!" I exclaimed firmly. "Most kings and princes are fools."

This was one of the most recent conclusions I'd reached, and I realized I couldn't just tell it to this ignorant girl without adding some suitable explanation.

"Just possessing a throne," I said, "isn't enough to make a man deserve the title of king. First of all, a king must be the bravest of his people. For instance, Alexander of Macedonia! Now he was a real king! He," I went on, rather enviously, "was the first of his people, not just because he was brave but because he was handsome. He was divinely handsome! He had fair curls that looked like a wonderful gold helmet!"

She was listening to me as usual with profound attention and respect. "You're younger than me, and yet you know so many things," she said admiringly.

I went on, impatient at the word *younger:* "But there are so few kings like him! And as for those who accept the title of king without being as brave as him, d'you know what they are? They're phonies, that's what they are — stinking, dishonorable usurpers!"

"Of course a man in command should be better than the rest," she agreed, humbly and timidly. "Because if important people don't give an example, how can the world keep going?" She thought a moment. "But that's what happens," she said. "Even important people don't always remember to pay what they owe Our Lord! The powerful sin, not just the poor. Not so many people have a clear conscience, after all. That's why the Son of God, up there in heaven, still goes around wearing the crown of thorns, and as for his passion, no one knows when that will be over."

A she said this, she sighed, like an imaginative little nun brooding on the age-old sufferings of her unhappy God, her curls drooping to match her sorrow. And she forgot that she was talking to an atheist, and looked at me with trustful, friendly eyes, as if her Absolute Certainties agreed with mine.

But all I did was look at her tolerantly. Then I went on, following my interrupted train of thought. "It's the fault of the people too! You can see that quite clearly if you read the *History of the World*, and even if you look at certain countries. The mass of the people doesn't know what's the one hope in life, and doesn't understand what it feels like to be a real king. That's why the best and the bravest are shunned like fierce bandits. No one goes near them, apart from their faithful followers, or just a single friend who follows them always and defends them with his life, the only one who really sees into their heart! The rest are separated from them like a heard of vile prisoners flung into the hold of the glorious ship! The *glorious ship*," I warned her at this point, "is just a phrase that I've used as a poetic symbol. They're not literal words. The *ship* means the honor of life!"

As I was explaining all this I sat up, astride the bench. It was the first time I'd unveiled the results of my solitary meditations to another human being. Her expression was rather grave, almost religious. I was silent for a while, glancing at her occasionally before deciding whether I should go on talking. In the end I continued. "The ideal thing in the World History would be this: for kings to meet people who felt the same as they did. If they did they could do anything — the most splendid things! They could even set out to conquer the future! It's not enough for a man to be brave if everyone else isn't like him and he can't make friends. The day when every man has a brave, honorable heart, like a real king, all hatred will be done away with. And the people won't need kings anymore. Because every man will be king of himself!"

This last grandiose and high-sounding idea was new even to my ears, as it had come to me that very minute out of the blue as I spoke, without my ever having thought of it before, and I was a pleased as if I'd made a really philosophical discovery worthy of a great thinker. When I glanced at her, I could see her face, like a devoted mirror, lit with radiant admiration! A new enthusiasm blazed up in me, and I proclaimed, boldly and definitely: "I want

to read all the books there are about science, all the really beautiful books; I'll be as learned as a great poet! And as for the rest —
well, there's this strength business. I'm all right as far as that's concerned. I can do any exercise. I started training when I was seven
or eight months old. Just wait another couple of summers, and I'd
like to meet anyone who could stand up to me; just let an international champion try! Then, as soon as I have the chance, I must
learn the use of arms, and get used to fighting. As soon as I'm old
enough, I'll volunteer to go wherever there's fighting, just to prove
myself! I want to do glorious deeds, so that everyone will hear of
me! The name *Arturo Gerace* must be known in every country!"

She began to laugh, with a little childish and enchanted
laugh, gazing at me with absolute faith, as if I was one of her
brothers come down to tell her of the wonders the Archangel
Michael was up to in heaven.

I no longer hesitated to tell her my most secret and ambitious
projects, not just those I still thought attainable, but even those that
had become legendary, which I'd thought about when I was small,
and which never could come true. At my age, of course, I realized
that some of my old plans were impossible, but I told her what they
were all the same, knowing perfectly well she'd believe me.

"Well then," I began, "when I become the bravest man of all,
just like a real king, do you know what I'll do? I'll take my faithful
followers and go and conquer the people of the world and show
everyone what real courage is! And real honor! I'll show all those
wretched, impudent creatures what fools they are! A lot of people
get scared the minute they're born, and go on being scared of everything for the rest of their days. I want to explain to all of them how
wonderful valor is, and how it overcomes that miserable cowardice!

"One of the things I'll do will be this. Soon, as I've told you, my
father and I are going away together for a very long time, until one
day we'll disembark at Procida at the head of a proud fleet. The
people will acclaim us, and the Procidans, with our example, will
become the heroes of all the nations, like the Macedonians; even
lots of haughty, grand people, will behave as if they were my father's
brothers, and be our retinue, and follow us into action. The first

thing we'll do will be to attack the Penitentiary and free all the prisoners; we'll hoist a flag with a star on it over the fortress, which'll be seen from the sea all around. The island of Procida will be covered with flags, like a beautiful ship: it'll be better than Rome!"

Here, I glared defiantly at her. Judging by what she'd said in the cab a few hours before, about prisoners and jails, we still had a bone to pick between us. But now when I looked at her I saw nothing in her face but exultant support, as if she were already impatient to see my flag waving on the island rock and had already promised herself a great celebration with singing and dancing. Then, to conclude my harangue, I went on, thumping the cover of the *Excellent Condottieri* with the back of my hand: "This isn't a book of invented stories; it's proper history, science! The historical condottieri, even the most famous ones like Alexander the Great, weren't people in fairy tales (they're invented); they were people just like everyone else in everything but their thoughts. And when someone wants to start being like them, and even better, he's got to have some true, great thoughts in his head . . . and what these thoughts are, I know!"

"What thoughts?" she asked me intently.

"Well," I confided to her after some hesitation, frowning, "the first thought, the greatest of all, is this: *Not to worry about death!*"

Well, that was how I let out the biggest secret of my famous Code; the boldest, that is, and the most difficult of my Absolute Certainties (and my supreme, most secret uncertainty as well).

"Yes, that's certainly the most important," she agreed gravely. "God teaches us that."

But by then I was hardly listening to her; I was so bursting with delight that I had no patience to stop there chattering.

I snorted. The kitchen suddenly felt like a prison. I wished it was a summer morning and that I was on the beach, climbing up on the rocks, diving, somersaulting in the waters; I suddenly longed to play, to do something extraordinary. Suddenly I whirled around on her.

"Look!" I yelled. And, slipping out of my shoes, I took a quick spring up the opposite wall toward the barred window, which was about six foot six high. In a single bound I grabbed one of the middle bars, and, almost at the same moment, gave a terrific leap with my legs and my whole body and landed with my feet between the two highest bars, flinging my head back upside down. From that position I could see her and all those curls of hers, applauding ecstatically.

I felt gloriously happy. I turned a kind of somersault, and hung from the bars with my hands; then I had fun twirling and swinging; and then I cried: "Look! I'm a flag!" And, holding on to the bars with only one hand, I pushed so hard with my arm muscles that my body stood out like a standard. I held this position for several seconds, like a virtuoso holding a note, and finally dropped to the floor, and from there gave an enormous leap as if I were crossing a bridge in the air, and landed, feet together, straight on the table about three or four yards away.

She was gazing at me as if I'd jumped, not onto a kitchen table, but onto the deck of a conquered ship. And I was so excited by my leap that I really felt almost like some storybook cabin boy flying with fantastic nimbleness from quarterdeck to conning tower to lookout. I showed her other tricks like it, and she admired them all, pretty much.

At last I returned and sat down beside her on the floor. I was barefoot because socks were one of the things my father and I often did without. My shoes lay on the floor a short way away from me, and I stretched out a foot and picked them up one after the other between my big toe and my second one and said proudly: "Look! I've got prehensile feet!"

She admired this ability of mine no less than my others, and I explained that I'd only managed to achieve it a short time before, with practice. Here at Procida, I told her, I'd lived a real sailor's life from the time I was born. And according to a book I'd read, a sailor must have *the nimbleness of a monkey, the eye of an eagle, and the heart of a lion!*

I told her the story I'd read as a boy about a pirate who'd lost his hands in battle, and from then on, instead of the missing members, he always wore two loaded pistols closely tied to the stumps. He'd learned to fire the pistols by pulling the trigger with his toe, and was a first-rate shot, so good that in the novel he was always called *Hell-stumps* or the *Killer of the Pacific.*

"What a lot of things you know!" she observed, with admiring humility. Then, lifting her head as if she were singing, she exclaimed, smiling joyfully, impulsively: "When you've become like a king, we'll all come and honor you. I'll bring my mother and my sister too! I'd like to bring the whole of the Pallonetto! And the whole of Chiaia! And the whole of Naples!"

She paused to imagine it a moment, then went on almost secretly: "Will you believe me, Artù, if I tell you that when you told me about wanting to become like a king, I really felt I could see you as if it was already really true, and natural — splendidly dressed, in a lovely silk shirt, with gold buttons, and a mantle, and a golden crown, and lots of beautiful precious rings . . ."

"Oh, pooh!" I broke out, proud and indifferent. "What are you talking about? The crown and mantle and all that rot! If one says the word *king*, you start thinking of the title of king. The kings I'm talking about are special kings; they don't go around dressed like idiots the way you say."

"And how are they dressed?" she asked, dumbfounded, but still curious.

"They dress without caring how, just as they like," I said at once. Then straightaway, because it really didn't take much thought, I said more precisely: "In summer they wear a pair of old pants and a ragged old shirt, with all the buttons missing. And — mm — well, a sort of flowery handkerchief around their necks . . . And in the winter some old jacket, say a checked one — well, anyway, a sport coat!"

She seemed a bit disappointed, but after a minute looked again at me with ingenuous devotion and said, quite convinced and wagging her head: "Well, yes, it's true. You may be dressed like a beggar, but you look like a prince . . ."

I didn't answer; I kept my lips closed tight to show how casually I took it; when suddenly — bang! — I burst out laughing on the spot, I liked her compliment so much.

Soon afterward we heard my father's steps on the stairs, and *the mystery man* reappeared among us.

We then saw that half the water in the saucepan, which had been boiling for some time, had boiled away and neither of us had noticed, and the fire had nearly died. This held up the supper, and while we waited my father began drinking his favorite Ischian wine. He had got up feeling rested, and was feeling gay; and he seemed glad to play at having supper, the three of us together in the castle of the Gerace. His gaiety enlivened us all, and the evening seemed like a party.

At supper

The bride had at last taken off the coat she'd worn on the journey. With her velvet skirt she wore a red woolen sweater that was short and tight like the overcoat. And in these clothes you could see the shape of her body better. Even to my inexperienced eye, she seemed very well developed for her age, but, womanly as she looked, there was still a kind of roughness, a childish ignorance about her, as if she herself hadn't realized that she was grown up. Her bust seemed too heavy for her immature figure with its narrow shoulders and small waist and inspired an odd and even kindly feeling of pity, and the heaviness of her hips, which were wide and rather badly shaped, instead of making her look strong, simply made her look clumsy, ingenuous, and vulnerable. The sleeves of the sweater left her arms bare to just below the elbow, and the white skin of her arms contrasted with the little swollen, winter-reddened hands. This too aroused pity for her. And her wrists, which were rather coarse, just because of their coarseness had — I don't know why — a kind of tender and innocent look about them.

She was proud of having cooked the pasta, and seemed to forget her fear of my father, which had made her shudder during the afternoon. But his present mood didn't seem alarming: he gave her no disquieting orders, refrained from rumpling her hair, and in fact didn't even go near her, or bother about her at all.

At supper he ate a lot and drank another glass of Ischian wine. And the wine, as usual, without making him the least bit drunk, made him quite unpredictable, and so more mysterious to me than ever. Wine might have one of several effects on him, even contrasting effects. Sometimes it made him more expansive, sometimes sleepy and dismal. And sometimes it filled him with regrets or longings, or else set him searching, violently and extravagantly, for things on which to vent himself (he never vented himself on me, except that he was sharper than usual; obviously he considered me too small, someone not worth the trouble).

That evening the wine matched his carefree mood and made him more loquacious and imaginative. Instead of glaring, he seemed to take pleasure in everything he saw, even a scrap of bread or a glass. He told us cheerfully that he'd had a very good sleep upstairs; he'd slept for more than two hours. Then he looked at his wife with a sort of sly expression, as if he'd been plotting some childish crime without her knowing, and added: "And do you know what I've been dreaming about? That ancestor of mine, the one in the portrait — the castle ghost."

"Oh, him," she murmured.

"Yes, him. He was wearing a dressing gown embroidered with the moon and stars, like a wizard. And he told me, 'You just wait and see what happens to you, now you've brought a woman to my house. Tonight I'll come with my knights and throw her out!'"

His wife laughed with an incredulous air, but rather nervously, all the same.

"Laugh away. You won't be laughing much longer. I think the time has come to reveal to you something that I've kept dark until now. D'you agree, Arturo? Ought I to tell her, now that she's Signora Gerace? Well then, my girl, here it is: there's a mystery in our family! Everyone knows it around here: the house is haunted by ghosts. The point is that ancestor of mine's a rather grand old man, who still keeps on giving dances and entertainments to all the smartest young people, the way he did when he was alive. The only difference, of course, is that now his guests are all ghosts, or even SOMETHING WORSE. Of course he doesn't invite the ghosts of women, because, as you know, he hates women. His guests are all male — young men and boys who died in their prime, and all of them, if you want to know, DAMNED SOULS! You see they were all the most frightful types you can imagine, and when they died they all turned into devils. The gang of them turns up every night from every corner of hell; they come in through the windows, from underground, by the hundreds. You can bear witness — it's true, isn't it, Arturo?

My reply was just a smile of agreement and also (because it was my duty) of loyalty, but it seemed to encourage her as well; and she smiled back, the small smile of someone wise and experienced and shook her head at my father.

"Ah, now you're trying to tease me," she said. "You're really making a fool of me. But there are some things that I understand, you know, better than you!"

"What's that? Mind your language, you! You understand better than me!"

"No . . . not exactly better than you. The word just fell out by chance, it doesn't mean a thing. What I meant to say was, you're really treating me like a goose if you think you can tease me, and think I don't know a few things! Really! As if everyone didn't know that child devils can't exist! Because if anyone dies when he's a child, he can't have been a great sinner. Suppose in his short life he has actually done something like stealing or killing — well, it just doesn't count! There's nothing very dreadful about it! In someone as young as that, all sins only count as venial sins. The very most a child could have would be twenty or twenty-five years in Purgatory; and then afterward, little boys become cherubs, and bigger boys seraphim. That's why people go and console their mothers by saying: 'Cheer up, my dear; he's really been very lucky. God has chosen to make him into an angel.' You can never make a devil out of a child. It takes old people to make devils."

Her arguments, which in themselves might sound rather comical, were put forward so gravely that it would have been too boorish to laugh at them. So we took them fairly seriously, and even my father laughed a very little.

"Well then," he told her, "these comfortable views of yours make you feel quite snug, don't they? Quite convinced that these knights are angels from heaven! And you don't believe even what my ancestor told me in a dream, about coming to attack you with them tonight!"

"Oh, who'd believe that old thing? He was the one that went around saying all women were ugly!"

"So!" exclaimed my father, rising proudly. "Well, this is really the last straw. Am I to listen with my own two ears while you go saying my ancestor was capable of telling stories?"

"No . . . no, really, I didn't mean to say that . . . about your relation . . . No, I made a mistake . . . But wasn't that man . . . wasn't he the one who said all women were ugly? Wasn't that what he said?"

My father stretched in his chair, laughing heartily. "Yes," he said, "that's just what he did say: that they were all ugly."

She looked at me as if asking me to confirm this very odd business.

"D'you want to know exactly what he said?" my father went on, and began straightaway declaiming like Romeo. "Ugh, how ugly they are! Better not think, Wilhelm my boy, just how very ugly they are. And they pop up everywhere, all over the world, they multiply by the thousand — by the million — these insults to nature. I wonder if they exist on other planets, or on the moon! And the more they come out stock size — the more perfect (if you can call it that) they are — the uglier they are! Poor wretches, it's just their breed that's stamped as revolting. But why? How can you explain it? Everything has something attractive, something pleasing, about it, something that makes you say: oh, what a wonderful, beautiful world! How splendid to be alive! Even when you see a cripple, the sort of poor creature who can't get into the army — you know, twisted somehow, or a dwarf — and at first you think well, he really is rather hideous. Yes, sir, even then, if you look at him again you always find something to make you say no, he's not really so bad. Yes, if you look at any scorpion fish or spider properly you can recognize the mark of that enchanted artist's hand that made everything in the universe. In just one case it was pitiless: in the case of women. All they got was ugliness, nothing else. They must be another product altogether; it's the only possible explanation."

The two of us burst out laughing at what he said, and at his comic tone. Then my father flung some orange skin lazily at me.

"Hey, little Moor," he said. "Instead of laughing so much, tell us what your views are on the beauty of women. What d'you make of this wife of mine, for instance? D'you think she's beautiful or ugly?"

I wasn't prepared for the question and felt my face flaming. And actually, I didn't even know myself what I thought of his wife, exactly. Before giving an opinion, I glanced at her as if to sum her up on the spot. But at the very moment I did so I realized it was no use my looking at her again, because, without realizing it, I'd already formed an idea of her. And this was it.

As for this business of women's ugliness in general, from what I knew and could see for myself, I felt Romeo had, on the whole, been right, and this particular woman couldn't be said to be any less ugly than the rest. and yet, in spite of her undeniable ugliness, I personally found her quite gloriously pretty.

I felt that my view was too personal and unmotivated, though, and was ashamed to come out with it. On the other hand, I didn't want to lie. So, scorning to look either at her or at my father, I looked down crossly, and almost ferociously answered: "I don't find her ugly."

"Oh, come on now!" my father exclaimed, shrugging his shoulders. "Now you're trying to be gallant and pay compliments. You don't find her ugly, indeed. Then what on earth do you find beautiful in her?"

She laughed, gentle and confused, and without resenting the way she was called ugly. I looked hotly at my father, and exclaimed firmly: "She's got beautiful eyes."

"Beautiful eyes, my foot! They're just big, much too big! Get along with you, Blacky. What are you talking about?"

She looked at me just then, and her eyes, brimful of shyness and gaiety and gratitude for the praise they'd received, looked so stupendous that she seemed to be wearing a diadem on her brow.

I laughed, and sat down again, and kept quiet.

And my father, turning to her and jerking his chin haughtily, said: "It's no good preening yourself, Signora Gerace: because we know you're pretty ugly . . . and something of a slut . . . Little old Blacky just wants to be polite, wants to play the courtier this evening. Now, my lady, instead of rolling those great big eyes of yours at him, tell us your views on this beauty business. Take Blacky, now. What d'you make of him? What d'you think, eh?"

She was shy of answering out loud; she went close to my father's ear, and, looking solemn and conscientious, said softly (I heard her, though): "I think he's handsome."

I looked away, feigning indifference. My father laughed.

"Well, this time I agree," he said. "He's a handsome little chap, and that's a fact. He's not my son for nothing, you know!"

I pretended not to notice, as if I didn't even know they were talking about me. He kicked me lightly under the table to provoke me, and went on laughing almost sweetly, looking at me; and then I began to laugh with him as well.

He poured out some more wine; and while he drank it we all remained silent, for about two minutes. Below, the waves crashed into the little gulf; and as I heard them I saw in my mind the shape of the island laid in the sea, with its lights, and the House of Guaglioni standing on an almost vertical peak, with the doors and windows closed against the long winter night. Like an enchanted forest, the island hid its fantastic summer creatures, fast asleep. In secret holes underground, or in cracks of the walls and the rocks, lay serpents and turtles and families of moles and blue lizards. The delicate bodies of crickets and cicadas were crumbling to dust, to be born again in their thousands, leaping and humming. And the migrating birds, scattered about the tropics, were remembering all this beauty with longing.

We were the lords of the forest, and this kitchen, lit up in the darkness, was our marvelous den. The winter, that until then had seemed to me like a stretch of dreary moorland, that evening suddenly turned rich and splendid.

Night

There was still a trace of his former attractive high spirits about my father's mouth, and I thought I heard his breath, continuous and reassuring as the sea's. The present seemed to me eternal, like a magic feast.

Supper was long over, yet we still sat on around the table. My father still had wine in his glass and went on joking with us for a bit, but he soon grew tired of it. Every now and then he stretched out his arms, or gave enormous sighs, which weren't a sign of sadness in him at all, but of a deep, almost bitter enjoyment of life. Once he moved, as if to stretch out his arm and draw his bride to him, but she leaped up hurriedly and stepped back, saying that she had to clear the table, and I saw the fear, which seemed to have left her for a bit, reappearing in her face.

Looking scared and zealous, she piled one plate on top of another and started taking them to the sink, but without getting up from his chair, my father grabbed her around the waist as she went, and, imprisoning her in his arms, held her close.

"Where are you off to?" he said. "Clearing the table, indeed! The servants will see to that tomorrow morning. You're the Signora Gerace, remember! And our wedding night is now about to begin."

Without daring to struggle, she watched my father with terrified eyes, trembling visibly, looking, with all that hair, like some black-furred wild beast caught in a trap.

"Scared, are you? Scared of your wedding night, are you?" exclaimed my father, bursting out with a free, fresh, pitiless laugh. "Stay here. Don't move." And he pulled her more tightly to his side, enjoying her terror. "You're right to be frightened. You know what happens to girls on their wedding night, don't you? But the worst of it is, Nunzià, that it's pretty rare to find a husband quite as awful as I am. The usual husband is an ordinary little man . . . No, it's no good trying to escape now; you can't save yourself, your done for!"

She had begun to struggle feebly, instinctively, as if she really believed she could escape. And her desperate efforts made my father laugh even harder. "You're done for!" he repeated, with childish harshness, gripping her easily with one arm, as in a vice. "The times when you could escape and hide so as to avoid meeting me are over. Oh, don't think I've forgotten! I'll make you pay for it all tonight!"

Carelessly, but threateningly, he began playing with her curls, intimate, gay malice gleaming from his face.

"D'you know," he declared, "she refused me! This lousy creature refused a man like me. And that's why I took her from her mother — because she refused a husband like me, who owned a castle, among other things."

As he said this, he assumed a judicial air, as if all the island's inhabitants were gathered around the table to decide on the bride's fatal punishment.

She said, in a tearful, lost little voice: "I wanted . . . to become a nun."

"Liar! Confess the truth! You wanted to become a nun so as not to marry me. You decided to marry me only to obey your mother. You said you were frightened of me. And if I'm not mistaken, someone heard you say I was ugly. Is it true or not? D'you think I'm ugly?" He laughed, looking indescribably attractive and bold, and she stared at him with her huge eyes, which fright seemed to darken still further, as if she really did find him ugly.

"And now, prepare to pay for it all to me, Signora Gerace." The hour struck on the church tower, and he looked at his watch. "Ah, it's ten o'clock! Time to sleep . . . nighttime. Oh, I'm sleepy, Nunziatè, I'm sleepy, Nunziatè!" And he pressed her to his heart without any kisses or caresses — on the contrary, he almost hurt her and rumpled up her hair. Then the fear that had crouched waiting for her all day seemed to rise over her like an enormous cloud.

"I . . . before going upstairs," she said, "we must . . . close the shutters on the French window."

"All right, then, close them," said my father, and unexpectedly freed her. And, as if he meant to give her a respite, he lit a cigarette and inhaled the first mouthful. But it looked as if he was just pretending, for the fun of it, the way cats do. She had just lifted the heavy bolt of the door with nervous hands when he put down his newly lit cigarette on a plate and got up from his chair.

"That's enough!" he said shortly. "Don't you worry about the door! Let it alone!"

As he spoke I thought I heard a kind of rhythmical drumming, like a troop of horses approaching from somewhere, and I realized with amazement that it was the pounding of my heart. My father went up to her with a kind of furious joy, seized her by the wrists, and, the way a male dancer does, made her twirl around in a half-circle. His eyes were searching for her, and looked even harder than usual; yet there was another look in them at the same time — a kind of declaration at once violent, and enchanting, and innocent. Maybe he was sorry, or maybe he wanted her to pity him; anyway, his voice softened.

"Can't you see how tired I am? It's nighttime; let's go and sleep!"

She looked up at him defenselessly. "Come on! Get a move on!" he urged her harshly, and she followed him obediently. Before going through the doorway, she looked around in my direction, but I felt a strange upsurge of hatred and anger and looked quickly away.

I remained standing by the table. When I looked at the door again, they had disappeared down the passage, and I could hear their footsteps on the stairs. Then I looked down, and when I saw the crockery and glasses from supper, and the remains of the food and wine, I felt a sudden revulsion.

I stood motionless by the table, thinking of nothing for what seemed to me a very long time, but actually, when I made a move to go up to bed, the cigarette my father had left was still burning on the plate among the orange skins. So only a few minutes had passed! And that day, that just-ended evening, seemed to me — I wonder why? — already years past. Only I, Arturo, was just as I'd been before, a boy of fourteen, with ages to wait before I became a man.

As I passed my father's room, I heard excited whispers through the closed doors. I almost dashed into my room: suddenly I felt, sharply but incomprehensibly, that I'd been injured by someone — I couldn't see whom — in an inhuman way I could never avenge. I undressed quickly, and as I whirled into bed and shoved my head under the blankets, I heard her shriek through the wall — tender, strangely ferocious, childish.

That reminds of me something; it's this: that I couldn't use her name when I was talking to her, and even now, when I'm writing about her — I don't know why, but I can't call her by name. Some mysterious difficulty bars me from using the simple syllables: *Nunziata, Nunziatella*. And so I'll have to keep calling her *she*, or *the wife*, or *my stepmother*, even here. So if I sometimes have to name her — for the sake of style, that is — maybe instead of her full name I'll just put the letter N., or even *Nunz*. (I rather like the sound of that. It reminds me of some animal that's half wild and half domestic, a cat, say, or a goat.

Family Life

Family life

THE NEXT DAY I got up as soon as it was light. My father and his wife were still sleeping, and the weather was splendid. I wandered about, and when I came home it was already the middle of the morning.

I went around to the back of the house where the kitchen was and saw her through the French windows, alone, and busy making pasta on the empty table, energetically twirling around with her fingers some yolks she had poured into a heap of flour. She hadn't noticed me, and I stopped outside the windows, astounded to see how her looks had changed since the previous evening.

How could such a strange transformation have taken place in such a short space of time? She wore the same red sweater as she'd worn the day before, the same skirt, the same slippers, but she'd become unrecognizable. Everything that had made her seem pretty to me yesterday had vanished.

She was wearing her hair loose again, to suit my father's whim, but her untidy curls, which yesterday had looked like an enchanted garland, today made her look just messy and plebeian, and there was something quite morbid about their blackness, in contrast to the pallor of her face. Yesterday's fresh cheeks were now pale, and heavy, and soft, and the skin under her eyes, whose untouched delicacy had made me think of the petals of a flower, was smudged now with great dark circles. Occasionally as she mixed the pasta she pushed her hair off her forehead with one arm, and as she did this she looked up a bit, and I could see her eyes, which I remembered as so beautiful, now clouded, and bestial, and abject.

When I saw her now, I was ashamed to think I had confided in her so much the previous day and let myself go so far as to tell her my secrets. Forgotten on the bench lay my book on the *Excellent Condottieri*, and the sight of it increased my shame. Angrily I flung open the French window, and then at last she saw me. Joy and friendliness lit up her face, and with a sweet smile she said: "Artù?"

I didn't even answer her greeting. I just glared at her as I might have at a stranger or an inferior who had presumed to treat me with improper familiarity. Her trustful, happy look vanished, she stopped smiling, and I saw her gazing at me strangely, disappointed, questioning, untamed, yet not at all humiliated, and without a trace of entreaty. I said nothing, not a single word, but took my book from the bench and left her.

All that day, and the days that followed, I avoided her; I even gave up being with my father when it meant sharing him with her. I spoke to her only when I really had to, and on those rare occasions my tone was so cold and disagreeable that I made it quite clear that she was less than a stranger to me. She was hurt, of course, by the way I behaved, and could think of no good reason for it, and answered me quickly, unsociably, hardly looking at me, and then giving me shadowy glances. But sometimes, generally in the evenings, when the family was gathered together, she gave me a timid smile of appeasement, or else her eyes seemed to be asking me humbly what she'd done wrong to make her lose my friendship. When she did this, she really made me shudder. Her mouth, above all, revolted me: it no longer looked the same as it had on the first day. It had turned a sort of bloodless pink, and it opened and closed with her breathing, in the softest, stupidest way.

My father dragged her around the island with him; they spent the whole time together. I never went for walks with them, and always avoided their company. The weather was fine, and I did as

I'd always done when I lived alone — went out as a rule in the morning with a big hunk of bread and cheese and didn't come back until dark. I'd take a book with me too, and when I was tired of wandering, I'd go to the café in the port, the one where the widow made Turkish coffee in the enamel pot.

I had money to spend in those days, which was something quite new and extraordinary, because my father had given me fifty lire before he left for his wedding, the morning he'd seen his tenant. With this unusual — and to me enormous-looking — wealth in my pocket, I'd order coffee with anise peremptorily, and fling the money down on the counter in advance, not deigning to chat at all; then go and sit down in the corner and stay there reading as long as I liked. At that time of day I was the only customer, and the old woman either dozed or played endless games of solitaire. Every now and then, with the dark and disdainful look of an outlaw, I'd bring out Silvestro's famous illegal cigarette lighter, and though, alas, without a flint it didn't light, I'd click it noisily. While I read I always kept a package of Nazionali cigarettes that I'd recently bought clearly visible on the table, though I didn't touch them: I'd sometimes taken a puff or two at my father's cigarettes and thought tobacco pretty foul.

In the evening, the widow lit a lamp on the counter and went on playing her solitaire. The flame of the little candle burning before the portrait of her dead husband glowed almost sinisterly in its dark half of the café, and then I really felt proud. I felt really like a pirate in some one-eyed smuggler's den, maybe in some village on the Pacific, or in the old part of Marseilles.

But the light was too feeble to read by, and after a bit I grew bored, and without saying good-bye to anyone, left and went up through the night to the House of the Guaglioni.

When I got in, I never went to see the pair of them, but marched straight to my room and shut myself up in it, and then a feeling of loneliness I'd never known before began to creep over me. Even my mother, the beautiful golden canary of the stories, who used to come at my first call, was no longer of any help. And the worst of it was that I hadn't lost her through any infidelity of hers, but simply because I myself had suddenly stopped wanting to see her, had denied her mysterious existence. My lack of faith, which at one time had spared her, and her alone, now shoved her underground with the other dead who no longer existed, no longer answered. Sometimes my longing for her tempted me, but I always told myself roughly: "What d'you think you're doing? She's DEAD."

I was going through a difficult time. But even in moments like that I preferred being alone to being with them. The only time all three of us met was in the evening at supper.

My stepmother decided that we'd have a hot supper every evening at home, and kept the kitchen fire going all day. To tell you the truth, this was about the only reform she'd brought into our domestic routine. She wasn't a great housewife and didn't do much but pull the bedclothes up on the beds, and sketchily though energetically sweep the kitchen and the other rooms. And so, luckily, the house remained more or less as it had been before, in all its age-old filth and natural disorder.

With my father married, Costante had thankfully resigned his job as our cook and general servant and had gone back to his life on the land. And actually, as far as looking after the house went, she was perfectly adequate. He turned up just once or twice a week to bring us fruit and other things from the farm.

At suppertime my father would shout for me and I'd come down. After that single gay evening the first day, our suppers together were generally silent. My stepmother was always frightened of my father and completely dominated by him, but unlike the first day, she now kept coming up to him all the time as if involuntarily, and even pushing up close to him. Sometimes my father took no notice and let her stay there; sometimes he pushed her off, as if she annoyed him. But, as I said, in those early days he never left her.

After supper we all went to bed. Usually I went first, hurrying up to my room, where, as soon as I'd shut the door, without even turning on the light, I shot in under the blankets. It wasn't long then before I heard the sounds of their footsteps in the passage, and of a door closing after them. Then instinctively I covered my ears with my hands for fear of hearing that shriek again from their room. I couldn't explain the reason, but I'd sooner have seen a wild beast rise up before me than have heard it again.

The head of the house gets bored

After a week of fine weather, it started raining. All the same, I went out every morning, and sometimes came home soaked through. My lonely life went on a bit longer, and then, toward the middle of the second week, my father began to talk of leaving. I then found I couldn't bear to lose the few hours of his company still left to me, and was forced into being with him, even though it meant putting up with my stepmother's company too.

It was afternoon, and, as on the day they had arrived, we were all three in my father's room while he smoked, half-lying on the bed as usual. The air was thick with the smoke of Nazionali cigarettes he had been chain-smoking since morning, and outside the dirty windows the great sirocco clouds went sailing past. None of us wanted to talk. My father yawned, shifting about continuously like a man in a fever; his eyes were a strange cloudy blue. Boredom seemed to weigh on him as bitterly, and as tragically, as disaster. And even in that I saw the mysterious laws of his which I worshiped, laws beyond reason, which once, when I was a child, had made him almost faint under my very eyes when a jellyfish bumped him.

And so I found something fascinating even in his killing boredom. I could see that he was now longing to leave the island, and I regretted those last lost days bitterly, days when he'd been there, and I could have spent my whole time with him, but had avoided him instead! All this was my stepmother's fault, and I felt vindictively angry with her.

(It is now so long since then, and I am trying to unravel the feelings that were then so strangely tangled in my heart, yet I find I cannot distinguish what they were really like, muddled untidily as they were within me, without a gleam of thought to light them. When I look back on it, I seem to see a deep, lonely valley in a night of heavy cloud, where a herd of wild beasts — wolf cubs, or lions — began fighting playfully, and then turned serious and ugly, while the moon soared beyond the clouds in a heaven clear and far away.)

For half an hour or more there wasn't a word from any of us. My stepmother sat quietly on a chair, complying, perhaps rather apprehensively with my father's mood. It was he who at last broke the silence.

"That's enough!" he exclaimed exasperatedly. "I can't stand this island any longer! I must have a change of air." And with a grimace of disgust he flung on the floor a cigarette he'd just lit.

He'd been talking about his travels for a couple of days now, as I said, but had left the date of his departure vague. It was understood, of course, that even this time he'd leave alone: his wife would wait for him at Procida, as it was her duty to do. She knew that perfectly well, and at his angry exclamation she looked down without making any objection. As she sat there quite composed, her small shoulders, which were too narrow in comparison with her large bust, made her look, somehow, pathetic and vulnerable. But her sensitive, downcast eyes seemed, with their dark lashes, to make her face look faintly mysterious and severe, and you could see that under her red sweater she was breathing calmly.

My father glanced at her, half angrily, and at the same time with a kind of confused tenderness, as if, though he wanted to leave, he felt rather sorry to leave her, but blamed her for keeping him on the island, blameless though she was. "That's enough!" he repeated capriciously. "Why the devil am I waiting to get off?"

Just then she looked up and their glances met, and she murmured, looking up at him gravely: "We haven't been married a fortnight, and you're already going away!"

Her tone was one of submissive regret rather than objection, but her words were enough to extinguish promptly any glimmer of friendliness in my father's eyes. "Well, and what's odd about that?" he burst out rudely. "I can't help wanting to go, even if I have been married only a fortnight. Are you scared the big bad wolf will eat you if you stay in Procida without me? Arturo," he went on proudly, "has stayed here without me hundreds of times and never made a fuss when I left. That's what happens when you get mixed up with women."

She shook her head. "But . . . Wilhelm . . . I . . ." she said, playing nervously with her curls.

"What's the matter with you? What d'you want?" my father interrupted. When she said his name, Wilhelm, he made an impatient face, and even that small jittery movement with her curls seemed to annoy him. "And leave your filthy hair alone," he went on at last. "Concentrate on getting those damn fool ideas out of your head instead. But . . . Wilhelm . . . I! What d'you think you are, now you've become *my wife?*"

Silently, sulkily, my stepmother listened to him, but her eyes unconsciously expressed dependence and fidelity.

He flung his feet off the bed and stood before her. I could see welling up in him the old dark anger that only his wife seemed able to arouse, and I'd already seen the first day in that very room. But that time I'd defended her deep down in me; whereas today I was glad he was ill-treating her, and, what's more, hoped he'd vent his rage on her physically, fling her on the floor, even, stamp on her. I almost felt I'd find peace in an outrage like that.

"Remember," he went on, growing more and more violent with every word, "that, married or not, I'm always free to come and go as I please, and that I don't answer to anyone about myself! I acknowledge no obligations and no duties: I AM A DISGRACE! And it certainly won't be you, my girl, who'll keep a check on me! The greatest ruler on earth can't keep Wilhelm Gerace in a cage. And you, you wretched, lousy little doll, if you think that a wedding's going to keep me tied to your apron strings, you'd better think again."

His glorious blue eyes, darkened by frustration, boredom, and angry longing, looked across at the window. "Oh, why aren't there any steamers this evening?" he exclaimed. "Why must I wait until tomorrow? I want to get away at once on the very first steamer, and I shan't show a sign of life for ages." He looked at his wife with a look of impatience and hatred, and it seemed as if the very fact of existing and taking up space before him was intrusive, an invasion of Wilhelm Gerace's right — the right to feel as free as the angels. I considered my father's childish stubbornness in defending it perfectly proper; in fact, this right appeared to me the basis of all his attraction, and of his immortality.

"I . . . really I didn't mean to go against what you wanted . . . that would be a mortal sin!" my stepmother said, quite persuaded. "You're my husband, and I've sworn to obey you . . . You're the head of the house, and must command me . . ." But she was so scared by his raging that her eyes began filling with tears. She'd always, since I'd known her, resisted the temptation to cry; this was the first time she gave way.

At the sight of her tears, my father lost the last vestige of pity and indulgence he might still have had for her. "What's this!" he exclaimed, with a kind of horror. "So we've got to the point of crying *because I'm leaving!*"

He was peering at her suspiciously, not just hating her, but really loathing her, as if she'd suddenly taken off a mask and showed the face of a devilish creature trying to imprison Wilhelm Gerace.

"I order you to answer this question," he said, with a surly air, as if accusing her of a crime. "Are you crying because you're sorry I'm leaving? Eh? IS THAT WHY YOU'RE CRYING?"

She looked at him with remarkable courage, her eyes sullen and proud, even through their tears, and answered firmly: "No."

"I don't want anyone to cry *for love of me*, I don't want *love*," my father warned her, his voice altering with hatred as he said the word "love" (which, with his rather hybrid way of speaking, he pronounced *ammore*, the way Neapolitans do). "D'you know, my girl, I'd never have married you if I hadn't been certain of one thing: that you had NO feeling for me. It was your duty to obey that mother of yours that made you accept me. You didn't love me, luckily! The fun I had seeing your mother and your godmother think they were so cunning the way they hid it from me, whereas in fact it suited me perfectly! You'll do well, my girl, *never to feel anything* for me. I don't know what to do with the feelings of women. I don't want them, I don't want your love!"

While he was speaking, my stepmother swallowed her tears and gazed at my father with enormous eyes, but without surprise, as if she was listening to some barbarous, incomprehensible language. And he began marching from the bed to the window, glaring aggressively at her.

"My ancestor, the one in the picture, said that women are like leprosy — when they get hold of you they want to eat you up completely, bit by bit, and isolate you from the rest of the world. Women's love brings bad luck; they don't know how to love. My ancestor was a saint, I tell you, and always told the truth. Ah — he!" And suddenly my father took Romeo's portrait down from the wall and pressed it affectedly to his heart. And in this operatic pose he suddenly gave a ringing spontaneous laugh, as if to mock both my stepmother and the man from Amalfi.

Against mothers (and women in general)

My stepmother suddenly shook back her hair, and her chin jutted forward, with a rebellious, scornful look about it.

"Him!" she burst out, sounding strangely aggressive. "That old wizard forgot his mother when he talked about women like that. Wasn't the mother who bore him a woman?" And she began swaying in a proud, boastful way that looked almost brazen. "The biggest fool on earth knows how lovely a mother is," she continued. "No one ever forgets her, because she's everyone's first love of all! And even . . ."

"Shut up, you ugly slut, you devil, you!" interrupted my father.

He flung himself down on the bed and laughed again, but tremulously, as though put out, quite differently from the way he had laughed awhile before. "Mothers!" he repeated. Then he turned to his wife again. "My ancestor," he declared triumphantly, "never had a mother! He was born of an encounter between a cloud and a thunderclap!"

"I bet!" my stepmother skeptically said. "A cloud and a thunderclap!"

"Yes, lucky man! If only everyone could be born like that . . . from a tree trunk . . . a volcano's crater . . . from a flint stone . . . from anything without female bowels to it!"

"But . . . women . . . sacrifice everything . . . for their children," my stepmother tried to object (though terrified by his invective).

"That's enough! I told you to shut up!" my father interrupted again. "*Sacrifice!* Shall I tell you an important Eternal Truth, you she-devil, you tiger, you? Well, learn it then: SACRIFICE IS THE ONE AND ONLY REAL HUMAN PERVERSION. I loathe sacrifice. And as for mothers' sacrifices — aah! Of all the wicked women you can meet in a lifetime, the worst of all is your own mother! That's another Eternal Truth."

I was so perplexed by this that I couldn't help sighing, but I don't think my father heard me. He had buried his head in the pillow again, and as he spoke he whirled around so violently on the bedspread that the bed heaved like a ship in a storm. Having silenced my stepmother, he carried on a monologue about mothers, without caring who heard him. Sometimes he talked between his teeth, sometimes roared, laughing or making pointless remarks; and I soon noticed in his voice that special tone (at once sly, and spiteful, and dramatic) that he sometimes used to provoke the dead with, for fun. And I remembered that old group photograph in which one girl among several of the same age was marked with a cross in ink, a big, blooming girl in a sentimental pose . . .

"With other women," he was saying, following his own train of thought, "you can save yourself, at least. You can discourage their *love.* But who's to save you from your mother? Sanctity's her vice . . . she never stops expiating the *sin* of having made you, and as long as she's alive she won't let you live, with that old *love* of hers. And of course, the poor insignificant girl has nothing but that famous *sin* in her past, and in her future there's only you, her unlucky son, as the only expression of her destiny; she has nothing else to love. Oh, what hell it is to be loved by someone who doesn't love happiness, or life, or herself, but just loves you! And if

you want to get away from an abuse of power like that, from per-
secution like that, she calls you Judas! The whole point is, you're
a traitor because you want to get out in the streets and conquer
the world, while she'd like to keep you with her forever, in a home
that consists of a bedroom and a kitchen."

I listened eagerly, yet with pain, to what he was saying. While
he was speaking, I had a strange feeling that a large, mysterious,
blooming mother had come down from the unknown north to
persecute him dreadfully as a punishment for speaking ill of her.
And in spite of the fact that talking of mothers always fascinated
me, I hoped he'd stop; but not at all — on he went, angrily, endlessly, as if he were going to while away this long dull day by
telling himself a dreary story.

"And while you grow up, and become handsome, she de-
clines, and good fortune can't be bothered with misery — that's
the law of nature. But she doesn't hold with that. She'd sooner
have you more wretched than herself, but always with her — old
and ugly, even mutilated, paralyzed, so long as you were always
with her. She's not free — that's her nature; so she'd like to have
you enslaved along with her. That's *mother-love* for you!

"When she can't enslave you, she cheers herself with the old
tale of the martyred mother and the heartless son. You, of course,
can't stand that old tale and have a good guffaw at it: other tales
and other hearts are what you're after . . . So she weeps, and gets
more boring, older, sadder for herself. Everything around her's
soaked with tears. And so, of course, you keep away more than
ever. The minute you turn up, she starts accusing you in the most
highfalutin, biblical way; the mildest insult is *frightful murderer!*
Not a day goes by without her chanting this litany. Maybe she
hopes to make you hate yourself with all these accusations, to rob
you and set herself up as a gloomy usurper of all your glory and
your pride. Wherever you escape to — miles away into town —
you can't escape that everlasting parasite, her *love*. Suppose you
hear thunder in the sky, or it starts raining, you can just swear that
at that precise moment she'll be in a state of despair at home in
the old hovel. *He'll get wet, he'll catch cold, he'll be sneezing . . .*

But if the sky clears, you can be perfectly certain she'll be moaning: *Oh, dear, now that it's fine that wretch won't set foot inside the house before nightfall . . .*

"No natural or historical event means anything to her except in relation to you. And so, the whole of creation threatens to turn into a cage. That's what she wants, that's all that *love* of hers dreams of. What she'd really like would be to keep you always prisoner, the way you were when she was pregnant. And when you run away, she tries to pull you back from afar, to set her stamp on the whole of your world, so that you will never forget the humiliation of having been conceived by a woman!"

(My stepmother and I had listened to my father's great outburst without daring to breathe. I didn't dare to say so, but it worried me, rather. What he said certainly hadn't cured me of my unlucky natural love for mothers; on the contrary, as I listened to him I surprised myself more than once thinking involuntarily: "People never know when they have good luck, and those who long for it never get it."

The fact was, our Chief's arguments to show the evils of mothers were — at least most of them — exactly those which made me always regret being an orphan. The idea of someone loving Arturo Gerace only, to the exclusion of all other human beings, for whom Arturo Gerace would be like the sun, the center of the universe, was certainly something I took to. Even the idea of someone weeping and wailing for me didn't seem to me the least bit unpleasant. And things already fascinating in themselves — like going out fearlessly in a storm or marching on to the battlefield — would have become, now that I came to think of it, even more delightful if someone were desperate about me when I did so.

As for the insults my father mentioned, I was sure that some insults wouldn't have seemed poisonous to me, but honey-sweet. Besides, he was arguing from his own experience, which meant his big fat German mother. But mine was a dear little Italian, and came from Massalubri, and as far back as anyone can remember, the women of Massalubri have been creatures with charming manners — too gentle, even, with nothing harsh about them at all. I felt certain that my mother would never have said anything unpleasant to me, even if there'd been a law passed to force her to.

Then there was this business of her decaying while her son grew up handsome, but this seemed to me an absolutely guaranteed advantage. When a woman was past her own youth, her son — even if he wasn't as perfectly handsome as my father — must seem the most glorious creature on earth. This, in fact, would have been the very best thing about it: there'd have been someone to think me marvelous, invincible, splendid! My father was perfect anyway, so obviously that didn't matter much to him, which made me admire more than ever his casual superiority.)

My stepmother sighed and finally plucked up courage to speak. But her voice sounded wild and remote, like the wail of a cat lost in the night. "Then," she murmured, "if the feelings you've talked about are an insult, then people shouldn't love each other . . ."

My father looked around at her. "You shut up," he answered. "You were born only yesterday, and stupid at that. If you say another word, I'll kill you! There are some feelings I can do without. I leave them to wretches who are only free on Sundays. I don't like love stories of any kind; but women's love is the OPPOSITE of love."

He began another monologue, and as he spoke again, boredom and restlessness made him keep yawning, laughing, and tossing on the pillow, like a sick boy half asleep.

"Women want to degrade life. That's what the Hebrew legend meant when it said men were chased out of the Earthly Paradise because of a woman. It's women's fault that we're destined for nothing but birth and death, like animals. Women hate everything unnecessary, undeserved, unlimited; they're ugly creatures who want drama and sacrifice, and time, and decay, and magic, and hope — who want death. If it weren't for women, life would be one long eternal youth in a garden. Everything would be beautiful and free and unoppressed, and *loving* would just mean: *revealing one's beauty, one to another.* Love would be something delightful and disinterested, perfect and glorious, like looking at oneself in the mirror . . . a natural, unremorseful sin, like a splendid hunt in a royal wood. That's what true love is like; it has no object and no reason, and submits to no power except human grace. But woman's love is a slave of destiny, and toils in the service of death and shame. Expediency, blackmail, excuses to back them up: *that's* what its vile feelings consist of . . . Aah! . . . What's the time? Look at my watch, here on my wrist. I don't want to life my arm."

I saw what the time was and told him, and he peered at me through half-closed eyelids and said lazily: "Arturo? . . ." Then, after a pause, "You heard what I said about women. What do you think of it, now? Am I right?"

I decided that this was a good opportunity to mortify my step-mother. "Yes," I said firmly. "We'd be much better off without women. You're quite right."

"Maybe, though," he said, voluble and peevish, "I'm not right or wrong. I spoke of everlasting life, a life without limits . . . as if immortality were something desirable and delightful. But sup-pose the idea of living eternally became a frightful bore in the end? Maybe death was invented to outweigh boredom . . . What d'you think, Arturo?"

"No. No, I don't think so. I think the dead must suffer horribly from boredom," I said, shuddering at the hateful thought.

My father laughed. "You like living, don't you, Blacky?" he said. "But d'you know what boredom is? Tell me, were you ever bored?"

I thought for a moment. "Actually bored," I answered, "no, never. Sometimes, though . . . sometimes I've been fed up."

"Oh. When, for instance?"

Well, I'd been fed up during the past few days when I shut my-self in my room to avoid meeting him and my stepmother to-gether, but I wasn't going to confess that, and was silent. Besides, my father wasn't bothering about my answer; distractedly, he rolled his head over on the pillow again, and soon afterward we realized, from his heavy breathing, that he was asleep.

My stepmother rose, took a woolen blanket from the small bed, and covered him as he slept. Her movement was so natural that it seemed almost automatic, and its very naturalness hurt me all the more. Its fatal simplicity meant: "He may have run women down, but nothing can cancel two sanctioned laws, one that gives me the right to serve him, and the other that gives me the right to protect him. These two laws are: *that I, being his wife, belong to him; and that he, being my husband, is mine!*"

I don't mean, of course, that I understood this movement of hers (with its two meanings) rationally, and with the logical clarity with which I now recall it. No, I never even stopped to wonder exactly *why* her doing so hurt me. But I felt something definite and precise, as if I'd been wounded in the heart with a mysterious barbed weapon.

The stab was so quick that I soon forgot it, but it must have been deep for me to remember it at such a distance. In fact, without realizing it, I was enduring trials more bitter than Othello's. In his tragedy the unhappy Moor at least knew what he was up against, and why he was fighting: the woman he loved on one side, the enemy on the other. While Arturo Gerace's battlefield was one great confused dilemma, without the relief of hope or of revenge.

Alone with him

She whispered that she must go downstairs and light the fire for supper, and went down right away.

I didn't move from my father's room until suppertime. I felt I loved him more than usual, and at the same time I was suffering in a way I'd never suffered before, a way that might, perhaps, if I try to put it into words at all, be translated as something like anxiety at not knowing what the future held for me. None of us ever knows his destiny, and this had always seemed to me something joyful and adventurous, but that day it weighed on me. I looked at my sleeping father and felt an almost savage affection for him, but the fact that he never answered me, never consoled me, made me feel childishly forlorn. I longed for him to kiss me and caress me, as other fathers kiss and caress their children.

It was the first time I'd felt this longing. There had never been any demonstrativeness between us, as obviously that was a womanly business, and had no place with us. The only kiss between us had been the one I'd secretly given his package of cigarettes one night in a dream, but not even in a dream had there ever flashed across my mind the idea that his mouth might give kisses. Who'd think such a thing about a god? The first kiss I'd ever seen him give anyone in my whole life was the one he'd given Romeo's portrait that day. And when I saw it, a kind of jealousy seized me. Why should a dead man's portrait have what I never had? All my life, as far as I could remember, I'd never even once known what a kiss was (except for Immacolatella's, and she used to give me a lot, the exaggerated kind dogs give). To tell you the truth, Silvestro told me afterward that when I was very small, and he used to feed me and look after me, he often kissed my cheek, just the way nurses do; and he has assured me that I used to kiss him back a lot. This must obviously be true, because Silvestro isn't the sort of person to make things up, but I don't remember them. As far as I can remember, at the time I'm talking about I had never kissed anyone or been kissed by anyone.

I wished my father would give me a kiss, even without waking completely, even sleepily, confusedly, or by mistake; or at least, I wished I could kiss him, but didn't dare to. Crouched like a cat at his feet, I watched him sleeping. Even the soft sound of his breathing or snoring, seemed to me something precious to hear because it was a sign of his fleeting presence on the island; of this visit which I had lost — and which now was over, I was certain.

In my room

And so it was: my father left the next day. My stepmother and I saw him off on the steamer. When we turned back from the dock,

I left her and took a separate road, and then wandered about the countryside on my own.

Never had my father's departure disturbed me so much as it did that time. Although there was no reason to doubt his return (for sooner or later he always came back to the island), I felt sad in a desperate, final sort of way, as if seeing him off on the dock a short time before had been a permanent farewell. There had been no kisses in this departure, any more than there had been in the others; the childish longing that had surprised me the previous day had not been appeased. Moreover this longing seemed quite futile that day. I felt dry and lonely, and from the depths of this loneliness I felt rising in me again the unnatural suffering I'd felt the previous day for the first time: the pain of not knowing my destiny.

The weather was as beautiful as in spring, and it was dark when I got home. I went in through the French window and found my stepmother in the kitchen, singing as usual while she lit the fire, and her carefree air struck me as rather unbecoming. Until a few hours before, I'd been indignant with her because she was always hanging around my father like a bitch, and stealing him from me. But now, I felt bitterly indignant that she wasn't sad at being separated from him and felt an ugly urge to punish her. While she was laying the table, I turned on her nastily.

"Now that my father's left," I said, "You'll have to learn to sleep alone at night."

It was clear that she hadn't yet stopped to think of this trial that obviously awaited her. I saw her face change and grow frightened, as if only what I had said had reminded her of it. (This was one of the many signs of childishness still remaining in her: that her imagination, which was always quick enough when it was a matter of stories and childish things like that, was pretty slow when it meant facing something that might bring her pain or disaster. It looked as if she had an ingenuous trust in what the days would bring, and attributed a kind of conscious benevolence to them, as if even time had a Christian heart.)

During supper, which lasted only a few minutes, she was silent with anxiety. I ate quickly without saying a word to her and went to bed immediately afterward. I was tired after the day's excitement and felt very drowsy. As often happened in winter, I wasted no time in undressing, and just took off my shoes; and the minute I got into bed I fell asleep.

About an hour later, or maybe less, I was wakened by some small nervous knocks on the door and by my stepmother's low voice calling desperately from the passage: "Artù! Artù!" I don't know what I'd been dreaming in that first hour of sleep, but I must have been very far away, because I'd forgotten her completely. Still half-asleep, and not taking anything in, I sat up and switched on the light beside my bed, and at that same moment the door opened and she appeared, looking terribly upset, on the threshold. "Artù, I'm scared," she said in a small voice.

Fear seemed to have chased her out of bed exactly as she was — in her petticoat and without shoes. On her feet she had her usual woolen socks, full of holes, which she wore even in bed; her hair, tied up in a single topknot for the night, reminded me of the crest of curly feathers you find sometimes on tropical birds.

When I came back to reality, I stared at her with remote, disdainful eyes. It wasn't the first time I'd seen her in her petticoat. I'd already caught glimpses of her like that — crossing the passage or moving about in my father's room. And she hadn't covered herself up at all, but had appeared perfectly calm and natural, as if she wasn't the least bit embarrassed to be seen in her petticoat by a boy of fourteen. It annoyed me, this behavior of hers!

"I hadn't meant to wake you up, Artù," she explained, her lips pale. "I tried to get to sleep . . . I even said prayers to Saint Rita to help me to drop off . . . But I can't manage it. I'm too scared to sleep alone without anybody in the room . . ."

She glanced suspiciously around the dark passage, and moved a little into the circle of light, as if seeking protection against the darkness. Sullen and scornful, I didn't invite her to sit down or to come in, and she remained standing, leaning against the door-jamb like a servant. Her slip left her delicate shoulders bare; they were very white, very pathetic and sweet; and the material of her petticoat revealed her breasts exactly as if they were bare, and their mysterious, mature heaviness appeared to me as something tender and vulnerable, something to arouse pity in me. I had a strange intuition of the terrible pain she'd feel if she was wounded cruelly there . . . For some minutes I turned this imaginary suffering over in my mind; it seemed almost incredible that someone as defenseless, as vulnerable, as ignorant, and as stupid as she was could go through life without getting hurt . . .

"You're over sixteen," I told her, looking enormously scornful, "and you can't even sleep alone at night. You try to act like an old lady, as if other people were children beside you! You make me laugh. Some fears really make people laugh, you know, once people are grown up! Just you look around at other people, and see if they're scared of sleeping alone!"

"Other women," she apologized, humbly, bewilderedly, "sleep with their husbands after they're married . . ."

"AFTER THEY'RE MARRIED. But what about before? And when their husbands travel? Whom do they sleep with then? With nobody!"

"What d'you mean, with nobody? They sleep with their mother, with their sister. With their brothers and their father. They sleep with their whole family. Everyone in the world sleeps with the family."

She begged me to let her sleep on the sofa in my room, at least for just that night. From the next day on she'd learn to sleep alone, but this evening she had nearly fainted at being in a room at night for the first time in her life without any of the family nearby. She just couldn't get used to it all at once, but she would in time. Unwillingly, I had to put up with the idea of having her in my room for the night. She went next door for a minute to fetch her blankets, and then came rushing back, dragging them along the floor, as pale as if she was escaping from a house on fire. When I saw her quite extraordinary terror, a fantastic suspicion came into my head, and while she was getting to bed on the sofa, obviously feeling heartened, I asked her if the Castle Ancestor had by any chance appeared to her with his knights — the wicked youths . . .

She shook her head, as if hurt at my talking such nonsense.

"D'you think I don't realize," she said, "that your father made it all up? But of course," she added sincerely, conscientiously, "when you're alone in a room at night, even stories are enough to scare you."

When the light was out, I couldn't get to sleep at once. Curiosity kept me awake. I was wondering if women slept like men, if, for instance, they breathed and snored like men when they were asleep. I had never seen a woman asleep, whereas I'd seen plenty of men sleeping, and all of them snored, though in different ways. Our old servant Costante, for instance, gave such loud, lengthy snores that he sounded like a siren. And my father's snoring was a light, amusing, voluptuous little noise, like a cat's purring.

A few minutes passed, and I heard nothing from the sofa, not the slightest snoring. Maybe she wasn't asleep yet. I called out softly: "Hey, you! Are you asleep?" No answer. Well then, she must be asleep.

A minute later I went to sleep too, and had a dream. I seemed to be swimming in a deep shadowy cave. I dived in to get hold of a beautiful branch of coral that I'd seen on the bottom, and when I pulled it away, I saw with horror the water turn red with blood. I jerked myself awake, and as soon as I opened my eyes, instinctively switched on the light with the confused idea that I had to dash somewhere and stop some unknown crime or tragedy . . . But everything was quiet, and near me on the sofa my stepmother was sleeping so soundly that not even the light suddenly turned on and shining full on her face disturbed her. For a moment I couldn't understand why she was in my room; but I soon remembered, and looked at her with curiosity. She was sleeping slightly curled up, to fit the size of the sofa, and was wrapped up to her chin in blankets, her face vague and innocent, her lips moist and fresh from her silent breathing, and even the faint color of her cheeks seeming to come from her tender breathing. It looked as if she wasn't dreaming of anything, that once asleep she left behind even the simple thoughts she had in daylight, and became even simpler, no longer living through her mind, but only through her breathing, like a flower. I recognized in her face the fairy-tale look

she'd had the day she arrived but which had vanished the following day. The delicate lines of her eye sockets, which a single
day had been enough to spoil, were hidden under the long pitiful
eyelashes. The bunch of curls on her cheek seemed just like the
corolla lopped from a great black flower.

She seemed to me prettier than when she was awake. Maybe
the famous beauty of women, which novels and poetry kept
talking about, appeared when they were asleep at night? If I
stayed awake until morning, should I see my stepmother growing
stupendously beautiful, like a fairy-tale heroine? Of course, I
wasn't really serious; I was just making things up for fun. Yet as I
dozed off a little later, my thoughts were mixed with a kind of anxiety. I felt that there was some foreign presence in my room, subject to peculiar changes.

I fell asleep again without remembering to put out the light, and
it wasn't a full, deep sleep; in fact, I still felt that I was in my room
with my stepmother sleeping on the sofa. But in my dream, she
seemed to me wicked and beastly: she'd got into my room by fraud,
pretending to be a boy like me dressed in a shirt that fell quite flat
on her chest, as if she wasn't shaped like a woman at all. But I'd
guessed she was a woman, all the same, and I didn't want women
with me in my room. Armed with a knife, I went up to her as she
slept, to punish her imposture, and found she was lying when I
opened the shirt and uncovered her innocent round breasts . . . She
gave a shriek. It wasn't new to me; I had already heard it, I didn't remember when or where, and I knew no sound so horrifying, so capable of piercing my mind and nerves, as this one.

I woke up with a start, hot and sweating, as if it were summer.
Dazzled by the light that was still burning, I saw my stepmother
sleeping peacefully in the same position as before. Senseless, uncontrollable hatred seized me. "Wake up!" I shouted suddenly,
jumping out of bed and shaking her by the shoulders. "Get out of
my room, do you hear me? Get out of my room!"

I saw her rise bewilderedly from the blankets, showing her small
bare shoulders and the shape of her bosom; and I hated her more
furiously than ever. I suddenly wished that she was really a boy like

me, that I could punch her until my anger was satiated. What enraged me most just then was the fact that she belonged to the weaker sex, which prevented me from venting my anger on her.

"Why don't you cover yourself up, you slut?" I roared. "Why don't I embarrass you? I want to embarrass you!"

She looked at me with innocent, astonished eyes, then looked down at the neck of her petticoat and blushed; and, not having anything to cover herself with, crossed her arms shamefacedly across her breast.

Her eyes returned to me, confused, uncertain, as if she didn't know me. Yet — and this was what maddened me — in spite of my hatred and my beastliness, she wasn't afraid of me. Deep in her eyes there still remained (and had always remained, the whole of that time), a kind of trustful questioning, as if my enmity was not enough to make her forget a single afternoon when I had been friendly; and she still believed in that Arturo. What she ought to realize was that that Arturo no longer existed as far as she was concerned, that I was ashamed of that afternoon and wanted to cut it out of time completely. I was seized by a dry pitilessness that could only be satisfied with cruelty and denial.

"I don't want you here in my room, do you hear?" I cried, chokingly. "Get out! You give me bad dreams . . . And you're a dirty, ugly, lousy beggar, that's what you are . . ."

She had withdrawn to the door, which had stood open from the time she came in; she looked gloomy and sullen, so that I thought war was at last declared between us. Then I felt, exquisitely, the will to wound, or rather the pleasure of wounding, and seized her blankets and pillow and flung them all outside into the passage and banged the door hard behind her.

For a while I could still hear her panting, scared and breathless, through the door. "She's crying because she's scared of the dark," I told myself with harsh satisfaction. Finally there was silence. The next day I discovered she'd slept in the room next to mine, which had once been Silvestro's. Obviously in that tiny room, which wasn't as isolated as my father's, she felt more protected against darkness and solitude. She took all of her Madonnas from the room where she'd put them the first day and set them up on the soapbox, on the chair, and on the windowsill, all around the camp bed like a guard keeping watch over her sleep. And while my father was away she slept there every night.

Sleeping women

Because she was so frightened, she never dared shut herself up in her room, and always left the door slightly open, and while she was getting into bed, she hurriedly recited out loud all the prayers she knew. From my room I could hear her voice repeating by heart what sounded like a meaningless monotonous tune, at once melodious and harsh. Occasionally her voice would rise, unexpectedly emphatic, and I'd hear distinct phrases like *Hail our life, our sweetness, and our hope . . .* or *Turn then, most gracious advocate . . .* The house was so profoundly still that sometimes I even heard the ardent, smacking kisses she gave her Virgins when she'd finished her prayers.

I didn't bother to find out how she spent her solitary days in the House of the Guaglioni; generally I appeared only in the evening, when she called me for supper. At table I always had a book and went on reading while I ate, letting her serve me without deigning to speak or to take the smallest notice of her. When I glanced fleetingly at her, she seemed to me paler than before, more melancholy and sad. It must have been the fear of being alone that made her suffer. But I didn't care what she suffered. Wasn't I always alone as well?

I began writing poetry at that time. I remember one poem called "Sleeping Women"; I felt as proud of it as if I'd written the sublimest lyric, and it included these lines:

> Women's beauty glows at evening,
> Like night flowers
> And proud owls that flee the sun;
> Like crickets, like the moon, queen of heaven.

But because they are sleeping women cannot know
The lofty eagles in their nests
That fold their wings on a rocky cliff
Breathing in silence.
No one, perhaps, will ever know
The grandeur of their beauty.

Every time I passed her room when she wasn't there I looked disdainfully away. But on one of those mornings, three or four days after the famous night when I'd kicked her off my sofa, I happened to wake up very early and she was still asleep. When I saw that the weather was wonderful, I flung open the windows of my room at once, and soon afterward, as I was going down the passage, a gust of wind caught the unlatched door of the little room and left it half open. And I happened to glance in at her, distractedly, while she continued to sleep peacefully, bundled up in blankets right up to her chin. The rising sun lit up her face the way those spotlights they have in the theater shine on dancers to allow people to see them better. And I saw that as she slept she smiled with joy; in fact, she was almost laughing, showing her small front teeth.

This rather surprised me and left me curious, because the night I had seen her asleep for the first time I had thought from her expression that she slept without dreams, and lived only in her breathing, like a plant. But this smile could obviously come only from some beautiful dream. Whatever sort of dream could she have, someone like her? This had always been one of my crazes: when I saw people asleep, I often wanted — I was even tormented by the longing — to guess their dreams. Making them tell them afterward when they woke up wasn't the slightest use (even if they didn't lie about them).

Sometimes the secret of those who slept didn't seem to me too mysterious. Immacolatella's dreams, for instance, were easy enough to guess. The very most she could dream was that she was a real hunting dog, as the rabbits on Vivara thought; or else that she had learned to climb trees, like a cat; or that she had found herself with a tray full of lamb bones. But obviously the best thing she could dream about was me. It wasn't hard to see all this.

And what about her? What dream could she possibly be having to make her laugh with joy? Maybe she thought she was home in Naples with her whole family in the one bed, and her godmother as well. Or at a great party in the middle of heaven among carts and lights and a crowd of little boys turned into cherubs. Or else that my father was bringing home a basketful of jewels from his travels. I wondered whether I came into any of them, too. It was irritating not to be able to see behind her closed eyes; as if she, who was so stupid and inferior, possessed something that cut out Arturo Gerace. I was tempted to infiltrate slyly into her dream. Sometimes in summer I went to sleep on the beach after bathing, and my father, bored with being there awake and watching me asleep, would tickle me for fun with a sharp piece of seaweed or blow gently into my ear. And in my dream a fish, say, appeared at once, tickling me with its fins as I swam in the depths of the Pacific, or the American gangster Al Capone pointed his murderous pistol at my ear.

I was all set to go into her room and play the game my father played with me, so as to creep into her dream. But . . . was I mad? How could I possibly think of getting involved with this stupid intruder? The idea that I had sunk to such friendly playfulness about her annoyed me the whole day long, so much so that later on, to give vent to my irritation, I tore up the poem called "Sleeping Women." Every time I found myself giving way to less hostile feelings about her — either from sheer absentmindedness or for some other involuntary reason — I became even more difficult to deal with, as if out of revenge.

Bad temper

My father's first absence proved much shorter than I had imagined it would be. It was less than a week since he left when, to our great surprise, he turned up again, quite unexpectedly as usual. I happened to be near the gate, and was the first to see him, but he was so impatient to see her that all he bothered to say was: "Hey, Blacky!" Then he asked me at once, anxiously and fast, where she was. I growled that she was in the kitchen, and he dashed around to the back of the house and went in through the French window. Surly and reluctant, I followed him; my joy at seeing him again had vanished in a moment when I felt so neglected and so unimportant to him.

At his unexpected appearance my stepmother flushed scarlet with delight, and, when he saw it, he grew radiant. He marched in without greeting or embracing her. "Phew, what a mess your hair is in!" he said, glancing at her with an air of security and possession. "Haven't you *done your head* this morning?" Then at once he handed over the presents he'd brought: a wooden bracelet painted in various colors and a belt buckle made of little bits of mirror. He hadn't brought anything for me, but when he noticed me scowling in a corner, he gave me fifty lire.

Then he asked the question he always asked when he arrived. "What's the news?" But this time it wasn't as it had been in the past; this time he really seemed rather eager to hear the answer. Still confused by the suddenness of his return, she answered: "We're all right . . . the weather's been fine all the time . . . I had a letter from my mother, signed by my sister too . . . and they say that they're all well at Naples too, and the weather's fine . . ."

And while she was telling him this sort of thing, he kept asking: "Did your godmother write to you? Did you go to Mass?" as if some momentary whim made him take notice, quite pointlessly, of her affairs.

At the same time, he kept wandering around the kitchen, looking around and recognizing objects with an air of enjoyment and conquest, as if it was ten years since he had been home. She shook her head a bit, with two little curls that looked like bells on her forehead, and, her quick black eyes laughing, said timidly: "I wasn't . . . I wasn't really expecting to see you back today . . ."

"I always do what I want," he said, carelessly, regally. "When I want to go, I go. When I want to come back, I come back here, and you'll just fit in with it."

Soon afterward he went upstairs with his suitcase, and we tagged along behind. As soon as we were upstairs, the first thing she did was take her blankets from Silvestro's room and put them back on her bed in my father's room.

While he was unpacking the suitcase, I stayed in the bedroom with the two of them. I was lying on the big bed, my arms behind my head and my legs crossed, looking silently at the ceiling with a surly, absent air. But soon I felt so useless there that I felt violently out of place; I jumped off the bed and ran wildly to the door, with the sidelong lope of a tiger.

My father gave a small malicious laugh. "Hey, Arturo, where are you off to?" he shouted after me. "Why are you so peeved? What's eating you?" But he made no effort to stop me or call me back.

"All right, I'll go out," I thought. "I've got plenty of money. I can go to the café or the inn, or even go and get drunk if I want to!" But every place I thought of seemed to me empty and hopeless just then, and I ended up downstairs in the Guaglioni's great drawing room, which we hardly ever used, and stayed there in the dark, sitting on one of those flattened-out sofas without thinking of anything or anybody.

My father stayed with us a couple of days and then left again. After about two more weeks, he reappeared for another day or two. And so it went. During the first months of his marriage he kept appearing at frequent intervals, though for rather short visits. But I was indifferent to his comings and goings; he clearly didn't come to Procida for my sake.

He must have noticed right from the start my obvious, flaunted dislike for my stepmother. In fact, sometimes it seemed to amuse him, but, like an idle despot, he left me alone with my whims and tempers, without taking much notice of me. Only once did he mention her to me, when I happened to be alone with him in his room for a moment while he was packing. I was looking at him without speaking.

Kicking under the bed some old shoes he didn't want for the journey, he glanced at me and observed in a haughty, absent tone: "Hey, Blacky, aren't you in rather a foul mood, by the look of things?"

I shrugged my shoulders scornfully, without answering.

With a half-smile, looking through his eyelashes at me, he went on: "Why have you got your knife into her so much? Why does poor old Nunziata get on your nerves so?"

I frowned and drew away from him; then he laughed and made a small ironical grimace, his eyes clouded over mysteriously.

"Oh, come on, cheer up, Blacky!" he exclaimed. "Poor Nunziata certainly isn't the dangerous rival that'll steal my heart from you."

As he said this, his voice and features had a hint of brutality about them; then he smiled, as if to himself, his mouth closed and the corners of his lips tilted up; and I recognized that fairy-tale goatlike smile I remembered having seen before.

I looked at him uncertainly, not quite sure what he was aiming at. "I don't care in the least!" I answered haphazardly, childishly.

He burst out laughing again, boldly. "Oh, so you don't care . . ." he said, looking down at me with beetling brows. "But my dear Spanish grandee, I happen to have come to a different conclusion, you know . . . Shall I tell you what I really think? Don't worry, I'll only tell you. I won't tell anyone else. My opinion is that YOU'RE JEALOUS! You're jealous of Nunziatella because before you had me all to yourself on this island, and now she's supplanted you. Well, what d'you think of that, Blacky?"

I colored as if he'd discovered a dreadful secret.

"It's not true," I exclaimed angrily. At that moment, she turned up and I made to leave him, but he grabbed my wrist quickly, as hard and ferociously as if we were wrestling, and said between his teeth: "Where are you going? Wait here." And without freeing my wrist, he put his other arm around his wife and began to play affectedly with her curls. "What beautiful curls," he said, while she looked at him very gravely, not understanding what it all meant. "What a shame Arturo hasn't got beautiful curls like these!" While he was saying this, he kept glancing at me and laughing to himself for the fun of provoking me to jealousy; but at last, seeing how violently I was trying to free myself from him, he got bored and said: "All right then, get out." And I left the room without even looking at him, seething with anger.

That word *jealous* had hurt me terribly. I was so upset at the charge that it never occurred to me to ask myself if it might be true, if the feeling that had made me live like a hounded animal since my father's marriage might not, perhaps, be called jealousy. At that time, however clever I was at pondering on ancient history, or destiny, or the Absolute Certainties, I wasn't in the habit of peering deeply into myself. Some problems were quite outside the scope of my imagination. I knew that I was hurt, and that was all. I was so hurt, in fact, that I thought of getting on a boat and leaving the island forever, and never seeing my father or my stepmother again. But I had hardly thought of it when I realized from the cold revulsion that immediately took hold of me that I would never be able to do it: I found the idea of the pair of them staying alone on the island without me completely unbearable.

My rage, with nothing to vent itself on, became such a torment that I began to moan furiously, as if I'd been wounded. I thought that it was all provoked by his insult and nothing else, but perhaps I was unconsciously suffering for my heart's impossible longings and for the interwoven, contradictory jealousies and complex passions that were to be mine.

Pasta

My father kept his word and told no one that he thought I was jealous. Besides, as far as my stepmother was concerned, he obviously wouldn't have confided anything so serious and important to her, and about a Gerace, too! As far as I was concerned, he didn't follow up his malicious remarks, but at once returned to his normal indifference without bothering in the least about me. And so the memory of his insult was soon buried.

My dislike of my stepmother showed no sign of diminishing; on the contrary, it grew worse every day. The result was that the life she led with me during my father's absence from the island wasn't exactly gay. I never addressed her except to give her orders. If I wanted to call her to the window for some order while I was outdoors, or wanted to warn her of my arrival, I just whistled. And at home, too, I whistled when I had to call her, or at the most, if we were in the same room, I'd say: "Hey you — listen!" When I talked to her, I'd look away in a slightly insulting way, as if to show her that she was something so vile that it simply wasn't worth my while looking at her. And when I went past the little room, I looked away from the unlatched door as if some ghost or monster lived beyond it.

I hated her so much that even when I was out of the house it often tormented me just to know that she was up there, living in our house, which had now become her home, and I tried to forget her existence, to pretend that she was nothing, less than a shadow, to me. When I looked back to the days before she had come to the island, they seemed a sort of happy limbo. Oh, why had she come? Why had my father brought her?

The days were lengthening and growing warmer. It was no longer cold those beautiful starry evenings, and often, what with the sea, the streets, and the widow's murky café, I let suppertime go by without going up to the House of the Guaglioni. But however late it was when I got home, I always saw the lamp still lighted in the kitchen window and knew I'd find her there, that she wouldn't have had supper yet, and was waiting for me before putting the pasta in the saucepan. I might be very late and hungry, but sometimes when I saw that lighted window I wanted, cruelly, to prolong her waiting on purpose. Cruelty like that was something quite new in me. I'd creep up silently, like a thief, right up to the glass door of the kitchen, and from outside, without her seeing me, I'd watch her as long as I felt like it. Lurking in a dark corner, I could see her beyond the glass, dropping with sleepiness, glancing hopefully at the door at the slightest rustle from outside, and every now and then yawning like a cat (cats open their mouths as wide as they'll go, the way tigers do, and make one laugh), or sighing, her breast heaving slightly. In the end I'd burst in like a wild beast hurtling

into its den and startle her dreadfully. Then I'd take my book off
the chest at once and wait somberly for her to serve me.

Once when I arrived I saw her through the windows writing on
a sheet of paper, looking deeply meditative and inspired, like a
proper author. After supper she went upstairs ahead of me and left
what she'd been writing on the sideboard, so I happened to see it.
It was a letter to her mother, and went something like this:

> Dearest Mother, — Here's hoping this letter finds you
> in good health, and Rosa too, please hand on my news
> to her. Here we're all well, please give my love to my
> dear godmother, and tell her to remember me, and
> love to my dear friends Irma and Carulina, and darling
> Angiulina, and tell them to think of me. Please give
> my regards to Father Severino, and Mother Conzilia,
> and is my dear San Giovanni still ill, it must be old
> age, though, and give my love to Maria and Filumena,
> and darling Aurora, and tell her the dress is very nice,
> and ask all my other friends if they remember me,
> maybe they've forgotten Nunziata, I don't forget them,
> day or night, and ask Sufia and the other Nunziata,
> Ferdinando's, if they remember me. Just think, Ma,
> dear, here at Procida we eat without paying, everything
> grows on our land, oil and potatoes and greens, and at
> the shops they trust you to pay later. Well now, Ma,
> dear, here's a thousand loving kisses from your little
> girl, and a thousand kisses for Rosa from her sister, and
> another thousand to my godmother, and lots of kisses
> to all the other friends I've told you, remember I'm al-
> ways thinking of you, that's all for now. Nunziatella.

Another evening when I came home at about ten o'clock, I
found her asleep as she sat up waiting for me at the kitchen table.
One arm was crooked on the table, and her cheek lay on her hand
as if it was a cushion. The heavy curls hanging over her forehead
shaded her face from the light, and this time while she slept, her

face looked strange, grave, and mysterious. I started beating on the windows and singing noisily to wake her up brutally and at once.

Two or three times it happened that when I got home later than usual I collided with her just outside the gate, where she'd come to wait for me. "What are you doing out here at the gate?" I asked her crossly, and she said she was there to get some fresh air.

Besides, she had nothing to complain of. I hadn't asked her to wait for me. But obviously, compared with the boring and lonely days she spent, those suppers with a dumb companion must have seemed an important occasion, a kind of party, like dancing or the movies to rich people. Right from early morning, she was in a whirl of preparations, making fresh pasta with eggs every day. As soon as it was smooth, she hung it out to dry on some beams by the door, like a banner. One morning early when I'd gone down to the kitchen feeling rather cross, and saw her busy at it as usual, I told her shortly that if she was doing it for my benefit, there wasn't any point in making pasta every day, because actually I didn't like it and never had liked it.

I said this just to humiliate her; it wasn't true. The fact was that I liked pasta just as much as any other food, and ate with equal pleasure anything humanly edible. The only thing I cared about was quantity, because I always had an enormous appetite.

"What?" she said softly, as if she couldn't believe her ears. "You don't like pasta!"

"No."

"Then what do you like?"

I wondered what the worst answer would be, the one that would upset her most. And remembering her onetime scorn of goats' milk, I made up an answer on the spot.

"Goat meat!" I said.

"GOAT meat!" she exclaimed, bewildered. But a minute later a kind of understanding, obliging enthusiasm appeared through her bewilderment, as if she were already thinking of getting hold of goat meat to please me and of preparing goaty dishes . . .

This gave me an irresistible longing to laugh, and I hid my face quickly in my hands, thinking: "If she sees me laughing now, she'll presume we're good friends again . . . like . . . that after-noon," and I shuddered at the thought. But however hard I tried to smother it, I felt my laughter bursting out in my chest. So, as I couldn't think of any other way of hiding my amusement just then, I flung myself down on the floor, knelt with my face in my crossed arms, and pretended to sob my heart out.

It was at times like that that I realized I could become a great actor if I wanted to. She came up to me, hesitant, solicitous. Un-derneath the arm hiding my brow I could see her small feet in their old house shoes . . . and as the act I was putting on increased my amusement, my fake sobs grew more desperate, more rending. The acting was perfect. "Artù?" she murmured anxiously, and then, a little later, she repeated, "Artù . . ." I could feel her tender, almost animal breath on me. Then, unable to hold back any longer, she said tremulously: "Artù! . . . Something's wrong! . . . What's the matter? Tell Nunziata!"

There was a kind of grown-up presumption mixed with her pity as she spoke; something like the importance of an elder sister who has held all her small brothers in her arms. When I heard her speaking to me like that, I was suddenly seized with scorn and dis-gust. How dared she? I leaped furiously to my feet.

"I'm not crying, I'm laughing!" I exclaimed. She looked with dismay at my hard face, at my dry, flaming eyes, as if she had seen a dragon rise from the earth. "I don't cry!" I went on, proudly, threateningly. "Don't ever dare to talk to me like that! You're no relation of mine. Don't you see? You're nothing to me! Not a rela-tion, not a friend! D'you see?"

She looked down at her pasta again, fiercely, wrathfully, and stuck out her lips as if she was going to say something angry. But she was silent, and went on kneading and working the pasta with arrogant movements, as if she wanted to hurt it. Then she began rolling it out, unwillingly, and at the last moment, as I went to the door, still chewing the remains of my breakfast, she looked at me dimly, uncertainly.

"Well then," she asked, "if you don't like pasta, what do you want for supper this evening?"

I half turned, looking as indifferent as I could, and declared as rudely as possible: "Me? Well, who cares what the devil you make for supper? Do you really believe what I said about the pasta? You may as well know that whatever I eat is all the same to me — I can live on biscuits and salted meat. And if you were to cook ostrich wings or shark fins, or hippopotamus tongues, I wouldn't even notice, because whatever you cook tastes exactly the same. As far as I'm concerned, you can carry on making pasta every day, or whatever you like. I don't give a damn. And besides, my tastes are none of your business."

The point was that I didn't want her to look after me, or bother about me. I gave her orders for the pleasure of humiliating her, treating her like an automaton, an object, but when she was kind (as if she really supposed that she was a relation of mine, or my mother) I just couldn't bear it. More than once I told her: "We're not relations! You're nothing to me!"

Once she went slightly pale, flung back her hair, and answered: "It's not true that I'm nothing to you. I'm your stepmother, and you're my stepson!" And she said it in a rather bullying, passionate way, as if she was staking a kind of proprietary claim on me.

I laughed in her face, angry and scornful.

"Stepmother!" I cried. "A stepmother's less than nothing! *Stepmother's* the foulest word there is!" And I told her harshly that I didn't want her waiting for me to come to supper. If I was late, she was to have her supper by herself at the usual time, and then leave the kitchen, and put my meal aside. I told her it bored me to have supper with her, and annoyed me to see her every evening, and in short, that I was free to have supper alone.

Solitary song

She was hurt by what I said, more hurt and depressed than I had thought she would be, but she didn't answer or disobey. From then on I got into the habit of coming home late every evening,

on purpose not to meet her. If, when I got home, I happened to
see the kitchen light still on, I wandered about outside the gate
(no longer peeping through the French window, but keeping
clear of the house) until the light went out and the darkness was a
signal to me that my stepmother had gone upstairs. Then at last
I'd decide to go into the kitchen and would eat the supper she'd
left to keep warm on the embers.

My stepmother made no protests or complaints, although I
was then all she had of family and company. She still seemed foreign to the unfriendly islanders, knew no one, and had made no
friends. She spent her time cooped up in the kitchen or in her
little room without anyone at all to talk to. Often when I looked
up from my boat and saw the walls of our apparently uninhabited
castle, I half-wondered if she was a dream of mine and whether
anyone besides me really lived up there. But then, at whatever
hour of the day I happened to pass the house, it wasn't long before
I heard the familiar sound of those famous old slippers on the
stairs or along the passage.

Toward me she had a new manner: fierce, and upset, and
angry, and proudly refusing to beg for the friendship I had so cruelly refused her. But when our eyes met, in the stormy depths of
hers I saw, like a tiny star, that eternal, unanswerable question:
But what have I done to you, Artù? What have I done to you?

Sometimes I saw her from a window tightly embracing the
bitter orange tree in the garden out of loneliness and the need for
friendship, or even the gate posts, as if those inanimate objects
were a sister, or a beloved friend. Or else she'd start cuddling one
of those wicked, mangy old cats that came looking for scraps,
pressing it to her heart and covering it with kisses. Sometimes I
even heard her talking to herself, joyfully, absorbed, with a sweet
humming voice that wasn't addressing anyone. For instance,
looking out on the terrace one moonlight night, she observed:
"The moon's high, and the boats are out fishing for squid." Once,
eating some sea urchins from a basket, alone on the front doorstep,
she said: "Ooh, isn't it delicious; it's like a pomegranate . . ."
Sometimes, as she combed her hair, she talked to the knots in it,

grumbling and insulting them as she tugged violently with the comb: "Oh, you nasty old beasts, you!"

She really preferred being shut up indoors to being out in the open and in the streets, just as a canary may love its cage more than its freedom. And although the House of Guaglioni was hardly hospitable, she left it very rarely. Sometimes I saw her dashing off to Mass early in the morning, bundled up in her black shawl, as if she were escaping secretly; and sometimes I happened to meet her in the streets with her shopping basket on her arm, her curls tucked under a handkerchief, a bulging purse clutched in her hand. When I saw her bustling around the shops with her clumsy walk and her small ineloquent hands clutching her purchases, she seemed like a poor little gypsy servant girl in the service of some mysterious abbess or great lady who had been bewitched. For she looked dark and reckless, and aggressive, too, as if she shared the secrets of a fascinating master who was universally disliked (in some way she must have come to know the evil tales and gossip about the Gerace family).

I felt that she was fading away in her loneliness, day by day. Sometimes I heard her singing around the house, singing the old songs she had learned from the neighbor's radio in Naples, the one about the apache, or another with the refrain: *Tango, you're like a rope round my heart.* Or else she'd sing a hymn that went: *We adore you, divine Host, we adore you, oh Host of love.* Her strident, vulgar notes dragged gloomily along, as if all the songs she sang were sad. But I don't think she worried; I don't think she even realized that she wasn't happy. If a carnation or a rose has to grow in a pot on a windowsill, it doesn't start thinking: *Things might be different.* And that's what she was like, just as simple as that.

As I listened to her singing, I remembered the famous Neapolitan song I had learned as a child, and often heard some musician singing down at the harbor below: *You're a canary . . . you're ill and you sing . . . alone, alone, you're going to die alone . . .* In fact, when I saw her suffering face, with those great black eyes burning in it, I really wondered if she was getting ill. I almost suspected that the fatal magic of the man from Amalfi was working and was going to kill her off.

But I hardened my heart against her, and refused to pity her; in fact, I persisted in my cruelty. One thing exasperated me increasingly above all, as the days went by, and that was that though she was so scared of my father, she never showed the slightest fear of me. When I hurt her and abused her, though she never answered back, she stood squarely before me, as bold as a lion. Her attitude was just another obvious proof that she treated me like a child whom a married woman like her couldn't possibly fear. And yet, since her arrival, the difference between our respective heights had already lessened a lot, and her boldness was like a slap in the face to me. I wanted to make her fear me the way she feared my father; it would have satisfied my pride. With him, she trembled if a shadow crossed his face. Often I forgot all my other ambitions; I had dreams of becoming a brigand when I grew up, a gang leader so terrible that she would fall down in a faint the minute she saw me. Even at night, I sometimes woke up thinking: "I want to frighten her," and imagined myself treating her with the most barbarous, unheard-of cruelty, in my longing to make her hate me the way I hated her.

When I gave her orders and made her work for me, I had the air of a surly emperor ordering a common soldier. And she was always gentle and quick to serve me, but there was no sign that this obedience of hers was a result of fear. Not a bit! When she was busy working for me, she revived, and even took on an important air, and her pale, ugly face became as fresh as jasmine. Maybe she hoped that our roles as master and servant meant the beginning of a reconciliation. There was no way of making her see the pitilessness of my soul.

Queen of Women

The hairstyle

M Y FATHER HAD come home fairly often when he was first married, but as the months passed his visits grew rarer. During the spring we saw him maybe only a couple of times, and he was always in a hurry, like a tourist dashing through; and sometimes, on those visits he took to wandering about the island with me again. My stepmother had been pregnant from early spring, and waited for us at home.

June went by without any news of my father, but in July I began looking for him, because in high summer he always longed for Procida, wherever he was. And in fact, he reappeared at the beginning of August and spent almost the whole month on the island as usual. The very morning he arrived he went out sailing with me in *The Torpedo-boat of the Antilles*, and we took up the old summer life we had always spent on the beach and out at the sea. I became his only companion again, all the time, while my stepmother in her pregnancy drooped around the shadowy rooms of the House of the Guaglioni.

The summer days continued, unchanging and glorious, shining like stars. My father and I never spoke of her, and in those happy hours together, the House of the Guaglioni, with its solitary inmate who had no part in our buoyancy and fun, seemed almost like an extinguished planet outside the orbit of the earth. But I no longer felt the childish happiness I had known in other summers with my father: my stepmother's existence came between us. The very fact that she was condemned to her dark slavery often made her seem more present than if she had been there playing with us, not a woman, but some lucky, lighthearted creature like ourselves, an equal of my father and of me. It was as if there was a great mysterious idol hidden away in a small room in the House of the Guaglioni, an idol without will or splendor that yet had a magic power to change the whole atmosphere and light of summer.

Pregnancy had changed her face as well as deforming her body, giving her an expression that was almost mature. Her features seemed to sag, her nose had sharpened, and her cheeks were pale and grayish, as if she had some blood disease. She moved listlessly and hung her thin, sweet head like a tired animal, her eyes dimmed to mildness — peaceful, unquestioning, unworried. Suddenly I thought I saw in her a strange resemblance to my mother. For months I had avoided looking at the famous little portrait I kept jealously hidden in my room, forgotten by everyone but me. And now when I saw my stepmother, the picture with its unfailing gentleness kept coming into my mind. I felt something vague and unfamiliar that changed my hatred for her into a kind of possessive curiosity, and more than ever, as if I was avoiding a hopeless temptation, I avoided looking at the portrait I adored.

Early in the summer, before my father came back, I heard my stepmother once complaining that her great mop of hair was tiresome in hot weather. An irresistible impulse made me suggest that she should do it in two braids pinned up into two separate buns just above her ears (this was the hairstyle my mother had in the photograph, but of course she didn't know, and I didn't tell her). She was confused and pleased at my noticing anything connected with her, as for me to do so was quite unusual, but she objected slightly because of the length of her hair. I insisted almost violently, and she did it in the new style right away. And so, with their identical hair (the only difference was, she always had a few short curls straying over her forehead and neck), she and the picture seemed to me more alike than ever.

Sometimes I felt strangely comforted, forgiving, almost peaceful when I saw the little parting of her hair between the two braids; and a new way she had of smiling (with her lips pushed out slightly by her pale gums) overcame my old malevolence for a while. Maybe the girl in the picture — the queen of all women, had smiled like that too.

She was worried about my father's reactions when he saw her without her hair hanging loose the way he liked it, but when he came back, he didn't even seem to notice that she'd changed it, as if he didn't even remember that she had once worn it loose. It was some time since he had been interested in anything she did, and he now took less notice of her than he had taken of me or Immacolatella in the past. He was neither kind nor unkind, and the idea of joking with her, or giving her presents, or teasing her had completely gone out of his head. Sometimes he even seemed to forget her, as if she'd been there for centuries, something so inevitable and unchanging that he no longer saw her. But sometimes he looked at her with an uncertain, surprised, and at the same time sleepy air, as if wondering who this odd creature might be, what on earth he had to do with her, and what she was doing in our house.

Sometimes when he addressed her, instead of using her name, he suddenly used some slightly teasing nickname that referred to her present misshapeness, but even if these names sounded a bit coarse, he didn't use them maliciously, but with a kind of childish and almost affectionate detachment, for he found it quite natural to give people nicknames taken from some characteristic of theirs, the way he called me *Blacky* or Romeo *Amalfi*.

After his visit in August, he was away for a long time. The weeks passed without a word of news, as if he had completely forgotten that such a place as the island of Procida existed on earth.

Starry evenings

In the meantime, my life went on at sea (the weather was good until November that year). From dawn to sunset I was busy with my boat, and, now that my father was no longer there to remind me of her, my stepmother and her lonely kitchen went completely out of my head during the day, and I was back in my old unworried summer mood.

But as soon as the sun had set, and the colors of the sea began to fade, my mood changed at once. It was as if the happy spirits of the island, which kept me company all day, left, waving good-bye to me from the sun's rays on the horizon. And for the first time I was scared of the dark, as children are who later outgrow their fear. The boundless sea, the streets, the open spaces, seemed to have turned into a desolate waste, and a feeling that was almost like exile called me back to the House of the Guaglioni, where the light was then on in the kitchen. Sometimes, if twilight surprised me in some out-of-the-way spot, or far out at sea, the House of the Guaglioni, which was then invisible, seemed to have fled fantastically, unapproachably far away. I hated all the rest of that indifferent countryside, and until the high, shining point on top of the cliff appeared, I felt lost. I landed impatiently on the beach, and if it was dark all sorts of childish superstitions chased me as I tore up the cliff. Halfway up, I began singing at the top of my voice, to keep myself company, and when she heard me from high up beyond the terrace, she appeared at the kitchen door and called, in a singsong, almost dramatic voice:

"Ar-tu-rooo! Ar-tùùù!"

She'd be busy already preparing the supper, and I'd come in looking grim and reluctant, and while I waited for supper, I would stretch out on the bench to rest after the day's labors. Every now and then I'd yawn, looking bored and weary, taking little notice of her, and talking even less. While she was waiting for the water to boil, she sat on a low chair with her hands crossed in her lap and her head slightly bowed, and kept pushing back off her perspiring forehead a curl that had worked loose from her thick braid. Her thick body, which now had nothing childish about it, seemed to me girt with nobility and repose; like those statues that people in the east adore and to which the sculptor, to signify his impressive power, has given an odd, misshapen heaviness. Even the gold earrings on either side of her face seemed to lose their meaning as human ornaments, and to me seemed more like votive offerings hung on a sacred image. I saw her small feet peeping out of her slippers; they had not, like mine, played all summer on the beach and in the sea, and the whiteness of her skin at a time when every man and boy like me was brown, seemed to me another sign of her ancient and august nobility. Sometimes I forgot that she and I were almost the same age; she seemed to have been born many years before me, to be older, perhaps, than the House of the Guaglioni, but I felt so compassionate when I was with her that her great age seemed to me something gentle.

Sometimes I dozed a bit on the bench. And in that delicate drowsiness the minutest physical impressions became fantastic, like fragments of a fairy-tale, childish and caressing. I'd see the sea in daylight, glittering ceaselessly like some marvelous being who lay there smiling, washed by the tender currents, resting and thinking of me . . . Through the French window, the night air touched my dark body like someone slipping a fresh, clean linen shirt on me . . . The night sky was an immense curtain hanging over me, rich with historical figures . . . no, it was more, a great tree between whose branches the stars rustled like leaves . . . and among the branches was a single nest — my nest, where I was sleeping . . . while below me the sea was waiting for me — mine, again . . . If I licked the skin of my arm, it tasted of salt.

Some evenings after supper, I was drawn outdoors by the coolness, and stretched out on the doorstep or on the terrace in the garden. An hour before, the night had seemed menacing down below, but now, a step away from the lighted French window, it grew familiar again. The sky when I looked at it now seemed a great ocean dotted with innumerable islands, and I'd screw up my eyes and seek the stars I knew by name: Arturo first of all, and then the Bear, Mars, the Pleiades, Castor and Pollux, Cassiopeia . . . I'd always regretted that there were no longer any barriers in modern times, like the Pillars of Hercules in the ancient world, because I wished that there was something I could cross fearlessly for the first time, some prohibition I could defy; and in just the same way, as I now gazed up at the stars, I envied future explorers who would reach them. It was galling to see the sky and think that there were so many other landscapes, so many other colors, perhaps other seas colored quite differently from ours, other forests larger than our tropical forests, other fierce, gay animals more loving than those we know . . . other splendid sleeping women . . . other handsome heroes . . . other faithful followers . . . and I should never get there.

Then I'd look angrily away from the sky and deliberately stop thinking about it, and look back at the sea again, and see it panting toward me, like a lover. Black and alluring it lay there, telling me that it was no less great or fantastic than the stars, that its territories were innumerable and that each one differed from the rest, like ten thousand planets. Soon, at last, I'd reach the time I had longed for so much, when I should no longer be a boy but a man, and the sea, like a friend who had played with me and grown up beside me, would take me along to meet the oceans, and all the other countries, and the whole of the rest of life.

Queen of women

Autumn was well on the way; you could tell by the early sunsets. Every day the dreadful moment of darkness that chased me from the sea came earlier. Now, if I got home before nightfall, I often found visitors there. My stepmother had come to know two or three Procidan women, wives of shopkeepers or boatmen, who came and passed the time of day with her, and gave her help and advice while she made clothes for the baby. I don't know how she had managed to induce them to cross the threshold of the House of the Guaglioni, and at first their presence struck me as the most astonishing, unlikely vision. Generally they sat around the kitchen table, which was strewn with clothes and bits of material, and I noticed that my stepmother, who was so submissive with my father and me, showed a kind of matronly authority among them, an almost acknowledged importance, in spite of the fact that she was the youngest there. Compared with the others, who were all very short, she seemed tall, and she sewed with a serious, responsible air, composed and silent in the chattering, gesticulating circle.

Their lively voices would drown the sound of my footsteps when I arrived, but when I came in they would jump up at once, embarrassed and shy, and a few minutes later they'd all troop off together, because in Procida women are usually at home after dark.

Sometimes when I came up from the sea rather earlier than usual and enjoyed the sunset from the terrace, I overheard their chatter. They nearly always spoke of the same things: family matters, their relatives, or things to do with their husbands' work, their homes and children, and, most of all, the birth of the child. It was on one of these occasions that I heard my stepmother's voice telling the others the name she had planned for her first child. If it was a girl, she said, she would call it *Violante* after her mother, and if it was a boy *Carmine Arturo*. Really, she explained, she'd rather have called him *Arturo*, because that had been her favorite name since she was a little girl, but as there was already an Arturo in the house, and two brothers couldn't have the same name, she had decided on Carmine as the first name, in honor of the Madonna of Carmine, the protectress of Procida. *Carmine* sounded rather nice, she observed, especially if he was called *Carminiello* — CARMINIELLO ARTURO! And to this double name she was going to add *Raffaele* and *Vito* on his baptism certificate, the names of her father and brother.

When her friends had left, my stepmother usually went on sewing for a while and I rested on the bench. For months she had been saving the small sums my father occasionally gave her, and had done her best to get scraps of material in the Procidan shops so as to prepare the baby's layette. It was really only a matter of five or six little oddments that would have fitted into a shoe box, and besides, as far as I could see, they seemed to be rather poor quality. But her small brothers had always had to put up with handed-down clothes and women's shawls, so the very idea of making a layette like this took on the importance of a princely, solemn ceremony in her eyes. But the serious, concentrated air with which she sewed showed me how little experience she had had of such things.

I never thought much about the child. His birth was now approaching, but he remained unreal, like someone in China who means nothing at all. It was odd to think that in fact it already existed among us, in that very house. And as for my stepmother, though she was making his clothes, she never mentioned it, and I'm certain she never stopped to think about him. Sometimes it looked as if she lived almost without realizing that she was carrying the baby in her. Cats and birds, and wild beasts too, during the mating season run around looking busy and inspired, and hasten to prepare the nest, without wondering who tells them to.

Autumn — latest news of Algerian Knife

September had been fine, but as burning hot as August, and the first touch of autumn, instead of reviving my feeble stepmother, seemed to exhaust her. Her eyes became opaque and blank, as if the spirit that fed their splendor was fading day by day. And the majesty that awhile earlier had made her misshapen body almost divine now faded with her weariness. Even her hair had lost its raven black sheen and seemed brittle and dusty. She was ugly, terribly ugly, and the mysterious child who was making her so, seemed to me a kind of monster or an illness to which she succumbed without a struggle. Ringed around by an aura of sadness, one loose braid slipping down from its bun, she moved about the kitchen, and as she lighted the fire she no longer sang. Often she went back and rested on her usual low chair, and even looked at me with her great faded eyes and started talking about something — her mother, her sister, her home in Naples . . . She never said a word, though, about her engagement and marriage; it was a subject, like God or the child, that, as far as she was concerned, seemed to belong to some mysterious power that was not to be translated into words or even into thoughts. Only rarely and fleetingly did I hear her mention Wilhelm, and each time I thought I caught a glimpse, in some unconscious gesture of hers, of his mysterious life beyond the island. But even then my pride wouldn't sink to showing her that the conversation interested me. I was almost tempted to question her, to explore through her ignorance the fascinating secrets she herself couldn't possibly understand, but I restrained myself scornfully, and even made it plain that when she spoke of him, I took not the slightest notice, even less than when she talked of other things; and, as usual, her small voice, discouraged by talking to itself, soon stopped.

Once, my heart leaped: I discovered that she had met Algerian Knife. I don't know why, but she mentioned a man called Marco who had given my father the watch he always wore. The day they left Naples he'd come up to see my father off on the steamer a moment before the gangway was removed.

This was how I discovered that she'd seen him. The question: "What was he like?" slipped out before I realized.

"Who?"

"That man," I exclaimed brusquely. "What sort of person was he?"

"Marco!" she said, "Well . . . I really only saw him for a minute from the steamer. I have a feeling he was about the same age as Wilhelm, but maybe a bit younger . . . small and slight, with moles on his face . . . long, light eyes . . . a discontented smile, and little teeth, sort of separated . . ."

I realized at once that this was more or less the way I'd thought of him myself.

"Was he dark or fair?" I asked peremptorily.

"I think," she replied uncertainly, "he had black hair." I was glad to hear it, almost comforted. Well, then, I had found out his name: Marco. I wanted to ask if he was Italian or a foreigner, if he happened to be Arabian, or, even better, Jewish (I don't know why, but I'd always given him an Oriental slant, and I particularly liked to think of him belonging to that persecuted, wandering race). There was plenty more I was longing to hear about this man who, more magical and resplendent than Aladdin, belonged to the last happy period of my childhood. But I sternly refused to question my stepmother further, and shut myself up in myself and in my cloudy solitude.

Abroad

As the evenings lengthened, I made a habit of reading and studying in the kitchen, to pass the time while I waited for supper. My favorite book at the time was a big atlas with a very full written text and enormous colored maps folded up in it, which I unfolded every evening, kneeling on the floor with it before me or on a chair beside the table. It was these maps that aroused my step-mother's attention. She had been considering them with a puzzled air for several evenings, as if she couldn't make them out, and at last ventured to ask me timidly: "What are you studying there, Artù?"

Without raising my head from the unfolded map, on which I was drawing with a piece of charcoal, I answered that I was studying the routes I was going to take; because, I declared firmly, the time when I would explore the world was drawing near. Next year at the latest I was leaving, either with my father or alone.

My stepmother looked at the map without another word that evening. But from that day forward, not a single evening passed without her returning to the subject. Every time I settled down to work out my journeys, I heard her, after a while, padding up to me with her weary, heavy, almost animal step. At first she would keep quiet, gazing at the map unfolded in front of me, but finally, after long hesitation, she would pluck up courage to point out the places I'd marked in charcoal, and ask in a vaguely anxious tone: "Is this a long way from Procida? How far is it?"

Ungraciously I'd snap out an approximate number.

"And what about Procida?" She would ask, her eyes wandering uncertainly all over the map. "Where is it? *What!*" she'd say, echoing my reply. "You can't see it here because it's in the other hemisphere?"

And she tried to make me tell her something more precise about the mysterious configurations of the map, her voice hoarse with the effort of overcoming her shyness. I answered her shortly and impatiently, always in the same gloomy, remote tone that now seemed the only one that came naturally to me when I spoke to her. But when I named the most fascinating places on earth, those I most longed for — continents, cities, mountains, seas — my tone exuded pride, and triumph, as if they all belonged to me. Sometimes I had an irresistible urge to talk, and told her about the achievements that would one day immortalize every lap of Arturo Gerace's journeys . . . but I quickly shut myself up again in my usual disdainful reserve.

My stepmother commented very little on what I said. When I spoke, she was silent, but her face suddenly looked old and, in a strange way, untamed. I had already realized that she looked on "Abroad" with suspicion and dislike; now this old attitude of hers seemed to have developed into a frightful hatred, and the more she found out about other countries, the worse she seemed to hate them. Everywhere that wasn't Naples or near it was as unreal and inhuman to her as the moon, and if I mentioned even quite a small distance away — say two or three thousand kilometers — she turned pale to her lips, as if she had seen some dizzy height or a ghost. "Are you really going that far alone?" she would say; *alone*, for her, meaning without my father, without any of the family. She gazed at the Arctic Circle. "So you really want to go off to those freezing places all alone?" she said, and then looked at the mountains shaded in dark colors. "To think you want to go off into those mountains, a year from now, all alone!"

To hear her tone you would have thought that traveling was not something gay and splendid, but something dreadful and unnatural. In just the same way, a swan (say) mopes if it has to leave its pond; a tiger in Asia hasn't the smallest wish to visit Europe; and a cat would weep at the idea of leaving its balcony to go on a cruise.

Besides, I have a feeling that she can't have got a very reassuring notion of Abroad from me. Everything I said was clearly gospel truth to her, and I could have removed all her suspicions and convinced her that even foreign parts were all like a beautiful, peaceful garden, but I just didn't bother. Actually, I rather wanted her to believe the opposite. And I suppose that from these labored talks of ours she got the impression that everything beyond Naples was one long succession of pampas and steppes and gloomy forests overrun by wild beasts, Red Indians, and cannibals, so that only the very boldest would dare to set out and explore it. Sometimes my silent, fascinating study of the map was broken into by her hoarse new voice asking something like: "In those *Quatorial* places, can you post letters to Procida?" Or else, when she had gazed around and around the Pacific or the Indian Ocean looking for Procida, she objected in a small voice: "You say you'll go and become captain of a ship . . . and that over there beyond Africa it's quite easy, and not even very expensive . . . But will they be nice people? Just think of going off with them all alone in a ship. And suppose when you're out on the high seas with all those sailors much older than you . . . Suppose they mutiny? Suppose they say you're not old enough to be the captain? Who'll defend you? None of the family will be around!"

Finally, one evening I told her: "Look, do something for me: don't bother me with your chatter when I'm studying." And she kept quiet. And so, like a conqueror in his tent, I drew charcoal lines across oceans and continents, from Mozambique to Sumatra and the Philippines and the Coral Sea . . . and while I worked, a great silence reigned around me. I call it *work*, and maybe it was just a game, but to me it was more beautiful than writing poetry because, unlike poetry (which is an end in itself), it was a preparation for action, and nothing is finer than that. Those charcoal lines stood for the glittering wake of Arturo's ship; action, definite action awaited me like daylight after night. Night has its dreams, which may be beautiful, but day means perfect beauty. Tristan was mad to say that night is lovelier than day. Since the day I was born I have done nothing but wait for high noon, for the perfection of life: I have always known that the island and my early happiness were nothing but a cloudy night; even the glorious years

with my father, even those evenings with her, were still part of the
night of my life, and in my heart I have always known it. And now
I know it better than ever, and await my day, which will be like a
splendid brother whom I can tell, with perfect understanding,
about the long dark years of waiting . . .

The iridescent spider's web

But now, let me get back to that evening (the one when I told my
stepmother not to bother me). She sat with her hands in her lap, a
little distance away from me, saying nothing, but her glance kept
straying to my big blue maps, and her soul, which had seemed to
droop and grow ugly, peered out of her eyes again, full of childish
questions and ignorant fears.

Every time I happened to look at those eloquent eyes of hers,
they said something different. Sometimes they had a Cassandra
look about them, and — huge, barren, and lonely — stared at me
as if I had already left. Sometimes they glanced at the maps as if
dreaming in a playful and at the same time unhappy way. "What
fun not to have this body, not to be a woman!" they seemed to say.
"If only I were a boy like you and we could gallivant around the
world together!"

Once she spoke out loud. "But," she said, "if I was your mother,
I shouldn't let you go!"

I looked up, and saw that she was suddenly looking gloomy, almost like a policeman. Her cheeks flamed aggressively, and even
her ears had turned bright pink. "I wouldn't let you go!" she repeated, looking at me angrily, bullyingly. "I'd put the chain on the
door and stand in front of it, and say: 'You're not twenty-one yet
and you can't leave home without permission. If you want to
leave, you've got to get past me!' "

"Oh, dry up, won't you? What d'you think you're chattering
about? You make me laugh! Permission! I ask you! You're pretty
dim in the head, you know. You can say that sort of thing to some
people, but really, trying it out on me just proves that you're pretty

stupid. *Twenty-one!* I'm older than twenty-one-year-olds. And who cares what you think, anyway? Talking to you is about as interesting as talking to a Chinaman."

I had begun by being derisory, but had worked myself up into a lowering bad temper. "I can make twenty-one-year-olds obey me if I think they ought to serve under me, just as if they were small boys. Men of twenty-five and thirty, too. I suppose you think I'm inferior because of my age; then you're a fool and can just shut up."

The old, eternal injury of being considered a child, which had so much infuriated me during the past year, rose again, filling me with rebellion and suspicion.

"Stop poking into my affairs," I went on, surly. "Every blessed time I take a took at the atlas, you come bothering me with your cackle. *Are you really going off such a long way all alone? Are you really going off such a long way all alone?* As if I were still a child and couldn't look after myself. And I can, too — unarmed at that. What do you think you're talking about? *Other people* go off alone and wander around all over the place alone, and you don't bother the way you do about me. What's the idea? D'you think *other people* are cleverer than me, just because they're older? Is that what you think?"

She didn't see what I was alluding to, and hadn't even realized that my pride expected an answer. Silent and shaken at the thought of having upset me, she forgave me every insult, but between her eyelashes there still remained just a gleam of the strange ferocity that had urged her on to provoke me before. Her troubled eyes kept altering with all sorts of questions not even clearly formulated in her mind. Like clouds moving across a star, they seemed to pass quite near, but the innocent star went wandering to another part of the sky, as clear as a mirror.

"Is that what you think?" I repeated peremptorily. Then I faced her, glaring resolutely, and decided to speak plainly. *"My father,"* I explained, "always travels alone, and you don't see anything to fuss about in that. WHY? Tell me!"

She looked up, her eyes no longer fierce at all, but just smiling with childish surprise. "Your father!" she murmured. "Well, he's different . . ."And her face cleared completely, becoming as sweet and attractive as if a beloved sister were kissing and caressing her, and pleading for her with me.

"Oh, so he's different . . . Why?" I insisted gloomily.

But luckily she didn't see my appalling expression. She was looking down, smiling softly. "Because," she said simply, shrugging very slightly, "because he's not like you. Oh, I certainly don't get worked up about him: he doesn't go far, after all. He's like a goldfinch . . ."

I didn't see what she meant, right away, so she explained to me that when goldfinches go away, they never go far from their homes. They fly to the next cornice, to the roof, or to another windowsill, but they always stay in the neighborhood.

This fabulous remark about my father just seemed to confirm how astonishingly slow-witted my stepmother was . . . when suddenly, an idea came into my head. Did she really mean what she said, or had she made up this unlikely and ridiculous answer to avoid telling me what she really, insultingly, thought? Which was that she looked on my father as a grown-up, and me as a child. The suspicion was enough to make me roar like a wounded lion. I looked at that mysterious, saintly smile of hers again, and burst out: "You're not my mother, you're not a relation of mine, you're nothing to me. Stop poking your nose into my business, will you?"

And after that she stopped taking any notice of what I was doing. During the evenings that followed, she no longer came up to ask questions as I turned the pages of the atlas, but it was clear that she hated and mistrusted it, and at the same time found it hatefully fascinating. She avoided touching it, and if she just looked at it from a distance, her eyes became anxious, as if it were the book of Fate or a treatise on black magic. If for some reason or other I happened to say the words *next year*, I saw her eyes suddenly staring ahead like two terrified guests stuck on a threshold they didn't want to cross.

And in the meantime, as the days went by, I kept wondering whether to go away at once, without waiting for next year. This would show whether I was a child or not, and if I could go away alone, and what I was capable of. But when I was ready to leave the island, a terrible enchantment kept me there, as it always had since my childhood. All the splendidly varied continents and oceans that my imagination worshiped every evening suddenly seemed to be lying in wait for me beyond the sea of Procida, an enormous, freezingly indifferent expanse, hounding me as I was hounded when evening caught me away from home — in the port, in the street — calling me back to the House of the Guaglioni. And I couldn't bear the thought of leaving without seeing my father at least once more. Sometimes I almost felt that I hated him. But no sooner had I decided to flee from Procida than the memory of him — fascinating, insidious — invaded the whole island. I tasted him in sea water, in fruit; I heard him in the shriek of an owl or the cry of a seagull, calling, "Hey, Blacky!" The autumn wind whipped spray or sand at me, and I felt him fooling about and teasing me. Sometimes when I went down to the shore I felt someone shadowing me, and, half flattered, I imagined that it was a private detective trailing me on his orders. And then, while I was a prey to all these odd illusions, I found myself hating him more than ever because he had invaded and taken over my island like that. Yet I knew I wouldn't have loved it so well if it hadn't been his, indivisible from him. I was seeing mysteries, seeing much that was new and disquietening, indecipherable, unattainable, seeing my childhood fade as my poor repudiated mother had faded, but it all went to make up the ever-changing, ever-enchanting chimera I knew of old. The eyes that laughed at me had changed, the arms stretched out to me were other arms; prayers, voices, sighs, all had changed, but it was veiled in magic as before, in something I couldn't fathom, like an iridescent spider's web, which kept me prisoner on the island.

Murdered?

It was halfway through autumn, and my father had not yet appeared. My stepmother kept hoping that he'd be home when the baby was born. During the first week of November she said to me every evening: "I wonder if your father'll arrive tomorrow." Then, as the days went by, she said no more. But when it was time for the steamer from Naples to come into port, she went and stood almost furtively by the window, peering down to see if the old carriage was coming up at the entrance to the road.

She and her friends had calculated that my half brother would be born early in December. Instead, he surprised us on the night of November 22.

Her friends, who were coming oftener than ever just then, had left the house as usual toward evening, and after supper she and I went to bed without worrying at all. But late at night (it must have been about one o'clock), I was startled by a dull groan, sounding more animal than human, from Nunz's little room. It was followed by a shriek of anguish such as I'd never heard before, which made me dash out, still half asleep, and fling open the door of her room. The light was on, and Nunz, terribly disheveled, was lying on the bed, her clothes loosened and the blankets flung back. When she saw me, she grabbed them convulsively and pulled them over her, but immediately fell back writhing, with a yell like the one I'd heard before, a yell that made her voice unrecognizable. And she began struggling wretchedly, like an animal, and now and then glared at me, asking not for help but only to be left alone. "What's the matter? What's the matter?" I shouted roughly. I had no exact idea of what women had to suffer, and the scene before me appeared tragic and mysterious; my first instinct was to hate the mysterious power that was torturing Nunz. When she had a moment's rest, she turned to me with a small, embarrassed, and at the same time important smile. "It's nothing," she tried to explain. "But you mustn't stay here . . . You must fetch someone . . . Fetch Fortunata . . ." (Fortunata was the Procidan midwife.) A new shriek cut short what she was saying; pain snatched the sweet smile off her face and made it inhumanly dreadful, and she tore at the woolen shawl she wore pinned around her shoulders at night. And, as I left her to go for help, her movement suddenly reminded me of something: of poor Immacolatella, who, during the anguish of her labor, had occasionally made as if to tear her own body with her teeth. It was now nearly two years since the bitter day when Immacolatella was buried, but I still remembered every detail of the way she died, and, as I'd never seen a human creature die, that was still my only experience of death. Now, as I dashed downstairs, a suspicion — or rather, a dreadful certainty — crossed by mind: that my stepmother showed many signs of the fatal agony that had made Immacolatella end up underground, by the carob tree, and I thought that it meant that the same evil that had killed my mother and Immacolatella was going to kill her too — now, tonight!

I was a prey to childish fantasies; in the passage I half expected to meet Romeo's ghost, singing melancholy songs in his melodious bass voice, and was dismayed at having to leave my stepmother alone in the house without any protection against him. As I ran through the narrow, sleeping streets, I felt that I was in a crowded theater where voices were screaming the word I hated at me: *Death! Death!* I stopped at the doctor's house, near the little square, and started banging wildly on the door, but a woman's voice behind one of the shutters finally told me angrily that the doctor had gone to Naples. So there was nothing left but to carry on toward the district of Côttima, about three kilometers away, where Fortunata the midwife lived.

I had long had reason to hate and suspect her, and the fact that I had to ask her help seemed like an evil omen. But there was no choice, and I ran to her house like a maniac, fearing that every second lost might prove fatal to Nunz.

𝒯he mi∂wife

Fortunata had been a midwife on Procida for more than thirty years. One of the women she had attended had been my mother, and I blamed her for not having saved her, and despised the Procidan view of her as a great mistress of her art. Her huge dark hands seemed to me those of a murderess, and though I knew that she had brought me into the world, and had given my nurse Silvestro good advice to guide him in the early stages with me, that wasn't enough to reconcile me to her. Among all the island women, she was about the only one who never paid attention to the rumors about us, who took the accursed Gerace family quite calmly in her stride. But even this didn't seem to me to prove any special merit on her part, because though she wore dresses, she didn't really count as a woman. As she marched across the countryside with her midwife's bag under her arm, taking great military-looking yet casual strides on those vast legs of hers, she looked like a strapping soldier of the Turkish fleet reincarnated as a midwife. She was so tall and stout (angular in places, and in others very fat) that she found it hard to get through the door of her own house, and next to other women looked a giantess. She was dark and had a few whiskers on her upper lip and even a touch of beard as well. Her hands and feet were enormous, her teeth long and irregular; her voice was ugly, and somber, and rather hoarse. She wore glasses and always the same dress of faded fustian, with big flowers on it, adding a voluminous soot-colored overcoat in winter. And on Sundays she wore an embroidered veil on her head, and looked even uglier than usual.

Because she was so ugly, she had never found anyone to marry her and lived alone in a one-room house. She used the same crusty, unattractive, ill-tempered tone with everyone and never seemed to listen to what anyone said, as if her mind was busy elsewhere. When she brought forth one of her opinions, she generally did so without addressing anyone present, in a dark, emphatic grumble, rather as if talking to herself or to the air, reciting a mysterious poem. The only beings she sometimes talked to more trustfully and politely were newborn babies and her cat. The cat I knew by sight; he was famous in the whole village as a kind of centenarian, for he was nineteen. He always sat in the window of her house like a sinister sentinel, and often when I went by I tried to provoke him.

I don't think I took more than ten minutes to reach Fortunata's house (and it usually took at least half an hour). There I began banging and knocking at the door, and before long the midwife appeared at the window with a shawl thrown over her nightdress. "Come at once," I cried imperiously. "There's a woman at home who's sick . . . pretty sick . . ."

"Oh, so there's only one of you! I thought there were lots," she said in her hollow voice. "A *woman!* . . . It must be Nunziata who wants delivering; who else could this woman of yours be? All right, wait a minute. I'm coming."

"Hurry up," I told her again, and then as she drew away from the window, I shouted after her in a menacing, hate-filled tone: "And don't you get drunk, now! If you do, you'll pay for it."

Actually, though everyone knew that she was fond of wine and always had a bottle in her room, no on had ever seen her tipsy, and I said that just because I was burning to express my resentment in some way. But she didn't seem to notice and didn't bother to answer. In the same way, when we met in the street I deliberately turned my face away from her, but she showed no sign of offense, or even of having noticed. Probably as she'd brought me into the world, she still thought of me as a child and took no notice of my nonsense.

I sat down on the little wall, waiting for her, and was almost surprised when I realized that it was a beautiful warm night; the air was still, and a great moon was lightly veiled in fog. The sea and the gardens looked smiling, as in spring, and there was no sound of movement or of voices. Perhaps I was expecting the whole creation to whirl agitatedly around N., like a court around a queen. But one woman's agony in her room is something so insignificant that it casts no shadow across the great universe.

I lay down on the wall and pressed my face against the rough plaster, feeling inconsolably wretched. The wonderful landscape, the starry sky, the whole island suddenly seemed bitter, angry, even loathsome, because her room meant nothing to them and wasn't even visible from here, isolated as it was in the House of the Guaglioni. It mattered only to me. There, all this past year, guarded under their eyelids like two precious jewels in a case, two queenly dark eyes had slept each night, eyes that showed all the trust, and adoration, and honor, they felt in serving me and belonging to my family. But all I saw now was the agony I had seen awhile before in those enormous eyes, terrible and blank and ignorant. "Oh, this must be death!" I said to myself, horrified. "This must mean death!"

All I loved, all I regretted, was upside down and confused within me. Wilhelm I'd forgotten completely; he might have been a dream. I felt as if nothing existed on earth but me and Nunz. And as for the way I'd hated her and suffered from my hatred, there wasn't a trace of it left.

The midwife stood ready at the door with her old bag tucked up under her arm, and I jumped down off the wall. She bade her cat inside the hut a simpering, formal farewell, and then we set off, with her gazing at the moon's track, frowning behind her spectacles, and talking to herself as usual. "Fine time for boys and girls, both!" she said. "Boys born after midnight and early in the morning grow up handsome and lucky and healthy! And girls grow up healthy and pretty!"

Then, quite satisfied, she went marching off on her noiseless rope-soled shoes, determined as a hangman. I looked at her hands with loathing. In the moonlight they looked darker than ever, and enormous, and, to avoid looking at her, I ran on ahead of her and made my way home quickly alone. Occasionally I turned around to make sure that she was following me, and hadn't wandered off among the gardens and alleys, and yelled: "Hey, hurry up!" in a threatening tone. But when I reached the end of the village at the top of the long hill that wound out of the square, my heart seemed to jerk to a standstill. High and far the House of the Guaglioni appeared with all the windows on the near side dark, looking like some ghostly deserted ruin, with nothing left alive within its walls.

Rooster-crow

I started running even faster than I had run on the way out, without bothering about the old woman. All I cared about was getting up there again, at least arriving in time to say a few last words to N., if for a moment she could still hear me. I couldn't possibly have said what the words were to be; maybe I was trusting to inspiration, to a kind of sudden last-minute intuition so sublime that in one sentence all the awful nonsense I had ever said to her would be wiped out, and everything settled between us for all eternity. I ran to the house, in fact, as if eternity was in the balance — an eternity locked in that mysterious, tender sentence I had to say to her, at least in the face of death. I feel rather curious about it. What can I have meant to tell her when I still understood nothing? (And do I understand it now?)

One thing I knew for certain: that I was going to speak to her, even though, as I made that last spurt along the road, of all possible words I remembered only one: Nunziatella. With the desperate rhythm of my footsteps I kept repeating it: Nunziatella. And everything else was blocked out. I saw nothing, heard nothing, and the fields below the house, I remember, looked quite unlike themselves; I felt I was crossing a kind of enormous ruined square in a foreign city. And at the same time I felt that if N. were dead, wherever I was, here on the island or elsewhere, I'd never find anything but that forlorn square of iron and stone and plaster, mindless and completely indifferent to me.

The front door was open, and the light was on in the hall as I'd left it when I went out. I had just begun climbing the stairs when I heard from the floor above the cry of a newborn child. From her there was no sound at all. And when I reached the door of her room, the first thing I saw was Nunz lying still on her back under the blankets, and the bloodstained bed. I thought: "It's over!" and I think my face grew ashen and my knees gave way. Just then the baby stopped crying, and in the silence she must have noticed my presence. She lifted her head very slightly and turned to me. She was pale, but alive. And a smile full of secrecy and of fabulous joy transfigured her face. "Artù," she said, "he's born! Carminiello Arturo is born!"

The baby started screaming again. I glanced at him, but she kept him close beside her under the blankets, so I caught just a glimpse of a small fair head. Then, very frail, embarrassed and nervous, she tried to make me leave the room, and asked me again to fetch Fortunata. As I ran down, I met the old woman, "Get a move on!" I roared at her as I crashed into her in the hall. "Get along, you old slowpoke!"

I went upstairs behind her, and waited in the passage, and was just in time to see her try to take the baby out of the bed as soon as she went into the room. But Nunz flung out an arm to defend him, as if the old woman were trying to steal him from her, and gave her a black, jealous look, not unlike the look she had flashed at me on the day she arrived and I wanted to take her jewel case from her, or a few evenings before when she had said: *I wouldn't let you go!*

"Well, what are you scared of?" said the midwife formidably, in her abrupt military way. "I'm not going to hurt you!" Then Nunz laughed embarrassedly and handed him over.

The sight of that newborn creature yelling with that toothless mouth of his revolted me, and I went into my room, but I left the door half open so that I'd hear what was happening, as I was afraid the old woman might hurt N. somehow, or actually murder her. Her heavy, muffled footsteps sounded all over the house as she busied herself about the room and marched up and down the passage, moving confidently as if she was quite used to the house after a gap of nearly fifteen years. Twice I heard Nunz telling her what to do, but her voice was so low and weak that I could barely make out what she was saying. The old woman expressed herself as usual with authoritative grunts, or made grandiose oracular pronouncements. The only person she seemed to enjoy talking to was my half brother. I realized that she'd taken him with her into an empty room beside Nunz's to wash and dress him, so that Nunz could share in the proceedings through the open door. And while she lay there waiting for the moment when she'd have the baby with her again, the old woman seemed to be holding a kind of private audience with him while she got him ready, as if he were the only person she could get on with, and the rest of the family was no more important than the furniture.

"You must weigh over eight pounds," she said, her hoarse voice sounding grave and fascinated. "You're a lovely fellow, you are, a lovely little boy!" I could hear Nunz's small voice laughing when she said this, sounding pleased.

"You lovely little creature!" the midwife went on in the next room. "Oh, you great giant, you! Out you popped, as clever and as pretty as can be, all on your own like a rabbit! You'll learn to walk without a leash, my pretty, and women'll go mad for love of you, and you'll sing like the tenor Caruso. What beautiful hair, my pet — look, it's trying to curl already! You've got eyelashes too, already. Oh, you're a treasure, a rose! Look at these dear little legs, and this darling bottom! . . . What's your name, my precious?"

"Carmine Arturo," the voice from the next room answered for him.

"Oh, you've got two names, have you? I've got two names too — Fortunata and Emanuella."

"But," said the small voice from next door rather emphatically, "he's called Raffaele and Vito as well."

Here I felt I would die of weariness, and lay down and went to sleep. Twice in the night I was awakened by the baby's powerful yells, but as I heard N. whispering back to him, I went to sleep again at once, happy to think she was alive. Her whispers, which reached me through my half-open door, borne on the silence, seemed quite close to me, close enough to be at my cheek. Toward dawn I heard a rooster crowing in a garden, and then, half asleep and without opening my eyes, I saw the island growing light from the farthest edge of the sea to the sandy beaches with their mounds of icy seaweed, and the colors of the houses, the fine gardens full of oranges and lemons and dahlias. Because Nunz wasn't dead, I longed to race victoriously across my kingdom, like a king who has got his possessions back.

My body was gladly relaxed in sleep, but my heart was waiting for morning with a mixture of joy, and consolation, and curiosity. But even then I knew nothing. I could not foresee all the suffering and misfortune the future held in store for me.

* * *

The sea urchin

From the moment we awoke, the next day was one long celebration. The light was so clear that it seemed like April instead of November 23; and after I'd slept until late in the morning, I ran along the beach and down to the dock, and came up again through the square. The sea, the air, and everything I met in the road shared my happiness, as if the whole universe was part of the family. The gardens flanking the road, which during the night had appeared like mirages in a desert, drawing away from me, hailed me like friends that day. And I felt myself in love with my island again, and everything I loved before I now loved again, because Nunz wasn't dead. It was as if, since we were small, and I was on Procida and she was in Naples, she had made the indifferent world take heed of me, and without letting me realize it, the way a great lady would.

That same morning she and the baby moved from the small room into a bigger room, the one my father had planned that she should have the day she arrived, where she hadn't wanted to sleep. But now, with the baby's arrival, all her fears of being alone at night were over. As for the double bedroom, this remained my father's undivided property again, as she foresaw that when he came back he wouldn't stand for the baby's crying at night and other annoying things like that, which mothers don't mind in the least.

So that's how the old room from that first day *returns to our story*, as writers say. Right away, we moved a new bed in, chosen for the purpose from among a quantity of unused beds in the house. A double bed of heavy wood painted with pictures the way they're done at Sorrento (landscapes, boats, the tarantella, and so forth), and really rather smart. It had two mattresses and plenty of pillows, which her friends, who very soon turned up to see her, banged and pounded up assiduously. And there, like a queen, she received their congratulations.

Her hair was just tied with a ribbon, the way she wore it at night, and over her shoulders she wore her woolen shawl, fastened with an ordinary safety pin. She seemed proud of being the center of attention, and even slightly important (though at heart she was confused), and she kept up her air of gravity and discretion before these friends of hers. If one of them began lamenting her situation — "You poor little thing, having the baby all alone, all by yourself, without even your husband — just like a cat!" "Poor Nunzià, how that husband of yours leaves you on your own!" She replied with a grim silence, as if warning the meddler to mind her own business.

When her friends picked the baby up from the bed to weigh and cuddle him, her eyes clouded over with anxiety lest they hurt him, but at the same time, when she saw him lifted up in triumph like a hero, she gave a little chuckle of joy and still half-dubious delight, as if wondering: "Is he really *mine?* Really *mine?*"

When she suckled him, she was careful to cover her breast with the shawl, and if she happened to see me looking at her just then, she blushed and covered it even better. (It was different now from the old days, when she'd felt no embarrassment with me. But now I felt that even if she hadn't been embarrassed, I wouldn't have minded.) I kept going to see her in the new room all through the day, hanging about and sitting on the bench. I think I would even have acted as her servant that day, and gladly, if she had needed me, but one of her friends was always there, and often several, so I stood aside, silent and surly. Her friends had now grown used to me and lost their shyness, and they chattered away while I grew more and more irritated with their nonsense. As for Carmine Arturo, with that haughty face of his which couldn't even laugh, he seemed to me too hideous to deserve a second look.

Although so many others were there with us, she never forgot me. Occasionally, while the women were talking on and on, she would stop listening and turn to me as I stood there, silent and separate from them, and say to me, with a kind of timid trustfulness: "Well, Artù?" . . . Perhaps she meant to ask my forgiveness for the fright she'd given me the previous night. All she said was: "Well, Artù?" She was now a mother, but her voice still kept its old sharp, almost discordant tone — the tone of a child who hadn't finished growing. And when I heard that familiar little voice saying "Artù," when only a few hours earlier I'd thought her dead, I felt such a violent, turbulent happiness that I looked gloomier than ever. That's what I'm like. I should have rather liked to say at least: "I'M HAPPY!" Several times during the day I promised myself I'd turn up in her room and say, quite simply and even indifferently, "I'm happy." But in the end I never got to the point of bringing out even a couple of words like that.

The sight of Nunz alive, restored to health, and animated, smiling at me — at me alone — through her curls, suddenly seemed miraculous, glorious, as if the island was peopled by gods. And, as I couldn't control my heart's turbulent happiness, I left the room after a bit, for it had grown too magical. Until then happiness had always been my natural companion, something that went unnoticed, like a sister. But that day, at moments, I realized something new: the sudden, almost unhoped-for presence of happiness blazing up in me. I felt that we were embracing each other, and I was unable to think of anything else. My arrogant joy flooded the light and space around me, filled every corner of the house, and every dusty cranny. I decided to go out, to do something. I thought of going out hunting, and looked about for a gun belonging to Costante. I dug it out, and for fun, though it wasn't loaded, pretended to take aim at things about the house — a chair or a shoe. Then I grew bored with the idea of looking for cartridges, and left the gun and went out free and unburdened. I wandered about the countryside and climbed the first majestic-looking tree I found, and there, high up among the leaves, I began singing with all the voice I could find in my chest, as if the whole island was a corsair ship, and I, on the mainmast, was its captain. I couldn't have said that day exactly what I was expecting from the future: it was just that, as Nunz was still alive, I felt that the next day and every other future day would be a delightful surprise and could bring me the mystery of happiness. I felt grateful, but I didn't know to whom, didn't know whom to thank. And after a few minutes at peace I returned to my fickle anxiety.

I even started having gallant notions: the idea came into my head that Nunz would be pleased if I took her a present and that it would be a charming gesture on my part. One thing I knew she loved, and that was jewels, but I'd long ago spent the last fifty lire my father had given me. Now, as I was walking idly along the beach, I saw a beautiful purple sea urchin attached to a rock beside the river and almost level with the calm, transparent water, and as I remembered that she was very fond of sea urchins, I decided to take it home to her. I pulled my shoes off quickly, and with my penknife prized it off the rock. Then I wrapped it up in a piece of newspaper that I found on the beach and rushed up to the house, eager to hand it over.

But just as I was going into her room, I suddenly felt a sense of embarrassment, maybe even of mystery, and hid the package hastily inside my shirt. For over a quarter of an hour I stayed in her room, sitting as usual on the old linen chest without saying a word, while her friends chattered on. I could feel the sea urchin's spikes lightly pricking my chest through the newspaper wrapping, which was irritating, but I couldn't find the right moment or the right way to give it to her. (It wasn't, I must make it clear, that I thought the present too modest or absurdly small. No, I had odd unrealistic ideas about the values of things in those days and was convinced this sea urchin was a really splendid present. What made me shy was just the thought of offering her a present, and, what was worse, in front of all those women.)

I remember going back to the bedroom at least three or four times that afternoon, or urging myself as far as her door and then hesitating outside in the passage, always meaning to offer her my present in the end, even if it meant dashing in, putting it in her hand without a word of explanation, and taking flight. But every time I lacked the will to do it, and at last when evening came and I went back to my room to sleep, I found the sea urchin wrapped in its bit of newspaper and flung it petulantly through the window.

A surprise

That night, I remember, one of her friends stayed behind to sleep in the house, after they'd all muttered together about not being able to leave the poor soul completely alone the very day after the baby's birth, without even her husband . . . And the following day we had an unexpected visit. Looking back on it, I still want to laugh, irresistibly.

Let's start by reconstructing the facts, as they say. A few days earlier one of the Procidan women N. knew had had to go to Naples for the day, so N. had taken the opportunity of giving her her old home address and asking her to take her mother some dried fruit she'd saved for her, if she had time; she said to tell her mother she was well, and sent her love, and all the rest of it. Well, this mischief-making woman had gone punctually and properly to the Pallonetto di Santa Lucia, to see N.'s mother, but, not content with taking her fruit, love, and good news from her daughter, as she'd been told to, took it on herself, after chatting for a bit, to reveal the dreadful opinion the islanders, and especially the women, had of my father. It appears that the Procidans thought him the very worst sort of husband, and N.'s friends and acquaintances, when they talked of her among themselves, pitied her misfortune.

The first thing they accused my father of was leaving his young wife always alone. It was true, they observed, that at Procida quite a number of wives were left by their husbands for long stretches at a time. But the husbands were sailors; if they left their wives to go on trips, it was all the fault of their work. But my father wasn't a sailor; his job was enjoying himself, and if he behaved toward his wife the way he did, that was just because he was a bad lot, and so on, and so on.

It was hard to guess everything that this gossip told N.'s mother (after at least a dozen oaths on the part of N.'s mother never to breathe a word of what her friend who'd hatched the plot had told her). The two ladies' talk must have been long and exciting anyway, and I'm amazed that the woman didn't miss the steamer back to Procida. The days that followed she had work to do, and didn't come to see N. again; she just sent a message through the others to say her mother was well and sent her love, and so on. So N. was completely in the dark about the whole business (and always remained slightly in the dark, because her mother, after all her oaths of secrecy, was reluctant to admit the whole truth of what had happened).

N. and I suspected nothing when, two days after Carmine's birth, we heard a rather loud knocking at the front door. There were only the three of us in the house just then: N., the baby, and me. So it was I who went to the door, and I found myself facing a smallish woman who was fat in the puffing, excessive, enormous way that mothers of families have. Her bust, especially, quite astounded me by its vastness.

She wore a pair of large men's old shoes, without stockings, and the rest of her clothes looked neglected, shabby, and dirty. Yet I was impressed by a kind of powerful grandeur about her, a grandeur that came from her scorn. It was plain that she was filled, just then, with passionate scorn: her dark gypsy's eyes flashed, and she looked like a sultana determined to avenge an outrage. She was alone, but beyond the gate I caught a glimpse of various Procidan women who must have come with her that far, and who, when I appeared, drew back and hurried away down the path.

First the mysterious woman asked me who I was.

"I'm Arturo!" I answered.

"Arturo. Oh, yes, my son-in-law's boy," she said at once. "And I'm Violante. Nunziata's mother!" she declared.

Then she asked vehemently, though with just a trace of anxiety in her voice, about my father, but when I said he was still away on his travels, she looked rather relieved, and her boldness knew no bounds. She marched angrily through the door. "Where's my daughter?" she asked peremptorily. "Where is she? Where's my daughter?" And without waiting for an answer she began climbing the stairs, calling: "Nunzià! Nunziàààààà!"

Her manners shocked me, but I thought that it was up to me, as she was a member of the family, to take her upstairs. So I pushed her firmly to the wall — the staircase was too narrow for the two of us to go up together — and went ahead of her, up to Nunz's room.

Nunz was lying in bed with the baby, peaceful and happy, and surrounded by pictures of her Virgins. But when her mother saw her she shrieked "Nunzià! Nunziatè!" so tragically that it sounded as if she had found her in chains in a dungeon, living on bread and water, beaten daily, and covered with scars. Then, after at least thirty or forty kisses, she drew back from the bed.

"I've come to take you away, love," she announced with savage determination. "Get up at once, bring the baby, and come back home with me just as you are, in your nightgown!"

At this, N., who had gone scarlet with joy at the sight of her mother, changed color.

"Why, Ma? Has something happened? Something wrong . . . with my sister?"

"No, nothing's happened. Your sister's very well."

"Maybe it's . . . Wilhelm?" asked N., in a very small voice.

"Oh no. Don't you worry about him. He's always fine, I can tell you that. Come along now, that's enough, don't waste time, and just you listen to me. Look, we must see that the baby doesn't catch cold. Let's wrap him up in this blanket off the bed. And of course," she went on, rolling her eyes malevolently in my direction, "we'll send it back later — we certainly don't want to keep it. We'll send it back right away — tomorrow, by messenger."

Here I let out a scornful whistle. "You make me laugh!" I said.

She had gone up to N. again, and was kissing her in a rather bullying sort of way all over her face, but though N. was won over a bit by all those kisses, she didn't return them, and remained firm, as if protecting herself against them.

"If nothing's happened at home, Ma," she said, sounding progressively more suspicious and disturbed, "why do you suddenly come talking about my leaving the house . . . with this tiny baby, only two days old . . . without even being able to tell my husband . . ."

When she heard my father mentioned, N.'s mother stopped kissing her. "Your husband . . ." she said, somber-eyed. "Oh, yes, your husband!" she went on, her voice growing shriller. "Of course, I'd forgotten him . . . Tell me, though, why is he away just now? Where is he? Eh? That's what I'd like to know!?"

"Where is he? . . . Well, he's traveling . . . I don't know . . ." murmured N., confused by her mother's aggressive behavior.

At this her mother looked downright ferocious. "I don't know, eh!" she burst out. "There's a nice answer for a poor girl to have to give about her husband! *I don't know!* So the family's just rubbish to dump in a corner somewhere, as far as he's concerned! Yes, that's just what they told me, but I couldn't believe it; I came all the way from Naples on purpose to find out."

"Oh, Ma," exclaimed N., turning on her and looking really angry, her lips trembling. "We've been more than a year apart, and you've come to tell me these horrible things! Who's been maligning my husband? . . . It must have been that nasty old gossip Cristina, who doesn't know what she's talking about," she said after a minute, scowling as she guessed at once where the scandal had started.

"Cristina . . . who's that? That woman you knew here in Procida? Pooh, that poor little creature just had time to say hallo and give me the package of figs and say good-bye, or she'd have missed the steamer. What do you suppose she told me? She didn't talk to me about anything. I'll tell you who really told your mother, Nunzià: it was my heart, that's who it was. I felt a voice in my breast saying: *Hurry up, Viulante, get that three-and-a-half lire for the steamer at any price and go and see Nunzià, who's weeping bitterly on the island of Procida.* And now I see how right my heart was, when I hear that your husband doesn't let you know where he is. Not even a postcard, nothing."

"If he doesn't send me news it's not to hurt me — it's because he forgets. A man has so much to think about that he can't always be writing to his family," answered N., growing more and more indignant.

"Things to think about! And what's he got to think about? Why doesn't he tell you?"

"Pooh, he's not like a woman who hates keeping secrets."

"Well, why's he always traveling? He's not a sailor, is he, the way he keeps traveling all the time!"

"Oh, Ma, I can just tell who's been talking to you. People here — the Procidans — hate him just because they're sailors and they travel to make money, and he doesn't travel to earn his living, and doesn't have to answer to anyone. He travels because he's imaginative!" she concluded proudly. "And for fun!"

"Oh, for fun does he! And he's found a lawyer as well, has he? Get along with you. I know you from the time you were tiny and were called *Nunziata-who-wants-her-own-way!* And as my name's Viulante I'm guilty for giving my daughter to that murderer! You were against it; it looks as if your feelings were right, because though you were a child you had better judgment than your mother. Just think of it! I thought I had discovered America for you when I found you this husband; and now my eyes are opened and I see what a nice mess I've made of it. A hog, a criminal, that's who I married you to! A man who left you here alone and abandoned to have your baby as if you weren't any better than you should be. Who always leaves you alone, all on your own, as if you'd got the plague, while he goes around enjoying himself."

N. seemed not merely hurt at all this invective, but actually frightened, so much so that she turned pale and very cold, just as if she were ill. She had half risen from the bed, and put one small foot on the floor, and kept repeating dully, violently: "What are you saying? Keep quiet, will you, Ma?" And at the same time she kept looking around at me, worried to think that I was hearing what she was saying, and as she looked at me, I saw a friendly smile gleaming through her troubled eyes, as if she wanted to tell her mother, among other things: "It's not true that I was alone. Arturo was here with me. What you're saying is an insult to him more than anyone. Is my dear good friend Arturo *nobody?*"

I felt sorry for her, the way she was so ashamed of her mother, and glanced at her in reply, shrugging scornfully as if to say: "Don't bother about her, she's quite off her head and doesn't even know who she's talking about."

All the excitement had wakened Carmine, who started screaming desperately. At once she turned her trembling angry face to him, trying to console him, and as he wouldn't be quiet, she and her mother began talking the usual sort of nonsense that babies like. In the end she gave him her breast to make him happy, and while she suckled him, her mother was silent a few minutes. Then suddenly she looked passionately and bitterly at her daughter, burst out sobbing, and rushed out into the passage, cursing my father again, her arms held high.

Although I didn't think that she mattered in the least, I sauntered idly after her, my hands in my pockets, just to keep an eye on her. She was so furious with my father that, as she couldn't vent her rage on his person, she might go and damage his treasures — the underwater mask, the binoculars, the fishing gun, and so on, that he left at home when he went away — and ruin them completely. She might, in her rage, go and tear up my writings, my poetry. But, luckily for her, she didn't dare to do anything as bad as that; she just wandered about like a ferocious bear, looking around with tearful eyes. "So this is the famous castle!" she said. "This cave! Oh, the wretch, tricking me like that! You'd think he was a millionaire, to hear him talk — him and his castle. But this looks to me like a cave. Just a cave, that's all."

N. had appeared at the doorway with the baby at her breast, and when she heard this, she exclaimed, with angry tears at the insult to her castle: "Oh, Ma, how can you say that? You can't say this is a cave. It's a very valuable castle, it's terribly old, and everybody likes it."

I gazed curiously around at our dirty, crumbling walls, hung with ragged tapestries, and at the floor that looked like an uneven field, and realized that the comparison to a cave really wasn't too bad. A cave! Or else an enormous barracks. (Caves and barracks were rather fascinating places, I thought, so I must confess that even in the middle of a row like that I was pleased, deep down, because we had an interesting house.)

With these last words of hers, N. involuntarily provoked her mother into a dreadful discussion. When she heard N. saying "Everybody likes it," she turned to her with a half-angry, half-pitying expression. "Ah, Nunziatè, don't contradict your mother!" she exclaimed. "Your mother's here to defend her own flesh and blood. Oh, so this old cave is beautiful, is it? I can tell you, your mother's ashamed to think she sent you here, it's so ugly. No one comes near it — that shows how much they like it! And . . . devils like it, that's true! It's full of devils! . . . Lord give me patience not to say too much!" she added, raising her eyes to heaven and covering her face with her hands.

Her face soon appeared again, looking somber and at the same time knowing, as if she meant to imply that there were all sorts of mysterious insinuations behind what she was going to say. She came toward us at the end of the passage and began talking in a low, moderate voice. "You know there are some things I believe in, Nunziatè, and some things I don't believe in," she said. "I'm not saying they're not true; they probably are. It's just that I don't always believe in them. But you've got to know what all the women in the village say — they say this house is cursed, and full of devils! They're evil spirits, and as soon as they see a woman, great hordes of them come rushing in, sooner or later, and bring trouble to any woman, because they don't want to have her in the house. And do you know what they told me about your husband? That he's as happy as Satan himself in the middle of all those devils, and even (some of them say) he brings his wives here just to annoy them, because the angrier they get, the harder he laughs. But you must listen to your mother, my pet; you mustn't stay in this house any longer!" And as she said this, she began sobbing harder than ever.

When N. saw her mother crying, she couldn't hold back her own tears. All the same she broke out: "Oh, Ma, what a thing to talk about in front of the baby!" And she made the sign of the cross on Carmine's forehead with her fingers.

Here I decided it was time to interfere. "Come along now," I said scornfully and haughtily to N.'s mother. "When are you going to shut up? You make me laugh! These are things I shan't even bother to explain to you, because you wouldn't understand a thing about them. But if all the women around here believe in devils, they'd better stop coming to call. They make such a fuss, but there they are again — every single day, one behind the other, coming to see us."

N. looked at me, moved, feeling deeply, as if to thank me for my support, and as if this support aroused her to the extremes of defiance.

"That's right, they do! They keep on coming," she said in her grandest tone, a great lady even through her tears. "They keep coming! And they even drink our coffee!"

Lamentations

N.'s mother stayed with us four or five days and slept in the same room as N., where she'd taken Silvestro's camp bed. Right from the start, though, she had to accept that N. had definitely decided not to leave my father and the house, and there was nothing for her to do but take it quietly. And, resigned to her fate, she went back to Naples, where her other daughter was waiting for her.

After her dramatic start, she became more tractable and even pleasant for the rest of her visit. She spent hours and hours in N.'s room, talking to her about all sorts of people and goings-on in Naples; and N., who was never very talkative with women she didn't know, was very lively and chatty with her mother. She liked talking about her life before she married, and sometimes even talked of *Wilhelm*. But if her mother said anything against him, N. looked angry at once and drew back into her shell. She seemed to have turned into a sensitive plant, as far as insults to him were concerned.

All the same our guest just couldn't help her bitter feelings toward my father from breaking through occasionally, and, as she didn't dare to press the subject with N., she sometimes ended up venting herself on me. I didn't give her much satisfaction, of course; at the most I'd look bored, or growl impatiently. And yet, I stopped and listened — though reluctantly — because I longed so much to hear about him. And, of course, she couldn't say too much against him to me. But, however much she tried to keep calm, she always ended up, whatever tone she was using, by saying that in her unalterable opinion this marriage was nothing more nor less than a disaster for N.

"And to think," she'd keep saying, looking around her with bitterness and distress, as if she forgot I was there and was talking

more to herself than to me, "to think the poor little girl was dead
set against marrying him. It looks as if she realized, even though
she was a child. 'Oh, Ma,' she kept saying, 'I don't really want to
marry him!' 'You don't know what you're talking about,' I said.
'What are you looking for, the moon? There he is — a landowner,
a millionaire, tall, handsome, and mad about you . . .' 'He doesn't
seem handsome to me,' she said. 'When I look at his face he
scares me. I'm scared of him, Ma! I'd be quite happy not to get
married . . . I'd like to become a nun . . .' 'You're trying to hurt
your Ma,' I said. 'Stubborn as a mule,' I said. And I went on and
on until I persuaded her. And I thought it was all for the best, but
I was wrong, poor child! To think of all the fine young men who
admired her, who'd have cherished her like a flower! And look
what I arranged for her! With this . . . with this . . ."

Here N.'s mother remembered that I was listening, and controlled herself. But her eyes betrayed her hostility. It was obvious
that she held more firmly than ever to her view of my father as the
very worst of husbands. "It's not as if she were old or crippled," she
exclaimed at last, battling at every word with her shudders of indignation, "to be humiliated like this! Summer and winter alone,
and not even a line in the mail, worse than if she were married to
a convict! And if when he deigned to reappear, he at least made a
little fuss of her to cheer her up. But not a bit of it . . . Oh, I know
just what this marriage is like. She doesn't say anything and sticks
up for that husband of hers, but even if she doesn't want to tell
me, I know how to make her talk. I know just how to make her tell
me the way things are, when I want to!

"Oh, my poor Nunziatella, you didn't deserve a fate like this.
When a woman's married, it's not enough just to be married. A
young married woman wants more than that, she wants to feel
close to her husband, to be treated gently, honorably, with feeling,
to have compliments and pretty little things said, caresses and
kisses . . . Aaaaah! All those pretty things, all those kisses are so
sweet that even when your husband beats you it seems like Oriental pearls! Even when it's cold and raining, inside the house
you'd think you had central heating. That's all you want! Just that

sweetness! But a husband that doesn't treat his wife like that makes her look bad in the eyes of the world. A man shouldn't treat his wife like a woman in a brothel — flinging himself on her for a couple of minutes, then off and away.

"Yes, Viulante, you can tell anyone: that Raffaele of yours, whatever he may have been like, died with a clear conscience, because he was always sweet to you. He kept you like a doll, and never humiliated me in front of other people! But, my poor Nunziatella, how could I know you'd come to this when you were married? Never any nice soft words, never a compliment, never a caress or a kiss — treated like a woman in a brothel!

"Just to think how lovely she was, how she used to laugh, and how people fell in love with her just after saying hello! The boys in the street when they saw her curly head passing used to sing *Anella anella!*"

N.'s mother told me so firmly and emphatically about all this success that for a moment I was almost convinced that N. was really some sort of beautiful star, and I saw her greeted by the populace as she walked through the streets of Naples, while a crowd of young men in love with her opened up the way before her, singing serenades in her honor with mandolins and guitars.

The conversion

I was often with N. and her mother while they talked together, so I came to know something of their life in Naples — their ups and downs, friends and acquaintances, and so forth.

But the most extraordinary thing I learned from their conversation was something about Wilhelm Gerace. Though it seemed to me almost incredible, it was absolutely true, and when I learned it, I realized what Nunz had meant, that day she arrived long ago, when she had said: "But your father's now a Christian," which at the time I'd thought nothing of. The business was this: so as to marry N., my father had been converted to the Catholic religion.

By birth, as I've said before, he was a Protestant. Well, here's the story of his conversion, as I was able to reconstruct it from their talk.

It was more than a month after my father had asked N. to marry him, and, after a great deal of hesitation, she had just decided to accept him, to her mother's delight, and was going to tell him her decision at last, when she discovered that he wasn't a Catholic, and that they'd be married only at the Town Hall. When she knew this, she was so terrified that she wouldn't even see her suitor, and when her sister or friends told her he'd reached the corner of the street their alley ran into, she rushed out of the house shaking like a lunatic and took refuge with one of the neighbors. Her mother tried to stop her, and was even unpleasant about it, because she hated upsetting a suitor with a castle. But N. became as strong as a tiger, and wrenched herself free, and kept saying what she'd said once and for all, that it was impossible, that she wasn't going to have a husband who wasn't a Christian, and that she'd sooner be dead than married without the sacrament. But her mother just didn't dare to tell him this, and when he kept asking, again and again, "Whatever's happened to your daughter? Why is she never here? And when's she going to give me an answer, may I ask?" she tried to quiet him with all sorts of polite excuses, but without explaining anything. And he grew more and more impatient, more astonished than ever at never finding the girl. "What does it mean? Why's your daughter never at home?" he kept asking. And each time her mother had to invent a new excuse, which each time he seemed to find very implausible. Each time he settled down to wait for N., and her mother, hoping that N. would decide to turn up and at least come to greet him, made great efforts to entertain him as best she could, with conversation. But he never said a word: he just stayed there glumly without even looking at her, for half an hour or even an hour, outside the door on a chair in the road, kicking at the terra-cotta pots, or stretched on the bed inside, catching flies. Finally he left, looking glummer than ever. "Good-bye," he said. "Tell your daughter to be here at this time tomorrow, because I'm coming to hear her answer."

So much the better! This way he'd warned her in advance, and the following day, long before the appointed time, she took good care to get out of the way, and escaped to some hiding place in the alley. "She had to go . . . please excuse her . . . I can't say how long they'll keep her. She said she'd come back as quickly as possible . . . but how can I know when? It's out of her hands! You must forgive us," said her mother. And he'd wait for her, looking like a man plotting murder, but N. stayed in her hiding place until someone she trusted told her he'd grown tired of waiting for her and had left.

In the end he turned up one day without warning and caught her just as she was escaping to hide in the alley. He grabbed her and pushed her back into the house, and her mother back in with her. Then he shut the door. "Listen, you witches: if you don't stop this game you won't go out again except on a stretcher or in your coffin."

N. was already weakened by so many struggling, fear-filled days, and barely had the strength to answer. "Don't hurt my mother," she breathed. "I'm the one who ought to die. And rather than accept this marriage I will die." Her mother then intervened, and trying not to insult his religion, revealed the truth as best she could.

When he had heard her, he rolled over on the bed where he was sitting, and burst out laughing the way he did sometimes — as if he were watching something very funny and at the same time eating something very sour. Then he sat up again and looked at N. with a determined but mollified air.

"Well, then, all this fuss is because you want to get married in church, according to the Catholic ritual, is that it?" he asked, still looking threatening and ironical.

The girl said it was.

"Well, I agree. What do you think I care, then!" he exclaimed. "As far as I'm concerned we can get married in a mosque or a pagoda, according to the Chinese ritual. I can become a Jew or be converted to the prophet Mohammed. I don't believe in any god, anyway, so one god or another, it's all the same to me."

She sighed; he rose.

"Well, then," he said, "we've agreed."

Trembling, without daring to look at him, she moved her lips soundlessly. Then she sighed again. "But you don't know . . ." she said at last.

"Oh, what else should he know?" interrupted her mother. "He's told you he'll do what you want and marry you in church. Leave him in peace now! Why do you have to keep on at him?"

"Oh, Ma, do let me speak," N. begged her, almost in tears. "We'd better say everything at once today and not leave anything out." Then she turned to him and went on in a rather harsh, broken voice, pausing for breath occasionally, as if she were running: "But . . . do you know that for a real Christian to have the real ceremony of Christian marriage both the husband and wife have got to be Christians of the true Church, of the true family whose head is Our Lord. I've even been to the priest here at San Raffaele to find out all about the proper ceremony, and that's what he told me. Because with a real marriage, you see, it's not enough for it to be valid in this world — it's got to be valid in heaven as well. Because holy matrimony's a sacrament, and the sacraments aren't written on paper: they're written in heaven. There in heaven only the eternal truths are written, and blessed by the approval of God and of the chief of the Apostles. And so Our Lord has given us sacraments on purpose to guarantee us that something we do on earth will become an eternal truth there in heaven. Two people can't be joined together without the eternal truth: it would be a wicked union. So they must both be Christians, with Baptism, Confirmation, and Holy Communion of the true Church, governed by the Holy Father who sits in St. Peter's chair. Then a marriage really becomes a true Christian sacrament! And unless it's a marriage like that, I won't get married!"

This speech seemed to have exhausted all her reserves of courage. After that, it was all she could do to say four words in a row without trembling, when they met again.

In short, her dauntless suitor accepted her final condition right away, and agreed to become a Catholic instead of a Protestant, and to undertake all that was required of a convert to Rome, right up to the sacrament of matrimony. He listened, more curious than alarmed, to what she thought she should tell him about it with the small amount of breath she had left, and then he raised no objection, but only made some rather acid comments, as if some things really weren't his soul's business, but his body's. Among other things, N. told him he'd have to go to confession. "What do you mean, go to confession?"

"Yes, a general confession of all the sins you've committed in your life . . ." she explained, her voice hoarse with shyness. "And first of all you must make an examination of conscience . . ."

At this he grew thoughtful, as if undertaking the examination of conscience at that very same moment, and by the look of it it wasn't bothering him much.

"Well, that's agreed then," he declared, as though he were announcing something quite astonishing. "I'll make a general confession!"

This was how they became engaged. Now that she'd given him promise, she no longer tried to run away from him, even though the mere sight of him at a distance froze her with terror. What frightened her more than anything was being alone with him, and she couldn't even have said why, because really when there was no one else there, he treated her just the same as usual, not taking much notice of her or confiding in her, not even taking her arm when they went out for a walk. They looked quite different from other couples in love, who went about holding each other close; maybe he was different because he'd been born in a foreign country, she thought, and this was the way engagements went there. Sometimes he touched her, but it was only to hurt her — to pull her curls, say, or pinch her arm, or something unpleasant like that, nothing very dreadful, but enough to make her tremble. And then he let her alone and laughed violently. "If you're scared now, when we've only just got engaged," he said, "what will it be like when we're married?"

Meantime she watched his Catholic instruction, constantly, though secretly apprehensive, since she couldn't forget what he'd said — that he didn't believe in God.

He kept to his part of the bargain, and did everything he had to

do to join his new Church, and was so indifferent and so enigmatic that it was impossible to tell what he was thinking. With N.
he was always mysterious on the subject, and once when she
dared to express her anxiety, he turned ferocious and solemn and
scolded her for her doubts. Almost every day, he said, he had visions of angels flying through the air, and other prodigies of the
kind — so holy and sincere was his conversion.

The time came for him to make his general confession, on the
afternoon before their wedding. He made her come to the church
with him, and there was no one else there at that time; and while
he was at the confessional grille, she knelt and waited for him on
a bench a short distance away. He whispered away intensely, his
mouth hidden in the hollow of his hands close to the grating, and
occasionally forgot, and spoke a little louder; and N. was afraid of
hearing what he said, which wouldn't have been right, because
confession is a secret between priest and penitent, and no one else
should overhear it. But luckily she heard only one phrase distinctly: *Word of honor! Word of honor!* which he said more than
once during his confession. What he was saying on his honor only
the priest could hear.

As she knew that no living soul could sin less than seven times
a day, N. was prepared for a long wait, considering that he had the
sins of a lifetime to confess, and considering his age. But his confession took rather less time than she had expected; six or seven
minutes, not more, must have gone before he got up and joined
her, and told her to leave her bench, as he had finished. She
obeyed, but at seeing him marching firmly off to the church door,
she whispered anxiously: "D'you want to leave at once? What
about . . . what about your penance?"

"Penance?" he asked. "What penance?"

"Penance for your sins, of course. . . . I mean . . . the prayers
you've got to say. Didn't the priest tell you to recite some Our Fathers and Hail Mary's . . ."

"Oh yes, that's true," he answered. "He did give me two Hail
Mary's, but there's plenty of time before tomorrow; I'll say them a
bit later."

They were now outside the church, at the bottom of the steps, and she paused with one foot on the last step, she was so astonished at his penance.

"What!" she exclaimed, astounded and confused. "Two Hail Mary's? Only two Hail Mary's after a general confession?"

He looked hurt at her astonishment. "Well, Nunziata, what are you so surprised at?" he said. "Did you expect him to give me a bigger penance? Well now, that's a sign that you think I'm a sinner!"

"No, you mustn't think that," she said. "But everyone . . . even good people slip up somewhere in their whole life . . ."

"Now you're insulting me! Comparing me with everyone else, indeed! Just you remember, my girl, that I'm a rare example of perfection on this earth. I deserve compliments, not penance! What's more, the priest ought to feel sorry he gave me those two Hail Mary's! Apart from a few fibs and a bit of bad language I may have come out with, I've got absolutely nothing else to confess! And as for giving me penance to do for a few fibs . . . even big ones — even enormous ones . . . and a bit of bad language . . ."

At this point he suddenly felt so spontaneously gay that he flung himself down on the steps and burst out into such fresh, endless, irresistible laughter that she'd have joined in foolishly with him if she hadn't been just outside a church, and on such a solemn occasion.

Mysterious as he already was to her, his laughter made him seem even more so, giving him, strangely, even greater authority in her eyes.

"What are you laughing at?" she dared to ask at last.

"Because talking of fibs and swearing reminds me of something a friend of mine once told me . . ." This plausible explanation satisfied her; and the subject was closed.

All the same, this business of the absurd penance still worried N., and just to make sure she spent most of that night saying whole rosaries for all the sins that he might have forgotten in confession. The endless murmur disturbed her mother, who protested, so that N. had to tell her what had happened in church, to justify herself. (In fact, it was her mother I afterward heard describing it. Not only this last scene, but everything earlier connected with my father's conversion, and other less important things I'm leaving out, I heard mostly from Viulante, not from Nunz. Nunz said very little about it all, restrained by the same extreme reserve she felt in talking about things in heaven. And the little she did say she said as solemnly, respectfully, and importantly as if she was reciting a story from Holy Writ.)

Later, after Viulante had left, I returned to the subject with N., and couldn't help telling her that I thought my father's conversion meant nothing. In fact, as far as I could see, I thought he'd been converted without changing his ideas in the least, as a joke, as if playing a game that didn't matter in the least, or making a bet. And that, I felt, oughtn't to please the Church, but to offend it, and even (suppose he existed) God. When I said this, N. looked at me with an air of profound gravity even in her unwitting childishness, and, in a tone so definite that it admitted no reply, told me that at first she had thought something like that herself, but that afterward she had realized that this was a wicked thing to think, because it betrayed God's first thought, God's first thought being the sacraments. What would really have offended God would have been if my father had married without the sacrament of matrimony; but he had had the sacrament — that was the important part. To show me what God really meant in the sacraments, she gave me the example of baptism, which is given mostly to tiny babies who understand about as much as cats, and yet it saves them. And as an example of the extraordinary ignorance of babies, she told me about a boy she knew called Benedetto. This boy was taken to church to be baptized when he was a month old, and his family was so poor that he wore nothing but a little dress that left his legs free. Well, the first thing he did, right in the middle of the ceremony, was kick the priest on the chin. But the priest didn't mind in the least and baptized him just the same, because though the baby was too simple to understand the importance of the sacrament, the priest understood it, and God understood it, and that was what mattered.

Tragedies

Tragedies

MY FATHER TURNED up after Christmas, when Carmine Arturo was over a month old; as he arrived unexpectedly, he found three or four of N.'s friends there. You'd have thought he'd be surprised, or perhaps even a bit annoyed by such an innovation, but he seemed to find nothing odd about their being there and, in fact, hardly seemed to notice it. Carmine Arturo, though he didn't know him and had never even seen him, greeted him by laughing delightedly — most likely, I think, because he'd just learned to laugh and laughed at any excuse to, as if to do so was something tremendously clever. But my father didn't even bother to pick him up to see how much he weighed, as N.'s friends kept fussing around and urging him to do, but stood, dark and distracted, in the middle of their chorus of praise for his new son, looking like a boy who had grown up outside the family, whose small sisters were now pushing their dolls up at him. His behavior toward the baby cheered me up a bit, as I had expected to be hurt all over again when they met — for one reason especially: that C. A. was fair. But even this extraordinary thing about my brother didn't seem to deserve any particular notice from him.

But, alas, that was the only cheering thing about his return. This time he had come to the island feeling so gloomy and so taken up with himself that not only Carmine failed to interest him, but the rest of the family and everything else as well. He seemed cut off from everything around him, as if he recognized nothing; and if I remembered how he had been when I said good-bye to him in August, he seemed unrecognizable to me as well. I'd grown used to seeing him variable like the clouds all my life, but this time anyone watching him with faithful eyes would have noticed that he was hiding something completely new. During this last long absence of his, a curious change had come over his expression. A kind of gloomy mask covered his face, making it rigid as death.

Not that he was any uglier. On the contrary, he looked handsomer than ever. But he seemed all at once to have lost that look of secret and rather smug enjoyment that sometimes hovers about beautiful people. When he said *I* he made a face, as if naming someone who had little or nothing to do with him. He was lean and grubby; the colored handkerchief he had got last summer was still knotted around his neck, but it was reduced to a rag, a bit of string, and his clothes were so rumpled that you'd have thought he had gone to bed fully dressed for several nights.

The rest of the afternoon and part of the evening he spent flung down on the sofa in the big room without even bothering to turn on the light, and when I went to look for him and turned it on, he gave me an odd look as if he didn't like the light or my presence. His suitcase was still in the kitchen, shut, and I asked him if he wanted to unpack, but he answered, desperately impatient, that he didn't, and that it wasn't worth while anyway, because he'd soon be leaving. And in the shining eyes that avoided mine I saw tears trembling.

At supper he hardly ate at all and afterward he sat by the hot embers without saying a word. Huddled up like an animal, his handkerchief knotted around his neck, he seemed chilled right through, not there at all. One single thought was clearly filling his mind ceaselessly, hopelessly, and we couldn't guess it. His eyes were fixed on the ground, and occasionally he took long, weary breaths, as if short of wind. Sometimes his eyes lit up strangely, sadly, and their proud look softened, but then he quickly hid them with his fists as if he hated to let us see their expression, thought us unworthy of seeing it.

When the new year began (I didn't know it would be my last year on the island!), he spent a good deal of time at home, but never had his visits seemed so pointless. No sooner was he in the house than he seemed to regret it desperately, and dashed away again, even though, when it really was time to leave, he seemed sorry to be leaving Procida, and would turn up again after two or three days. He seemed to want our company and yet find it unbearable when he had it. One thing was obvious: we had all grown pale and insignificant as far as he was concerned, and N. more so than anyone else. He now treated her like some old relation who pottered about the place, absolutely unimportant and only too easy to forget. Generally he seemed to regard us from a tormented loneliness of his own, or not to notice us at all, but just occasionally it looked as if he could hardly forgive us for being alive at all, as if even our talking or moving about was something unruly and abusive. In this mood Carminiello's crying or N.'s voice singing in another room was enough to make him spew out the maddest insults, full of the blackest ideas.

Yet some days, when he could find no other way of escaping his own solitude, he might spend hours and hours in the kitchen right in the bosom of the family, and even of N.'s friends as well. There he'd lurk, aloof from us all, looking — with the beard sprouting all over his face — like some exile or deserter. For whole weeks he gave up shaving, and when he finally made up his mind to shave, he used the razor so roughly that he kept nicking himself. He seemed almost to enjoy ill treating himself, making himself bleed — he who had nearly fainted because of a jellyfish, at one time.

When he didn't come downstairs, he stayed in his room in a sort of lethargy, and remembered me only to send me out for cigarettes, which never lasted long and which all the same he always said were dreadful. A suffocating stink of smoke and stuffiness hung about his room, but he seemed to like it and even closed the shutters sometimes, so as not to see daylight. What strange thing had happened since last summer to reduce him to this martyred state? What mysterious, unchanging thought had for months been pursuing him, giving him no rest?

One day as I crossed the hall, I saw him through the half-open door, sobbing horribly and biting the bars of the bed. I crept quickly away on tiptoe, afraid that he'd be hurt if he knew that I'd seen him sobbing worse than a woman. I remember, too, that more than once I found him lying as flat as a corpse with an arm crooked over his eyes, smiling to himself. From the way his lips moved as he smiled, it looked as if he were having a conversation at once absurd and divine, but there was something sick and bitter about his smile as well, as if everything he asked was being refused.

Later, I thought back over these things a great deal, but in those first months of the fatal year, they were soon forgotten — mysteries, but secondary mysteries that passed me quickly by. I saw my father leave and return as if I were seeing a ghost, because as far as I was concerned he wasn't much more than a ghost just then. Wilhelm Gerace's troubles had become unimportant: I was too much taken up with my own to be interested in his.

My main person was no longer Wilhelm Gerace. That was quite certain (or at least, it seemed so to me).

The golden curl

I have written *my troubles* but I should really have written *my trouble*; because actually I had only one trouble just then, and it had only one name — jealousy!

At other times I had treated the suggestion that I was jealous as a piece of perfidious calumny. But this time, I had to admit the evidence. Of course, I'd rather have died than confess it frankly to anyone else, but to myself I couldn't deny it; I was sick with jealousy, sick because of a rival. And now, when I am ready to say who my rival was, I don't know whether I am ashamed or want to laugh.

Well, this was how it happened: my brother, Carmine Arturo, who had seemed so ugly at first, turned out to be beautiful, as the weeks and months went by, more beautiful than me, I'm afraid. His hair wasn't just fair — it was curly, and stood up quite naturally around his head in little tufts that looked like a perfect golden

crown and gave him a distinguished, aristocratic air, as if he ought
to be addressed as *Your Highness* or something of the sort just on
account of those curls of his. His eyes were pitch black, proper
Neapolitan eyes, but around the iris they were ringed with an enchanting dark blue, so that they looked a kind of blue-black. He
was fair skinned and rosy and round, and his hands and feet,
though tiny, were beautifully shaped, with tapering fingers and
toes, with a sort of little bracelets around his wrists and ankles.

According to N.'s friends, those natural little creases he had in
his skin were a sure sign that he was born lucky. In fact, according
to them, a baby's luck can be read in the beauty and perfection of
these little bracelets, which more or less all newborn babies have
because at that age they're fat. His were just perfect, and besides,
if you added up those he had at each wrist and ankle, you got
three, which is the perfect number. That meant that he would become a fine gentleman, who would be kind and accomplished,
and would succeed in everything he put his hand to. He would
protect the unfortunate and fascinate even his enemies; he would
live to be ninety, and always be as beautiful as a youngster, and his
beautiful golden curls would never turn white. Over land and sea
he would journey in showers of blossom, beloved by everyone.

While N.'s friends kept counting and recounting his little bracelets, so as to repeat this wonderful prophecy, Carmine would look
at them, still and serious, as if he knew it was a matter of his destiny. He seemed to think that these women were all marvelous
fairies of some kind, just because they were friends of N.'s and
when he saw them, he used to burst out laughing and hold out his
arms as if he was longing to fly. But if for some reason, N. had to
go away and leave him, just for a single minute, he'd burst into
desperate sobs, as if from radiant triumph he had been dashed
down to misery. And he struggled in the other people's arms in a
wretched, savage way that seemed to mean: "Well, I might as well
die! I might as well fall down and die!"

The only real beauty in the world, as far as he was concerned,
was N. It was the presence of this one beauty that enchanted
everything, that made all the others, even if they were ugly, seem

as lovely as angels, so that he loved the whole world, and won everyone by his enormous charm. But even his favorites meant little or nothing to him, basically. *She* was his one passion. And as the weeks passed and the months, he grew to love her more and more, and she returned his love. And so I saw someone else have that famous happiness I had always longed for and never had had.

He wanted N. beside him all the time; without her he even refused to sleep, and before he went to sleep he had to hold her finger tightly in his fist. Asleep, he kept his fists clenched, maybe persuading himself that he was still clutching her tightly. And his lips pouted a little, looking hurt and loving, as if to say: "I've got you, I'm keeping you, and you can't run away again!"

Now, when my father came home, things weren't as they had been in the days when she would dash back to the double room with her blankets from the small room. My father now slept alone, and liked it; Silvestro's old room was abandoned forever, and N.'s famous fear of the dark had become nothing but a memory. With Carmine I think she'd have slept in a desert without minding, as if that child, who was only a few months old, was some heroic paladin who could defend her from any attack.

As for Wilhelm Gerace's ever-present and enigmatic tragedy, you would have thought that, like all her husband's other secrets, this was taking place in a kind of mythical theater whose signs and symbols were quite alien to her simple sense of reality. Apart from being vain and futile, it would have been disrespectful for a mere spectator like herself, an outsider and an illiterate, to try to find any explanation of the obscure legend being played out; interference would have been far-fetched or even downright impious. And, in fact, it would really have been senseless and childish to worry very seriously about the great protagonist who there, on that unreal stage, was working out his own inscrutable and inescapable myth.

My father mattered to her only insofar as she could serve him and take care of him (always, of course, in her rather elementary way, as she never had the qualities that make a really good housewife). She never questioned his orders, and when he called, went flying to see what he wanted. But apart from that she left him to his thoughts, as if he were a tyrannical, solitary lodger. Her normal submissiveness toward him seemed like the faithful ignorance of animals, unquestioning, unworried, rather than any human kind of passiveness.

And so the secret fortunes of Wilhelm Gerace, who came and went encircled by suffering, never darkened her happiness with Carmine.

The attempted crime

Now that she had Carmine, she was so happy that she was singing and laughing from morning to night; when her mouth wasn't laughing, her eyes were. In a few weeks she had blossomed into such unexpected beauty that it really seemed like a miracle that had come out of happiness. The pallor that came from living indoors had disappeared, though she spent her time in the house no less than before. Her skin was now rosy, smiling, and healthy, and her old immaturity had given way to pleasant womanly curves; at the same time, though, she seemed taller and more slender than when we had first met, and walked more gracefully, more lightly on her small feet.

The clumsiness (a sign of her humble birth, I suppose) that had previously spoiled her movements, suddenly disappeared; as light as a cat she went running when she heard Carmine's voice. And when she carried him, she seemed not to feel his weight; in fact, the more he grew and the more he weighed, the greater honor it seemed to her. And when she carried him proudly about, she flung her head back a bit, joyously contrasting its darkness with Carmine's golden curls.

She always wore the same hairstyle, in buns, the way I'd shown her; but always half coming down because Carmine kept playing with her curls, with her curls and with her face, with the little chain she wore around her neck, with her whole body; and she would laugh impetuously, with an air of fresh, wild freedom.

Early in the morning I'd hear them from my room the minute they got up, laughing and playing together the way they did. I listened to the words better than a poet's she thought up to praise him, and as I listened I was flooded by a bitterness sometimes so great that I wished I had never been born.

It was the injustice, more than anything else, that got on my nerves, as I had never, in my whole life, had the satisfaction of hearing anyone praise me. And after all, though I was dark, not fair like him, I wasn't ugly. Even my father had said so more than once, as on that evening long ago, say, when he had said in front of her: "Yes, he's a handsome lad — he's not my son for nothing." And he had said the same sort of thing in passing on several other occasions. But at the most he had said things like: "Oh, get along with you, you know perfectly well you're not ugly," or "Let's see if you've grown handsome while I've been away. Well, that's not too bad." And that was all. Nothing to compare with the fabulous praises she gave Carmine, which, even if they were sometimes rather inconclusive, were perhaps for this very reason even sweeter. More than ever, I now realized how happy a man must be who has a mother.

It wasn't just that she kept praising and complimenting him; pretty often she talked to him seriously as well, as if he, who couldn't understand a word, really understood her, and the little inarticulate answers he gave were quite enough for her. Now that she had his company, she wanted no other; happy with him, she remembered no one else. When the weather had grown warm, she carried him around with her wherever she went, even in the morning when she went shopping, though she already had the weight of the basket and he enjoyed himself as much as if he was traveling in a carriage to see all sorts of exciting marvels — galleys maybe, ocean ports, bazaars full of jewels and gold.

Sometimes when she was talking to him as usual she'd pretend to dislike him. "Ooh, you ugly toothless old thing!" she'd say. "What am I going to do with you? D'you know what I'll do? I'm going to take you down to the square and sell you!" Then I tried to imagine, as if in a dream, the unlikely case that she really might not want to have anything more to do with him and would sell him or throw him away, or give him to a pirate ship. Just these dreams gave me a certain satisfaction, and even a feeling of relief.

I thought how offended I had been that day when she had suggested that I should call her *Ma*; and even now I realized that I had been right to be offended. All the same, it didn't seem fair to me that I had no mother, while she had a son. I haven't yet said, though, what aroused my most unbearable jealousy. It was this: that she gave him kisses. Too many kisses.

I didn't know there were so many kisses in the world, and just to think that I had never had any or ever given any! I watched those two kissing each other as, from a solitary ship out at sea, I might watch an unapproachable, mysterious, enchanted country, full of flowers and foliage. Sometimes she flung herself into the kind of mad game that small animals play together: snatching him up, hugging him, dropping him, without ever hurting him in the least, and finishing it all up with innumerable kisses. "I'm hungry!" she'd say. "I'm going to eat you up!" And she'd pretend to be as fierce as a tiger, but would end up kissing him instead. And when I saw her lovely mouth giving him those pure, those blessed kisses, I would keep telling myself what a wretched place this world is, where one person has such a lot and the next has nothing at all, and I felt transports of jealousy, delight, and melancholy all at once.

I would wander out, and it would seem to me that everything in all the world was kissing. The boats tied together along the beach were kissing each other; the movement of the sea was a kiss as it ran in to the island; the sheep as they cropped the grass were kissing the ground; the wind in the leaves and the grass was all a lament of kisses. Even the clouds in the sky were kissing each other. There was no one about in the street who didn't know the taste of kisses: the women, the fishermen, the beggars, the boys — I was the only one who didn't. And I had such a longing to know them that I thought of scarcely anything else night and day. Just to try, I would start kissing my boat, or an orange I was eating, or the mattress I was lying on. I kissed the trunks of trees, and spray from the sea, and cats I met in the road. And I realized that without being taught I knew how to give the sweetest kisses — really beautiful ones. But as I felt against my lips nothing but some cold vegetable, or rough bark, or the salt taste of brine, or saw close to me the nose of an animal that purred and suddenly dashed away, at once whimsical and dumb, I grew bitter to think of that divine, that laughing mouth of hers, which knew, besides kissing, the sweetest human words.

"Someday or other," I said to myself, "I'll kiss a person as well. But who will it be? And when? And who will I choose the first time?" And I began thinking of various women I had seen on the island, or of my father, or of some ideal future friend. But kisses like that all seemed insipid and valueless when I imagined them, so much so that, from a sort of superstition, I rejected them all, even in my thoughts, in favor of others more beautiful. It seemed to me that no one could ever know the real happiness of kisses who had lacked the first, the loveliest, the most heavenly kisses — those of a mother. And then, to get a little rest and consolation, I imagined a scene in which a mother was kissing her son with almost divine love. And the son was I. But the mother, though I didn't want it so, wasn't like my real mother, the dead woman in the portrait; she was like N. This impossible scene went on being played, over and over again, in my imagination, as if in a wonderful theater I owned. And I enjoyed it so much that I almost managed to persuade myself it was true, and then when I saw N. kissing my brother instead, he seemed to me an intruder, and she seemed to be betraying me. Angrily, I felt like insulting him, like bursting brutally in on their idyll. Only pride stopped me, while reason kept repeating, quite unheeded: "What right have you got?" Pride made me look indifferent, forced me not to look at them, to keep away. But a mysterious power soon called me back. I felt, mixed with my jealousy, a bitter curiosity to watch the beauty of her kisses. And at the sight of them, I guessed how they tasted — guessed to the point at which I could feel them on my own lips — a flavor that was all strangeness and all delight, a flavor unlike any other in the world, but miraculously just like N.

Not just like her mouth, but like her ways, like her character, like her whole self.

One day I went into her room when she wasn't there, and was tempted to kiss one of her dresses, but pride stopped me, as usual; it was just as if she were a great lady and I a beggar accepting charity from her. Another day, though, I yielded to a new temptation, and snatched from the kitchen table a piece of bread she'd already bitten, and secretly bit it. I felt a kind of backhanded sweetness in it, sweetness that hurt, like robbing a honeycomb.

If Carmine, who got all the kisses I envied, had only been ugly, had only lacked some quality at least, I might have been comforted by contrasting myself with him. But what happened instead — and increasingly — was that the more I compared myself, the humbler I felt, because the older he grew the more beautiful he became. He had inherited not only all my father's beauty, but also the little beauty of his mother, and, however hard you looked, there was absolutely nothing ugly about him. Their particular good points weren't exactly repeated in him, but combined in a surprising way that seemed like something entirely new and original — an invention, in fact, and full of charm. To be quite honest, I've never, either then or later, in Naples or anywhere else I've been, seen a more attractive child than my brother.

And his beauty was my cross. Even when I was alone, every hour of the day I seemed to see it floating before me like a flag — blue and white, blue and gold — which was trying to provoke me. One day (while N. was upstairs and he was asleep in his basket downstairs in the kitchen) I felt such a longing to be revenged on him that I was tempted to kill him. Among the few relics of the past that remained in the house, there was an old pistol in the big room, one of those loaded with wadding and now quite rusty and useless. I thought of using the heavy butt of the weapon to bang my enemy in the middle of his forehead so hard and so precisely that just the one blow would finish him off, and I put the pistol under my arm and approached the basket where he was sleeping. But it didn't seem fair to kill him while he was asleep, without his knowing, so I sat him up and tickled the palm of his hand a bit.

This made him move his lips in such a funny way that I laughed until I wanted to play with him more than I wanted to kill him, and went on tickling the palm of his hand, and his ears and his neck, making the sort of sound some exotic feline creature might make — until he began laughing in his sleep — maybe hoping to find a small leopard in the kitchen, or something like it. So everything turned into a game, and my murder just went up in smoke.

All this now seems so absurd that I can't keep a straight face telling about it. It's as if I were inventing funny stories, not telling the truth. But to think how much I was involved in it then!

My great jealousy

To me it was torture to see how his simplest action, like offering a crumb of bread to a chicken, or waving an exuberant rattle, seemed to her marvelously clever. And when he, who had never seen or known anything, found out something new, like the existence of rabbits, or the fact that fire burned, she treated him like a great discoverer every time. The minute there was anything worth seeing, she was impatient to show it to him. The moon would rise, and she would dash to pick him up and take him to the window and say, "Look, Carmine, look! Look at the moon!" A boat would pass out at sea, and she would be delighted, knowing that he loved to watch boats going by. And as soon as it appeared (at least according to her and to all his other female admirers) that he had learned to identify some object by name — say, a chair — the chorus of women would start yapping: "Wonderful! Wonderful! A chair, yes! That's right, a chair! That's wonderful! Wonderful!" in an important, ceremonious sort of way, as if the chair, by the mere fact (only presumed, at that, by the lot of them) that he knew it by name, had suddenly turned into a great lady, to be treated with deference. But if he happened to bump into the very same chair and hurt himself, they flung it down to the lowest criminal level, called it a terrible old chair, and banged it and beat it mercilessly.

I began to spend more and more time in the kitchen, where N.

spent most of her days with Carmine. I planted myself before her all the time, and to force her to notice me I took to marching up and down with an almost menacing air, or else flung myself down to lie yawning on the floor, or sat for ages just a step away from her, gloomy and proud, a living reproach. But you would have thought for all she cared, that I had become invisible. Again and again, those evenings, I would make a parade of unfolding the maps in the atlas across the table and scribble all over them, up and down with heavy pencil strokes, but nothing had the smallest effect. She would sit beside Carmine's basket, humming away to him, without taking the least notice of anything I was doing. I often picked up the book about the *Excellent Condottieri*, too, and pretended (as I really didn't feel in the mood for reading) to read; occasionally I'd purposely choose the most exciting parts to read out loud with noisy, emphatic comments. But she only bothered enough to ask: "What are you studying, Artù?" in an absent sort of way before turning back to Carmine and gazing at him anxiously because she thought she had heard him muttering in his sleep.

One day I found her actually looking at me, and I seized the chance. I rushed up to the bars of the skylight and started doing all sorts of tricks and exercises. And the only result was that she cried: "Carmine! Just look! Look what Arturo's up to!" as if I was an acrobat doing turns for Carmine's amusement. So I jumped down at once and left the kitchen, trembling with hidden rage.

This time I swore to myself I would leave the wretched woman with her old Carmine, and treat her as if she was invisible too, as if I'd completely forgotten her. But I couldn't resign myself to this; if for nothing else, because I had to punish her. In my heart I accused her of being as wicked as stepmothers always were, who flung aside their stepchildren as soon as they had children of their own; and I would have liked to do what castoff stepchildren did in stories — to go far away from my inhuman stepmother and seek adventures. But how could I, how could I? Now that I knew how faithless she was, I was certain that if I left she wouldn't even remember me; then, I shouldn't be even a stepson to her, not even some wretched relation. And I couldn't resign myself to that. So I planned to do something so wonderful that even at a distance she would have to admire me, be interested in me. I would lead an expedition to fly to the Pole, or write such a marvelous poem that I'd be famous even in America, and they would erect a statue to me in the main square at Naples . . . And then, at the height of my triumph, when I had her kneeling admiringly before me, I planned to tell her: "Go back to your blessed Carmine, then! Good-bye!"

But these plans were too uncertain and remote to console me in my daily disappointments. Besides, these disappointments, by their very cruelty, kept me chained to the island more than ever. Because she was on the island, and I couldn't help staying near her, if for no other reason than to bear witness, with my presence, to the past she had betrayed, and to her infidelity.

I was learning that poets were right who spoke of the inconstancy of women. And they were right, too, about the beauty of women, though none of the famous women they had praised seemed to me comparable to N. It is not hard, after all, to seem beautiful if you have golden hair, the way they had, and eyes like periwinkles, and bodies like statues, and, quite apart from all that nature has given you, if you have dresses made of brocade, garlands, diadems as well. But to have a body with nothing beautiful about it at all — rather a badly shaped one, in fact, thickset and graceless; to have dark hair and eyes, old shoes, ragged clothes; and yet to be as beautiful as a goddess, as beautiful as a rose. That was beauty supreme and triumphant! Beauty like that can't be described in a poem, because words aren't enough for it; or painted in a picture, because it's not something you can encompass. Maybe music could do it better; and I wonder if, instead of becoming a great leader or a poet, I shouldn't become a musician. The pity of it is, though, that I've never learned anything about music, and, though I have a fair singing voice, I know only a few Neapolitan songs . . .

Even things about her that were irrevocably ugly now seemed to me uniquely, matchlessly beautiful. What's more, I was sure that if by some future miracle her ugliness should be suddenly transformed into perfection, her looks wouldn't improve — on the contrary, I'd always regret the change. *That* was how beautiful I thought her. I thought everyone else must feel just as I did; in fact, I felt this so strongly that the simplest greeting, the most ordinary words addressed to her, seemed to me reverent homage, signs of adoration.

If I looked back to the time, a few months earlier, when this wonderful mother had treated me like one of her dearest relations, had longed for my orders as if they were an honor, had sighed for my company — then I rebelled against the vile upsidedownness of fate. I felt that I could never have peace if she didn't go back to being at least the same toward me as she had been before my half brother's fatal arrival; and yet, whatever happened, I couldn't betray this longing of mine to her. So I looked about desperately for a way by which, without damaging my pride, I could force her to take some notice of me; or else to show, once and for all, her irrevocable indifference toward Arturo Gerace.

Suicide

One morning as I went up from the harbor, I met her running down the hill, carrying Carmine for fun, and, as she ran, singing the Neapolitan song *Fly away my little pigeon* at the top of her voice like a gypsy. And as she passed me, she just didn't notice me.

I reached home alone, and so depressed that my heart ached. I felt that I could no longer bear the wretched way she had abandoned me, and at the thought of seeing her soon coming back to the house with Carmine as if nothing had happened, careless and indifferent to me as usual, I rebelled; and then felt almost beside myself with longing to break the sour old sameness of events. At all costs, I decided, I must punish her, and at the same time force her to notice me instead of my half brother — at least for a day, for an hour. And so I suddenly decided on a rather extreme piece of strategy that had flashed through my mind at times during those last wretched days.

I had one last weapon, only one: my death! Perhaps the sight of my lifeless body would still be a blow to her. I didn't, of course, mean really to die, but just to pretend — but making it look so real that obviously she would be taken in.

I thought of the time I had pretended to cry when in fact I was laughing, and the way she had been anxious at once (though she had been rather resentful a moment before) and had come over and said, so pityingly: "Why are you crying, Artù? What's the matter? Tell Nunziata!" When I remembered the success I had had, this new, much more impressive test seemed to me more tempting than ever. And so I decided quite firmly to put my plan into effect before she came back — she would be out shopping in the village for about an hour, I thought.

My father was away on his travels, and I went up to his room knowing I would find what I needed there. For some time he'd been suffering from insomnia and often took sleeping pills, and he had left an almost full bottle of them in his chest of drawers. From what people had said casually, I had realized how powerful these pills were. The dose my father took — one or two at the most — was a mild remedy, but if it was increased it became a poison. If you took a lot — say twenty — they could really kill you.

I emptied the pills from the bottle into my hand and counted them. There were nine of them, exactly the number that, by my calculations, I needed. As far as I knew, they wouldn't be able to kill me, but they would certainly be able to make me look tragically ill. What sort of illness it would be, I couldn't foresee, except in a vague sort of way, but I was sure it would be pretty spectacular.

I picked up all the pills and went down to the kitchen, and there I wrote this message on a piece of paper that I left on the table, unfolded and clearly visible:

MY LAST WILL
I WANT MY CORPSE TO BE BURIED AT SEA
FAREWELL
ARTURO GERACE

N.B. DESTROY THIS AS SOON AS READ
SECRECY!! SILENCE!!!

ARTURO

Then I poured some wine into a glass: I had a feeling the awful medicine had a very disagreeable taste, and thought the wine might improve it. And then I went out on to the terrace, because the kitchen didn't seem a very suitable place for suicide.

The terrace seemed to me the ideal place, especially because N. always came into the house that way when she got home from her shopping. I wondered what she would feel when, in a little while, she came in that way and bumped into my body, and I was sorry the sleeping pills would most likely prevent me from appreciating my own success. I wished I could undope myself, to be able to see the effect, and for a moment I was tempted to throw away the poison and just pretend that I was a corpse, trusting only to my theatrical talent. But I foresaw that if I did that, I'd never be able to stop laughing at the crucial moment of the tragedy, and that would ruin it all. So I gave up the idea.

The Pillars of Hercules

I put the glass on the step outside the door and sat beside it on the grass, closing my hand over the pills. Just as I was ready to take this odd step, I hesitated between the decision I had taken and an instinctive fear. It's true that I was quite sure my imminent suicide wasn't going to be fatal in the least. My father had told me what I knew about the doses of this particular poison. It was a matter of science; there wasn't the smallest doubt about it. And yet I looked at the pills I was holding in the palm of my hand as if they were barbaric coins to pay my fare to some final, unknown place.

The fact was, I had no experience at all of chemists, or illnesses, or poisons, and that all the laws of science that I had never learned about seemed to me mysterious, almost religious, like magic to a savage. What separated this poison's evil sleep from death was confused in my mind. I felt I was making a kind of advance right into death's territory; then, like an explorer, I'd turn back. But I had always hated death so much that the thought of touching even its wide shadow appalled me.

A kind of affective weakness came over me. I wished some faithful friend at least were there beside me to say good-bye in this fake suicide of mine. A friend, not a woman, because women as a race were inconstant and I had never been in love with one. The only woman I would have liked near me then was a mother, but a living mother, not the old one who once upon a time had floated above the island in her Levantine tent. That day I pitied that old idea of mine. I had learned, since then, that death is harsh, not gentle. The beautiful landscape I had imagined as a child was unsuitable for its severity.

The first Signora Gerace, no less than poor Immacolatella, recoiled from this radiant morning. It was several days after the March equinox, which, in Procida, means almost summer. And air and water were both so clear that Ischia appeared twice, sparkling with its small houses and its lighthouse, and also reflected in the sea below. Everything looked clear and precise, isolated — but those innumerable separate points of color mingled as well into a glory of green and blue and gold, and every moment that passed changed, dissolved, imperceptibly varied and reunited the colors, like a cloud of exotic insects whirling endlessly in the light. Even the gloomy Penitentiary across there on the hilltop was a rainbow of a thousand shifting colors from morning until evening. And now from the bay came a seagull's cry, from the port a ship's siren, from the town a peal of bells. Even the convicts across there in the prison were listening to the music, even the owls that cannot see in the daylight, even the stupid anchovies dying in the nets . . . Blessed, blessed sounds, glowing, shimmering reality! Every living heart responded to the enchantment of it all.

I was curious to know whether these sleeping pills brought dreams with them too. And suppose there were dreams in death as well? That's what that ass Hamlet wondered. But I wasn't an ass like him — I knew perfectly well what the truth was — that there was nothing in death. No rest, no waking, no great vault of heaven above us, no sea, no voices. I shut my eyes and for a moment forced myself to pretend that I was deaf and blind, imprisoned in my own body and entirely unable to move, divorced from every thought . . . But no, it wasn't enough; life was there in the depth of me, there like a point of light multiplied in a thousand mirrors. I could never imagine, could never conceive, the narrowness of death. Compared with its wretchedness, a miserable prisoner in a cell — no, a shellfish stuck to a rock, a moth — has a limitless, noble existence. Death is something senseless, unreal, meaning-less, something that muddies the marvelous brilliance of reality. And I felt that, like sailors long ago before the Pillars of Hercules, I'd soon be sailing on an unclean current, dragged from my own beloved landscape to some twilight hollow.

I wondered, meantime, if the poison would taste very bitter. From the grimace of disgust my father used to make, I rather thought so. And, after all, he always kept to the prescribed dose, while that day I meant to take a good deal more. The thought of beating him suddenly made me proud, and beating him, the whole fun of this business, became the most important reason for this whim of mine, almost canceling my original object and com-pletely canceling the memory of N. Like King Ulysses when he had avoided the siren's rocks, I felt free and alone before a choice: this test, or renunciation. And I suddenly felt that I wanted to play some mysterious and unfamiliar game, something bold and de-fiant, as if I was a daring officer making a skirmish into the enemy camp while the sentry was asleep, on my own, without an escort, trusting to the moonless night to hide me.

I can still feel the taste of the first of those pills on my tongue: it was quite ordinary, slightly salty, a little bitter. I swallowed it down with some wine, and everything around me remained ex-actly as it was. All I felt was a rapt silence to the very ends of the horizon, the silence you get at the circus when a brilliant trapezist flings himself forward in the mortally dangerous double somer-sault. Impatiently and carelessly I went on swallowing the pills with the wine, two or three at a time, and I think the wine had an effect before the pills did, because I soon began feeling drunk. A distant buzzing, which made me imagine that thousands of swordfish were cutting off the island at its roots, started up, and I expected the whole landscape to crumble, a possibility that somehow seemed almost restful. The splendid morning I had delighted in now seemed merely ugly and boring, and the immense, dazzling sun got on my nerves; it was torpid and sulfurous as a plague. I wanted to be sick on the grass, to throw up the wine and all the rest I had taken, but I kept it down, and with the absurd notion of going to rest in the shade, managed to get to my feet and, I think, even to move a few steps. I felt I was wearing a heavy metal helmet pushed down as far as my eyebrows, a helmet I should never get off, which would darken my sight with its visor. That was the last thing I knew. I didn't even realize when I fell, and from that moment the whole universe vanished. I knew nothing more. I didn't remember, or think, or feel another thing.

From the other world

Later I found out that this complete absence of mine lasted about eighteen hours, but as far as I was concerned, it would have been just the same if it had lasted five hundred years. Although afterward I hunted about in my mind for some trace of those eighteen hours (which were absolutely packed with excitement, voices, comings-and-goings — of which I was the center) I haven't been able to find a thing. The time wasn't even a dream, wasn't even confused and shadowy to me: it was nothing. And from the time I tried to move from the sun on the terrace until I first came to at dawn the following morning seemed like less than a moment.

My first impression, after what had seemed to me a moment, wasn't that I was coming back to life, as in fact I was, but just the opposite. I felt that I was slipping away, and dying. I didn't know where I was or the circumstances I was dying in. I knew nothing but that I was dying. I felt a horrible nausea, and all my senses were extinguished — silent, blind; the only thing I knew was the agony of taking breaths that were wrenched painfully out of me, and gradually growing too weak to rise to my lips. "I didn't think I was destined to die today," I told myself. "But look, here is death. This is the end. I am dying." And as I thought this, I fell back into unconsciousness for another long period. I do have some sort of memory of this time, though, a kind of thread on which my consciousness wavers, like a tightrope-walker. I realized that I was lying with my eyes closed, and this seemed quite natural, as I thought I was dead. Sharp voices reached me, scattered in a monotonous roaring, like the sea. "Well, I'm no longer alive," I thought, astonished, "and yet I can still hear. That means that death doesn't finish us off." And, ill as I was, I felt, deep down in me, a very small, very tremulous sense of adventure. "Now I'll see what death is like" I thought. "I wonder if we really don't meet other people? Suppose I meet my mother, Immacolatella, Romeo . . ." And it seemed likely, because among all the confused voices I heard a woman's voice sobbing distinctly: "Artù, what have you done?" and I knew perfectly clearly that I was answering her out loud: "Is that you, Ma?"

Every now and then I fell back into a torpor, quite deaf, and then I'd hear that little tearful voice again. A confused idea was taking shape in my mind: maybe the eternal task of the dead was always to grope about looking for one another and never meeting. There was no way of getting one's bearings. My darling mother could hear me near her, could call me, and I could answer, but our voices returned in space like unheard, undirected echoes.

More than once I think I cried: "Here, Ma! Here!" when, unexpectedly, the same voice kept saying: "Artù, what have you done?" clearly and definitely into my ear. "Here she is at last! Here she is!" I said to myself, and opened my eyes again. And then I realized at once what was really happening. I was alive, this woman calling "Artù" wasn't my mother, but my stepmother. And the supreme point of my existence was — to kiss her.

Now or never! I thought, fast and impulsively, and though I still felt pretty lifeless I raised my arms and pressed her to me. Her curls, her tears, all her young freshness, I felt on my face — tender and wonderful, like spring. And I was shaken with a great deep shudder of joy. "Now," I told myself, "even if you die of this suicide, you can die happy!"

And I offered my lips, but I was too weak, and as I did so, I fell back on the pillow, half fainting, without having kissed her.

Insipid kisses

I was sick for another two days. What happened, I found out afterward, was that the dose of sleeping pills I had taken, which as far as I had known wasn't enough to kill a man, was quite enough to kill someone of my age, more or less a boy that is, whatever I might claim to be. So, without meaning to, I had really risked dying, and only my tough constitution had saved me. I was sick in bed for nearly half a week, though, something that had never happened to me before, as far as I could remember. I had headaches, felt exhaustedly sleepy, and every now and then sick and dizzy, which made it seem as if the bed were rolling like a boat. And if I wanted to get up and walk around, something absolutely new surprised me: my body no longer obeyed. My knees wobbled and folded up, and my heart thumped. I no longer felt like Arturo Gerace, with a whole battery of muscles at his command, but like some small, bloodless, languishing girl, with limbs as weak as stalks.

Hour by hour, though, I felt my strength returning. And, though I had always thought that being sick was the dreariest business, I almost wanted to prolong this illness, as N. was always near to look after me and didn't worry about anything else. To say that she was a perfect nurse wouldn't, as far as I can judge, be strictly true. She didn't by nature have the particular qualities (rather pedantic ones, anyway) that you need for nursing, and it wasn't her fault. But she had all the right intentions, and besides (which was much more important) you could see from the way she looked and behaved when she was with me that her whole soul was then, as it were, suspended in a sort of exquisite torment, over one single object: the dear, precious existence of her stepson, Arturo. At the head of my bed, to keep an eye on my recovery, she had thought of hanging one of her Madonnas; and it was the most magical, the most foolproof, of the lot — the Madonna of Piedigrotta. Sometimes I'd peep at her when she thought me asleep and surprise her in the act of whispering to this famous old Virgin of hers, her hands clasped, her great beseeching eyes wet with tears and lighted by the most heavenly superstitions. And who was she praying for? For me! When she wasn't praying, she spent hours sitting on the sofa opposite my bed, watching over my breathing, and spying out every sign of life with the religious expectancy of a savage tribe awaiting the sunrise. I shall always see her angelic loveliness, uncombed and untidy as she was, those disorganized days as she sat there before me, her two small hands lying in her lap with that faithful, passionate idleness of hers. Beside her was a big basket, where Carminello slept, and when he wasn't asleep, she tried to keep him as quiet as possible in some other room, alone or with those women friends of hers, for fear he might disturb me. He would shriek away for her, of course, but if she happened to be busy looking after me then, she let him cry without taking any notice of him for as much as five or six minutes at a time.

Sometimes I caught drowsy glimpses of her pacing around barefoot with him in her arms, as she couldn't abandon him all the time, or sitting on the sofa with him on her knees, suckling him, or rocking him and murmuring little persuasive lullabies. If he did not respond, but made his usual gay little noises — chuckles and so on, she scolded him quite severely. "Be quiet, love! Arturo's ill!" And on one of these occasions, she even went so far as to give him two little slaps on his fingers. Yes, she smacked Carmine for my sake! This really was far, far beyond what I had ever hoped for, even in my wildest dreams.

When I thought back over the way I'd been jealous of the baby, it now seemed like a ridiculous dream. As I lay tranquilly there in the half-light, I'd hear now and then the sweet sound of the kisses she gave him, and I wondered if such a thing was really possible, that someone of my age could be jealous of those kisses. You might as well envy a baby his toys, his rattle, his little bells and things. The jealousy that had provoked this fake suicide now seemed to me like a storm late in March, after which high spring, with its long days, begins. And as I slowly came to from my deadly drowsiness, I felt (as if new senses were being born in me) that the real flavor of life should be much more serious, much more sumptuous, than those childish kisses.

Atlantis

By the fourth day of my illness, the unpleasant dizziness had disappeared altogether, leaving me feeling just weak and languid, and early in the morning I realized that I was very much better. But I wanted to profit from my suicide just one day more. So when she asked me, "How do you feel, Artù?" I murmured, scarcely opening my eyes: "Oh, I'm feeling terrible . . . really terrible."

And the whole morning I pretended to be suffering and half-conscious, though in fact I was wide awake. Every now and then, I said in a gravelike voice, *Water . . . Drink . . .* Or else I'd lift my head up for a minute and then fall flat again and pretend that I had fainted, peeping through half-closed eyes just for the pleasure of catching a glimpse of those great frightened eyes bending over my face. But toward noon I began to get sick of playing at dying and, as I started feeling hungry for the first time since my suicide, I let myself be fed quite willingly (she simply had to feed me then, I was so weak and helpless).

Then I went to sleep, this time into a real sleep, and opened my eyes again early in the afternoon, feeling deliciously surprised and fresh. N. came up at once, and seeing my clear eyes fairly trembled with delight. "You feel better, don't you, Artù? Do you want anything?" she asked me, and sounded as if she were singing.

I stretched, and said I was better, but that I didn't want anything. I just wanted to rest. And she went back to sit in her usual place on the sofa, without another word, so as not to disturb me.

Carmine was asleep in his basket. The shutters were drawn so that the light wouldn't bother me, and the afternoon silence was complete: no voices, no church bells. I have never enjoyed such fantastic silence as we had at home in Procida. It seemed as if the village and its people were no longer outside, but a great deserted estuary of a calm sea, at a time when even seagulls and all the other creatures on land or sea are at rest and no ships are passing. Between the shutters, outside the midnight window (the one I had once seen a real owl perching on), I could see a tiny cloud moving across the blue sky. For a moment it looked like a shell, then like a little balloon, then like an ice-cream cone, then like an old man's beard, then like a ballet dancer. And in this last shape, stretching and lengthening like a real ballet dancer, it moved away. The cloud passing by brought back to my mind — I don't know through what association — exactly what I had thought and done on the morning of my suicide until the moment when I had fallen on the grass, and without even looking at N. I suddenly said loudly: "I say, you know that bit of paper I left — did you tear it up?"

The sound of my voice after my illness surprised me a little when I heard it; there were rough, deep notes in it which hadn't been there before. N.'s small voice, though, was just as it had been. "Yes, I tore it up . . ."

"Did you read it? I'd written: *Secrecy! Silence!* You didn't talk about it?"

"No, I didn't."

"Well, be very careful, no one must ever know the truth. They mustn't think it was done on purpose — just a mistake, that's all." "That's what they thought . . . But Arturo, what were you doing?"

"And you've got to shut up with my father as well. If he hears anything about it, you must make him believe the same as the others."

"Well, who does he ever talk to? He'll never hear anything from anyone."

"In any case, you must never tell him the truth. He, above all, must never know it."

"I'll never tell him the truth. But Artù, what did you do? What did you do?"

At this point I realized that I ought to give her some explanation, to compensate her for involving her in my secret. But of course whatever happened I didn't want to reveal that my suicide had been a fraud and she the whole reason for it! Right at that moment I could think of nothing better than to invent some other explanation, just to give her an answer. Imagination came to my rescue, and, as one of the many thoughts I had had that fatal morning happened to flash through my mind, I said, without thinking: "Well, I'll tell you the truth: I wanted to go beyond the Pillars of Hercules."

"The . . . Pillars of Hercules!"

I buried my head in the pillow to hide my half-smile. All the same, I rather liked what I had thought up. I knew by experience that my stepmother believed everything I invented, however incredible, and it's never a bad thing to show you're clever where women are concerned. So I carried on, inspired, bold, and perfectly natural, in a thoughtful, narrative tone to which my breathing, which was still rather labored, added a certain majesty.

"I said the Pillars of Hercules," I began, "just to make a comparison. You know the Straits of Gibraltar? Well, in ancient times they seemed fantastically far because people had to go about in smallish boats, with oars. And the passage through the Straits went between two great walls of gigantic rocklike pillars set up as a frontier. Every ship that had gone through it had been lost with all its crew to the last man, and had never been heard of again. People said that as soon as boats came out into the open sea on the other side, a cloud engulfed them and they were flung to the bottom in a whirlpool, because there the earthly world ended and an eternal mystery began. That was what the ancients thought first of all, but people later discovered that their idea was just a story, because beyond the Straits the great Atlantic started, and when they went on they found the West Indies full of people, and houses, and mines . . . Anyway, if you want to know, my comparison is this: that our fate in an eternal death where everyone ends might be just another story, like all the others, so that if, instead of hanging around and getting scared like a miserable coward, one decided to explore it, one might find out if it was all a lie . . . Well, that's what I decided. And I did it."

When I began this mystifying explanation, I vaguely had the idea of taking it to its final and most brilliant conclusive nonsense; to get as far as asserting that my strange cruise had led to some grandiose discovery that would make Columbus, Vasco da Gama, and the others green with envy. Say, that as soon as I'd passed the limits of the grave, I had turned up at a kind of Atlantis or something like it, and that I had disembarked at some magnificent port, crowded with girls and marvelous nobles, with pirates and captains, and powerful carriages of gold and copper, and so forth. But instead, when I had got to the words *that's what I decided*, I just didn't want to carry on with the second part of my story. After so many hours of sickness and silence, I had already talked too much, and I was tired; besides, my voice, with those unexpected harsh notes in it, sounded out of tune and almost foreign. N., who was listening intently to me from the sofa, asked no questions, made no comments. Maybe, although she was a bit stupid, she wasn't so stupid, I thought, as to believe all this rot; maybe she hadn't believed me. I felt a bit ashamed of inventing it all, but on the other hand, I wasn't going to deny it. And then, as if to revenge myself on myself and answer her silent questioning in the cruelest way possible, I suddenly ended up, quite without planning it.

"Well, and so I found out just what I suspected . . . D'you know what there is in death? NOTHING, that's what there is. Just blackness, without a single memory. That's what there is!"

I remembered the horrible dizziness when I had first come to after my fall, and I turned over in bed revolted. I heard a sigh from the sofa, and thought that it was a sigh of bitterness. I wondered if she was getting ready to accuse me of blasphemy and wanted to talk about eternal life and Paradise . . . But I was wrong. Her sigh was a sigh of relief, not of bitterness at all! After a while I heard her voice, and though it was still tremulous with anxiety, it betrayed obvious relief . . .

"Well, then," she said, "now that you know . . ."

She stopped a moment.

"Know . . . what do I know?" I drawled.

She gave another little sigh, a little sigh of damnation, it sounded. Then hurriedly, brokenly, she concluded: "Now that you know it, now that you know there's absolutely nothing there, you won't want . . . *to go back there!* Will you?"

I burst out into such gay, natural laughter that in two seconds I felt completely well. Really it was almost incredible — my good luck. So N., to save my life, had got to the point of denying her old Paradise! This was even better than slapping Carmine for my sake. It was an absolutely extraordinary proof, something far beyond my hopes. I was tempted for a moment to answer, "Well, who knows?" . . . as basic cunning told me (if I wanted, even in the future, to go on exploiting the success of my suicide) to leave her always a little in doubt . . . But the memory of that horrible dizziness still haunted me. Death was too hateful to me, and the idea of using its loathsome face as my accomplice (even if I was only lying) filled me with horror. I couldn't pretend about that.

"Oh, no, never again!" I said, with violent revulsion.

The catastrophe

That same evening I wanted to get up for supper. I was still a bit unsteady on my legs and had difficulty getting downstairs. But when I went up again after supper, I already felt better, and the following morning I got up alone at dawn, feeling impatient and hungry. My illness was over: nothing was left of it but a kind of drunkenness that gave my steps a sort of inspired and rollicking solemnity. The first sounds of the day echoing through the fresh air outside seemed to give me a wonderful answer, as if they were the instruments of an orchestra accompanying me. And when I went out into the open on the terrace, this ridiculous feeling of mine increased, crossing the whole arch of the morning landscape. The great theater of my suicide seemed to gather me up with kindly, exhilarated surprise, just as if I'd acted out a tragic pantomime, and then come back to act again, safe and sound, on the stage. But then, when the sun came up, the pantomime gradually seemed to recede into a past that kept growing more and more remote, as if it was back in the childhood of the world. Carmine's happy shrieks told me that he was coming downstairs in her arms, and when I heard them I didn't even care that, in prehistoric times, he had ever been my rival.

I don't know what sudden whim made me hide behind the outside corner of the house just then. She was clearly surprised when she arrived to find the French windows open and no one in the kitchen or on the terrace. I heard her leave Carmine in the kitchen and go upstairs again to find out if I had really got up and gone out so early. After a moment she came downstairs again and on to the terrace, hesitating. She didn't think of looking around the corner, but instead leaned forward over the slope that led down to the beach and began calling without getting an answer: "Arturo! Artù!"

She was wearing a red dress and was barefoot, as she had got into the habit of being while she was looking after me. At that hour of the morning the shadow of the wall was still long on the terrace. The rays of the sun, which was rising behind the house, reached only to the farthest corner of it, where she was standing, and in its rosy light her bare legs had a childish color that oddly made me want to laugh. She walked about a bit, gazing around with the worried air of a mother cat, the wind catching her curls and her dress. Then, again, she began calling me from the top of the slope.

Suddenly I jumped out behind her, saying: "Here I am!"

She started with surprise and turned around delightedly; then burst out: "Where were you? Are you running around already?" Then, perhaps bewildered by something aggressive about me, she murmured as she looked at me: "Artù, you've grown taller, these last few days . . ."

When she said this (whether it was true that I'd really grown a little during my short illness, or whether, being barefoot, she looked smaller than usual) I noticed for the first time that I was

taller than she was. This seemed to me a sign of my power —
something ancient, and proud, and joyous. And meantime she
was drawing imperceptibly away from me, which was like con-
fessing to me that her heart was beating fast . . . Suddenly I
pressed her to me and kissed her on the mouth.

Her lips had a cold, unripe taste to them, and my first feeling
wasn't very different from the feeling you get when biting a piece
of grass or tasting sea water. My first thought in that moment was:
"Well, now I know what kisses are like! This is my first kiss." And
this thought, which was all mixed up with a rather boastful feeling
— something curious, and surprised, and at the same time
slightly disappointed — almost distracted me from her. At first,
though she didn't respond to my kiss, she was so confused, made
so vulnerable by her surprise, that she didn't try to draw away. I
heard her murmur "Artù" between my lips as if she didn't know
me, and, strangely, she grabbed hold of me, as if to beg my help;
and I only pressed her more tightly to me, growing bolder and
more demanding, crushing my lips against hers.

She had grown pale, quite colorless and weak around her soft
eyes, and her lips, which at first had been cold, were now burning.
I felt the sweet taste of blood in my mouth and in a moment it de-
stroyed all thought in me. My voice said, "Nunziata! Nunziatè!"
but as I said it, she jerked away from me in ferocious denial, and
started shaking her head — tenderly, stubbornly, excitedly.

For a moment she stood like that, a step away from me, as if
she were still half dreaming, and wasn't yet conscious, as if she
were questioning some mystery; but her curly head (which had
never appeared to me so angelically lovely) went on refusing
fiercely, and her eyes were already avoiding mine, and already
looked guilty and afraid. Well, my old longing was being satisfied
— to frighten her, to frighten her no less than my father did! I realized, though, that the two fears were not the same, though how
they differed I was still ignorant enough not to know. Her fear of
my father, which I had never forgotten, was something agonizing,
something that seemed to freeze her limbs entirely, while her
present fear (a strange new kind I'd never seen before) seemed to

contradict itself and to glow in this very contradiction. At the very moment when her desperate will was refusing my kisses, her body (which suddenly obtruded on me, as if I were seeing it naked) was begging me to kiss her again! This wild, throbbing prayer ran through all her limbs, from her rosy feet to the tips of her breasts jutting sharply out under her jersey. And in her frightened eyes was that same startled look — that wonderful, wet look, tinged with misty blue — that a little earlier I had glimpsed while I was kissing her.

I cried again, "Nunziata! Nunziatè!" and was just going to run to her. But when she heard me call her name, she answered with a diabolical, brutal, terrified shout. And then, covering her face, she cried with pitiless certainty, as if swearing a sacred oath: "No! No, my God!"

And with a harsh, glassy look, quite unlike herself, she fled away from me as from an enemy.

The Fatal Kiss

Ricerco un bene
fuori di me.
Non so chi'l tiene
non so cos'è.
    aria of Cherubino

The fatal kiss

*A*ND SO, WITH that kiss, I had again undone our friendship; and this time, quite hopelessly!

After that fatal morning I had only to go into a room where she
was (even if I didn't say a word to her, even if I went there simply
to do something on my own, something that had nothing to do
with her) — I only had to appear before her for her at once to lose
all confidence and spontaneity. Her normal manner, in which
pride and gentleness were so touchingly mixed, vanished immediately, overlaid by a curious fear. This fear of hers, I repeat,
seemed rather unusual, and not at all like the fear she had shown
on other occasions in the past — for instance, when she was with
my father. If I had to invent an image for this new fear, the only
thing I could compare it to would be a small flame that suddenly
lit her up with its faithless rosy glow and shone in all her limbs, a
light she tried to escape from in terrified, unexpected ways of behaving. First she colored, then turned pale; then she wandered
around the kitchen picking things up pointlessly and dropping
them with trembling fingers; then she sat down again beside
Carmine and began singing him her usual little songs in a shy,
cold voice, as if she wasn't listening to her own words. These
songs were an excuse, or actually a little magical singsong to distract herself from her own fear and from the embarrassment my
presence caused her. At times it looked as if she went behind

Carmine's basket, or clasped him in her arms, in order to defend herself against an intruder who frightened her. And I was the intruder! But the oddest thing, which I haven't yet said, is this: that in her presence I, too, was afraid.

I say *afraid* because in those days I wouldn't have known how to define my confusion more accurately. Although I had read books, and love stories among them, I was still a half-savage boy; and perhaps too, without my realizing it, my heart was taking advantage of my immaturity and ignorance to protect me against the truth. If I remember the whole of what happened with N., right from the beginning, I can see that the heart, in its struggle against the conscience, is shrewd, and inspired, and imaginative, like a skillful costume maker. It can make masks out of nothing at all and dress one thing up to look like another just by changing around a couple of words . . . And conscience, in this odd game, behaves like a foreigner reeling tipsily round at a fancy-dress ball.

After I kissed her, I couldn't see her without my heart pounding fearfully (and it started right in the street, as soon as I saw the House of the Guaglioni from down there, growing nearer at every step!). Then when I was with her this anxiety turned to longing, to a sense of almost bitter unfairness, to rage. What had happened was this: of the innumerable moments that made up our common past, I remembered only one when I looked back — the one when I had kissed her. I felt that my kiss had left its mark on her, quite visibly all over her body, had surrounded her with a kind of aureole — radiant and partisan, tender and sweet and, above all, mine! — and that was where I longed to nestle again, as if she was now the enchanted prisoner of my kiss, and I was called to share that prison of love with her. I could no longer see her without feeling a violent, an irresistible need to take her in my arms and kiss her again. But how could I do it, how could I achieve my longing — no, my right — if she had become my enemy because of that very kiss? And if that single kiss of ours, which to me seemed something so glowing, appeared to her threatening and terrible? I had the feeling (so great was her fear) that if I took her in my arms and kissed her another time, I would kill her! One day when she was cutting bread with a knife, I met her glance as I watched her with thudding heart, as usual, and thought I read in her sweet, trembling face these words: "Be careful now. If you come near me, I'll stick this knife into myself and fall down dead!"

And so her fear became my fear too. And she and I, together in the same room, moved like two lost beings around something that burst out roaring to hit us, to fling us together and then separate us, to prevent us from ever meeting. After a while I would go out without saying good-bye, incapable of expressing the bitterness of my longing and disgust. Her refusal of my kisses seemed to me nothing but a denial of our friendship and relationship, something that condemned me to languish unfairly alone.

The injustice I accused my stepmother of had a solemn, mysterious power and prestige that fettered my will, but I hadn't the smallest scruple or feeling of guilt. I found nothing forbidden in my feelings for her, not even in my kiss! When I had kissed her, I was obeying a joyful, glorious impulse, without forethought or remorse. Among my Absolute Certainties there was nothing that said: *It's a crime to kiss friends and relations.*

I knew, of course, that kisses weren't all alike. I had read the canto of Paolo and Francesca, for instance, not to mention that I knew dozens of love songs all talking about caresses and kisses. And, besides, I had seen illustrated movie magazines down in the village, with photographs of couples kissing each other (and I had even learned the names of a few movie stars from the captions). But I had got so used to being thought a child that I couldn't suddenly put myself in the place of Paolo, who was damned in hell, or of a hero like Clark Gable (whom, anyway, I'd never liked because he had a squashed-looking face, and was dark besides). The love that they talked about in songs, and books, and magazines, had seemed to me something remote and legendary, something outside real life. The only woman in my thoughts had always been a mother, and if I had ever dreamed of kisses, they had always been a mother's holy kisses to her son.

So now when N., by being frightened of me, gave me the

enormous honor I had always longed for (that of treating me as a man and not a child), I couldn't even recognize the honor!

Forbidden

Well, I'm clever these days and I wonder if maybe it wasn't my heart's old wickedness that pretended not to recognize the obvious, so as to leave me free. These days I can conjecture and dig around better than a philosopher. And what I suppose is this: that maybe if I had questioned my conscience like a man, it would have answered (not being completely savage, however immature it was): "Don't be a fraud! You're a cheat and a seducer." But what really happened was that the calm clear days of the Procidan spring had spread a kind of shining cloud around me, through which strange gleams and mysterious figures glanced, and in which I lived wrapped like an outlaw, so much so that I didn't even remember that conscience existed, and at times I didn't even notice that I was myself.

Maybe at that time of life everyone experiences something like that.

I had begun to spend whole days outside the house again, seeing N. as little as possible. And while we were separated, my mind, without any effort of will, was separated from her image. I never thought of her face, still less of her body; even my thoughts seemed to have fled from the sight of my stepmother. But even without looking at her, my thoughts, like those of a blindfold pilgrim, returned to her.

That is how it was. Well, the fact is (though I never said so) that in my capricious memory the fatal kiss had become more ingenuous than it had been in fact (like music of which you remember only the simple theme). All that was odd, and fierce, and violent in the kiss, had been almost wiped out in my memory (and so I was less likely than ever to see myself as guilty for having given it!). But there was something else I did not forget, and that was that on that one occasion I'd called N. by name for the first time (instead of saying *Hey, you,* or something like it). I don't know what visionary notion prompted it, but whatever it was, this one thing seemed to me a crime, this single thing. And now the taste of it often returned to tempt me.

I don't know how many times a day I'd surprise myself repeating softly, without even thinking of her — Nunziata, Nunziatella, with a feeling of delicious but foolhardy lightness, as if I were confiding a secret to a false friend. Or else I'd trace her name with my finger on a piece of glass or in the sand, and then rub it out at once like a criminal leaving clues that might implicate him. But suddenly the sound of the waves, the whistle of boats, all the noises of the island and of the sky seemed to cry out together *Nunziata, Nunziatella!* It was like an immense intoxicating revolt against the famous rule (which, in fact, I had invented myself) that always denied me her name, and at the same time a tremendous denunciation of my crime, so terrible that it almost overwhelmed me.

The name *Nunziata, Nunziatella* had changed, as far as I was concerned, into a secret password, the sort that, used by conspirators in secret plots, loses all its original meaning. And so not even the sound of her name, which now symbolized an obscure, violated law, brought her face and her physical presence into my mind again. When I wasn't with her, her person seemed to hide itself from me in a cloud; as soon as I was with her again, the cloud was torn aside to show me always the grim face of her refusal.

Even in my dreams, N. held aloof. Or at least I don't remember her coming into them ever, in those days. I remember, though, that I had dreams like the *Thousand and One Nights.* I dreamed of flying. I dreamed of being a splendid nobleman flinging coins into the air by the thousand. Or a great Arab monarch crossing a burning desert on horseback, while, at his passing, the desert rocks sent fountains of fresh water soaring up into the sky.

In actual fact, though, I suddenly seemed to have become the bristling foe of everything that existed.

The kingdom of Midas

This was an odd time for me, as I have said. The quarrel between me and my stepmother was only one aspect of the great war that seemed suddenly to have broken out between Arturo Gerace and the whole of the rest of creation with the flowering of spring. The fact was that when the fine weather returned that year, it brought with it, I think, an age that in smart families is called the *awkward age*. Never before had I felt so ugly; in myself, in everything I did, I noticed a curious unattractiveness that started in my voice. I had acquired an unpleasant voice — not the soprano I had had before, or the tenor I got later, but something that sounded like an instrument out of tune. And everything else was like my voice. My face was still fairly round and smooth, but my body wasn't. I couldn't fit into my clothes; so, though she was my enemy, N. had to get busy altering to fit me some sailor's trousers that her friend in the shop gave her on credit. And meantime I had a feeling that I was growing most unattractively, completely out of proportion. My legs, for instance, grew so long in a few weeks that they got in my way, and my hands had become too big in comparison with my body, which had remained thin and meager. When I closed my fists, I seemed to have those of an adult brigand, who wasn't me at all. I didn't know what to do with those murderous hands, I always wanted to hit out with them, so much so that if pride hadn't stopped me, I'd have fought with the first man I met — with a goatherd or a laborer, with anyone. But I didn't talk to anyone or fight with anyone, and I kept my distance from everyone even more than before, if possible. In fact, I felt so discordant, so hateful, that I almost wished I could shut myself up in some den where I'd grow in peace until the day when from a rather handsome boy I'd turn into a rather handsome young man. But it was all very well to talk of shutting myself up. How could I have borne being shut up when I felt I had an infernal spirit about me that turned me into a kind of wild beast, all day hunting a prey I didn't know? The beauty of the weather soured my mood; in winter, in a storm, I'd have been happier. The glory of the island in spring, which in other years I had loved so much, filled me with a sense of angry derision as I clambered on my long legs up and down the rocks and through the fields, like a chamois or a wolf, in a perpetual ferment that found no relief. Sometimes the triumphant joy of nature overcame me and pitched me into a strange ecstasy. The fantastic volcanic flowers, which crowded every corner of uncultivated ground, seemed for the first time to unfold the glory of their forms and colors to me, to invite me to share their joyous, varying delight . . . But at once the old hopeless anger would seize me, grown even sourer from shame at my pointless transports. I wasn't a sheep or a goat, to be satisfied with grass and flowers! And to revenge myself, I'd ruin the ground, tearing up the flowers, and stamping them ferociously underfoot.

My despair was like hunger and thirst, though it was something different. And, after longing to grow up, I was now almost sorry to have left what I had been before. What had I lacked, in those days? Nothing. If I wanted to eat, I ate. If I wanted to drink, I drank. If I wanted to have fun, I went out in *The Torpedo-boat of the Antilles.* And what about the island — what had it been to me until then? A realm of adventure, a beautiful garden. But now it seemed like a great voluptuous haunted house, where, like the wretched King Midas, I found no fulfillment.

I kept wanting to destroy; I would have liked some brutal job like stone breaking to occupy my body from morning to night in some futile, violent action that would somehow have distracted me. All the pleasures of summer which had once satisfied me now seemed laughably inadequate, and I did nothing without wanting to be aggressive and ferocious about it. I hurled myself into the sea as if going in to fight, the way a savage flings himself on his enemy clutching a knife between his teeth, and as I swam I wanted to smash and devastate the water. Then I would jump into my boat and row madly toward the open sea, and there on the waves sing desperately in my discordant voice, as if I was swearing violently.

When I came back, I lay down on the sunny sand, whose carnal warmth made it seem like a beautiful silken body. I abandoned myself, as if rocked in a cradle, to the slight weariness of midday, and wanted to clasp the entire beach to me. Sometimes I said soft words to objects, as if they were people. I'd start saying: "Oh, darling sand! Darling beach! Darling light!" And other more complex, tender things, really quite lunatic things. But it was impossible to embrace the great body of the beach, with its innumerable glassy sands that escaped through my fingers. Nearby lay a heap of seaweed steeped in the brine of spring and exuding a sweet, fermenting smell, like mould on grapes; and as if I'd turned into a cat, I bit the seaweed and scattered it furiously about for fun. I wanted to play too hard — to play with anything, even with the air. I would wink at the sky, opening and shutting my eyelids hard. The pure blue spread out above me seemed to approach, speckled like the starry firmament, then to burn up into a single great flame, then to turn black as hell . . . I'd roll over laughing on the sand; the pointlessness of those games maddened me.

Sometimes I would feel an almost brotherly pity for myself. I'd write my name on the sand: ARTURO GERACE, adding IS ALONE; and then afterward, ALWAYS ALONE.

And later, as I went up to the house, knowing that I'd find no one up there but an enemy, I'd be seized with infernal longings. I would decide to grab my stepmother by the hair, fling her to the ground, and hit her with my enormous fists, shouting: "I've had enough of your disgusting way of carrying on. You've got to stop it!" And then, in her presence, my evil ideas would vanish, and I would feel full of embarrassment and shame, as if there was no place for me there in the kitchen. The old bench on which I'd once loved to stretch out had grown too short for me. My long legs, my unnatural voice, and my hands encumbered me more than ever, and a gloomy sense of disaster filled me, a feeling that my present ugliness, and nothing else, was the reason why N. was avoiding me.

From a distance, I know, tragedies like that seem comical more than anything, and at this distance I can laugh at them myself. But you must admit that it's not easy to cross the final limits of that dreadful *awkward age* without anyone to confide in — not a single friend or relation. For the first time in my life, I really felt the full bitterness of being alone. I began to miss my father's presence desperately (he had now been away an unexpectedly long time — about two and a half months — after that period when he was so often on the island). In my longing I made a romantic portrait of him, not really very much like him, I must admit. I forgot completely that we had never confided in each other, and that there were some things I could never have told him — him above all. I even forgot the way he had behaved recently, which certainly wasn't conducive to conversation. I thought of W. G. as a kind of great affectionate angel, my only friend on earth, someone to whom I could confess all my worries, even the unconfessable, and who would understand and explain what I didn't understand. Gradually as that treacherous spring advanced (the last spring I was to spend on Procida), confusedly, tormentedly, I clung to the angelic vision of my father as to my only refuge and hope. All that was unreal and utopian in the dream I refused to admit. Hope sometimes saps the intellect like vice.

And I began to wait for Wilhelm Gerace every day, just as I had waited when I was a child, though for other reasons. I'd find myself on the beach every time the steamer arrived from Naples — faithfully, stubbornly — until, one fine day, he turned up. He arrived on the second afternoon steamer, which came into port about six. It was halfway through May, the days had lengthened, and at six o'clock there was still bright sunlight.

On the dock

When I saw him appear on the covered deck, listless and alone, holding back a bit from a small group of passengers who were to land, I began calling him from below with uncontrollable delight. But from his expression I realized at once that he was almost annoyed to find me there. And when we were together, he simply avoided greeting me, and asked me to go up to the house without him because he had to stay on there and would come up later on his own. "See you quite soon at home," he said. Then taking a look at me, although absently, he went on: "Hey, what's happened to you, Arturo? How you've grown these last months!" And actually when I stood before him I no longer had to look up as I had before, and his surprise had a note of coldness in it, as if he no longer recognized me, changed as I was.

That cold, quick remark was all the attention he gave me; in fact, even then he hardly seemed to be seeing me. "All right then," he said. "So long." And his confused and rather excited behavior betrayed his impatience to get rid of me.

This sort of thing had never happened before, on similar occasions. He was usually quite content to let me see him off when the boat left, and even happier if he had the surprise of finding me when he arrived. This new, inexplicable desire of his was worse than if he had hit me. I was so astonished, so humiliated, that I nearly asked him to give me his suitcase to carry up to the house, as if it was a favor; but immediately I was ashamed to the depths of my soul of such a servile temptation. I hadn't gone there to be his porter. And without asking him to explain his attitude, without a word, I left him, looking sneeringly indifferent.

I did not obey his order to go home, though; a kind of defiance made me want to stay on the dock. I took a few indolent steps and stopped a short distance from him beside a crate, and leaned against it sideways, like a crook in a horror comic. At all costs I didn't want to show him how bitterly mortified I was. But he was so pleased to be left alone that he didn't even bother to notice whether I'd obeyed him or not. He stood beside the gangway with his suitcase at his feet, as if waiting for someone who was soon to disembark from the steamer, and at the same time looking down disdainfully, without taking the least notice of me or of anything else. Who could this late passenger be he was waiting for? Could it be that this time he hadn't come to the island alone? As I wondered, I kept staring at him, deliberately arrogant, and noticed how much thinner he had grown. His suit, which was still his winter one, seemed twice as big as it had before. Underneath it, his unbuttoned shirt showed his white, white skin; obviously in spite of the wonderful warm weather, this year he had never been out in the sun.

He lit a cigarette and threw it away at once. I then realized that his hands were trembling, and that in spite of itself his stiff manner betrayed a determined effort to hide his anxiety — a dreadful, excited, childish anxiety. Obviously the mysterious person he was waiting for just then had a powerful hold on him, but, as a final effort of pride, he was trying to pretend to himself that he wasn't really waiting too vigilantly or attentively, too faithfully or too fascinatedly, which was why he kept looking down, fiercely determined not to look at the deck or the gangway toward which his tense nerves were yearning.

Who was he waiting for, then? As far as I could see, the few passengers landing at Procida had all disembarked from the steamer — in fact, those who were leaving had been allowed to go on to the boat and were just waiting for the signal to weigh anchor and set sail. "Perhaps," I thought sarcastically, "he's waiting for a convict!" In fact, the new inmates of the Penitentiary disembarked last of all, when all the other arrivals and departures were over, and the small crowd had cleared off the dock.

A suspicious character

I had thought *he's waiting for a convict* only as a kind of ironical guess, without realizing that I had actually hit on the truth. Just then I noticed that the van from the Penitentiary, which I hadn't seen before, was waiting at the entrance to the square, and that a guard in a grayish green uniform and with a bayonet was walking up and down near the steamer. This was a sure sign that some new guests for the castle of Procida were on board, shut up in the strong room in the hold, waiting for the two guards to bring them to land. There was another short wait — perhaps a minute long — during which my father, with an extreme effort of will, seemed to turn cold, still, and apathetic, as if what was just going to happen, or anything else on earth for that matter, meant nothing at all to him.

He still kept looking down, though suddenly I saw him look up and turn his flashing, childish blue eyes instinctively toward the covered deck. At that same moment, the trio he had been waiting for, which the islanders were by now quite used to, appeared on the deck and made for the gangway. And then an unusual feeling — a kind of wretched, devilish feeling — came over me.

As a rule, whenever a trio like that appeared on the island, my heart immediately went out to the prisoner. He might look like the most abject, frightful, wretched sort of rascal, but that didn't matter. He was a prisoner, and so, as far as I was concerned, he was an angel. As soon as I saw him, I felt a sense of brotherhood, had visions of escape, and while as a sign of respect I looked away, wanted to call out how much I sympathized. This time, though, I had no sooner glanced at the new prisoner than I felt a really savage dislike for him, a dislike that kept me from making out what he really looked like, or considering him anything but horribly ugly (a judgment that simply wasn't true!). From the very first moment, in fact, I loathed him. I almost longed, viciously, that the prison rules would make the guards treat him cruelly, hurt him and insult him as they went along the dock instead of escorting him with that protective air of theirs.

As, with hostile eyes, I watched the prisoner going quickly past, what I noticed most about him was that he was extremely young; he looked even younger than a convict was allowed to be. His face and handcuffed hands were tinged with that kind of grayish pallor which dark skins get in prison, but even this gloomy shade had not managed to make him look any older. Instead it hardened the air of young plebeian brutality — a common quality, but in him very striking — that showed in his face, particularly in the curves of his lips and in the way his dark hair grew. This dark vitality — something worse than impudence, and to me seeming downright savage — at once appeared to me to be his true form: an oblique image, mysterious because of its blackness, and one that from the start filled me with angry, contradictory feelings.

His head was drooping forward on his chest with a very remorseful look that seemed, in him, just a matter of his particular circumstances at the time, or perhaps only ironic. And, in fact, his body contradicted the expression on his face, for his walk and movements were all those of fresh, gay, aggressive adolescence. He was of medium height, but, being so much more vigorous than my father, at first sight looked no shorter. For the journey he had put on his best civilian suit (snappily cut, brand new and flashy), as prisoners, especially new ones, sometimes do, just out of impudence, but in those clumsy clothes his body moved as if he had been dressed like a jockey — free and untamed, happy and lithe.

He looked as if at heart he regarded his own sentence as something to be proud of, something that united the two most arrogant, most envied things imaginable: self-assertion and adventure. (Later on I was able to explain this attitude of his quite reasonably, as his vaunted imprisonment in the end seemed to me rather laughable. And I should think his crime must be, too . . . But in those days, I thought that green youth must be a murderer, with a real life sentence. And his very casualness seemed to me to have a promethean air about it, which I'll tell you about later.)

Apart from various romantic images, during the few moments the scene lasted I was given a sensibility that was like insight, the sort of thing found sometimes in women, or in animals. I realized, for instance, immediately and for certain, that my father already had known that prisoner — not just that day, but before; he look he gave him will always remain in my heart. His eyes (which to me were still the most beautiful in the world) were like two mirrors when some celestial form was passing, and had grown clear and fabulously blue, without a trace of their usual shadow. Their expression might have meant faithful greeting, imaginative understanding, or wretched, desperate welcome, but, more than anything, it meant imploration. It seemed that Wilhelm Gerace was asking him for charity. But what on earth could he be asking from that wretch, who wasn't even allowed to say a word or make a sign? One look, in answer to his look of adoring friendship, was all that he could be asking. And this single thing that my father begged, and that could have been given him, was refused. What's more, though the convict saw him as he passed, his childish face

deliberately looked as insultingly bored, disgusted, and scornful as
he could make it, and his dark eyes turned away. All this lasted
only a few seconds, the time it took for the dreary trio to reach the
prison van. I saw my father break away from where he was, as if unconsciously trying to follow them. The policeman on guard
pushed him back, and only when the wagon door slammed was he
allowed to pass; when he reached it, the wagon was already starting
up. Then I saw him stop a moment, as if uncertain, then run a few
steps in the direction of the wagon waving desperately, with almost
comical pointlessness — the gesture of a mother made sick by suffering, who flings herself from the restraining arms about her, and
with a cry of denial dashes down the steps into the street below
where the mourners, carrying their small burden, have already left
the street door and are disappearing around the corner.

Then he stopped, and stood there idly for a while, without remembering the suitcase he had left near the gangway. A boy
came and tugged his coat to remind him of it, and he went back
mechanically to pick it up. I was still there before him, beside
the crate, but he just didn't notice; probably he hadn't noticed
me the whole time I had been there. I saw him walking up
through the square, alone with his suitcase and drooping at the
shoulders, which seemed to have grown curved. And then after
a few minutes, feeling numb and sluggish, I left the dock.

Assunta

As far as I could remember, that was my father's longest stay on
the island; he arrived, as I said, about the middle of May and
didn't leave until the winter. A wonderful, unchanging summer
reigned on the island the whole time; while in the House of the
Guaglioni the weather rose, dark and inconstant, toward the final
storm . . . I'll start at the first important thing that happened to me
that summer. It happened a few days after my father's arrival, perhaps in the third week of May.

* * *

One of N.'s friends was a widow about twenty-one called Assuntina. Although I saw her often, I had never noticed that she was more attractive than the others who came to the house. The only thing that distinguished her from them, and that made me notice her, and perhaps be less churlish toward her, was the fact that she limped a bit because of an illness she had had as a child. This handicap of hers seemed rather attractive to my skeptical and peevish eyes, especially because, out of some kind of basic vanity, she often enjoyed posing as a melancholy invalid, though she was now bursting with health and youthful exuberance. Her friends and relations, to console her for what she had suffered and then later for her widowhood, had always spoiled her, had given her special attention, special affection, and she had grown up with vulnerable soft ways, like the Oriental languidness of a favorite cat.

Although she was very short and had tiny bones, her body was well formed and rather plump, but, as I've said, I had never even noticed. To me she was just like a bundle, neither more nor less than other women.

Her skin was dark, and rather olive, and her black hair was long and straight.

From our kitchen window, looking out across the sloping countryside, you could see a long lane going down into the valley, curving like a stream, and down at the bottom you could make out the hut where she lived with her family. They were peasants with some land of their own who went to work every day where it lay on the other side of the island, but because of her illness she was excused from farmwork, and so, as she had no children, in summer she often spent most of her time alone in the hut. If I happened to pass it, I often saw her sitting outside the door, slicing vegetables for the family's soup or combing her hair in front of a little mirror, wetting the comb in a basin. When she saw me, she would fling back her hair, smiling uncertainly, and lean her head a little on one side while she waved me good-bye with her hand. Sometimes I would answer her with a quick *good day*, and sometimes I didn't answer at all.

She had always been one of N.'s friends, but that spring she

came to the House of the Guaglioni much more often; N. was
pleased enough to see her and so was Carmine, whom she often
held in her arms while N. was busy in the kitchen. Almost every
day when I went home at about three or four in the afternoon to
have something to eat, I'd find her there, and she would greet me
when I came in with the same silent smile that just touched her
closed, full lips and veiled her black almond-shaped eyes. But I
took no notice of her smiles or of her. I had other things on my
mind. And as the spring advanced and I began staying out of
doors for the whole day, I very rarely met her.

One afternoon a few days after my father's arrival, I was wandering around the countryside, a prey to that terrible mood which
had been hanging over me for some time like a curse. No
summer had ever been so lonely, so miserable, and my father's
presence on the island, instead of consoling me as I had dreamed
it would, increased the strange feeling I had of being a sort of
wretched animal hated by the whole universe. Now that he was
back, Wilhelm Gerace obstinately avoided my company as he
never had in past summers. And ever since the evening he had arrived, after the disappointment I'd felt when he disembarked, I
suspected that he was repudiating me because of the change (so
very much for the worse) in my appearance. Every time he looked
at me I thought that I could see him judging me critically, feeling
surprised and antagonistic as if he no longer recognized his son
Arturo in such an ugly creature. And his eyes, like two frozen
pools, seemed to reflect back to me every clumsy thing I did, so
that, unlike Narcissus, I fell furiously out of love with myself. I
ended up longing to return to the time when W. G. at least used
to say, "Well, you're not too bad. You're not my son for nothing!"
After I'd sighed for so many years to grow tall enough to catch up
with him, now that I was near him, my height embarrassed and
shamed me. I got the impression that he considered it oddly intrusive, something to be regarded with dislike or suspicion, and I
wished I could go back to being small.

   I didn't, of course, give up my pride in the meantime. I returned coldness with coldness. And as I wanted to get away from his insulting treatment — voluntarily, at least without giving him the initiative — I behaved as if I was avoiding him no less than he was avoiding me.

Well, that's what my life had come to: my father pushed me away, my stepmother kept away from me, as if I'd been a snake. Anyway, anything is better than arousing pity, and I aroused pity in no one. In the evening I came home with a bold, mysterious air, as if I had spent the whole day captaining a band of robbers or a fleet of pirate ships. At times I wished that I was a real monster of ugliness — say an albino with fangs for teeth and one eye hidden under a black patch — so that, just by appearing, I'd have made everyone shake with terror.

On one of those afternoons I happened to pass Assuntina's house. I caught a glimpse of her greeting me from behind a window, and I don't think I even answered her, but as I went on, I heard her little limping step running close behind me and her voice calling: "Gerace! Gerace! Arturo!"

The corals

I turned around. "Hallo . . ." she began. "How on earth are you here? It's so long since I saw you . . ."

I noticed that she was using the formal *voi* for the first time in addressing me; and remembered that in the past she had always used the *tu*. "Hallo," I answered, and, not knowing what else to add, I eyed her from head to foot with the dark, disdainful air of a tiger meeting a family of lion cubs in the jungle.

Her bare feet on the dry dust were as dirty as if she had been walking in mud. She explained to me at once that she had been busy washing her feet when she saw me pass, and had run to catch up with me without even drying them. And as she explained this, she looked down at her tiny feet in an eloquent way that was meant to mean: *Excuse this mud, or rather accept it gratefully as a sign of my interest.*

Then she looked at me again, but still half looking down, shyly, with an expression that was half reproachful, half servile. "I was just getting ready to go up to your house," she went on. "But, anyway, I already knew you wouldn't be there at this time. At one time I used to see you there, but now, absolutely never! Not now or at any other time!"

Her singsong voice seemed almost complaining as she said this, and in its gentle weakness sounded like the noise dogs or donkeys make when they're accusing you or wrongs you don't understand.

"I have a feeling," she went on after a pause, "that you must have a girlfriend down in the village, to make you stay away from home all day!"

"I haven't a single girlfriend!" I declared, glum and haughty.

"Haven't you? Haven't you really got a girlfriend? Oh, I don't know that I really believe that . . ."

She was daring to disbelieve me! All the same, this wasn't as insulting from a woman as it would have been from a man, and all I did was pick up a stone and hurl it far away, threateningly, without deigning to answer.

"And if you really haven't got a girlfriend, why are you out all day? I've been to your house a hundred times, and a hundred times not found you there. Not in the morning, not in the afternoon."

"And what business is it of yours?"

"Mine? . . . Oh, now, you mustn't be offended. If you are, I'll feel small and won't know what to say. But I don't want to lie to you. What business is it of mine? Well, it is just a little bit, just a very little bit, my business. And the reason is a secret of mine . . . a secret I could tell you alone, and not anyone else . . . You know, if you really wanted to know it, I'd almost — almost, mind you — tell you this secret now, but if you don't want to know it I won't tell you."

I made a face in answer, that clearly meant: *As far as I'm concerned, you can say it or not say it, I don't care in the least. Do just what you like.*

"Well, then? Shall I tell you or not? All right, I'll tell you because I really can't go on bottling this up any longer. Well, this is the way it is," she began in her slow singsong soprano. "When I enjoy coming to your house (and I go there every day, every morning and evening — even with this bad leg of mine), I come for just one reason and no other. Of course I come because I'm friendly with Nunziata, and then because I'm fond of your little brother, Carminiello. Of course. Everyone knows that, but it's not the real reason. The real reason is something else (and that's the secret I was telling you about). I go there mainly in the hope of seeing you!"

At this my face was aflame. I had never thought a woman could make such a bold declaration so naturally. But she didn't even blush. No, she looked at my cheeks and laughed instead — sweetly, sensually — and I caught a glimpse of her wet pink gums that made her teeth sparkle.

"Well, now, you know my secret and no one else need know it. Oh, yes, it's been ages since I've thought of anything else — since before Easter, I swear. You must have seen that I'm always here alone in the afternoon, so every day I start brooding about it . . . and brooding. You're a man, of course, and so you don't brood. Men have got only one idea in their heads and that's to run round in circles the whole time, drinking in cellars, in taverns . . . They don't brood. But women do! And when I saw you dashing past, like today, I always thought: *He might just stop in sometimes and cheer poor Assuntina up a bit, as she's here all alone.*"

There was a pause. She glanced fleetingly at me through lowered eyelids. "But then," she went on at last, "I thought that maybe I'd do better to forget this idea. I even seemed to hear an old wise woman's voice telling me: *Oh, Assunti . . . he's dashing off because he's got a date with a girl. Who knows how many pretty girls he has? After all, you're not very attractive (even not counting your bad leg). And then, compared with him, you're pretty old already.*"

When she had said this, she was silent again, looking almost proud of her sadness, and remained there looking down virtuously, her small dark hand playing meantime with a string of corals around her neck.

I didn't know what to say, so I exclaimed in a rush, boldly, aggressively: "What lovely corals you've got!"

"Yes, it's true, they're really rather nice," she said, pleased, yet a little melancholy. "And this isn't all I've got in the way of coral. I've got some others that match this necklace exactly: earrings, a bracelet, and a beautiful pin, in fact a complete *parure*." (She actually used this French word, I remember exactly.) "Of course, I can't put them all on together, especially when I've been in mourning," she said regretfully. Her voice softened, grew languid. "I keep them at home," she told me. "Upstairs in my little bedroom. If you like nice coral, why don't you come sometime, and I'll show them to you. Whenever you like, some time or other . . ."

And she glanced at my face. I showed no sign of accepting or refusing her complimentary invitation. As if treacherously, then, she asked me: "Well, where are you going just now?" And her dark face was suffused with a blush that looked quite unlike shame or modesty — rather the opposite, I'd say.

I didn't know what to answer. In fact, I didn't even know where I was going or, rather, I wasn't going anywhere in particular. "Well, it's certainly very hot at this hour," she went on, "and everyone's asleep . . ." As she said this, under her oblong, very thickly lashed eyelids, which seemed to weigh down on her eyes, she gave me a look that spoke clearly as if she were an odalisque and I a sultan!

The little bite

And, taking my hand with an important, mysterious smile, she led me with her into her little house. And there, under my very eyes, the first thing she did was finish washing her feet, very carefully. Then she took off the coral necklace, which she put on the table beside the bed, and then she took the pins out of her smooth, neatly parted hair (it looked like untying the ribbons of a raven black bonnet).

And so, that day, I first made love. While the great hour lasted, my eyes would stray, now and then, to the coral necklace lying there beside the bed, and since then the sight of coral has always brought back my first impression of love, with its flavor of blind joyous violence, of precocious ecstasy. The fact that I tasted its flavor with a woman I didn't love doesn't matter. I liked it all the same, and I like it still very much, and occasionally at night I dream of those corals again.

As the afternoon wore on, Assunta advised me to leave, as her family would soon be returning. Before seeing me off, she held a mirror out and a comb for me to do my hair, and when I saw myself in the glass, I noticed that I had a tiny wound on my lower lip, from which a drop of blood was trickling. With a shock I realized what had caused it so recently: a little while before, at the very moment when I was making love to Assunta, I had had to bite my lip until it bled so as not to shout another name, Nunziata!

From that moment it was as if, there in front of that small looking glass, I had had an extraordinary revelation. I thought, that is, that only then had I understood what in fact I wanted from my stepmother: not friendship, not motherhood, but *love* — what men and women do together when they're in love. And so I made this remarkable discovery; that therefore, without any doubt at all, I was in love with N. So it was she who was the *first love* of my life that novels and poetry kept talking about. I loved Nunz, and clearly, without realizing it, had loved her from that famous afternoon when she arrived, maybe from the very moment she appeared to disembark on the dock with her shawl over her head and her smart little high-heeled shoes. I was now so certain of it that I remembered all the unlucky ups and downs, all the difficulties and sufferings that had kept me prisoner from that distant afternoon until this day, and everything that I hadn't been able to explain before now seemed to me quite clear. I looked back on all the months we had gone through like a crazy haphazard journey through storms and upheavals, the ship heeling over, until I was shown, to give me my bearings, the Pole star. Well, here was my Pole star: she, Nunz, my first love. The discovery at first flooded me with radiant, thoughtless exultance; then at once I realized my desperate fate. Of all the women who existed in the world, if there was one who was completely impossible for me, supremely inaccessible to my love, it was N., my stepmother and the wife of Wilhelm Gerace.

Until a moment before, when I didn't yet know that I loved her, I could allow myself the hope of going back to her, of deserving her sweet friendship again, but now I was allowed no hope at all. What is more, I should have been thankful for the state of war which N. maintained between herself and me, for at least it did not give my criminal impulses any opportunity to show. And that wasn't all: thanks to the war that divided us, I could still without too much danger or remorse stay in Procida, in the same house as my love, and avoid the unbearable punishment of never seeing her face again.

Intrigues of love

This was how I found a way again of putting off a farewell that now seemed to me a duty and a necessity; and the summer, which as usual crowded my days with variety and movement, helped me to put it off. Each day after lunch I went to Assuntina's and found her waiting, and there in her small room I stilled my restlessness a little. She was astonished that, though I always made love to her, I never gave her a single kiss, not even the smallest and simplest, the kind you would give a sister. I told her I didn't like kisses, that I thought them sloppy. But the truth was quite different: the truth was, I couldn't ever forget that first and only kiss of mine, the one I had given N. I'd have felt that I was betraying N. if I had kissed this other woman, whom I didn't love, anyway.

My memory (setting me straight where I had been mistaken in the past) filled that kiss I'd given N. with all the glowing flavor of love, with sensual delight, with passionate understanding. I felt that in the short moment I had kissed N., I had known all the divinity that belongs to true love alone, all that I could never feel with Assuntina. When I saw the shameless way she behaved I thought of N.'s behavior — how modest, how pure it was — and my heart was torn with regret. And then, seeing my face darken, Assuntina would ask me: "Well, what's the matter?"

"Let me alone," I'd say. "I'm feeling sad."

"Can't I cheer you up?" she'd ask.

"No, you can't cheer me up," I'd say. "And neither can anyone else. I'm just a miserable wretch."

All the same, although I didn't love Assuntina, I was pleased to have a mistress, and proud above all, so proud that I wanted to tell everyone the news (apart from just my father; him, I'd have been ashamed to tell — I don't know why). Assuntina, instead, did nothing but urge me to keep it absolutely secret, and I submitted to this sacrifice, as was proper and honorable. But I found a way of making it clear (by my rather fatuously conceited air) that there was something in my life . . .

There was someone I specially hoped would get to know about it . . .

One day, I remember, I had the notion of buying a few yards of lace (on credit, of course), or some women's garters, or something like that, from the shop where the owner was a friend of N.'s, warning her not to breathe a word about it to anyone, particularly to my stepmother: in such a way that she would realize there was a mysterious woman in my life. But alas, when I got to the shop door, I lacked the poise to go in, and turned back without doing anything about it.

Of course when I thought up the idea, I certainly had no illusions about the shopwoman's discretion; on the contrary, I was quite sure in advance that she'd never be able to keep it from N. I say *quite sure*, but it would be truer to say: *I was counting on it.*

Assuntina remained Signora Gerace's eagerly loyal friend, but was careful to keep her own romance with her stepson Arturo hidden. So, thanks to her discretion, my stepmother was completely in the dark about this important bit of news — no less than Carminiello. Morally and logically, this ought to have cheered me, but instead, it rather irritated me.

In fact, my ambition to display my conquest to everyone (so much that I'd gladly have printed it in the newspapers) was aimed rather specially and precisely, I think, at my stepmother. At the thought that some gossip, some spy, for instance, might go and breathe a hint of it into her ears, I actually burst out laughing all by myself, without wanting to. Well, that's all; my tormented heart would have felt it was a kind of success if, somehow or other, she had come to know about it . . .

The Lano

But why *a success?* Why the devil would that have been a success? There's no doubt about it, answering this question would have set me a deep problem. But I didn't worry much about problems when I had got my dreams.

While I pretended to respect Assuntina's discretion with N., in fact I was nursing quite contrary plans myself. These plans took deceitful and complicated forms. Every now and then when I was with N., I let fall some half-revealing phrase, or I gave Assuntina burning looks, or made small conspiratorial signs to her, pretending that I thought my stepmother wasn't looking at us just then . . . Assunta, being cunning, would look like a saint; and later, in the hut, she would take it up with me. "Do be careful! Do be more careful!" she said.

But I'd answer reassuringly. "Oh, go on, don't worry, my stepmother knows nothing about anything, she's got no more brains than Carmine. All she thinks about is prayers; she doesn't know or see anything else at all. Can you believe it, if she were to turn up at the door this very minute she'd think we were in bed together just sleeping peacefully like brother and sister."

As far as this, at least, went (that my stepmother was too slow to understand), I wasn't lying; no, that was exactly what I thought.

One day as the afternoon drew to a close and the time drew near when I had to leave Assuntina, I started pressing her with various excuses, to come along the road toward the House of the Guaglioni with me. And along the road, especially the last part of it, I suddenly began embracing her, putting my arms around her waist.

"Look out! What are you doing?" she protested, trying to free herself. "Not here, not in the road! Someone might see us!"

"Oh, who do you think's going to see us?" I answered. "There's no one around." But, in fact, a moment before I took her in my arms, I had seen, up there at the kitchen window in the House of the Guaglioni, a furtive curly-headed shadow that drew quickly back behind the grating as soon as the pair of us had passed the last curve in the road and emerged at the top of the lane, right under the window.

My stepmother's attitude in those days was rather peculiar, as even a not very sharp observer would certainly have noticed. She seemed to have fallen into a kind of absentminded daze, and her face was sad and pale, almost livid. She did the housework with her usual familiar movements, but heavily, wearily, and at times with an absent, incoherent air, as if her body was moving unwillingly and was quite detached from her mind. Her mildness had given way to a nervousness that was almost bad temper. I heard her scolding Carmine; she even went as far as to answer my father shortly; and her friends complained that they found her irritable and quite unlike her usual self.

One day when I looked up, I surprised her looking at me. For a moment her eyes, when they met mine, instinctively kept on looking at me, full of crude, throbbing pain; then she quickly became self-conscious and withdrew under her pale eyelids.

I don't remember if what happened afterward took place on the afternoon of that same day or on one of the following days. I was going up the lane with Assuntina, and as usual kept glancing up at the window in the House of the Guaglioni until I caught a glimpse of that familiar little shadow hiding up there behind the grating.

And then, on the spot, I seized Assunta passionately, and though I had never kissed her before, planted a beautiful kiss right in the middle of her face.

The quarreling women

Sometime the following morning, landing my boat on the beach after I had been out at sea, I had the notion of going up to the house for a minute — to change an oar, I think, or for some other reason of the kind. And right from the bottom of the terrace I was surprised to hear coming from the kitchen shrill feminine shrieks mingled with Carmine's crying. When I reached the French window I saw something completely unexpected. In the kitchen, besides my brother, who was yelling desperately in his basket, I saw my stepmother beside herself with rage and screaming at Assunta as if she wanted to tear her to shreds.

Assuntina, who looked completely astonished and confused, burst into tears when I came in and begged me to watch what was happening, as she couldn't understand the least thing about it. She explained that she had turned up there a short while before to say hello to Nunziata as usual, and had taken Carmine from his basket to rock him in her arms, as she so often did, and that at this point my stepmother had leaped on her like a wild beast and snatched Carmine away. And then (as Carmine began crying because she'd snatched him so brutally), Nunziata had unfairly started scolding her — Assunta — accusing her of just that, of making the child cry. And so she'd gone on yelling and scolding, and had ordered her never to pick him up from then on, because he (the baby) loathed her (Assunta) as much as smoke in his eyes, and if she just touched him he wanted to cry. Well, at that point I had turned up, Assunta concluded through her tears; now that I was here, I could bear witness to her sworn testimony that it wasn't her fault my little brother was crying. She certainly wasn't going to stand for that sort of treatment, as if it was a crime to pick up a baby.

While Assunta was justifying herself, my stepmother, instead of being soothed, was growing more and more furious, until her face was suddenly transfigured, like a fury. "Don't show yourself in my house again!" she burst out, yelling; and shook her head in the atavistic way of quarrelsome women in the slums. "I don't want you here! I'm mistress in this house!" she shouted, completely beyond herself. And suddenly she got ready to hurl herself on Assunta.

Luckily I came between them in time to stop her, seizing her by the wrists and pushing her hard against the wall. There, nailed against it, she was too proud to struggle. Through her wrists I could feel all her muscles trembling, developing a desperate ferocity, and her eyes looked just like the glow of two sublime and wretched stars flung about in a storm. White beneath the tumbled hair stuck to her forehead with sweat, she turned her face from me and stuck it out toward her enemy. "Get out!" she yelled, as if carried away by hatred. And added: "Get out, you're *marked by God!*"

This *marked by God* is something heartless villagers say with malicious vulgarity to insult the lame, the crippled, and other unfortunates. Assunta burst into sobs at her viciousness, and limped toward the door. And I marched off indignantly, leaving my now ugly-looking stepmother where she was, and taking Assunta a little way down the road, as seemed to be my duty.

Although she seemed grateful for my gentlemanly care of her, as soon as we were alone she began blaming me for my indiscretion. "If you had been as careful as I told you, your stepmother would never have suspected a thing, because she isn't malicious. And now look what's happened. I believe she's found everything out. And though when I was there with her I pretended to believe her excuse about Carminiello, I'm not such a fool as not to realize that it was just an excuse not to fling the truth in my face. Besides, now that I come to think of it, she's been looking at me nastily for several days! The truth is — you take it from me — that you've been too careless and she has seen us meet. And according to her way of thinking, what we're doing is a terrible sin, and a woman like me who does it is loose and dishonored. And so, as she's a good woman, she's disgusted with my friendship and doesn't want to know me any more. Well, all right, whatever she likes! But she's wrong, you know; because I'm not unmarried, I'm a widow, and if a widow lives with someone, it's not so much of a sin as if she were unmarried. Oh, not nearly so much! Oh, well, I already knew she was a dreadful prig . . . but I didn't know she was so vicious! Who'd suppose such a sweet woman, who looked as gentle as a dove, could turn into that fierce, ugly eagle!"

My stony stepmother

While Assunta was letting off steam we got a good way down the lane, and so, as from a distance she saw one of her relations going back to the hut, she begged me to leave her so as not to arouse any unpleasant suspicions, and I left without arguing and went off by another path.

I was glad of this chance that allowed me to be alone a little and to abandon myself, without anyone to see me, to my deep, irrational exultation.

I shouldn't have felt exultant, actually, but remorseful. Assunta didn't dream how guilty I really was. She accused me of being indiscreet without ever having guessed what was worse: that my indiscretion hadn't been a matter of carelessness, but quite deliberate. All the same, though I was conscious of my guilt, in my heart I felt no remorse; no, I felt an intimate, triumphant joy that made me walk so lightly that I felt as if my feet weren't touching the ground.

Almost without noticing it, I took the road up to the house. It was about noon; in the kitchen Carminiello was sleeping peacefully in his basket, and my stepmother was standing by the table, where things were laid out as usual for her to prepare the pasta. The scene a little earlier had interrupted her, and now her hands were moving weakly over the layer of pasta as if they wanted to get busy with it but hadn't the strength to do so. And her face was so white, so staring and stupefied, that it made me think of a serious illness.

I asked her if my father had come down from his room yet, and as she couldn't find the strength to speak, she moved her eyelids a little to answer no, but even this small movement seemed to cost her such an effort that her whole face, and especially her lips, began to tremble.

Then, scared by her appearance, I asked her: "What's the matter? Are you feeling ill?" (Since she'd started keeping me at a distance because of that famous kiss, I had begun a new habit: that of using the formal *voi* when I spoke to her. And I couldn't have said whether I meant to be deliberately respectful or just sulky.)

She looked at me tremulously, without answering; but as if my pity had removed her last power of resistance, she suddenly fell on her knees and, hiding her face in a chair, burst into terrible dry sobs.

"What's the matter?" I said. "Tell me what's the matter!" I felt a tender longing to caress her, at least to stroke her hair, but her forehead and her hands, ruined by housework, looked so pale that I didn't dare to touch her. I was afraid I would make her die. Meantime, between her sobs, she began to say, in a tone of voice that didn't seem like hers — an adult, rending voice: "Oh, I'm damned, I'm damned. God . . . won't forgive me . . . ever again . . ."

Words of adoration came crowding instinctively to my lips. I wanted to say: "You're a saint in heaven to me, though! You're my angel!" But I realized I'd frighten her. Just now, I thought, it would be better to talk to her like a father, or something like that. And, though in a voice that, in spite of myself, expressed only a laughing and brazen passion, not a fatherly severity, I said to her: "Oh, come on, now! Damned? Get along with you! Drop it! Don't be a silly!"

At last her cruel sobs turned into tears, and her small voice was recognizable again, though overwhelmed by a secret torment. "And how could I," she said accusingly through her tears, "have used those wicked words to that poor creature? It isn't as if it's her fault, having a disability! Oh, saying that's worse than murder! I'm ashamed of living! And what shall I do now, what shall I do? I must go and find that poor girl and beg her to forgive me, beg her to forget what I said to her, and to come back here like before . . . But no, I can't! I can't!" And as if she was afraid of herself, she hid her mouth between the palms of her hands, while her eyes, at the thought of Assuntina, grew larger with a perfectly savage hatred.

"Oh, what shall I do? What ought I to do?" she murmured.

And between these questions she turned on me with a tearful, lost look that seemed to implore my help or advice, as if I were God. But her eyes had grown so beautiful just then that I no longer noticed their sorrow; in their black depths I seemed to find two magic mirrors, distant points of light, of absolute happiness. And I exclaimed in a rush: "D'you know what you ought to do? You ought to leave Procida with me. Then you'll never have to see Assunta again, if you hate her so much. Let's escape together, you and I and Carminiello. Anyway," I added rather bitterly, "my father doesn't care a hoot about any of us — he won't even notice, very likely, if we leave. We'll all three go and live in some marvelous place far from Procida — I'll choose it for you, and there you'll live like a queen!"

At my words she made a sudden movement and covered her face with her hands, but the violent blush that covered her right down to her neck and her bare arms was visible all the same. For a while she couldn't answer me, and her short breathing, rising to her throat, turned into a harsh, savage lament. At last she said: "Artù! . . . As you're still a boy, God will forgive you the dreadful things you're saying, the wrong . . ."

Perhaps she was going to say *the wrong you're doing,* but it seemed too severe a word to use, and she didn't finish. And at her rebuke, instead of being sorry, I was filled with a sense of revolt that was full of joy, that more than ever made me careless and crazy, and her voice reached me from behind the mask of her hands like a fabulous sound that hopelessly betrayed, still more than pity, the anguish of renunciation, and with it the balm of sweet gratitude.

I rushed up to her, and exclaimed: "Oh, please, look at me, look at my face, look into my eyes!" And armed with sweetness and with power, I took her hands from her face. For a moment her dismayed face flashed before me, still sweet, still rosy from its blush, but she had already jumped to her feet, and was so pale that she looked disfigured. She backed toward the wall.

"No! No! What are you doing?" she said, "Go away . . . Artù . . . Don't come near me if you don't want me to . . ." And then, turning her head around a little, she laid her forehead against the wall, frowning hard, as if in her weakness, which almost made her slither down to the floor, she was gathering all her nerves in a gigantic and desperate effort of will.

And without looking at me, she turned her face around to me, and it had become unrecognizable — furrowed, extinguished, with thick black eyebrows joining on her forehead, she looked like an image of some dark, soulless barbaric goddess, a real wicked stepmother.

"Artù," she said in a small toneless voice, that might have belonged to a woman of forty. "Before, I loved you . . . like a son. But now . . . I no longer love you."

Here her voice seemed convulsively stifled, and then she went blindly on with a sharper sound, discordant and almost hysterical: "And so, the less we see each other, and the less you talk to me, the better. Think of me as if I'd always been a stranger to you, because our relationship is dead forever. And I do beg you to keep away from me always, because when you're near me it gives me the creeps!"

I suppose that someone more experienced than me would have thought she was lying. And would even have said to her: "You ought to be ashamed, you awful old liar! At least you might learn to pretend a bit better. You can't even sound convincing with those terrible lies of yours, and have to lean back against the wall as if you were expecting to be struck by lightning. And you're trembling so hard that even from this distance I can see the goose-flesh on your arms."

As I listened to her I wasn't absolutely certain, though I did wonder whether her words really reflected her feelings. And this was enough to plunge me into agonizing sadness, as if I had suddenly been condemned to spend my life in a polar night. Impulsively I felt tempted to say: "If what you're saying is true, swear it!" But I didn't dare to; I was much too afraid she really would swear and make me definitely certain. What hurt me most was that word *creeps* that she had used, and I supposed that the obvious shudders, which actually gave her goose pimples while she was talking like that, were just the natural effect of the horror she felt for me. I was now almost reduced to believing that Assuntina wasn't mistaken in attributing to moral disapproval the scene N. had made. And to think I'd almost been flattered to have assisted at a jealous quarrel, even feeling a secret satisfaction at the idea that two women had got to the point of pulling each other's hair out for my sake, under my very eyes! Nothing was sadder than to have to give up such a sweet, enchanted absurdity for the ugliness of a cold and serious reality.

The little Indian slave girl

So deeply was I wounded by what she said that I couldn't speak and didn't answer. It was just at this point, perhaps, that Carmine woke up or my father turned up — I don't remember exactly which — but what's certain is that with these words of hers our talk was over.

And from that moment her attitude toward me remained the same, fixed. As the days went by, she never showed me any other face than that kind of soulless, barbaric image, with opaque eyes, and eyebrows that met to form a dark cross with the lines of her forehead. Oh, I'd rather she'd treated me like the beastliest step-mothers in stories. I'd rather have seen her turn into a murderous wolf than into that statue.

In the hope of making her forgive me, I even pondered, among other things, a scheme I had to abandon Assuntina noisily (assuming that she was lumping us both in the same moral disapproval). But I realized at once that in fact her horror of me had sprung up before I got mixed up with Assunta: it had started on the morning of my fatal kiss. No, even leaving Assunta would get me nowhere. There was no remedy for me. N. had a horror of me, and there was no hope of forgiveness.

I felt such a need to tell someone, at least, to be consoled, that sometimes I was even tempted to confide in Assunta, to tell her everything: my secret love for N., my desperation, and so on. But I always held back in time, especially because I was afraid that sooner or later Assunta would go and tell N. all that I'd confided in her, and obviously N.'s horror for me would reach its climax if she knew I loved her. A revelation like that would confirm the idea she already had of me, that I was a terrible monster of evil, a real incarnation of Satan. The thought of this was enough to make every desire to confide in her stick in my throat. So luckily there were some things Assunta never knew.

After all this, my mistress seemed less attractive than she had been, and sometimes I even disliked her crippled leg, which before had seemed to me so sweet. I was no longer tempted to boast of her, and I enjoyed being with her less and less. All the same, I went on going to her every day, for that hut was the only refuge left me. Assunta even said that I had grown more passionate than before. Maybe because the desperate flames I hid in my heart ended by blazing wherever they happened to be.

Besides, it sometimes happened that, even without my loving Assunta, a feeling of pity rose in me which burned almost like love. Just because I didn't love her, and didn't even find her attractive, or was actually fed up at being with her, I felt pity. So little, so naked on the straw mattress, with her small olive breasts, which had nipples the color of geraniums and were somewhat loose and long, making me think of goats', and with that straight loose hair of hers, she sometimes seemed to me like a being from another country, perhaps a little Indian slave. And I was her chief and did what I wanted with her. Then N., up there in the House of the Guaglioni, seemed to me like a great white chieftainess, blazing with scorn, and to chase away this suffering, fascinating image, I vented myself on Assuntina, almost ill treating her in my harsh ardor.

But I never kissed Assuntina again; my kisses always seemed consecrated to N. by a kind of holy decree that I couldn't infringe without sinning against love.

When, toward sunset, I left the hut, I was ashamed to have amused myself with a wretched little slave, as if it added to my unworthiness in the presence of N. I would linger alone in the countryside around there, over which towered the crumbling, massive, pink-washed walls of the House of the Guaglioni, and would never look up at that famous window again, knowing that anyway I would find it deserted. There, behind those walls,

among its sinister prohibitions, my castle N. lived, mighty and remote. From a distance she seemed to me taller than she was in
fact, and it seemed to me that all the angels of her dreams were
flying around her like flocks of splendid owls, and storks, and
seagulls, telling her to shun me night and day.

The Walled Country

O flots abracadabrantesques
A. R.

Dearer than the sun

MEANWHILE, WHILE I was living under the same roof as N. and feeling like a sinner in the courts of heaven, another castle had begun to have an even stronger hold over my mind. The island's Penitentiary, which to me had always seemed the gloomy dwelling of darkness (only slightly less hateful than death), was suddenly lighted up for me that summer in a resplendent flash, as in a chemical change, where black becomes gold.

The sun that summer seemed to shine pointlessly as far as Wilhelm Gerace was concerned. Something completely new was happening; at the height of summer my father spent the most glorious time of day shut up indoors, as if to him the weather seemed like an everlasting winter night. Obstinately, he fled from all the delights of summer, which we had always enjoyed so much together, and his white skin in July and August seemed to me mournful and unnatural. I felt that I was assisting at some unwholesome overturning of the universe.

Often, especially at first, I went up to him and, frowning heavily, urged him to come down to the beach with me or to go out in the boat. These invitations of mine were always scornfully refused, with an air of rather theatrical suffering. From his responses it appeared that this year he had decided on a contemptuous and vengeful hatred of sun, sea, and fresh air, which he had always loved so much. But at the same time he meant to offer up the renunciation of them as a sort of holy and propitiatory sacrifice, not unlike that of a devotee who flogs himself to become worthier of a deity.

Anyway, however mysterious he was, he couldn't help giving himself away (here I could still recognize the unearthly grace of his heart, which even in the most desperate straits always rather liked being mysterious). And from various remarks of his I wound up knowing without a shadow of doubt what his secret reason was (and, anyway, it was just what I had suspected).

Someone dearer than any other friend spent his days shut in by those four accursed walls. And how could he enjoy the summer that his friend was denied? No, he wanted to act out, hour by hour, his friend's sufferings; what is more, he wished he could have received a similar sentence, and would have counted it an honor except that if he had not been free himself, he would have lost every means of keeping in touch with his friend. His freedom was worth only this one thing, and the earth, with the summer and the sea and the sky, with the sun and all its planets, seemed like skeletons to him, and made him shudder.

Conventional pearls and roses

When my father came out with things like that, I was tempted to answer that I knew perfectly well what he was talking about, that I had seen that precious person from a distance of four yards on the dock, that I despised him with all my soul, and thought him a stinker, so loathsomely ugly that he was unworthy not just of friendship, but even of a glance. But I didn't say a thing; I frowned proudly and turned my back on my father as if I had not even been listening, and went away alone as usual, down toward the beach.

After that famous meeting of ours when he had come off the steamer, I had always avoided remembering the unknown youth I had seen passing with two guards on the dock. The scene that afternoon, overlaid by my own sorrows after it, lurked in the bottom of my mind, just as he had been relegated to the prison up there. He was something that I felt was unlucky for me, and just as I had avoided looking closely at his features that day, so now I avoided remembering him. If, in spite of myself, my thoughts happened to dwell on him, I couldn't make out any precise human figure, but only a kind of shapeless clay, gray and muddy and hideous.

And yet at the same time there flashed into my mind, with a kind of soaring elegance, the impudent, ingenuous way he'd walked to meet his fate. This attractive vision, like a sword crashing down on my scorn of him, bit into my heart with anguish, startling me. Suddenly, instead of an unfortunate ghost buried in prison, I saw a fabulous bandit, to whom perhaps even the police and the guards acted as servants.

And to betray me, various romantic prejudices of mine returned from my childhood to adorn him. When I was a child, the title of *convict* meant more to me than a coat of arms; and, I might add, it still meant as much to Wilhelm Gerace, who was grown up! Indeed (as I now realize) Wilhelm Gerace's devotion needed the crude glitter of something conventionally seductive like that to kindle it, and the theatrical figure of that *convict* suited his melancholy very well because it was everlastingly childish. In just the same way the theater audience wants conventional heroines to believe in *La Traviata, The Slave Girl, The Queen*. And thus every pearl in the sea eternally copies the first pearl, and every rose the first rose.

Metamorphoses

And so, though I didn't realize it, I had really known for some time why Wilhelm Gerace had been longing and tormenting himself so strangely since the autumn, but my dim realization of it, hidden away below my thoughts, was unraveling and growing more complex all through that feverish summer.

My father's few remarks were all that we said on the subject. I stopped asking him down to the beach or anywhere else, and we said no more about his secrets. This tortuous, tenacious silence was something I wanted, rather than he: a proof — my own proof — of my scorn for that anonymous creature on the dock. Perhaps I deluded myself that I could really bury his existence away under a gravestone like that, and thus rid him of his mysterious power, so much so that once, when I happened — I don't know how — to mention the Penitentiary to my father, I blushed with disgust and shame at myself.

Every day (late in the afternoon, usually), my father would leave his dreary confinement and go out, always alone. I had no need to spy on him to know just where he was going; and the towering fortress, which in the past I had always avoided on my walks — out of a kind of religious sense of propriety — was now girded around by a new prohibition, something strange and monstrous. Even today, I find it hard to describe what I then felt and moreover refused to examine. Perhaps it was a bit like what the Mosaic tribes must have felt about the temple of Baal in Babylonia, or something like that.

My father's remarks had confirmed that he and the prisoner on the dock already knew each other and had been friends before the famous day when I'd seen them come off the same boat at Procida. And the mysterious privilege — it couldn't be chance — that had brought him to the place my father loved proved that there was a kind of magic complicity between them. The young man's boastful air when he landed was not enough to convince me that he wasn't a friend of my father's, for insolence obviously came as naturally to him as spots to a leopard.

I didn't know what our prisoner's crime was. But I had reason to think it was serious, for petty criminals were very rarely sent to prison in Procida. Most likely, I thought, he was serving a life sentence, so I ended up by calling him the Lifer, to myself.

The idea that he was walled up for life might have consoled me a bit, but it really was cold comfort, however cruel. What I really felt was, that while on the one hand his having a life sentence limited his hold over my father, on the other it always made him seem much more impressive to him, as well as to me.

My childish, superstitious belief in my father's authority (a super-human authority that could perform every marvel) meantime began to return. I knew the law was that prisoners could receive visitors from outside only very rarely, and then for just a few minutes in the presence of a guard. Yet in some unplumbed corner of my mind I began to have a feeling that when my father went out each day, he went to meet the convict — that, thanks to some hidden power of subtle bribery, they met and talked together every day in some underground secret passage. Now, in the same slumbering corner of my imagination, as in a thick mist, these meetings of theirs took on an imprecise shape that was somehow mysterious and horrible. A strange clayey image, viscous and fluid as lava, represented the young prisoner to me — I don't know how — and by some hideous magic it was changing into my father, dissolving and reforming into a kind of formless, variable, improbable sculpture. And this inexplicable change had for me the secret value of dreams that seem senseless when one wakes, but that while one dreams them seem like unlucky omens.

And through the tangled horror of it all I began to feel — and this was worse than anything — the matchless proud grace that transfigured the figure I had seen on the dock. It was as if the young prisoner flung me an ironic greeting and, as he did so, changed from a foul monster into a charming heraldic character who yelled "Impostor!" at my scorn of him. My old childish prejudices came back pitilessly to make him seem more attractive . . . and in a flash the prison seemed to me like a castle of the Knights of Syria. Fabulous legendary adventurers sworn to a terrible vow crowded the walled palace where only my father was welcome, and their tragic enchantment held the island in thrall. On their worn faces their crimes and captivity were something seductive, like makeup on women's faces, and they all hid, and loyally protected, the mysterious place underground where my father met the figure from the dock.

Although the prison was so near, it now seemed to me located in some inhuman, unattainable dimension, a kind of gloomy Olympus. I now avoided not only going near it, but also even looking at it, as much as possible. In the boat I never went close to the North Point, behind which the castle overhangs the shoreless sea from the top of its rock base. And when I passed it from a distance, I always looked out to te open sea, turning away from that great irregular hulk which from a distance looked like a mountain corroded by tufa. I was so superstitious about it that as I sailed by, I felt things that I knew were false but that seemed almost like hallucinations. From the tufa shape behind me, I seemed to hear strangely melodious echoes calling together. And I was terrified by the odd suspicion that among them I suddenly heard my father's voice, as unreal as that of a fetish or of a dead man. There, in funereal splendor, he wandered with his wasted white face.

The end of the summer

We had now reached the end of September. One day I stayed out at sea so long that, almost without noticing, I let pass the hour in which I usually met Assuntina. When I landed, I judged from the sun's position that it must be about four in the afternoon, and in fact, from a short way off, I heard a quarter past four striking from the church tower. So I decided that it was too late to go to Assuntina's, and gave up the idea for that day. When I had pulled the boat onto dry land, I dragged my torn jersey and rope-soled shoes from under the rock where I always left them in the morning, and began walking without any precise object along some country shortcuts that led to the village.

The shadows of tree trunks and plants had already lengthened, and the colors were soft and fresh. Two months before, the island had still been aflame at the same time in the afternoon. The days had shortened since then. Summer would soon be over.

On other days, when I had been with Assuntina, I had never

really stopped to consider it. Today it was as if some wan, sad apparition with half-closed eyes had profited from my solitude, and had appeared to me and greeted me as he ran through the grass with a rustle of autumn. This greeting meant good-bye, as if here, today, I knew quite definitely that this was to be my last summer on the island.

In fact, those last months I had always — though very vaguely — thought of the end of that summer as the end of my time in Procida. But when I thought *summer*, I thought of some indistinct, boundless season, like a whole lifetime. I cheered myself with thinking confusedly that somehow the summer, just as it ripened the grapes, and olives, and other fruits in the garden, would somehow ripen my sour fate as well, and settle my sufferings with some great consoling explanation. But to have reached the end with my sufferings as sour as ever — this was something I couldn't believe, yet which I saw in the light and in the delicate gusts of wind, like a chill, ambiguous greeting. *Question without answer* was what that greeting meant, translated into words, and nothing, no one, said anything else to me, not even N.'s beautiful, motherly eyes, which turned to stone when they looked at me.

I walked on thoughtfully until I found myself on the step hill of the Two Moors, which ends in the Piazzetta of Monument and has a plain balustrade along its seaward, west side. At that hour it glowed, splendid and calm, between the orange-pink of its walls and the great golden reflection of the water. I have often mentioned this attractive little square, but maybe I haven't yet said that four streets led out of it. One, of course, was the hill of the Two Moors. Another was the one we often went along in the carriage when we were going down to the harbor. It continued on the opposite side of the square under another name and became my famous little road between the gardens. The last street and the widest was a very well paved road on the west, which snaked up to the highest point of the rock like a twisting lookout tower; the same balustrade that ran along the side of the square ran along its outer side, so that at that time of day it was, like the square, open to the full blaze of the sun, which turned it a wonderful orange-pink.

The Walled Country

This was the only road on the island that led to the gate of the Walled Country. (This was what people called the district where the Penitentiary stood, in memory of the old fortifications.) The van bringing new prisoners up from the harbor passed along it. I don't know how long it was since I'd been along it myself, because then, as far as I was concerned, it might as well not have existed on the island.

But that day I chose it instinctively. I didn't hesitate, I wasn't surprised, all I noticed was the pounding of my heart. It was as if, by breaking my own restrictions, I was doing something at once brave and very serious. The long ribbon of road was empty as far as the last visible turning, and it gave me a feeling of repose to climb into that enchanted quietness; its dreadful melancholy seemed almost to offer me a refuge. Below, the dolphin shape of the island lay in the play of its foam, and, with the smoke of its little houses, with its murmur of voices, it seemed a long way away from me and no longer magical, for I was searching for more powerful magic. I was going forward to a place beyond the year, a place where the end of summer brought neither hope nor farewell. Up there in the unhappy buildings of the Walled Country they knew another climate, one of desperation, of maturity, of proud ruin, one that kept them far from the world in which mothers existed.

Near the top of the hill, on the left, opposite the balustrade, the first buildings of the Penitentiary arose — the houses of the men connected with it, the offices, and the hospital. At the end, the hill opened out on a terrace that on two sides showed the fresh blue of the open sea. Here arose the gigantic gate of the Walled Country, with its great stone arch, and with sentry boxes cut in its pillars. In front of one of the sentry boxes an armed sentry always marched, but he didn't refuse to let free people pass, because beyond the gate, apart from the prison compound, there was a good-sized village with old churches and convents in it.

When I reached the terrace, I saw my father a few yards away. He was half sitting on the balustrade with his back to the view, and with a kind of whimsical indifference was letting the west wind ruffle his hair. I stopped to look at him, but he didn't notice me. His thin, angular face against the light of the setting sun seemed almost adolescent under the golden fuzz of its neglected beard. After a while he moved away; his faded blue coat was unbuttoned across his white chest and now and then flapped in the wind. He went under the arch of the gate, and I followed him, walking slowly to keep at a distance. I now felt that right from the start I had gone there to spy on him, and I realized that, right from the beginning of the summer, perhaps, I had been getting ready to track down his mystery some time or other.

The hunt

The gateway was a gloomy passage whose plaster walls were painted from top to bottom with crosses in dusty black; past it, emerged the main square of the Walled Country, which was so big that it looked like a square in a large town, but was always strangely empty. On the left of this square, at the bottom of a small steep-sided paved hollow, a gate guarded a great bare yellow courtyard with enormous rectangular buildings around it. On the gate, HOUSE OF CORRECTION was written around a colored picture of Our Lady of Pity.

This was the entrance to the Penitentiary. From there on, beyond various low-walled buildings, the prison hill rose behind the Main Square as far as the old Castle, which towered on the right of the village cluttered below it. For a moment, my heart in my mouth, I expected to see my father march confidently down into the hollow and before my very eyes vanish, as if by a miracle, through the gate. But instead he turned to the right and went

around the square, making for the high ground where, on a terrace of ancient rock in a maze of cuttings, slopes, and hollows, the
village houses had stood for centuries.

Unlike the Main Square, which was now three-quarters in
shadow, this part was sunlit. Its small windows between old over-
hanging arches, uneven roofs, and balconies sprouting peppers
and geraniums, were flaming red, and through those noisy alleys
in the sunset my father walked lopsidedly, looking drunk. He was
wearing wooden-soled sandals, the sort that people often wear on
the beach in summer, and their clatter as they rang out on the
stone guided me through the confusion of alleyways. Thanks to
my rope-soled shoes, I walked silently, and, anyway, though I was
following right behind him, I was not in the least afraid that he
would discover me. I felt protected by a kind of cynicism, or by
destiny, as if I had swallowed the ring that makes people invisible,
and at the same time as if he was some elf or will-o'-the-wisp, and
there wasn't a single way we could communicate. I almost had a
feeling that the people in the streets, or looking out from the balconies, or sitting on the steps, calling and chatting to each other,
did not see us go by.

My mind had ceased to function, but, robbed of willpower and
of comfort as I was, I knew for certain that my defenseless father
was, without realizing, guiding me forward, and that soon, inevitably — I had no notion how — I should enter the very center
of the mystery.

I felt not the slightest curiosity; I felt ill and forgetful, the way
one feels in dreams. Five or six minutes, at the most, had gone by,
and it seemed to me hours since I had passed through the gate of
the Walled Country.

Up here, W. G. could have only one object — the old Castle.
It was there, it seemed, that the prisoner was lodged. He must occupy one of the little cells with windows of the kind called *wolf's
mouth* that looked out to sea without seeing it; the steamer passengers gaze at them curiously from the decks and stare glumly
across at Procida. Although my father could have only this one
object, for a while he kept wandering haphazardly through the al-

leys and lanes that cut across the one road (called Via del Borgo) leading up to the Castle. I wondered if he really had been drinking. His pointless meanderings made me think of moths beating crazily around a lamp at night. In the end he made up his mind, and, as I expected, took the Via del Borgo. There I suddenly lost track of him.

The Via del Borgo was a kind of covered gallery cut out of the rocky ground under the houses, and paved with nothing but a thick layer of dirt. Between its opening arch and the arch that opened out by the Castle (distance of about thirty yards, I'd say), it had no light except what came from a crack the size of a doorway, about half way along, which gave out on to the open air. And so for long stretches this road (which people called *the canal*) remained in everlasting darkness, with just occasional gleams at the side from small cavelike openings in the ground where ladders went up to the houses built above.

When I went down into the Via del Borgo, the blue splash that was my father had already been swallowed up in darkness a few yards ahead of me. At first, all the same, I continued to hear the clack of his wooden shoes, muffled by the dusty ground, echoing very softly under the arch; then nothing. From the village the sound of girls' voices calling their brothers home came down, for day was ending, and here and there, in the little dark entrances, you could see a small boy sitting on the ground near the ladder, playing among dogs and chickens, and sometimes the flutter of doves. My eyes had now grown used to the feeble light, but though I hurried on, and peered ahead, trying to make out the man I was following, it was no good. I ran down the rest of the Via del Borgo, and in a moment reached the exit and the great stretch of grass near the end of which, beyond a heavy gate cut in a kind of earthwork, was the base of the Castle. But there was not a sign of my father. On the dry grass before the barred gate there was no one but the soldier on guard, with his rifle on his shoulder, and he just gave me a glance that looked more sleepy than suspicious. Apart from him there was not a sign of any other human presence. I stood there dumbly for a while, but finally shrugged and went loping back along the Via del Borgo.

It seemed pointless to go all the way back along that gloomy old canal, so half way down it I stopped and went up through the space cut through to the open air. It occurred to me that maybe my father had gone out that way as well, which would explain his disappearance without any conjuring tricks. It might have happened. But even if he had gone out at this very point, where on earth would he be now? And besides, what business of mine was W. G.? What did I care about his old secrets? Suddenly, instead of hoping to find him, I found that I didn't want to. As I went higher on the rocks, I met a group of boys coming down carrying an eagle, and was tempted to ask them if they had seen a tall man in blue, but I decided that it wasn't worth it. By now I had almost given up the chase, and was going ahead without caring, without any exact direction.

The palace

From the crumbling walls of the canal, across piles of broken stones and rubbish, you reached an abandoned patch of land called the *Guaracino* that ran around the back of the village along the farthest edge of the Walled Country, vertically along the island's highest rocky points. At the end of the Guaracino stood the immense old Castle; in fact the far end of it consisted of a heap of ruined huts (dating back to the times of the Turkish corsairs, I believe), mostly buried away under piles of earth. This heap of ruins was divided from the Castle, which was built almost in a straight line with the rocks opposite, by a deep natural ravine that it was impossible to cross, the bottom of which was strewn with stones and rubbish; and on the right, between precipitous woods of briar and brushwood, it sloped down to the sea cliffs.

Below was the North Point, which I had been avoiding like a specter all summer every time I had had ot sail past it. The noise of the sea being sucked into the rock crannies was the only sound to be heard. The Guaracino was completely empty, and as I climbed that great heap of rubble, I felt wholly desolate.

The voices from the nearby town, which came to me hushed and softened by the calm air, seemed to me like the voices of a race of children, quite different from my own, and when I heard them, I felt what a sad knight errant must feel toward evening as he goes through woods and valleys alone, and hears the chatter of birds gathering in the trees to sleep all together. Regretfully I remembered other days when, at that time, I had idled about the harbor, sated with my afternoon's love-making and already half asleep; and I felt a little guilty about the little Indian slave who, that day, had waited for me in vain. Just then, I thought, down there in her little hut she would be busy preparing the supper for her family coming back from the country. And in the House of the Guaglioni my stepmother would be singing beside the basket to send Carmine to sleep. And Carmine wouldn't be sleepy, and would want to go on playing . . . Everybody was doing simple, natural things. Only I was on the trail of terrible and extraordinary mysteries, which maybe did not even exist, and which, in any case, I no longer wanted to discover.

Among the flowering ruins of those buried houses, the remains of taller buildings rose here and there — bits of wall about two or three yards high, with battered square holes in place of the old windows. At the foot of one of these walls, quite unexpectedly, I saw my father's wooden-soled sandals.

I backed away, and quickly hid behind a wall. Suddenly, after searching for W. G. so long, I was afraid of seeing him, or rather of being seen by him. I stood quite still, my heart thumping, without venturing out of my hiding place. Obviously he had left his sandals because on that hard ground he could get along faster barefoot, and he couldn't have gone far, because, with the rocks plunging down to the sea, there was nowhere for him to go. And yet, though I held my breath, the seconds passed without the smallest sign of a living presence.

On that side of the hill the Castle had no door or windows,

nothing but the gigantic blind walls reinforced with pillars, but-
tresses, and blind arches. It really looked more like a pier made of
natural rocks than a human dwelling. Only on one wing, which
stuck out vertically in a semicircle above the sea, could you see a
few *wolf's mouth* windows from there, but no sound or movement
came from them. It was as if the Castle's inmates in their dreary
white uniforms now lay in a lethargy inside it.

Unless you had wings it was quite impossible to get into the
Castle from this part of the Walled Country. And, in the empty silence around me, all sorts of fantastic notions about W. G. returned to me. Ladders, secret passages, incredible tricks — maybe
even death. I had a feeling of foreboding that, as he had taken off
his wooden-soled sandals, he had leaped down to smash himself
on the rocks below, and I felt then that even if he was dead, I
wouldn't care. Dead or alive, far or near, I simply didn't care. Suddenly I wished that I had already left the island, was already
among strangers, without hope of return, and I decided that in the
future I'd tell all the new people I met that I was a foundling,
without father, or mother, or relations, that I had been left in a
bundle on a doorstep and grew up in a foundling hospital, or
something.

I yawned, to insult the invisible shade of W. G. But without
knowing what I was waiting for, I remained there, weakly. The
sun had almost dipped into the sea; I don't know how many minutes passed; and then, just a short distance away, I heard him
singing.

The miserable voice and the signals

His voice, which I recognized at once with a shock, came from
the lower, hidden layers of the hill, so that it seemed to be coming
from the bottom of the sea cliffs. This illusion gave the scene the
disturbing solemnity of dreams, but to me the oddest thing about
it was the fact that he was singing at all. Usually he never sang,
and, indeed, he did not have an attractive voice (it was really the

only ugly thing about him) — sharp, almost feminine, inharmonious, it was. But the very fact that his singing wasn't musical or attractive mysteriously moved me all the more. I don't think that even an archangel's song would have moved me as much.

He was singing part of a well-known Neapolitan song that I had known ever since I could speak; to me, it seemed perfectly ordinary and banal after all the times I had heard it and had sung it myself. It was the one that goes:

> I find no peace
> And make night day
> Ever to be near you
> Hoping you'll speak!

But he was singing it with such persuasive bitterness, so harshly, so desperately, that I listened as if to some wonderful new song full of tragic significance. The four lines that he was yelling slowly, dragging them out, seemed just to sum up my own loneliness: the way N. had been avoiding me, and I had wandered around friendless, cheerless, restless, and the way I had ended up on this great mountain of misery today, in this dangerous spy hole, to meet the climax of my sorrows.

I could not see W. G. from where I was, so I climbed up onto a piece of the wall that jutted out, behind which I'd been hiding. And from up there, when I peeped through an old broken window, I could see the singer. He was alone there, half stretched on a weedy patch of ground at the bottom of the steep slope going down toward the cliff, and from that steep narrow patch of ground, like a wretched toad croaking at the moon, he was singing to the prison. His eyes were fixed on one of the windows visible from the ground, in the wing that curved around in a half-circle between the bottom of the little hill and the sea. It was a window on its own, about halfway up, and, like the others, it gave no sign of life through the small opening above the *wolf's mouth* — nothing but silence and darkness.

Just the same, it looked as if my father was waiting for some reply to his song. When he reached the end of the verse, he waited a little, silent, worried, and rolling glumly over on the ground like a sick man in a hospital bed. Then he began his song again from the beginning, the same verse as before. At this point I grew scared that he might see me, and left my spy hole and jumped down to the bottom of the wall. From there, if I leaned out a bit at the side, I could, without seeing him, watch the unchanging prison window. In fact, I did not look away from it again.

Twice or three times more I heard him from the bottom of the hill, repeating the song with somber, childish stubbornness, always the same verse of that familiar song. And each time his tone expressed a different kind of suffering: supplication, command, or tragic, demanding passion. But the window remained blind and deaf, as if the prisoner who lived behind it had left his cell, or was dead, or fast asleep at the very least.

The pointless song ceased at last, but after a while, instead of the song, I heard some short, rhythmic whistles rising from the hidden hollow in a new effort to call to the window. And I found that I was shaking with jealousy.

At once I had recognized in the rhythm of the whistles a secret signal language, a kind of Morse code, which my father and I had invented together during my happy childhood. We used this alphabet of whistles to send messages at a distance when we played by the sea in summer, and sometimes even at the harbor or in the café, to laugh at various Procidans who were there and didn't understand.

Now, it was obvious that my father must have told the prisoner about this mysterious alphabet, which I had thought belonged just to the two of us, me and Wilhelm Gerace!

Years of practice had taught me the signals so well that I could translate them into words the minute I heard them, better than an old hand at telegraphy. All the same, my jealous outburst made me miss the first syllables of the message my father whistled. I heard the rest, and it went like this:

NO — VISITS — NO — LETTERS — NOTHING
AT LEAST — ONE — WORD

WHAT — WOULD — IT — COST — YOU?

My father waited quietly again, but the window continued as silent and indifferent as the grave. My father repeated:

AT — LEAST — ONE — WORD

and then, after another pause:

WHAT — WOULD — IT — COST — YOU?

At last, through the little opening high up in the window where the *wolf's mouth* widened and left the end of the bars exposed, two hands appeared clinging to the bars. My father obviously saw them at once; he leaped to his feet, so that I could see him from his shoulders upward, running toward the edge of the cliff. There he stopped, almost below the Castle, from which he was separated by only three or four yards by the plunge down to the sea. He waited there in silence, as if those wretched, clinging hands were two stars that had appeared to announce his fate.

After a moment, the hands dropped from the bars, but the prisoner was obviously still there behind the window, perhaps standing on his bench in order to reach up to the bottom of it, and from there he put two fingers to his lips to send back his answer. His whistles came back promptly, sharp and rhythmic, one after the other with cruel monotony. And suddenly, feeling incredulous but quite certain, I recognized in them, as in a voice I knew, a proud, stinging voice full of youth and disdain, the unmistakable exasperated accents of the convict on the dock.

His message to my father, which I translated at once, consisted of just these words:

BEAT IT, YOU GROTESQUE

Then nothing. Only it seemed to me — perhaps it was just a trick of hearing — that from all the windows nearby came a low chorus of laughter, as if my father was being somberly mocked. Then there followed another gravelike silence all around, which a little later was interrupted by the guards on their rounds banging on the bars with their rods to check them before evening. The noise came closer and closer from the invisible windows facing the sea, and I saw my father move from where he was and prepare to climb up again slowly. Then, for fear of his surprising me, I hurtled down the hill, and hurried back the way I had come.

All the way home I kept repeating the word *grotesque* to myself, so as not to forget it; I wasn't quite sure what it meant. When I got home, I went to look in an old school dictionary that had been in my room for years; maybe it had belonged to my grandmother the schoolmistress, or maybe to Romeo's student. At the word *grotesque* I read:

> A caricature, in which what is serious in others is made
> ridiculous, or comic, or distorted

That was how Wilhelm Gerace set his last snare for me. If he had worked out the wickedest way of getting me back under his spell, if he had done it deliberately and with his eyes wide open, he could not have thought up a better way of getting me back than this one — which had drawn me to him without his even knowing it. It was now quite clear that on his trips up to the Walled Country, nothing awaited him but shameful loneliness, and that he was mortified and reviled like the basest slave. And when I realized that, I don't know why, but my love for him, which I thought had flickered and nearly died, rose up in me again more bitterly, more destructively, more dreadfully than ever.

Farewell

Non più andrai, farfallone amoroso,
notte e giorno d'intorno girando,
delle belle turbando il riposo . . .
. . . .
. . . Coi guerrieri, poffarbacco!

aria of Figaro

Hated shadow

TWO MORE MONTHS passed. It was nearly the end of November when I found out that Assuntina was betraying me.

There is no point in wasting time saying how I came to know it. I must hurry now and get to the end of these memoirs. I'll just say I was told about it without the slightest possibility of doubt, and that she wasn't betraying me with just one lover, but with more than one, and all these lovers had been carried over from before the time she had come to me. The day I found all this out I passed her house on purpose, and when she saw that I didn't stop, and ran after me, I turned and pushed her off with such suitable, violent insults that she drew back frightened. Later I went past there again. There was no one in front of the house and the door was shut. With my penknife I scratched a picture of a sow on the door and underneath it wrote: *Farewell forever.* After which I lost myself wandering around the countryside, and I finally flung myself down in a field and burst out sobbing.

I had never loved Assuntina, that was true. But lately I had even thought of marrying her because I so much wanted a woman who loved me, one who was really mine. I had decided that as soon as I had married her, I would even kiss her the way I had once kissed N. And had never kissed her. And then — and this was the main thing — we would have a child. I liked the idea of having a child immensely, and I enjoyed thinking what he would

be like, and making plans to take him with me on my future journeys, like a real friend. And then even this scheme of mine vanished, like so many others.

If at least my mother had still been alive, I could have unburdened myself by telling my troubles to someone. For a moment I
had a vision of N. as she once had been, but that earlier image of
her was blotted out at once by the present image, which was so
grim that even her curls looked malevolent. At this point what
that hateful Assuntina had once said really seemed quite true —
that under her lamblike appearance my stepmother hid the in-
domitable toughness of a wild beast.

That was all, then: I was absolutely alone. Then what was still
keeping me on that bewitched old island? What kept me from
abandoning it forever, as I had abandoned my foul and faithless
mistress?

The answer was Wilhelm Gerace, who in other years had left
on a trip in the autumn, but this year still honored Procida with
his presence.

Often the affections we suppose magnificent or downright super-
human are, in fact, rather insipid; only some down-to-earth bitterness can work like salt and, though atrociously painful, bring out
their mixed, mysterious flavor. All through my childhood I had
thought I loved W. G., and perhaps I was mistaken. Maybe I was
beginning to love him only now. Something extraordinary was
happening to me, something I should certainly not have believed
before if it had been predicted: I felt sorry for W. G.

I had felt compassion for others before in my life. I had felt it
for strangers, people I didn't know, even sometimes for someone
just passing by. For Immacolatella. For N. Even for Assuntina. In
fact, I already knew how incomparably dreadful this feeling is.
But the people I had felt it for, even if I loved them, had all been
united to me only by chance, by choice; they had not been related to me by birth. For the first time, though, I now knew the inhuman violence of pitying my own flesh and blood.

In spite of the winter gloom that reigned over the island, W. G.

had been less bad-tempered and more sociable for some weeks.
Not that he was cured of his fixation, of course; no, it looked as if
it had him more in its power than ever. It was just that now it was
shaking him out of his anguished half-sleep and seeming, as the
days went on, to bring him to a new mood — one of impatience,
a kind of new and obscurely gay impatience. He would stride
from room to room and through the village streets and country
lanes as if pursued by cruel omens and impossible longings.
Sometimes he went out in the mood of an exalted, ingenuous
gaiety, like a very young man. But that seemed to make him desperately tired, and then, because he needed to rest, he took refuge
in dreadful gloom.

I had noticed that his visits to the Walled Country had slack-
ened off, but that was not enough to take me in. I still saw in his
eyes, in his behavior, the hated shadow that possessed his mind.
And so I always looked hostilely, taciturnly at him. When he went
into the village or wandered about the countryside, and asked me
to go with him — as he had begun to, again, in the last few days
— I went ungraciously. If he spoke to me, I answered abruptly
and disagreeably.

When I think back, those last weeks really seem to have flown,
the fastest of my life. Maybe they seemed long to him, however,
he was obviously counting the days. All around him, in the air,
was the dramatic and impatient joy of waiting. I felt that something new was just about to happen, but I refused to share it with
him, so much so that I didn't even try to explain what he was
waiting for to myself, or perhaps even pretended not to notice it.
All the same, it was soon explained.

One evening

One evening early in December I got home very late. Since N.
had declared her unalterable aversion to me, I always went home
late in the evening so as not to sit down at the table with her. Before she went to bed, she left my supper hot beside the embers,

but for the preceding few weeks I had got into the habit of eating on my own in the village fairly often, at the Cock Inn or the widow's café. I was terribly rich that autumn; my father just poured money out. Not a single day passed without his giving me a fifty- or hundred-lire note, and that morning he had given me the absolutely crazy sum of five hundred lire. I didn't know what to do with so much money; I would forget about banknotes and leave them in books and in drawers among the rags. I always had at least seven or eight rumpled together in my pocket, and I gave enormous tips — so enormous that to find anything like them in their past the Procidans would have had to go back to the Spaniards in the seventeenth century.

Usually I went to have supper at the inn about seven, but afterward I stayed in the village until ten or later, so that sometimes when I went home, I felt rather hungry again and enjoyed eating what my stepmother had left me as well. This was why when I went home that evening I went to the kitchen. And there I had a surprise: the ashes of the logs were still warm, but the two little pots in which N. usually left my supper were there beside them, empty and uncovered. And on the table there was no sign of the plates and cutlery N. laid out for me every evening.

It was the first time that such a thing had happened. I took a piece of bread out of the drawer and went out on to the terrace to eat it. But there I no longer felt hungry and flung it away.

It was a dark night; the wind was damp and rather cold. I had gone only a few steps when the wind slammed the doors of the lighted French window which I'd left open behind me. Without a light or a moon, the terrace was so dark that you couldn't see where it began or ended. It certainly didn't seem very inviting, and after a short while I decided to go back to the house, which rose at the end of it, quiet and lulled in sleep. It was while I was going back to the house that I noticed a pinkish light behind the great glass window of the big room.

That huge, freezing room was always shut up and deserted by the family, especially in winter. The first thing I thought of, without even believing in them, was ghosts. The stories I had heard when I was little and had never believed came back to me — about the ghost of the man from Amalfi and his *guaglioni*. Perhaps, I thought, the ghosts ate my supper too ... And I went into the house, puzzled and skeptical, and made straight for the big room.

I saw at once that the reddish glow that I'd seen from outside came from the stove. Someone, hoping to warm that great barn of a room a bit, had lighted a few pieces of wood in the old convent stove, and the stove, which probably hadn't been touched for fifty years, had already almost filled the room with smoke. When I went in, a solitary figure moved on one of the flattened sofas near the stove, and in the dark I thought at first that it was a dog. But it got up, it was a man, and as I turned to the light switch, I recognized him at once. Even if I hadn't recognized his face and clothes (the same Sunday suit he had been wearing that day on the dock), I should have known him in the sudden uprush of harsh devouring hatred that I felt as soon as I saw him.

In the big room

The dim dusty lamp from the ceiling glimmered in that corner of the room, but even in its wretched light I saw at once, as if it had been painted very precisely before me, the warm, gentlemanly, exultant welcome my father had given him, a kind of untidy banquet, improvised clumsily, childishly. On the table, which had been pulled beside the sofa, were the plates with the remains of my supper, and olives, unwrapped sweets, dates, cigarettes, wine, even an already empty bottle of *spumante* and another of liqueur. There was a carpet on the floor, dug out from somewhere in the house, and on the sofa were a pillow and my father's woolen rug ... All this, to my savagely wounded eyes, took on an air of positively regal magnificence.

This time his features too (unlike that day on the dock) appeared to me with strange clarity, as if he had been lighted up by a beacon. As soon as I saw him I realized how mistaken I'd been to think him ugly when I had seen him before, and the sudden realization of his beauty cut into me like a knife. Maybe I wouldn't have hated his looks so much if he had been fair, but he was dark, quite as dark as I was, or even darker. And this, I don't know why, hurt me unbearably.

I remember my conversation with him in a haze of hatred. I hated the shape of his tall, well-developed body, of his muscles, which seemed quite unspoiled by imprisonment, and which showed when he moved. I hated his shoulders, and the strong neck that carried his head proudly, and the head itself, which, pale as it was from prison, was modeled with fearless beauty. I hated his splendid dark hair, which was carefully and childishly shaped to hang rather low on his forehead, as if sculpted . . . There was not a single feature or movement that could make me forgive him.

His deep-set, shadowed eyes looked scornfully, haughtily, and at the same time slyly out from under thick eyebrows; he never looked directly at the person talking to him, but sidelong, as it were. When he smiled, his hard, beautiful lips never parted; one corner of his mouth lifted slightly with a sort of suggestive coarseness, as if a proper, kindly smile would detract from his manhood. And his chin was very faintly cleft, which made his expression still tougher and harder.

Betrayal

"Where's my father?" I asked him, as soon as I was in the room. My noisy, aggressive tone must have told him that war was already declared between us.

He looked at me without moving a step from the corner where the stove was. "And who's your father?" he flung back, pretending not to know.

"My father? He's the owner here! I am Arturo Gerace!"

"Oh! How do you do," he said, with an air of lazy, false politeness. "He went upstairs just this minute, *the owner*; but he won't be long coming down again."

"Then I'll wait for him here," I declared. And I planted myself there in the doorway, standing up and leaning back against the door post.

"Come in and sit down," he said, making a face and looking completely indifferent, as if to say that as far as he was concerned I might have been a fly on the wall. Then, stretching out again on the sofa, he added: "Do put out the light while you're there, though. Your father told me not to turn it on. There's a danger of being seen from outside . . ."

I didn't move. He glanced up at me.

"Well, what are you waiting for?" he asked. And at my deliberate disobedience he raised himself on one elbow. A sudden gleam, half-jokingly mysterious and half-arrogant, came into his eyes. "It's dangerous, I tell you," he threatened vaguely. "The police . . ." Then lowering his voice, he said, with a wild and wicked air. "I AM A FUGITIVE!"

I looked at him without batting an eyelash. In his manner, his tone, I'd quickly smelled some mystery. But it might be that he was speaking the truth. It certainly went ideally with the image I had had of him from the very first day . . . And this was the only explanation for the presence in our house that evening of a man serving a life sentence, which was what I had supposed him to be right from the start.

For a moment, in spite of my hatred, I was fascinated by this idea of splendid complicity that flashed so startlingly, so unexpectedly upon me: to think of hiding a real escaped convict, searched for by the police, in our house! It was an honor, and at the same time it was something to use against him, to have him at one's mercy . . . Just the same, because I felt doubtful, I left the light on, if for no other reason, so that he shouldn't presume that I'd really believed him.

He looked at me. "What are you waiting for?" he said.

I shrugged my shoulders, looking disgusted. Then, from his arrogantly closed lips, as if in spite of himself, a short childish laugh escaped him, and at the same time he struck a sarcastic, superior, and condescending pose, and arched his eyebrows so that they lined his forehead.

"Well," he said, "do what you like as far as I'm concerned. *I am a Fugitive* is the name of a film. Did you believe it? I'm a free citizen from this evening and perfectly in order with the law. I was legally evicted from my home up here at the big house at exactly nine o'clock today, the 3rd of December, if you want to know!"

While he was speaking, he looked at me lazily, steadily, without stirring from his indolent position, but hinting all sorts of malice. "You don't care for that, do you?" he said. "Come on, tell me the truth. You swallowed the story of the escaped convict and rather liked the idea of running straight off to denounce me . . ."

From the moment I had planted myself there, facing him, I had promised myself I wouldn't say another word to him, and would take no more notice of him than if he had been an animal. But when I heard him come out with such a crazy piece of calumny, I couldn't help giving a proud, throaty snort of amusement.

All he replied to that was a smug half-smile, as if he wasn't changing his opinion. "Well, you can save yourself the bother," he went on undaunted, settling himself better on the sofa. "And as for the lights, I can assure you that as far as I'm concerned, lights on or lights off, it's all the same to me this evening. It's your father who's got this discreet idea of turning out the lights. The police, though, have nothing to do with it. It's just a question of private matters, family matters of yours."

At this point, he yawned and lit a cigarette. "Well, just to let you know," he explained more clearly. "Your father doesn't want to let the others in the house know I'm here. And that's why he hasn't given me a room upstairs, as you see. I think that he particularly doesn't want to introduce me to his wife . . ."

His way of speaking had different inflections from the usual Neapolitan ones I was used to, less singsong and more robust. He didn't speak in dialect, but in fairly correct Italian. In fact, he seemed to find a kind of malicious enjoyment in using rather unusual expressions, and his manners, which were of lowly origin, prickled with pride and challenge while he tried to behave politely. He drawled, between puffs of his cigarette; and every time he said "your father," there was a note of ironic deference and at the same time of repulsion in his voice, as if he was avoiding some wretched, tiresome object, and at the same time mocking the fatherhood of which I was so proud.

"Oh, of course," he went on, dropping the words from his mouth with the lordly air of a sultan, as if he thought himself the greatest gangster of the century. "I'm not a family type, I'm a dangerous ex-convict . . . At the trial," he said boastfully, "they gave me two years. But afterward they had to reduce it, because of these great international events in the meantime, and the amnesty resulting from them, given by His Majesty the King . . . Aren't you pleased at this lucky coincidence? If it wasn't for the march of history, I wouldn't be here in your mansion enjoying this beautiful evening!"

When I heard all this, I turned to look at him in spite of myself, perplexed, almost questioning. Not because of the *great international events* he mentioned: I knew nothing about them, and at that particular moment cared even less, but for another reason. *Only two years!* I felt disconcerted. Well, then, the man I had thought a genuine criminal serving a life sentence was, by the look of things, some petty criminal of no importance at all. And yet I now realized angrily that not even the fact that I knew that he was just a wretched back street bag-snatcher or a mugger, instead of a dreadful murderer or outlaw, was not enough to diminish his hateful black splendor in my eyes.

All the same, to show him that I attached little or no importance to what he had said I made a face, looking fed up. And he on his side began yawning exaggeratedly, as if this *beautiful evening,* just in being mentioned, had become a dreadful bore. But he said no more about it.

A few minutes of silence followed. I stayed there upright against the doorpost, my hands in my pockets, with the air of a gang leader facing an enemy gang leader in the middle of the pampas. In the end I broke the silence. "Well, are you sleeping here tonight?" I asked darkly.

"And where do you expect me to sleep? At the Grand Hotel?"

"Why," he asked sarcastically, after a bit. "Does it bother you?
Maybe . . ."

I gave a shrug of sophisticated scorn. "Pooh . . . I don't give a
damn about you anyway," I answered.

"Well, yes, I've accepted your father's invitation," he went on
in a mildly conciliatory tone, and with a kind of impenitent gen-
erosity. "Because, all things considered, this seemed the most
comfortable hotel here on the island, and I still have to spend my
last night on it. Until tomorrow there are no steamers going to the
mainland . . ." Here his face showed such longing, such long-
nourished impatience, that he appeared much simpler, indeed
downright childish. "But if it wasn't for your father poking his
nose into my affairs," he burst out suddenly, in a tone of excessive
antagonism, flinging his legs off the sofa, "tonight I'd be sleeping
with my girl in Rome. It's half an hour by car from the Viterbo jail
(where I was) to my home at Flaminio! And it was him (though
he even tries to deny it) who organized my transfer to his beautiful
oasis of Procida, heaven knows how; that's what he fixed up with
his important friends . . ."

Oh, so that was it! . . . When he said this, I pictured a kind of
court of brisk, discreet followers, the competent, mysterious, and
nameless society which from childhood I had imagined was entirely at my father's service, and I felt a kind of swanky pleasure at
my father's prestige, just as I had felt when I was a child. That explained why the famous Walled Country had entertained such a
petty convict, serving such a paltry sentence . . . It was my father's
will that had dragged him to Gerace territory, unwilling, arrogant,
like a slave . . .

But when I thought of that, I suddenly remembered with a
shudder — and was astonished not to have thought of it before —
the famous old promise my father had sworn when Amalfi died,
never to bring a friend of his to this island, into this house, which
was forever dear to a single memory. Still ringing in my ears were
Wilhelm Gerace's words: "If I fail in this, I'll be a traitor and a
perjuror."

Well then, that's just what he was.

My face must have betrayed my sudden, deep dismay. And perhaps it was my vulnerable expression that gradually brought a kind of courtesy into my enemy's manner. He indicated the loaded table with an absent nod, still frowning darkly, and said, with almost aristocratic politeness: "That reminds me. I haven't yet apologized for eating your supper . . ."

This apology of his made me shudder with rage, but I didn't want to give him the satisfaction of seeing it, so I glared at him like a pirate whose ugly face has been bashed to bits in the shadiest tavern brawls, and with furious casualness flung at him: "What supper are you talking about? I always eat out."

"Oh, of course, I hadn't thought of that," he answered, in his usual ceremonious way, but as he did so, he began to look at me curiously, his eyes full of laughter. "Tell me now," he went on quite differently, with an indiscreet, insinuating tone. "Why do you come home so late at night? Have you got a girl?"

"No," I said darkly.

"You haven't got a girl," he retorted with a sudden expression of complicity in his eyes, which had turned cheerful, "because you've got at least two or three girls. D'you know what your father told me a little while ago? That you have supper out because every night you go chasing after women like a tomcat! That you're mad about women! That you have mistresses already!"

I felt myself blushing. Well, then, without my realizing it, W. G. knew something of what I had been up to. In any case, luckily this fellow didn't notice my childish blushes. He had looked away from me, and suddenly instead of smiling he looked black again. He gave a big restless sigh, like a wolf's, and got up. And then, triumphantly, threateningly, as if with the last drop of his blood he defied anyone who dared to contradict him, he declared: "I like women too!"

And he backed that up, more threateningly than before: "I like women, AND THAT'S ALL!"

Then he started striding up and down the room with his proud, elastic jockey's walk. He glanced angrily at the walls painted with fake pergolas, vine leaves, and bunches of grapes, at the scribbles of the *guaglioni*, at the loaded table, at everything, as if he was still in the depths of a jail.

"I say, if you know a pretty girl here, why haven't you brought her up here?" he said complainingly. "Then at least we'd have some fun, this evening!"

He flung himself down on the sofa again, and it protested with a mournful squeak of its battered skeleton. The lamp in the middle of the room, which had stayed on in spite of my father, gave no more light than candles, and every now and then, because of the inefficient current, the bulbs wavered like insects writhing with pain.

My father didn't come. I kept deciding, minute after minute, to go upstairs; but some irrational, instinctive force — maybe something that warned me of new sorrows — kept me facing him in that beastly room.

It was he this time who interrupted the silence. Glumly, ill-temperedly, he cocked a disgruntled eye at me, and said: "Hey! Arturo Gerace!"

I grunted in reply. Then, without altering his sleepy position lying on the sofa, he put his hands to his mouth like a megaphone and began declaiming, in the artificial and crazy tone of a detective story: "ATTENTION! ATTENTION! We're looking for a dangerous criminal from Sing Sing! Here's a description of him: straight nose, straight mouth, Greek profile . . ."

Then he began laughing softly to himself, alluding, of course, maliciously (though almost pleasantly) to my credulity some time before. I was tempted to reply with some frightful insult, but he had already fallen back into his bored and languid silence, as if he were dozing . . .

And it was then that suddenly, into the silence, without even expecting it myself, I flung out a question which I had kept shut up too long inside me, brusque and peremptory: "Why were you inside? What had you done?"

Although he took some time to do it, he turned to consider me between his eyelashes, raising half a lip in a foppish, conceited smile that all the same seemed not to deny me an answer. "Oh, so you're curious to know," he observed as a preamble . . . And, in fact, I had even forgotten my dislike of him, and was gazing at him intently, waiting anxiously and with a sense of adventure for what he would have to say. There in the big room, waiting for his confession, I almost expected him to reveal to me some absolutely unique and extraordinary crime, something I had never heard of in my life before, had never read of in any book, something tricked out with all that was marvelous and terrible and seductive . . . And this aroused an extraordinary feeling in me, as if I was going to have some gloomy initiation, some promotion to manhood, something very important, fascinating, and repulsive. In the meantime, lying flat with half-shut eyes, he was stretching slowly, and keeping me waiting awhile for his answer. At last, gazing into the air, he said slyly: "Well . . . ah . . . Armed robbery! I held up a stage coach going at ninety (ninety yards that is) an hour . . . on the road to Buffalo . . . in Texas . . ."

Then he contradicted himself in the same tone: "No, that wasn't it. I raped and violated a maiden of fifty-seven . . . of royal blood!"

Then, after another pause: "No, I was wrong . . . I stole . . . the curate's gown!"

And he concluded: "Now you can choose."

"What do you think I care?" I exclaimed with a sneer. And from that moment on, I decided to keep absolutely quiet, as if as far as I was concerned there was a corpse or an Egyptian mummy on the sofa instead of him. But after a bit, as if trying to find an excuse to make friends with me, he offered me a cigarette. I refused it.

At this he rose to his feet and with a tone of quite religious seriousness, asked me: "Do you know who I am?"

Without speaking, I raised my chin as a scornful way of saying I didn't. Then he dipped his finger in the glass of wine, and with it drew on the wall, among the *guaglionis'* old drawings and signatures, the shape of a star. "I am Stella. Tonino Stella," he declared.

At my obvious indifference he announced, hurt, but proudly: "My name has been in all the papers!"

After which he came up to me and, as if to prove his identity, raised his sleeve a little and showed me a tiny tattooed star on his wrist.

But even before I had glanced at the tattoo of the star, I had seen something else on his wrist quite by chance, something that startled me when I saw it, a watch, only too famous and familiar for me not to distinguish it among all the watches of Europe. Apart from its mark *Amicus*, I even recognized a small scratch on the face and on the steel strap various marks made by salt water. There was no possibility of doubt, it was the famous watch my father had received as a present from Algerian Knife, that sacred pledge of their friendship from which he had never been separated for years. I remembered seeing it on his wrist that very morning, and for a moment I suspected that Stella had stolen it. But I quickly realized that the truth was something quite different. It wasn't a matter of theft, but of a present, a present from my father to Stella on this gay evening of theirs, with no thought for his old faithful friend.

So, in a single day, W. G. had airily denied first Romeo and then Mark, the two most faithful friends he had. He was a double traitor and perjurer. And all in the honor of this oaf.

Grotesque

I am almost sure that Stella must have realized at once, at the very first moment, that I had recognized the watch, but he showed no annoyance and no regret. No, without pausing as he spoke, he glanced casually at its splendor, as if with obvious pleasure at owning it.

"Oh, come, now," he went on haughtily. "Don't you get any newspapers here from Rome? My picture was in some of them too, about a year ago, when they were looking for me. Ask your father if you want to know about it. Yes, it was just about then, I think, when I was hiding around the place, that I had *the honor* of making his acquaintance! . . . Which reminds me," he observed, "his lordship's keeping us waiting this evening, isn't he? It must be half an hour since he went upstairs."

And with a jerk of his forearm, he pulled his cuff from his wrist and consulted the watch. "Exactly," he declared, "twenty-seven and a half minutes."

It looked as if he was determined to annoy me with that watch: he wound it ostentatiously, then put it up to his ear. At last, following the direction in which I was looking, he said sly and in a bullying tone: "Well? Do you think you recognize this watch? I may as well tell you it's mine now — *by right!*"

I shrugged my shoulders and, to show that I didn't give a damn, kicked the armchair there beside me.

"BY RIGHT!" he repeated. "Yes, that's it. It's *owed* to me by your father. And apart from the watch he owes me a pair of marine binoculars, a fishing gun, and an underwater mask that he says he's got here in the house, shut away upstairs. And besides that, tomorrow he *owes* me a brand-new suit, to be bought at the best tailor in Naples, and a pair of new rubber-soled shoes. Then his obligations are that he'll owe me a sum of money, as much as I need to open a garage in Rome, so that I can marry my girl."

He was sitting quite calmly there, leaning back on the sofa, looking quite regally imposing and self-possessed. But as he finished speaking his brow suddenly clouded. "Which reminds me," he said, perplexed, "is your father really as rich as all that?" It was clear from his tone that he had a nasty suspicion, and at that my anger, which I had masked too long with indifference, began to boil. Yet I now felt more than ever that to unmask my casualness would give him the satisfaction he longed for, and so I limited my reply to a hefty grunt.

"Because, to listen to him," he went on, curling his lips with a skepticism he hardly attempted to disguise, "you'd imagine he could spend what he likes, and that he's a millionaire . . . but to look at him, you certainly wouldn't think him a millionaire. He doesn't really look a gentleman . . ."

"Oh, so that's what you're saying . . ."

"Yes, that's what I'm saying . . . But so would any respectable person, even if he didn't say it. What sort of a gentleman is he, anyway? He goes around dressed in rags, not even patches, and he doesn't shave, and never washes, so that he stinks . . ."

"Hey! Watch what you're saying!"

"Well, sorry."

"Watch what you're saying, I tell you!"

"And I tell you I'm sorry . . . Besides," said Stella, "if I'm interested in his finances, it's a business matter. It's all a matter of business, what your father's proposing to me. He's going to give me what I've told you, in money and in kind, and in exchange I'm to go on a two-week trip with him . . . But he's going to hand over the loot (the money he's promised me, I mean) only after the fortnight, not before, because if he coughs it up ahead of time, he says he'll lose the only guarantee he's got that I won't run away from him. All right then! I'll trust him! But I advise him not to cheat me, for the sake of his own good health!" Here Stella looked at me threateningly and severely, as if I was a witness and a pledge. "Obviously," he concluded, making a scornful face, "if I go looking at sunsets with him instead of heading straight for my girl in Rome, it's not going to be because of his pretty face!"

At that, he seemed to plunge into an exacting and tormented train of thought, as if the very idea of the trip he had been promised was torture to his nerves. As for me, from the moment I heard the word *trip* I remained colorless, breathless, silent.

And I hardly recognized my own voice — it sounded suddenly so lost and weak in the question that, from some childish depth in me, rose to my lips: "Are you going far? . . ."

Stella raised one eyelid. "Far? . . . What's that?" he said, slow-wittedly. "Oh, you mean me? With your father? Oh, you mean on our trip! Not likely! We'll go wandering around on more or less the same old track . . ." His lips curled again in a half-smile — bored, skeptical, mocking. "Your father," he went on, as if it was something everyone knew, "isn't the type to run around a lot. He'd be heartbroken, terribly upset. He's the sort that always putters around the same places. You know the old captive balloons? Well, that's him . . ."

I looked up uncertainly at Stella, as if to ask him if he was se-

rious. It wasn't the first time an unexpected view of my father like
this had struck me. I remembered that I had heard someone else
say something not very different in the past. And what now seemed
to me something bewitched (almost as if it had some mysterious
and complex connection with my own nature and destiny) was the
fact that two witnesses, who didn't know each other, who were exact
opposites and completely remote from each other, should find
themselves in agreement on something that I (maybe I was the last
in the whole world — was I?) still persisted in treating as heresy.

"You don't know a thing about my father!" I shouted.

"Oh, well, maybe you understand him better . . ."

"You can't even imagine the trips my father's made!" I shouted.
"He's spent his whole life traveling through the remotest parts of
the world! Always! His whole life!"

Stella looked at me with light, ironical, but quite sincere surprise, and arched his eyebrows the way he did, so that they made
lines across his forehead.

"Oh, really!" he observed. "That's something quite new to me.
And what, may I ask, are the most important trips he's made? All
right — there was Germany to Italy about forty years ago, that we
all know. But apart from that . . . Well, of course, he's been on the
trip around Vesuvius . . . He's got a season ticket for that . . ."

"You make me laugh!" I declared, flaming with scorn.

"Oh, really! I make you laugh . . . Well, to get back to the
point, just satisfy my curiosity on another point, if it doesn't bother
you too much. Why on earth has he spent his whole life on these
terrific cruises? As a tourist? . . . As a missionary? . . . Or what?"

My nerves were on edge and my blood was boiling with the
disgust and bitterness burning in me. "Why?" I repeated, *"What's
the reason?* Well! For his own freedom! To get real knowledge —
that's the reason! To learn about the whole world, and every nation, without end . . ."

Stella laughed again. "Come on, that's enough," he interrupted
me, raising the palm of his hand with an air of having taken quite
enough. "I've been teasing you. Now I've got proof that what he
said is true — that you're nuts about him."

"Who said that?"

"He did. He said: 'I've got two children: a little fair one and a dark one, and lovelier children than mine no one could ever produce. And the dark one, from the minute he was born, was *nuts* about me'"

"It's not true that he said that!"

"Yes, it's true; he said it. And it's true you're nuts."

"It's not true!"

"Not true that you're nuts?"

"No."

"Well, then, if it isn't true, how can you explain these tales you're telling me about him? To hear you, one'd think he was some kind of long-distance flier, or . . ." — he rose solemnly to his feet — "a real *space man!*" he went on in a tone of cruel mockery. "But the truth is he's the typical baby who's never been weaned from his mother and never will be! And as for his travels, from the time he was kicked out of his savage den up north and found his cot here in this pretty volcano, I should think it extraordinary if he ever got as far as Benevento, or even Viterbo!"

And for the first time in speaking of my father Stella laughed strangely, as if with irrepressible, friendly, and scarcely veiled indulgence. "Maybe," he went on, "he's scared that this precious treasure island of his will fall into the sea if he loses sight of it. The minute he gets three or four stops away from it he starts to get homesick like an orphan, and when he remembers it he makes such a face . . . He's even jealous of it, like of a woman. D'you know he's even nicknamed 'Procida'?"

This last bit of news (whether it was true or false) I certainly didn't dislike. And I waited almost thirstily for Stella to continue. But he suddenly abandoned the subject and, flinging himself down on the sofa in a kind of brutal and vicious joy, shook his head so hard that all his smooth oiled hair was disarranged. A new expression appeared on his face — childish, plebeian, attractive — and all sorts of thoughts and fun, intrigues and mischief contrasted with his arrogance. Obviously he was suddenly following a train of thought from which, though present, I was excluded, but it was impossible to know if the thought attracted or repelled him. It was like watching a cat chasing a feather and not knowing whether its mood is playful or gloomy.

He got up impulsively and stretched with an air of boredom, then flung himself down again and sat. Then suddenly he laughed — seriously, almost dramatically, and exclaimed: "Your father is *grotesque!*"

That was enough. Anger overwhelmed me — sinister, fatal, uncontrollable. I went up to Stella with clenched fists. "Now I'm going to spit in your face," I said.

A harsh, oddly sly shadow fell on Stella's face. And he turned to me as well and said, weighing his words: "And whose face are you spitting in?"

The final scene

I was beyond myself with rage, and just about ready to leap on him when I heard a well-known step hurrying along the passage. Then my father, who had turned up in the doorway behind me, seized me by one arm.

He had just overheard Stella's last words, and he echoed them: "Whose face are you spitting in?" while he gave me a penetrating look, threatening and apprehensive, and turned pale. This pallor and his distress disarmed me. But I shook him off brusquely, violently, and gave him no explanation, and then turned loweringly away from Stella, who retired from the fight and sat down on the sofa again, looking indifferent and sarcastic. I stayed in the corner where the stove was, a few steps away from the two of them.

My father had come down from upstairs with a heap of things in his arms — linen, blankets, a pillow. *Like a servant*, I thought. I noticed at the same time, with bitter surprise, that he had put on new clothes that I had never seen before — corduroy trousers, a gray woolen jacket, and around his neck a blue silk handkerchief. He had shaved carefully, and even combed his hair and smoothed it back. Clean and elegant like that, he seemed to me as handsome as a storybook prince, and yet, as I looked enchantedly at him, I realized that I was searching desperately, absurdly, for the comic or grotesque side of him which might deserve Stella's epithet.

I was really longing to find something really ridiculous in him, but, alas, I could see nothing but beauty. His nervous thinness, which looked odd under his smart clothes, made him seem younger and more delicate; beside him Stella's boyish robustness seemed insulting or trivial.

Again he looked with alarm from Stella to me, but he asked no more questions. Then he seemed to forget our mysterious quarrel at once, as if nothing had happened, and hurried over to the sofa to drop the linen and blankets beside Stella.

"Well, everything's ready," he said with a kind of ingenuous vivacity. "I've packed the suitcase too!"

Then he turned to me and said in quite another tone, proudly and sharply: "That reminds me, Arturo. I was looking for you to tell you this, but you weren't in your room. I'm leaving on the first boat tomorrow."

Tomorrow! Until that last word I had refused to accept the nearness of what was to drag tomorrow, and all the days that came after it, into ruin and sorrow for me. I stared at my father with lost eyes.

Frowning, he went on: "We'd better say good-bye now, because I won't have time tomorrow."

"You're leaving . . . with him!" I burst out, choked with disgust.

"That's none of your business," my father answered.

"You can't do it! No! You can't do it!"

My father glanced at me sidelong, dominating me with his flashing splendor.

"I'm going with whomever I please," he answered. "And Your Mercy can just put up with it."

I felt that he was being as overweening as possible so as to shine in Stella's eyes. Maybe, too, his high-handedness with me was a revenge for the base slavery Stella held him in. Stella himself seemed to understand all this, and looked at him stealthily, ironically, critically. But my father didn't notice the irony: he was much too worked up and theatrical.

"Well, Arturo, are we agreed then?" he asked, half turning around to me with a sharp look that meant a definite dismissal. I was just going to say: "Of course! Good-bye!"and turn my back on him. But an instinct that was prouder than my will (something like the instinct of self-preservation) shouted like a thunderclap in my ears that everything between him and me would be over after this, and that there, just outside the big room, a bottomless night awaited me. I took a step forward, with just a glance of disdain at Stella, as if, as far as I was concerned, his presence there was something to be ignored, and stood before my father.

"I'm sixteen!" I exclaimed. "You promised that when I grew up, you'd take me on trips with you. And now the time has come. I'm grown up. I'm a man!"

"Oh. Well, I'm glad to hear it," my father said. Then, moving over to the stove, and leaning on it with one hand in his pocket, he said in a tone of false calmness: "Come here, Arturo. Stand here in front of me, please." He was scared that I'd offend Stella again, of course.

Scornfully, I obeyed.

Then, looking intently at me, he said: "Shall we part politely, Arturo?"

I frowned without answering.

"Well, in that case," he went on, hardly able to control his stormy impatience, "be so good as to postpone the discussion to another time and get along upstairs. I quite agree about the promise you mention. Every promise is sacred, of course, between gentlemen . . . but this doesn't seem to me the best hour to discuss it — at midnight when I'm ready to leave . . . We'll talk about it calmly when I come back."

I gave a desperate, cynical laugh. His face darkened again.

"And so, in the meantime," he went on, in a gloomy, altered voice, "you'll have time to grow up a bit more, I hope. For instance, you'll learn not to make such a fool of yourself as you have here this evening, or else, if you carry on this way, everybody'll

know that even if you're grown up in years, you're still a boy —
no, still a baby . . . Good night!"

I felt my face was aflame, then pale as death. "Yes," I answered.
"I'm going. You can have your old promises. I don't want them . . ."

I noticed confusedly that I was starting to shout. My voice had
now become a real man's voice, no longer discordant as it had been
a few months before. But when I heard it I had the strange feeling
of listening to a stranger, a savage talking through my mouth. I
wasn't thinking what I was saying, and saw nothing beyond W. G.,
who was looking at me with a kind of curiosity in his cloudy blue
eyes. My eyes, sharp with bitterness, went to his bare left wrist.

"You've got no loyalty," I went on shouting. "Either to your
promises or to your oaths! You've even betrayed friendship! I
know you now! You're a traitor!"

I felt that I was being swept along by a terrible cyclone, and that
the ground was rolling horribly under my feet. I saw W. G. move
slowly away from beside the stove with his deliberate but slightly
tired walk and come up to me, and I waited for him to hit me. It
would have been the first time in my life he'd done so, and in a flash
I had time to think that in any case I wouldn't hit him back. He was
my father, and fathers have the right to beat their children. Although
I was grown up, it was still through him that I had been born.

But he didn't really hit me after all. He just seized my arm up
near the shoulder, and said: "Hey! You old Blacky, you!" Then he
jerked me free, proudly, his face grim, but with a small, almost
amused laugh. "Well, so now you know me!" he added. "That's
what you said, isn't it?" He took two or three steps away from me.
"Well, and if you know me *now*," he said, "I've known you for
quite a long time, my Blacky!"

"No, you don't know me at all," I murmured. "*Nobody*
knows me."

"Oh, really, the mystery man! But the fact is that I know you
pretty well, know you like the palm of my hand. And what's
more, I'm going to tell you what you are — here and now, before
witnesses."

"Go ahead then. Who cares?"

He stopped one step away from me, in a warlike and pitiless po-sition. And at that very moment all sorts of expressions dawned on his face — magnificence, and gaiety, and complicity, judgments of me, duplicity, jokes, and magic. In fact, all the old airs he had when you didn't know if he was preparing (perhaps) something important and murderous, or hatching (perhaps) some infernal mischief.

"Very well then," he said. "Then I attest, and all the world can know it, that you Arturo, are *jealous*. What's more, I might say more accurately that your highness deserves the title of King Jealous. You're the great Hidalgo, you're Don Giovanni, you're the King of Hearts — oh, yes! And you keep falling in love and shooting your arrows about like Venus's son Cupid, and if you don't catch people, then you get jealous . . . According to you, the whole world should be in love with Arturo Gerace. But you don't love anyone, oh no! Because you're capricious and vain, and selfish, and a rascal, and love nothing and no one but your own sweet self. And now run along and go to bed. Get out!"

"Yes, I'm going," I said in a low voice. Then, my voice growing louder, and darker, and more desperate, I repeated: "Yes, I'm going! And I want to forget you! Forever! Pay attention! These are my last words!"

"That's fine," he said. "I agree. Your last words!"

I turned furiously to the door, but as I did so I saw Stella looking at me, half flung across the big sofa against the wall. All the way through our row he had been listening from there, quite comfort-ably, without putting in a word, as if he had been at the theater, and during my father's speech he had laughed softly several times.

In fact, I caught him with his mouth still ready for a laugh, and that, just then, made me lose my last gleam of reason. I took a step backward and, quite beyond myself, without even knowing what I was doing, grabbed a piece of cutlery quite haphazardly off the small supper table and flung it at him. Rage and astonishment kept my father motionless for a few seconds, while Stella, having neatly avoided the blow, put the piece of cutlery (I don't think it was a knife — I rather think it was a fork, but I can't say exactly) down on a chair there beside me.

I stopped halfway between the stove and the door and waited there resolutely. After all, I couldn't dash away without a word after such defiance and risk their thinking I was running away from Stella. But he didn't even get up from the sofa; he just smiled at me seriously and said, in a conciliatory tone: "Well, what are you fighting with me for? I really wasn't laughing at you."

Then he turned to my father and said, sounding attractively patient and superior: "From the very minute he set foot inside the door, he's tried as hard as he can to quarrel with me."

"Get out of here! Get out, and don't let me see you again! Do you hear me?" my father roared, trembling with really dreadful rage.

I glanced harshly around the big room, and it seemed to roll around before me like a revolving stage that was just going to disappear forever; and then I rushed out. When I was in my room, I didn't even bother to turn on the light. I flung myself on the bed with my face against the pillow, and for several minutes stayed like that, waiting for an apocalypse, an earthquake, or any cosmic disaster that would resolve this hateful night. In one way, I wished that the morning would never come, but in another, I was measuring fearfully the interminable hours of the night, as I was certain that I wouldn't be able to sleep.

The letter

I should have liked to spend the whole night awake, but at the same time wanted to fall into a great lethargy lasting days, months, even centuries, as happens in stories. My eyes were burning, but I wasn't sleepy. After a while I turned on the light and wrote a letter to my father.

I can't remember, of course, just exactly what I said in the letter, but I remember the gist of it very well. Briefly, it said more or less this:

> Dear Pa, — This is my last word; you were wrong this
> evening if you thought I still wanted to go on trips

with you, the way I did when I was little. Maybe it was true then, but I don't want to any more. And you're quite wrong if you think I'm jealous of your friends. When I was little I was jealous — that's true; but now I've found out they're jailbirds and terrible stinkers. And I hope that one day in some town where you're around with them, one of them will kill you, because I hate you. And I wish I'd been born without a father. And without a mother, and without anyone Good-bye. — Arturo

I don't know how long I stayed awake with my ears cocked, listening to hear if my father came up to his room, because I meant to go out and give him the letter without saying a word as soon as I heard him in the passage. But outside my half-open door no step or noise interrupted the silence of the night. I could, of course, have taken the letter into his room and left it well in sight on the suitcase, which is what I thought of doing. But the idea of venturing into the corridor and into that great empty bedroom frightened me. It seemed to me that its walls, and all the familiar things inside it, would be marked at night and made unlucky by the wrongs I had suffered, and that to face their silent presence alone would be another insult to me.

So, without making up my mind about the letter, I flung myself down on the bed and gradually went to sleep with the light on. Before it was day I woke up with a start, and, seeing my letter folded on the table, hid it under my jersey, which I was still wearing. Then I went back to bed and, with the light out, wrapped myself up completely in the blanket because I felt very cold.

Farewell

But I didn't sleep again. I could hear the roosters crowing, and not long after, the first glimmer of dawn appeared. Then, through the closed window, a noise of wheels and horseshoes stopping below in the street, by our gate, came up to me. "That's the carriage that's come to take them down to the port," I said to myself. I thought of the letter for my father which I'd put under my jersey, but by then I wanted him to have it rather less, and kept still under the blanket. I cocked my ears spasmodically for small sounds around the house. Usually when my father left, the whole family was running around, but this time my stepmother obviously had not been called. The bedroom and the passage upstairs were silent and still. From the street, every now and then, came the murmur of the driver talking alone to his horse.

Suddenly from the passage I heard someone striding along, trying to walk softly. The door was pushed gently, noiselessly, open. And my father came into the room, shutting the door behind him with his shoulder.

At first I shut my eyes tight, pretending to sleep. He shook me a bit, his lips forming the usual little whistle he always used when he wanted to wake me up in the morning. Then he called softly: "Arturo . . ."

"Arturo," he repeated. I opened my eyes, hard and set, without looking at him. "I'm leaving in a few minutes," he said.

I didn't bat an eye. I didn't move. Even without looking at him, I caught a glimpse in the cold light of dawn of the blue of his eyes. I could feel a hesitant anxiety in him, which kept him poised above me in the bustle and nervous gaiety of leaving. That was dividing his heart. I could feel the fresh flavor of his breath close beside me, and I felt he was bringing into my small stuffy room, like a second body made of air, all the cold gay freshness of the winter morning on the dock, in the excitement of departure.

"Hey! Are you listening Arturo?" he said, talking softly but insistently. "I'm leaving soon. I've left the others asleep, and anyway, I said good-bye to them last evening . . . I came to say good-bye to you."

"All right," I said. "Good-bye."

"That friend of mine," he went on, "has already gone down to the port on his own. He's waiting for me on the steamer. I'm going down alone in the carriage."

I could hear the horse clacking its hooves by the gate. "The carriage is down there, ready," he said. I curled up inside the blanket, and as I moved I felt the letter hidden under my jersey scratching my skin a bit. Now was the moment — now or never — to give him my letter. But I couldn't give it to him.

"Well, and what are you going to do now?" he asked. "Aren't you getting up? Aren't you coming down to the harbor with me as usual in the carriage?"

"No," I answered.

"Don't you want to?" he asked me again, in a tone at once angry and inviting, at once scolding, smiling, and disappointed. But even as he said it I could feel his nerves bristling with impatience to get away down to the harbor, where Stella was waiting for him on the steamer.

"No," I repeated, and turned over on to the pillow with an ambiguous movement that looked as if I wanted to turn my back on him, like some irritated sleeper who wants to be left in peace. Although I was avoiding his eyes I could still see him bending over me, his hair flopping untidily over his disappointed brow. And just then, when I saw his hair close to me, I caught a glimpse of a few white hairs among the blond.

"Well then, see you soon," he said, sounding quite casual.

"See you soon," I answered. And as he left the room I thought: *See you soon indeed . . . I'll never see you again!*

December 5

When the door shut behind him, I wrapped myself up in the blanket to my nose again, and covered my ears with my fists so as not to hear his retreating footsteps or his movements as he left the house or the carriage rumbling away down the hill. For a long time I remained deathly still. When I shook myself and threw off the blankets, the sun had already come into my room and the house was plunged in silence again.

I opened the window and, leaning out as far as I could, looked between the bars out into the roadway outside. The small terrace below the gate and the roadway were deserted, and even the distant echoes of wheels or hooves had faded. Only the scattered, distant voices of strangers sounded in the fresh, limpid morning, but to me these real voices were overlaid by another sound I seemed to hear in my brain, an unreal high-pitched noise on a single sharp note, a kind of deafening, incredible shout that might be translated as "Farewell, Wilhelm Gerace!"

I felt a mad temptation to dash down the street in the hope of catching up with the carriage and being with him for at least a little while longer. But even while that temptation was rending my heart, I stayed where I was, letting the minutes slip by until all hope was over.

I began to hear noises, familiar voices, about the house. My stepmother and Carmine were up. I ran angrily to the door and locked it. I wished just then that I had a dog to keep me company in my room, to be friendly and lick my hand gently with his rough tongue without asking me any questions. But every human presence, and even the sight of the countryside and all the places I knew, seemed to me intolerable. I wished that I could turn into a statue so as never to feel anything again.

So I shut myself up in my room as if I were dead. For several hours no one bothered about me. Then in the afternoon I heard someone knocking, and my stepmother asking, very softly and uncertainly, if I didn't want to eat and if I felt ill and why I hadn't gotten up. I chased her away, yelling rudely; and yet, a few hours later, I heard her knocking again, and the same voice, grown even softer and more uncertain, told me that if I wanted it, there was something to eat on a chair outside the door. I shouted that I didn't want anything. I didn't want to eat or drink, but just to be left in peace.

For the first time in my life, though I wasn't ill, I wasn't hungry. Every now and then I dozed, but woke up again at once, as if I'd had a horrible shock or heard a frightening uproar. I realized right away that nothing had actually happened: no uproars, no earthquakes. Suffering was using those evil tricks to keep me awake and never leave me. And, in fact, it didn't leave me the whole day through. It was the first time in my life that I really knew suffering. Or, at any rate, I thought I knew it!

I knew quite definitely then that these were the last hours I would spend on the island, and that the first step I took beyond the door of my room would be to leave. And perhaps that was why I stayed firmly shut up in my room — to put off, for a few hours at least, the irrevocable step that threatened me.

I didn't want to cry, but I cried. I wished that I could forget W. G. as I would forget some insignificant person I had met just once in a café or at a street corner. But through my tears I found myself calling "Pa" like a child of two. At one point I took out the letter I still had hidden under my jersey, and tore it up.

Hunger was obviously making me weak as well. I thought of my father so intensely that I ended up by making myself believe that he was thinking of me at that very same moment, and that while I was calling "Pa!" he was saying to himself: "Arturo, dear old Blacky!" or something like that, wherever he was. Finally, (though it sounds impossible), as the hours went by, a last hope came to me toward evening, one that seemed so reasonable that I was almost persuaded by it. This was the way it was: I haven't yet said that the following day was December 5, and that it was my birthday. I'd be seventeen. Out of pride, I hadn't reminded my father of it the previous evening, and he certainly wasn't the sort of person to remember birthdays and things like that as a rule. But this time I began to hope that suddenly on the trip his memory would jog him, as if inspired by a miracle, and he would remember the day he had forgotten, and would decide to turn back and wish me many happy returns, even spend the day on the island with me. Maybe, I told myself, he hadn't gone far yet; maybe he was in Naples, and from there it would be quite simple to come back for a day. I thought of his regretful expression a few hours earlier when he had leaned over me there in my room, and I could almost have sworn now that this regret, together with his despair because I hadn't seen him off on the dock, would bring him back to the island the next day. By nightfall my hope had turned to certainty, so much so that, from sheer relief, I felt at once exalted and weary. I looked outside the door to find the food that my stepmother had left for me on the chair: bread, an orange, and even a bar of chocolate (an unusual treat for us). I ate it, and went to bed, and fell asleep.

I woke up as I had the previous day, toward dawn. And so the second morning started, which was to turn out even worse than the first.

As soon as I was awake, I remembered that it was my birthday, and felt a joyful certainty that Wilhelm Gerace would arrive. While I waited for him, I remained as I had the previous day, a voluntary prisoner in my room with the key turned twice in the lock. But this morning my imprisonment was in the nature of a spell I was casting rather than anything else, and I foresaw that I would be going out gloriously very soon. I felt a kind of magic certainty that my father would arrive on the first steamer that stopped off at Procida at eight o'clock sharp.

But when I gazed out of my window and heard nine o'clock strike without any news of him, I passed from certainty to doubt, and from doubt to thinking not only that he would not arrive on the second boat at ten, but that he wouldn't arrive at all. But hope still clung to me like a parasite and refused to leave, and for another two hours I counted the quarters of the church tower, going from the window to the bed and back again, sometimes blocking my ears, sometimes straining them, wondering and wondering if he mightn't come on some small private boat, marching up and down the room, jerking around at every noise, every whistle, every rustle. In fact, the usual business of waiting and hoping. In the end, when eleven o'clock had passed, I realized definitely that I had been mad and taken my sentimental fantasies for heaven-sent prophecies, and that W. G. hadn't even dreamed of turning back, and certainly wouldn't be coming.

Then, for the first time in my life, I really felt that I longed for death.

Noon tolled its usual great peal. All through the morning,

luckily, no one had dared to call me, but soon after the clanging of the bells there was a knock at the door, as on the first day, only this time it was even fainter than that one and almost imperceptible. From what I heard, I realized that it was my stepmother with Carmine beyond the door. Not daring to do it herself, my stepmother had held the baby's hand while he knocked, and now she was showing him softy how to say "Happy birthday to you," which he was repeating obediently to me in his Ostrogoth sort of way.

Familiarity like that just at that moment disgusted me more than an atrocious insult, and in reply I merely kicked the door, to show them plainly that I didn't want any happy birthdays and that I sent the lot of them to hell.

For about an hour and a half there wasn't a sign of life. But it must have been just before two in the afternoon that I heard that obstinate knocking at the door again. This time it was she who knocked, and harder, almost roughly. I gave no sign of having heard, and then, in an uncertain voice that was almost frozen with fear and timidity, she called out, "Artù . . ."

The earring

I didn't answer. "Artù," she went on, faster, breathlessly, as if talking while she ran. "What are you doing? Why don't you get up? I've made you a sweet pizza like I made for your birthday last year . . ."

Although I had always thought her pretty stupid, her stupidity had never struck me as it did then — immeasurable, worse than infinite. How could she come chattering about nonsense like sweet pizzas at such a tragic moment? Her very kindness, which I hadn't seen many signs of lately, and which a few days earlier would have softened my heart, now simply hardened it. I would rather have had her hostile and severe as usual, and I felt that she ought to have realized this herself. "Get out, you stupid idiot!" I shouted, and, in a desperate rage, flung open the door.

There she was, with the baby in her arms, pale as death and with her lips trembling. I noticed at once (made sharper-eyed with fury) that she had put on that famous velvet skirt of hers and had dressed Carmine up in his party clothes as well, to celebrate the day, of course, as it ought to be celebrated, all of which, instead of softening me, only increased my resentment. In the meantime, I ran straight into my father's room, moved by some angry impulse that I couldn't understand.

The room was still untidy, more or less as he had left it. My stepmother was never one to tidy up in a hurry, and she had just collected in a heap all the old suits, shoes, newspapers, books, empty cigarette packages, and so on, which my father had left scattered about on the floor in the rush of packing. On the bed there was only the mattress, without blankets or pillows, and a quick glance into the open wardrobe was enough to show me what I had foreseen — that the place where W. G. usually kept his and my historic treasures, the fishing gun, the sea binoculars, and so on — was empty.

Unconscious of it all, the portrait of Romeo smiled as usual, with his dear blind eyes, from the wall beside the bed.

I moved feverishly about the empty room, while from the doorway my stepmother watched me with wretched, anxious eyes.

"Do you know who he's left with?" I shouted at her. "He didn't leave alone, the way he told you. He went off with Stella."

She looked at me, ducking her head to avoid Carmine as she did so, because, as my odd behavior had scared him, he was trying to get back his courage by playing with her curls. Vengeful and obstinate as a small boy, I went on: "He prefers Stella to you!"

She came into the room anxiously and put Carmine down on the big bed.

"Who's Stella? Is she a woman from here?" she asked, her face completely altered by a lowering savage rage. I realized from her question that, hearing the name Stella for the first time, she thought that it was a woman's. But as soon as she had heard that it was someone called Tonino Stella, her face cleared with relief.

When I saw these changing emotions in her, I felt an old, un-confessed jealousy stirring in me.

"But he loves him!" I yelled, suffering cruelly, racked by a double jealousy. "He's in love with Stella! HE'S IN LOVE WITH HIM!"

"He's in love with him . . ." she repeated, and her voice was inexpressive, an innocent, cold echo of my words. As soon as she had spoken, though, she stopped, her mouth suddenly trembling with shame. She looked at me for just a moment, questioning, waiting, then quickly looked away.

"Yes, he loves him! HE LOVES HIM! He cares a lot more for him than for you or Carmine, or me! Or anyone!" I went on, like a madman.

She moved her lips in protest, but was silent; her expression fragile and sorrowful, like that of a child precociously matured. For a moment she tried to escape me, and seemed to curl up entirely in herself like a sick bird that gathers its feathers around it to protect itself. Then she recovered, and turned on me almost brutally. "You shouldn't say that . . ." she exclaimed, breathless and trembling, and glanced down at Carmine, perhaps afraid that his year-old brain might have understood the dreadful things I had said about his father.

"This Stella who's gone away with him," she went on angrily, frowning, "can't be like a relation of his . . . This is just friendship . . ." Suddenly she raised one shoulder a bit. "That's quite different!" she concluded with an odd air of vulgar skepticism, halfway between indulgence and scorn.

Here a glowing, almost splendid maturity returned to her, and she was silent, proud and calm, frowning as if to show me that the argument was closed.

Then, in a mad spasm, I shouted: "But what about you? Do you love him?"

At this unexpected question she looked startled and bewildered, as if her heart had suddenly missed a beat.

"What . . . I . . . who?" she stammered.

"Him! My father!" I said. "Do you love him?"

Her cheeks had turned dark red, as if her skin was flaming, and she stood before me beyond the big bed that separated us, taking no notice even of Carmine, she was so overwhelmed.

"What are you saying?" she repeated two or three times. "He . . . he's my husband."

Maybe she thought that I was accusing her of not loving my father. Instead — poor wretch that I was — I was accusing her of just the opposite.

"I know!" I broke out at last, my bitterness freed all at once. "I know! You love him!"

Instead of giving her courage, what I said made her tremble as if I was shaking her, and, with her big eyes wide and defenseless, she gazed at me in a kind of confused supplication.

"I know! I know you love him!" I repeated. "*Why* do you love him?"

"Oh . . . I can't . . . I can't listen to you . . . I'm . . . I'm his wife . . ."

"He's wronged you! He's wronged you!"

"Oh, Artù . . . Why are you speaking of him like this? He's your father . . ." she broke in. A sudden emotion took all the color from her face, and the fiery blush turned to a nervous, timid pink. "And besides," she added, "he's more unfortunate . . . than you."

"My father . . . unfortunate?"

"Yes, you're luckier than he is . . ." she said, shaking her head slowly. Automatically, as if without realizing, she'd turned back to Carmine again, and, to distract him from our wicked talk, I'm certain, was making him play with a lock of her hair. "You're much luckier than he is," she repeated, "because — well, just think of all the beautiful women you'll have in your life . . ."

Her chin trembled a little as she foretold this, like a little girl's. And her dull, slightly sharp and quite unsophisticated voice became melodious with hidden tears, like the crude music of some poor undeveloped instrument.

"But then — well, women don't really like him much," she went on, still hanging her head. "He's . . . too natural . . . doesn't say the right thing . . . he doesn't know what makes a good im-

pression on women. Well, you see, lots of women don't really like
a man who's hardly ever with them . . . and then he forgets . . .
And he never has any nice little ways or pretty little compliments
. . . and, besides, he behaves as if he was with a bad woman, you
see, and lots of women think that is rather unpleasant . . ."

All this (which was necessary to illustrate what she meant)
she dragged out with visible reluctance, between blushes of
clumsiness and innocence, and echoes too, perhaps — just per-
ceptible in her breathing — of secret, involuntary sighs . . . yet
gravely, like someone very experienced. And in it I recognized,
almost with amusement, some of her mother Violante's topics of
conversation.

"And that's why I told you he's unluckier than you are," she concluded. "Because he can never be lucky with women, you see."

"But," I objected, "he's terribly handsome!"

"Yes, quite handsome . . . I don't mean to say he's ugly . . . No,
not a bit. He's not bad . . . But he's old."

"Old!"

"Well, of course. Isn't he? Do you know how old he is?" She
counted on her fingers. "He's over thirty-five. Yes, he's thirty-six.
He's got wrinkles and white hair already . . ."

I had noticed this myself, but I had never thought of my father
as really old.

"And that's why," she continued, "I asked you to remember the
respect you owe your father. Besides, apart from being his son,
you're rich and splendid compared with him. You're so lucky!
Think of all the beautiful women you'll meet in your life — rich
girls and foreigners who . . . who'll . . . love you . . . And the beautiful wife you'll have . . ."

She swallowed once, twice. Her voice broke again. But she
went on at once, bowing her head gravely and looking mild and
sweet and persuasive.

"But think of him. If he hadn't found me, what other woman
would have loved him, now that he's old? If it wasn't for me, I
don't suppose any other woman would take him on . . . And as he
was born without a family, poor soul, the way he was, he'd have

been alone like a gypsy his whole life through, like someone in the Foreign Legion . . . The only person to do things for him now is me . . ."

She didn't say this humbly, but in a rather pleased, matronly, and superior sort of way, with an air of childish courage mixed with it. And in this comical mixture her unobtainable beauty seemed to me so magnificent that it was worthy of a king, a real king. For a moment I watched her; then I burst out: "If you think I'll ever get married, you're wrong."

"Artù! . . . Why? . . ."

"You're wrong. There's only one woman who could ever be my wife. I know who she is! And I want no other! I'll never marry anyone!"

She stared straight at me, growing frightened, as if I had shouted a curse at her. But her eyes were unintentionally filled with glowing, smiling gratitude, even though it was veiled by incredulity, as if in her heart she wasn't displeased at the thought of my staying unmarried in honor of a certain woman.

Then all my love for her seized me again in a great blaze of regret, and duty, and revolt. All the sweet things I would have told her if I had been her husband suddenly flamed in my imagination like a great whirl of fireworks: all the kisses, all the caresses I would have given her and the way I'd have slept close, close to her, naked every night, to feel her breasts near me, even in sleep. All the fine clothes I would have bought her — silk petticoats, silk dresses, even, all embroidered so that I could see them when I undressed her. I'd have taken her to see her mother, Violante, wearing a fur coat and a hat with feathers like the grandest lady in Naples. And when I traveled, it would only have been so as to send her letters that were like great poetry, every day. And I'd have gone as far as America — no, to the farthest corner of Asia — to bring her jewels no other woman had. But not for her to keep hidden away: for her to cover her neck and her ears, and her little hands, as if they were all of them kisses of mine. And all her friends, when they saw her go by loaded with gold and precious jewels, would say: "Oh, isn't she lucky to have such an important husband!"

These thoughts (which I had already had more than once, and with great difficulty had gotten rid of during the preceding few months — since the famous day when I had discovered that I loved her) went whirling around in my head, as I said, like a firework display. The impossibility of it all, which turned these joyful ideas of mine into sorrow, was unjust, unnatural, destructive, but with N. before me, breathing and sensual, it seemed absurd to think of impossibility. Violent with happiness, I rushed round the bed to her, and said: "I love you!"

It was the first time in my life I had said these words, and I felt that, hearing me say them, she must be as moved as I was in saying them. But instead, the old fantastic denial (which just then seemed to me more loathsome than the vilest superstition) altered her whole expression. She shouted: "No, Artù! We mustn't do wrong!"

And I, with the rage that demands its rights, took her in my arms, pressed her to me, and sought her mouth to kiss.

But she was ready to avoid my kiss. She twisted her head and leaned back feverishly, repeating, "No! No!" in a sort of wild call for help, as if there was anyone in the room, apart from scared, defenseless Carminiello, who could have helped her. Then she began defending herself, struggling with knees and elbows and fists, even with her nails and teeth. A wild beast in the desert trying to kill me could not have grown as ferocious as she grew in refusing me a kiss. Then my love turned to hatred, and before I let her go without having kissed her, I began to hurt her, blindly, furiously — her cheeks that were pulling away from me, her neck, her hair. And finally with an amazement more innocent, oddly, than remorseful, I saw through her tumbled curls a small pink ear stained with a few drops of blood.

Thoughtless with rage, I had tugged her earring so violently that I had unhooked the clasp, which had torn the lobe a little. And when I let her go, I found the pitiful little prize in my hand — her golden earring. Meanwhile, as in a dream, I heard Carmine crying, clearly convinced that I was trying to murder his mother. And I saw her, deadly pale, going up to the child and holding his dress to stop him from falling to the floor. She was so alarmed that I don't think she was even complaining; she simply stared at me with her great soft sorrowful eyes wide open as if expecting some new horror from me. I flung the earring at her feet. "You beast, you murderess!" I shouted. "Don't worry, I'll never kiss you again." And as I dashed out of the room I said. "Goodbye! Good-bye forever! It's all over."

In the cave

She had remained quite still and silent, leaning against the bed, but when I reached the staircase landing, I heard her calling, frightened, from the bedroom door: "Artù! Artù! Where are you going?" Then I heard Carmine crying harder in the room, and N. hurrying in and trying to quiet him. Again, as I crossed the hall, I heard her calling breathlessly from the top of the stairs: "Where are you going? Artù!" And her clogs clattering down the first steps, and Carmine babbling in her arms. But in a moment I was away and out in the road, and the voices from the house faded behind me in the distance like sounds from another world.

I didn't know exactly where I was fleeing to. I had no friends on the island, and besides, in my hurry I hadn't brought any money with me, and having left all I had in my bedroom. Besides, except for the bread and chocolate and fruit that I had had the previous evening, I had been fasting for a day and a half, and obviously that was why I had this strange, rapturous sense of unreality which relieved my suffering a little. I was now firmly, irrevocably resolved: the island would soon be a part of my past. There were no more steamers leaving for the mainland that same day, but I didn't worry about the details of how and when I would be going. All I asked for the moment was just to creep into some quiet corner of the island for a time and hide my loneliness there. "Well," I told myself bitterly, "this is the end of my birthday!"

I crossed the piazza of Christ the Fisherman, then the big pier, and left the dock behind me. I had no particular object in mind and was just looking for somewhere lonely and uninhabited, when I turned left to the little gray beach that, against a background of earthy rocks, shuts in that part of the island. On the open space in front of the lighthouse, which was cluttered like an arsenal with boats that were unused or undergoing repairs, some small village girls were playing a game that involved jumping in squares they had drawn on the ground with chalk. I marched brutally through them, nearly knocking one of them down, and I went on toward the beach without taking the least notice of the girl's protests and those of her friends.

At the end of the beach, some natural caves are hollowed out of the rock, and two or three of these — an opening not much bigger than an ordinary door, but fairly big and comfortable inside — were used as storehouses for tools, oars, and so on, by some of the boatowners, who paid the town council a rent for them and put stout doors at the openings, which were usually kept firmly locked. But as I went down the beach I realized that one of the doors was open. Maybe the owner of the cave had left the island, and it was unused; inside there was nothing but a mass of half-rotted old rope, and several pots of glue covered with mold.

Chance had brought me to that beach, and chance was now helping me. This small abandoned room was exactly what I needed. I went in and shut the door, which, stretched by the dampness, fitted perfectly into its square, and from outside looked as firmly shut and locked as the others. To secure it even better against the wind, I barricaded it with a heap of rope on which I then flung myself down, feeling, on that bed where no one knew me, as free and alone as some wretched vagabond.

My long fast, and the way I had been running, began to produce faint rumbles in my ears and a kind of confused exhaustion. I wasn't worried about what was to happen to me, not even in the next few hours: it was as if they belonged, not to me, but to someone I didn't yet know and didn't much want to know. I no longer hated my father, no longer loved N. The dramatic sufferings I had known up to a short time before had given way to an amorphous sadness in which I no longer felt anything for anyone.

The goddess

The wind had changed to sirocco, and the weather was warm, blustery, and lowering. The cracks in the door let a ray of dusty light into the cave, mingled with the heavy salt smell of the air. At that time of the year the small beach was as empty as the farthest reaches of the earth, and for several minutes I heard nothing but the sound of the sea beaten by the African wind. But after a while I heard approaching through the wind the voice that had followed me to the hall as I fled from it, and it was still shouting, broken with running and breathlessness: "Artùùùùro! Ar — tùùù!"

My stepmother had obviously run after me the moment she had put Carmine safely down. Someone who had seen me go by, and finally the little girls playing with the chalk, must have told her the direction I had taken, but no one had seen me going into the cave. Feeling fairly safe in my hiding place, I got off my heap of rope and crouched behind the door, peering through the cracks in the wood.

A moment later I saw her running breathlessly from the far end of the beach, and from her behavior I guessed quite definitely, and without much difficulty, what she was thinking. When she heard my exalted "Good-bye forever" in the bedroom, she must have suspected that I was going to pass those famous Pillars of Hercules, this time without returning (besides, I must confess I rather wanted to make her think something of the kind). And now, on this gloomy, empty beach, her suspicion was growing enormous.

She passed the caves without stopping, as obviously she thought them private property and locked, and it never occurred to her that I might be in one of them. She ran along the beach to the farthest barrier of rocks, then turned back, more overwhelmed, then went back there again. At one point she even started banging at the cave doors with her fists, but I'm sure that she was just venting her violent feelings on the wood, without any real hope. The wild, unsystematic way she was banging showed how sure she was of beating on emptiness. I even thought that I heard her small hand trying to force the door of the cave next to mine, but she soon stopped trying, as it must have seemed absurd and pointless.

She prowled up and down the beach again like a murderess turned desperate. Perhaps at that very moment she saw me leaping into gorges, rolling unimaginable distances. She ran about shouting "Artù" in all directions in a strange new sensual voice that was heartbreakingly high-pitched, letting the wind tug at her dress quite without shame. Her black shawl had slipped off her head, disclosing the tousled curls I had untidied when we struggled, and as she ran against the wind, her hair covered her face, stopping her mouth and stifling her shouts. Occasionally she slowed down, her knees gave way, and her lips, which looked pale and almost swollen from all the shouting, were still, looking brutal, disheartened, violent. In the few minutes since we had parted up at the house she seemed to have developed into a woman of thirty, and her innocent soul seemed suddenly to have changed into a sinner's. And from her ruined, earthly, old woman's ugliness shone a splendor at once sweet and barbarous, as if her soul was speaking, was begging me: "Oh Arturo, don't die! Pity a poor woman who loves you! Come back to me alive and I'll fling myself down on these stones and give you, not just kisses, but all you want! And if I go to hell for you, my love, my own darling, I'll be proud of it!"

I peered out at her, but felt cruel and dry and dispirited. "Go away," I thought. "It's over now. I no longer love you and no longer hate anyone else. I have no feeling for anyone. Go home, go on, go away, I don't even find you attractive."

And I lay down again with my head on my arms, hoping that she would soon go away and leave me alone.

I heard her wandering about the beach a little longer, still repeating "Artù," but softly, muttering it in a depressed sort of way. At last her unhappy voice trailed away along the road to the village, and the beach was empty again.

Then I nearly felt that I was really dead at the bottom of the sea, as she feared. As soon as she had gone I heard in the wind the whistle of the three o'clock steamer coming into the harbor. But it meant nothing to me, I was no longer waiting for anyone. I knew that my father certainly wouldn't come back for my birthday, but I no longer suffered; in fact, something worse happened — I knew that even if he came, it wouldn't cheer me up at all.

In an hour or a little more, it would be evening, I thought, and felt pleased, for no one else would come along that forgotten beach, nobody would come to bother me. A timeless, unconscious night was perhaps the only bearable way the day could end.

As the minutes passed, I felt my still muscles slacken and my mind become enchanted, as if I was turning into a vast sea turtle inside its stony black armor. I heard the steamer's second signal as it was leaving the harbor after its brief stop there, as if it came across a distance of centuries, part of a fabulous tale I no longer cared to listen to. From nearby, beyond the door of the cave I had taken over, came the noise of the wind and the waves, a natural, voiceless chorus settling my fate in a language as incomprehensible as death.

Just then (when the steamer's parting hoot had just faded into the distance) I heard a voice again, approaching from the end of the beach — not a woman's voice, but a man's this time; not anxious, but sure of itself and almost gay — calling the name Arturo. It wasn't the pitch of my father's voice; it wasn't his footsteps coming across on the stones of the beach — fast, with heavy shoes — no, it certainly wasn't he.

I got up as I had before, to peer through the cracks, and there outside, a few yards away, I saw a soldier going by — a rather short dark man, with a round face, a pair of small black whiskers, and lively black eyes that were gazing around. I couldn't quite place him at once, but I recognized something oddly familiar about him, something that made me start with a feeling of mystery and surprise.

"Hey! What Arturo are you looking for?" I shouted from behind the door.

"Why, Arturo Gerace!" he answered.

I opened the door. "Arturo Gerace," I said. "That's me!"

"Arturo!" he exclaimed, and rushed up to me, glowing with pleasure. And right away he kissed me on both cheeks.

"Don't you recognize me?" he asked. And, with a mysterious, significant smile, he showed me on the third finger of his right hand a silver ring set with a cameo of the goddess Minerva.

The enchanted pin

Maybe our nature makes us see the unforeseen tricks of fate as more pointless and arbitrary than they are. In a story or a poem, for instance, every time the unexpected happens to fit in with something that fate secretly intended, we accuse the writer of being too fictional. And in real life, too, unforeseen events that in themselves are natural and simple appear to us, just because of the way we happen to feel at that particular moment, extraordinary or downright supernatural.

Supposing that on my fatal birthday my one friend on earth had unconsciously and intuitively realized my desperation from a distance, and so had come to me . . . Well, even if that had happened, it wouldn't rationally and scientifically have seemed a miracle. Even swallows and other simple migratory creatures like them know by intuition, and quite alone, the moment they must leave, find their way with no one to direct them.

But the sudden, startling arrival of my unexpected visitor on the shore seemed to me so romantic that at first I thought him a hallucination rather than a living presence. When I unexpectedly saw the cameo, my famous present to my nurse Silvestro, and an obvious proof of his identity, I felt quite breathless, as if the beach had suddenly opened up to show me a Valley of the Kings or some buried legend like it. But after a minute I realized what was happening, murmured "Silvestro!" and promptly returned the two kisses he'd given me on the cheek, joyfully sure that he at least, being my proper nurse, would not accuse me of sending his soul to hell for a couple of kisses. And as I kissed him, I realized that actually his presence here on my birthday, even though something quite new, wasn't as odd as all that. What was odd (and ungrateful too) was the way I had completely forgotten that he never let my birthday go by without getting in touch with me, even if he just sent a greeting card. But lately I'd been thinking too much of other people to spare a single thought for him.

He explained that as he had been drafted again, he had taken advantage of some leave and the reduced fares on the steamer for troops to make this trip (which he had been promising himself for about ten years) and bring me his greetings himself. He told me that awhile before, as soon as he'd gotten off the boat, as he crossed the square, he had kept hearing the name "Arturo" repeated excitedly by a group of women and girls. And when he found out that one of the women was my stepmother out searching for me, he had introduced himself and suggested that he patrol the beach while she continued searching the piazza. The little girls kept saying that I might have climbed back to the piazza through various difficult shortcuts across the rocks, over by the storehouses . . .

Here Silvestro advised me to let my stepmother know at once that I'd been found, as the poor woman was in a terrible state. She must be rather a nervous character, he added.

"No," I said, laughing, "she's not at all nervous. But of course she's in a state. I should say so! She thinks I'm dead!"

"Dead!"

I shrugged slightly, thinking it best not to explain too much. All the same, I thought Silvestro was right, and went to the lighthouse point with him right away, where from a distance I saw one of the little girls I knew by sight still hanging about, jumping around in the chalk squares all alone. We called her, and she came across to us.

"Go to the piazza at once," I said, "and look for Signora Gerace. Tell her you've seen me here with my friend, and that I was up there among the rocks before, resting behind those bushes . . . Tell her my friend and I want to talk a bit on our own, so that she must go home quietly and we'll join her later."

I managed to get the whole of this out in one breath, but as soon as the child had left with her message, I flung myself down

on the ground and begged Silvestro for pity's sake, before anything else, to run to the shop on the corner and buy me something to eat, because I was ready to faint from hunger. I would pay
him back whatever he spent at once, I added, because I had
plenty of money at home.

My perfect nurse at once fetched fresh eggs, fresh cheese, and
bread from the shop, and I felt as if I had drunk the elixir of life.
Then we went back to my cave, which I now regarded affection-
ately as my commander's tent on the field, or something stirring
and important like that. And there we sat down on the heap of
rope and talked comfortably.

He told me that he'd have to leave Procida the next day on the
first steamer, at dawn, because his leave was over, worse luck. I
asked him why he had been drafted again.

"They're starting to call people up," he said, "because of the war."

"What war?" I asked.

"What, don't you know about the war? Haven't you heard
about it on the radio? Or read about it in the papers?"

Actually, I never read the newspapers. My father said that they
stank, that they were full of vulgar lies and idiotic gossip, and it
was an insult even to use them in the toilet. And as for the radio
— well, it's true that there had been at least one in the village for
some time, owned by the shopkeeper who once had kept an owl,
and sometimes I had heard talk and singing when I passed, but
those few times it had always been light music or vaudeville,
nothing serious. The fact was that the history I knew took me up
to the ancient Egyptians: I knew about the *Excellent Condottieri*
and plenty of battles long ago, but of our contemporary life I knew
absolutely nothing at all. The few signs of current life that had
reached the island I had hardly bothered to glance at. I never felt
the slightest curiosity about what was happening — it all seemed
like newspaper chitchat, far removed from the excitement of History and of the Absolute Certainties.

And now when Silvestro told me what was going on in the
world, I felt that I had been asleep for sixteen years like the girl in

the fairy tale, in a courtyard of wild grass and spiders' webs and owls, my brow pierced by a magic pin.

He went on explaining to me that in spite of a recent peace pact, grandly signed by the Powers (these must be, I now realized, the famous *international events* that Stella had meant, which had brought about the amnesty and his freedom), the World War was properly and hopelessly upon us. It might break out from one month to the next, even from one day to the next. And even those who were against it, like him, were going to get involved in the whole hellish business.

I sat still for a few minutes when I heard this, thinking my own thoughts. Then I told Silvestro what I had decided. First of all, I told him that for very secret, very serious, and even tragic reasons I could not stay on the island a single day longer, and so I intended leaving with him by the first steamer the next morning at dawn, never to return to it ever again. And so, I went on, if war was really on the way, I had definitely decided to volunteer on the first day we entered it. Whatever happened, I wanted to take part in the war, even if it meant getting secretly onto the battlefield (supposing my request to join up was refused, because of my age).

Silvestro listened very seriously to what I said. He discreetly avoided asking questions about my secret reasons for leaving Procida, but he had no need to know them to realize they were grave and justified. And he was pleased — or rather delighted — to hear that I had decided to leave with him the next day. But he wasn't too keen, it appeared, about the second part of my program — my idea of volunteering for the war. I saw that he was puzzled and set against it, so I declared, as fervently as I could, that I felt that a man wasn't a man until he had proved himself in war, and that to stay at home without fighting while others were fighting seemed to me the most disagreeable and dishonorable thing that could happen.

He looked unconvinced and reluctant as he listened to me. In the end he said that my ideas might have been all right in ancient wars, but that modern wars were quite another kettle of fish. As far as he could see, modern war was nothing but mechanized butchery, a loathsome ant heap of destruction and not a matter of courage. As far as the war we were talking about was concerned, he thought that on general principles (that is from the point of view of its *real cause*) neither side was right. But of the two, the one that was definitely wrong was ours. And fighting like that, for no reason but the wrong reason, was like singing with a thorn in your throat, a disaster, with nothing to be said for it.

These commonsense words of his made me stop to think a moment, but they made me laugh as well. In any case, I answered stoutly that for the time being I didn't care much about the rights and wrongs of the business. What I wanted was to fight so as to learn fighting, like a samurai in the East. The day I was sure of my valor, I'd choose my cause, but I had to test myself before I could be sure, and the test that had turned up was this war. I didn't want to miss it, and it was all I cared about.

"That's like saying you're trying to get killed for nothing," he said glumly, hesitantly. Then he looked at me seriously: "Why the devil d'you want to get killed for nothing?" he asked.

I blushed, as if he was shouting about some mysterious scandal that was always hushed up, but took hold of myself at once, clung to my old ideas, and told him passionately that from the time I had been little, death had been a challenge to me. Some boys were afraid of the dark, and that was how I was afraid of death; only of death. My revulsion at the thought of it poisoned the certainty of life for me, and until I had learned to be casual in the face of it, I couldn't know if I had really grown up. Or worse: whether I was a brave man or a coward.

Then I explained my views of life to him briefly, and even the Absolute Certainties, which I had almost forgotten in the preceding few months. As I told him all about them, I felt that I was redressing a betrayal, and grew as excited in telling him as he grew in listening. Suddenly, with a confused, ingenuous smile, he confided to me that my ideas were wonderfully like his — that is, his ideas about the people's revolution. Because, he said, he was a revolutionary, and was delighted to hear that all alone in Procida, without having spoken to a soul, I had hatched the same thoughts as the finest thinkers. As he said this, Silvestro's face and tone clearly showed his enormous admiration for Arturo Gerace. Besides, it was obvious from the way he behaved that this admiration for A. G. wasn't something new, but something that must have existed before — you might say forever. It might have waited forever for a chance to confess itself — limitless and almost magical, in a way it was rather like what I felt for W. G.

In the end my enthusiasm won Silvestro over and even convinced him of my moral need to fight in the first available war that turned up. Maybe, we dreamed hopefully, we might even end up in the same regiment. (But our hopes weren't realized. I was put with boys of my own age, and he with an older bunch of conscripts.)

Finally he took my birthday present from his pocket, where he had forgotten it until then under the pressure of so many other emotions; it was a red woolen scarf his wife had knitted, which I delightedly tied around my neck right away. He told me that a short time earlier he had married the girl he'd been going with for years, and that now that he was in the army, she had gone to her mother's in a small village near Naples. If I wanted to, he said, I could go there at first as their guest. And it was only a few minutes' tram ride from there to Naples.

While we had talked, evening had come on us, and Silvestro reminded me that it was time to go up to the house, as I had promised my stepmother. I felt myself blushing as he said that, but luckily it was dark and he didn't notice. I thought my voice would tremble when I spoke; but I spoke up resolutely.

"Listen," I said, "for reasons I can't tell anyone, I can't go back to the house. You go alone and talk to her, and make her believe this whopper: tell her I left on the half-past four steamer for Ischia, and that tomorrow you'll be joining me there, and then we'll go on to Naples, and from there I'll embark at once for abroad. Tell her that I'm saying good-bye because I won't see her for a long time, perhaps never. Tell her to remember me and to forgive me for hurting her. And give my love to my brother, Carminiello, too.

"Ask her to give you a suitcase. Tell her you'll bring it to me to-morrow at Ischia. And go to my room and take all the paper you can find with writing on it, and all the money you can find as well — there is a bunch of it in my room, strewn about among the books and in the drawers. But do be careful, won't you; bring *all* the paper that's written on. Don't leave any behind. It's important, because I'm a writer.

"If you like, you can sleep up there at the house tonight. Your room is just as it was, with the camp bed and everything. But before you go to sleep, you must bring me some blankets and something for supper. The fact is, until I leave tomorrow I don't even want to cross the piazza, because there are too many memories there. Tonight I'll sleep in this cave, where I'll be fairly comfortable. Anyway, it's not cold, luckily; there's the sirocco."

Silvestro promised that he'd do everything exactly as I told him, but, he said, as I was sleeping down there in the cave, he'd sleep there with me instead of up at the house, so as not to leave me alone. As he was a watchman on building sites, he had slept in huts almost his whole life, and now, as a soldier, he must be ready to sleep in foxholes. Caves, indeed! A cave like ours was like the Vatican Palace, compared with a foxhole.

And so I waited for him to get back as quickly as possible with all the things we needed.

Contradictory dreams

It wasn't more than two hours later when I saw the wavering glow of a candle lantern coming up from the dusky end of the beach and ran to meet Silvestro, who was holding the lantern out in front of him and was loaded up like St. Nick. Besides the suitcase full of manuscripts and provisions, and several heavy woolen blankets, he was carrying a blanket filled with things, and even a bag of charcoal to warm the cave's damp air a little. Some of these reinforcements my provident friend had got from the House of the Guaglioni, but the rest of them he had preferred to borrow in the village so as not to arouse my stepmother's suspicions, as she mustn't know that I was spending the night on the island.

The moment I met him I spoke. "You talked to her . . . the way I told you?" I asked.

"Yes," he said.

"And did she believe you?"

"Yes," he said, "she believed me." And for the time being that was all I asked.

We put the lantern on a jutting piece of rock in a corner of the cave, laid the bundle on the heap of rope spread out on the ground, and on this improvised bed sat down fairly comfortably and prepared the supper. Among the food that Silvestro brought out of the suitcase was a large sweet pizza wrapped in thick paper. He told me my stepmother had asked him to take it to Ischia for me, as she had made it for my birthday and didn't feel the least bit like eating it now.

Besides the sweet pizza, she had sent me all her savings as a present, in case I needed money — about four hundred and fifty lire, which Silvestro gave me knotted up in a rather grubby handkerchief. And finally she had given Silvestro, asking him to tell me to keep it in memory of her, a broken earring, of gold.

When I took the little gold ring from Silvestro's hand, I colored, flung myself down on the bundle, and with my face in shadow, asked him to tell me exactly what had happened when he saw my stepmother.

He said that when she saw him turn up alone at the House of the Guaglioni, she looked at him uncertainly, but didn't ask about me. Then at his first words, "Arturo's sent me to say . . ." she began to turn white, but managed to murmur: "Please don't keep standing there. Do sit down," and herself sat down on the chair beside the kitchen table. After this, he quickly told her what he had to say, and when she heard that I had already set sail and left Procida, she looked at him with two great cold grave eyes that seemed to see nothing. Suddenly her pallor grew unnatural, green, deathlike, and without a word or an exclamation or a sigh, she fainted, hitting her forehead on the top of the table.

In a few minutes she was on her feet again, though, and in fact told him not to tell me what a shock she had had. She stammered and grew confused, as if it was something to be ashamed of. And she even helped him to pack the suitcase for me at Ischia, moving about like a bloodless shadow as she did so.

At this point I broke in. Lying there with my face still in darkness, I begged Silvestro please never to speak of her again. I never wanted to hear her even mentioned by anyone from that time on.

When supper was over, Silvestro and I stayed awake talking until late. Luckily he had thought of bringing a pair of extra candles for our lantern. We talked of a thousand things: of the past, but above all, of the future, of the Absolute Certainties, of the revolution, and so on. Silvestro asked me to read him some of my poetry, too; and of course I chose the best and most effective poems, and saw that while he listened he actually had tears running down his face.

The lighted brazier between the two of us gave out a pleasant warmth, and in the mysterious light of the glass lantern, sitting there in the cave on that splendid orange bundle, we really might have been in some Arab or Persian tent, and the barking of dogs in the distance might have been the roaring of exotic wild beasts. Wind and sea had quieted down, promising us a calm crossing the next day. At about ten o'clock we put the brazier outside the door so as not to risk being poisoned with the fumes, fixed the door, put out the lantern, and then, rolled up in our blankets, settled down to sleep.

In contrast to the wonderful evening I had just spent, I had the most disturbing dreams, in which N., Carminiello, and my father all appeared muddled up. Then armored cars, black flags with skulls on them, and black-uniformed fighters all mixed up with dark kings and Indian philosophers and pale, blood-splashed women came rumbling past together, a great crowd that roared over the walled trench in which I was crouching. I wanted to climb out of it and get into battle, but there was no way out, and all around me I felt the weight of sand swallowing me up, sucking me down with a kind of horrible human sigh. I shouted to all the people passing above me, but nobody heard.

I woke up with a start in the middle of the night, to hear a tremendous roaring noise echoing from the rocky walls around me. For the first few moments I remembered nothing — neither what had happened during the day nor how I happened to be in that little stone room. But I wasn't long in collecting my wits and realizing that the astonishing noise was only Silvestro snoring, and snoring so that you'd think it wasn't just a single soldier, but an entire platoon. The discovery cheered me a lot. I tried to remember the thousands of times I must have heard the same symphony when I slept with Silvestro as a child; and I laughed to myself when I imagined the thoughts I must have had on listening to my nurse produce such curious music. And I decided to tease him about his accomplishment as soon as he got up in the morning, and laughed in anticipation.

His high-powered snoring, which a little before in my sleep had turned into the terrible sounds of death, filled me, during the short time I lay awake, with a trusting, peaceful feeling; and, as if lulled by its pleasant, friendly rhythm, I fell asleep again, tranquilly this time.

The steamer

I woke up naturally, but rather early. It was still very dark, and by the light of a match, I could see from the alarm clock (which Silvestro had borrowed in the village) that there was still over half an hour before we needed to get up. But I no longer wanted to sleep, so, taking care not to disturb Silvestro (he was still snoring, though rather more softly), I slipped out of the cave.

I kept the blanket on my shoulders, using it as a cloak the way they do in Sicily, but actually it wasn't cold, though the sirocco had dropped. From the gleaming stones I could see that it had been raining in the night. The small December stars were scattered about the ragged sky, and the tail end of a quarter moon gave out the palest twilit glimmer. The sea lay under the windless rain, moving very slightly, rhythmically and monotonously. And as I went along the sea edge in that great cloak, I felt like a kind of highwayman already — homeless, countryless, with a skull embroidered on my uniform.

Roosters were already crowing inland. And suddenly my heart was heavy, inconsolably heavy, at the thought of the morning that would rise over the island, just like other mornings, of the shops opening, the goats leaving their stalls, my stepmother and Carminiello going down to the kitchen . . . If only this sick, wan winter could have continued on the island. But no, the summer, too, would return, inevitably, just as always. You couldn't kill it — it was a dragon, an invulnerable dragon ever reborn into its first marvelous childhood; and a dreadful jealousy seized me when I thought of the island glowing with summer again, and without me. The sands would be hot again, the caves would gleam with color again, migrating birds would cross the sky on their way back from Africa again. And in all this glory that I worshiped, no one — not the commonest sparrow, not the smallest ant or the meanest fish in the sea — would care that summer had returned to the island without Arturo. In the whole immense landscape around me not a thought for A. G. would remain; it would be just as if, as far as this place was concerned, Arturo Gerace had never been there.

I lay down in my blanket on the wet pale stones, and shut my eyes, and for a while pretended that I had returned to a past summer and was lying on the sand of my little beach, and that the murmur close by was the sweet calm sea below, ready to receive *The Torpedo-boat of the Antilles*. The fire of that everlasting childhood summer rose in my blood so passionately, so terribly, that I nearly fainted. And the one friend I had had all that time returned to bid me farewell. As if he were there beside me, I said out loud: "Good-bye, Pa!"

The memory of him came to me at once, not as a definite figure, but as a kind of blue-and-gold cloud; or a bitter taste; or something like the noise of a crowd, though it was just the echoes of all he had meant and said to me at every part of my life that returned. And some of his features came back to me, too — but casually, and some of the way he shrugged, his absent laugh, the shape of his large, neglected nails, his finger joints; one of his knees scratched on the rocks. All these came back to me separately, making my heart pound as if they were single perfect symbols of a multiple, mysterious, infinite glory, and of a pain, the sharper because I knew it was childish, which, like the meeting of whirling currents, rushed headlong through this brief valedictory present. Later I would forget him, of course, and betray him. From here I would pass on to another age, and look back on him as on a fairy tale.

I now forgave him everything. Even the way he had left with someone else. Even his harsh final speech in which, in front of Stella, he had called me, among other things, a stealer of hearts and a Don Giovanni, which at the time had hurt me quite a lot.

Afterward, when I thought back on it from a distance, I wondered whether in fact he wasn't right, or at least partly right. Maybe while I thought I was in love with this or that person, or with two or three people at the same time, I really didn't love anyone. The fact was that, on the whole, I was too much in love with love; this has always been my real passion.

Maybe the fact was that I had *never* really loved W. G. And as for N., who was this wonderful woman, after all? A poor little thing from Naples with nothing special about her, just like so many others. Yes, I have a suspicion that what he said wasn't completely wrong. Suspicion, not certainty . . . And so life remains a mystery, and to me the chief mystery of all is still myself.

From this infinite distance, now, I think back to W. G. and imagine him older, uglier, lined, and gray-haired, coming and going alone, always alone and adoring a man who calls him *grotesque*. Loved by no one — for even N., who wasn't even beautiful, loved another. And I wish I could tell him: it doesn't matter, even if you are old — to me you'll always be the most beautiful.

Later I had news of her from travelers who came from Procida to Naples. She was well, though very much thinner, and she car-

ried on the same life in the House of the Guaglioni, with
Carmine, who grew more attractive every day. But she no longer
called him Carmine, she preferred calling him by his second
name, Arturo. And I like to think that there is another Arturo
Gerace on the island, a fair boy who now, perhaps, races along the
beaches happy and free . . .

From the cave, which I had left half open, I heard the alarm
clock shrilling, and went back, just in case it hadn't managed to
wake Silvestro. But I found him already half sitting up among the
blankets, rubbing his sleepy eyes and grumbling curses at the
wretched noise. I went straight up to him and said, triumphant
and impatient: "Hey! D'you know you snore?"

"What?" he said, sleepily, without understanding properly.
And then I roared into his ear, in a voice like thunder, with
laughter breaking through the words: "DO-YOU-KNOW-YOU-
SNORE-WHEN-YOU'RE-ASLEEP?"

"Hey! Your breath tickles!" he protested, rubbing his ear.
"Snore . . . Well, what about it? Of course I snore," he continued,
beginning to wake up. "Oughtn't I to? Everyone snores when
they're asleep."

"Of course!" I exclaimed, rolling on the ground with laughter.
"But there are ways and ways! You'd beat the world champion!
You're like an orchestra going full blast on the radio!"

"Oh, I am, am I? Well, I like it!" he retorted, now fully awake
and rather offended. "Maybe you think you snore softly, do you? I
can tell you that last night I had to go out on the beach and take a
leak, and ten yards off I could still hear snoring from the cave, like
a fleet of cars in low gear."

I was delighted to hear it. If I snored like that, it was obvious
that I could consider myself grown up, mature, really manly on
all counts.

We picked up our luggage, blankets, and so on, and went to
the village along the beach, which was starting to lighten in the
dawn. In the east, a red sky under dark strips of cloud foretold a
variable day's weather. When we reached the square, Silvestro
went to the boat office, which was already open, to take the things

he had been lent the day before to a man he knew, who would give them back to their various owners; he also undertook to buy the tickets for our crossing while I went ahead of him toward the dock. The first flashing, criss-crossed rays of the sun were lengthening on an almost smooth sea. I thought that soon I would see Naples, the mainland, cities, crowds. And I longed suddenly to get away from that square, from that dock.

The steamer was there already, waiting. And as I looked at it, I felt all the strangeness of the childhood that was slipping away from me. To think that I had seen this boat arrive and leave so many times, and had never embarked for the journey. As if, as far as I was concerned, it wasn't just a poor little freight boat, a kind of streetcar, but a distant, inaccessible ghost destined for unknown icy deserts.

Silvestro came back with the tickets, and the sailors were setting up the gangway for us to go aboard. While he was talking to them, I took out of my pocket the gold earring that N. had sent me the previous evening and, without anyone seeing me, kissed it, in secret.

And as I looked at it, an intoxicating weakness suddenly blurred my eyes. At that very moment I saw just why she had sent me the earring, saw that it meant farewell, and trust, and coquetry at once harsh and marvelous. Well, now I knew that she was a coquette, my darling love — without realizing, of course, but a coquette all the same. What farewell from a woman could ever express a lovelier coquetry than this, which in her ignorance she had sent me? Not the sign of a caress or a kiss to remember her by, but the sign of my vile ill treatment. As if to say: even when you hurt me, it's part of our love, to me.

I had a wild temptation to rush back to the House of the Guaglioni, to get into bed beside her, and say: "Let me sleep with you a little. I'll leave tomorrow. We won't make love if you don't want to, but at least let me kiss you here on your ear, where I hurt you."

But the sailor at the bottom of the gangway was already tearing our tickets for the conductor, and Silvestro was already climbing the gangway beside me. We heard the parting whistle.

When I was on the seat beside Silvestro, I put my arm on the back of it and hid my face there, and said to Silvestro: "Listen, I don't want to see Procida while it's receding, and growing dim and gray . . . I would rather pretend that it doesn't exist. So I'd better not look until it can't be seen any longer. You tell me when it can't be seen."

And with my face on my arm, as if I were sick, as if I had no thoughts, I waited until Silvestro shook me gently and said: "Come on, Arturo, you can wake up."

Around our ship the water was as uniform and boundless as the ocean. The island could no longer be seen.